Allan and the
Holy Flower

Allan and the Holy Flower

H. Rider Haggard

MINT EDITIONS

Allan and the Holy Flower was first published in 1915.

This edition published by Mint Editions 2021.

ISBN 9781513277622 | E-ISBN 9781513278032

Published by Mint Editions®

 MINT
EDITIONS

minteditionbooks.com

Publishing Director: Jennifer Newens
Design & Production: Rachel Lopez Metzger
Project Manager: Micaela Clark
Typesetting: Westchester Publishing Services

Contents

I

Brother John

I do not suppose that anyone who knows the name of Allan Quatermain would be likely to associate it with flowers, and especially with orchids. Yet as it happens it was once my lot to take part in an orchid hunt of so remarkable a character that I think its details should not be lost. At least I will set them down, and if in the after days anyone cares to publish them, well—he is at liberty to do so.

It was in the year—oh! never mind the year, it was a long while ago when I was much younger, that I went on a hunting expedition to the north of the Limpopo River which borders the Transvaal. My companion was a gentleman of the name of Scroope, Charles Scroope. He had come out to Durban from England in search of sport. At least, that was one of his reasons. The other was a lady whom I will call Miss Margaret Manners, though that was not her name.

It seems that these two were engaged to be married, and really attached to each other. Unfortunately, however, they quarrelled violently about another gentlemen with whom Miss Manners danced four consecutive dances, including two that were promised to her fiancé at a Hunt ball in Essex, where they all lived. Explanations, or rather argument, followed. Mr. Scroope said that he would not tolerate such conduct. Miss Manners replied that she would not be dictated to; she was her own mistress and meant to remain so. Mr. Scroope exclaimed that she might so far as he was concerned. She answered that she never wished to see his face again. He declared with emphasis that she never should and that he was going to Africa to shoot elephants.

What is more, he went, starting from his Essex home the next day without leaving any address. As it transpired afterwards, long afterwards, had he waited till the post came in he would have received a letter that might have changed his plans. But they were high-spirited young people, both of them, and played the fool after the fashion of those in love.

Well, Charles Scroope turned up in Durban, which was but a poor place then, and there we met in the bar of the Royal Hotel.

"If you want to kill big game," I heard some one say, who it was I really forget, "there's the man to show you how to do it—Hunter

Quatermain; the best shot in Africa and one of the finest fellows, too."

I sat still, smoking my pipe and pretending to hear nothing. It is awkward to listen to oneself being praised, and I was always a shy man.

Then after a whispered colloquy Mr. Scroope was brought forward and introduced to me. I bowed as nicely as I could and ran my eye over him. He was a tall young man with dark eyes and a rather romantic aspect (that was due to his love affair), but I came to the conclusion that I liked the cut of his jib. When he spoke, that conclusion was affirmed. I always think there is a great deal in a voice; personally, I judge by it almost as much as by the face. This voice was particularly pleasant and sympathetic, though there was nothing very original or striking in the words by which it was, so to speak, introduced to me. These were:

"How do you do, sir. Will you have a split?"

I answered that I never drank spirits in the daytime, or at least not often, but that I should be pleased to take a small bottle of beer.

When the beer was consumed we walked up together to my little house on which is now called the Berea, the same in which, amongst others, I received my friends, Curtis and Good, in after days, and there we dined. Indeed, Charlie Scroope never left that house until we started on our shooting expedition.

Now I must cut all this story short, since it is only incidentally that it has to do with the tale I am going to tell. Mr. Scroope was a rich man and as he offered to pay all the expenses of the expedition while I was to take all the profit in the shape of ivory or anything else that might accrue, of course I did not decline his proposal.

Everything went well with us on that trip until its unfortunate end. We only killed two elephants, but of other game we found plenty. It was when we were near Delagoa Bay on our return that the accident happened.

We were out one evening trying to shoot something for our dinner, when between the trees I caught sight of a small buck. It vanished round a little promontory of rock which projected from the side of the kloof, walking quietly, not running in alarm. We followed after it. I was the first, and had just wriggled round these rocks and perceived the buck standing about ten paces away (it was a bush-bok), when I heard a rustle among the bushes on the top of the rock not a dozen feet above my head, and Charlie Scroope's voice calling:

"Look out, Quatermain! He's coming."

"Who's coming?" I answered in an irritated tone, for the noise had made the buck run away.

Then it occurred to me, all in an instant of course, that a man would not begin to shout like that for nothing; at any rate when his supper was concerned. So I glanced up above and behind me. To this moment I can remember exactly what I saw. There was the granite water-worn boulder, or rather several boulders, with ferns growing in their cracks of the maiden-hair tribe, most of them, but some had a silver sheen on the under side of their leaves. On one of these leaves, bending it down, sat a large beetle with red wings and a black body engaged in rubbing its antennæ with its front paws. And above, just appearing over the top of the rock, was the head of an extremely fine leopard. As I write to seem to perceive its square jowl outlined against the arc of the quiet evening sky with the saliva dropping from its lips.

This was the last thing which I did perceive for a little while, since at that moment the leopard—we call them tigers in South Africa— dropped upon my back and knocked me flat as a pancake. I presume that it also had been stalking the buck and was angry at my appearance on the scene. Down I went, luckily for me, into a patch of mossy soil.

"All up!" I said to myself, for I felt the brute's weight upon my back pressing me down among the moss, and what was worse, its hot breath upon my neck as it dropped its jaws to bite me in the head. Then I heard the report of Scroope's rifle, followed by furious snarling from the leopard, which evidently had been hit. Also it seemed to think that I had caused its injuries, for it seized me by the shoulder. I felt its teeth slip along my skin, but happily they only fastened in the shooting coat of tough corduroy that I was wearing. It began to shake me, then let go to get a better grip. Now, remembering that Scroope only carried a light, single-barrelled rifle, and therefore could not fire again, I knew, or thought I knew, that my time had come. I was not exactly afraid, but the sense of some great, impending chance became very vivid. I remembered—not my whole life, but one or two odd little things connected with my infancy. For instance, I seemed to see myself seated on my mother's knee, playing with a little jointed gold-fish which she wore upon her watch-chain.

After this I muttered a word or two of supplication, and, I think, lost consciousness. If so, it can only have been for a few seconds. Then my mind returned to me and I saw a strange sight. The leopard and Scroope were fighting each other. The leopard, standing on one hind leg, for the other was broken, seemed to be boxing Scroope, whilst Scroope was driving his big hunting knife into the brute's carcase. They went down, Scroope undermost, the leopard tearing at him. I gave a wriggle and came out of that mossy bed—I recall the sucking sound my body made as it left the ooze.

Close by was my rifle, uninjured and at full cock as it had fallen from my hand. I seized it, and in another second had shot the leopard through the head just as it was about to seize Scroope's throat.

It fell stone dead on the top of him. One quiver, one contraction of the claws (in poor Scroope's leg) and all was over. There it lay as though it were asleep, and underneath was Scroope.

The difficulty was to get it off him, for the beast was very heavy, but I managed this at last with the help of a thorn bough I found which some elephant had torn from a tree. This I used as a lever. There beneath lay Scroope, literally covered with blood, though whether his own or the leopard's I could not tell. At first I thought that he was dead, but after I had poured some water over him from the little stream that trickled down the rock, he sat up and asked inconsequently:

"What am I now?"

"A hero," I answered. (I have always been proud of that repartee.)

Then, discouraging further conversation, I set to work to get him back to the camp, which fortunately was close at hand.

When we had proceeded a couple of hundred yards, he still making inconsequent remarks, his right arm round my neck and my left arm round his middle, suddenly he collapsed in a dead faint, and as his weight was more than I could carry, I had to leave him and fetch help.

In the end I got him to the tents by aid of the Kaffirs and a blanket, and there made an examination. He was scratched all over, but the only serious wounds were a bite through the muscles of the left upper arm and three deep cuts in the right thigh just where it joins the body, caused by a stroke of the leopard's claws. I gave him a dose of laudanum to send him to sleep and dressed these hurts as best I could. For three days he went on quite well. Indeed, the wounds had begun to heal healthily when suddenly some kind of fever took him, caused, I suppose, by the poison of the leopard's fangs or claws.

Oh! what a terrible week was that which followed! He became delirious, raving continually of all sorts of things, and especially of Miss Margaret Manners. I kept up his strength as well as was possible with soup made from the flesh of game, mixed with a little brandy which

I had. But he grew weaker and weaker. Also the wounds in the thigh began to suppurate.

The Kaffirs whom we had with us were of little use in such a case, so that all the nursing fell on me. Luckily, beyond a shaking, the leopard had done me no hurt, and I was very strong in those days. Still the lack of rest told on me, since I dared not sleep for more than half an hour or so at a time. At length came a morning when I was quite worn out. There lay poor Scroope turning and muttering in the little tent, and there I sat by his side, wondering whether he would live to see another dawn, or if he did, for how long I should be able to tend him. I called to a Kaffir to bring me my coffee, and just was I was lifting the pannikin to my lips with a shaking hand, help came.

It arrived in a very strange shape. In front of our camp were two thorn trees, and from between these trees, the rays from the rising sun falling full on him, I saw a curious figure walking towards me in a slow, purposeful fashion. It was that of a man of uncertain age, for though the beard and long hair were white, the face was comparatively youthful, save for the wrinkles round the mouth, and the dark eyes were full of life and vigour. Tattered garments, surmounted by a torn kaross or skin rug, hung awkwardly upon his tall, thin frame. On his feet were veldschoen of untanned hide, on his back a battered tin case was strapped, and in his bony, nervous hand he clasped a long staff made of the black and white wood the natives call *unzimbiti*, on the top of which was fixed a butterfly net. Behind him were some Kaffirs who carried cases on their heads.

I knew him at once, since we had met before, especially on a certain occasion in Zululand, when he calmly appeared out of the ranks of a hostile native *impi*. He was one of the strangest characters in all South Africa. Evidently a gentleman in the true sense of the word, none knew his history (although I know it now, and a strange story it is), except that he was an American by birth, for in this matter at times his speech betrayed him. Also he was a doctor by profession, and to judge from his extraordinary skill, one who must have seen much practice both in medicine and in surgery. For the rest he had means, though where they came from was a mystery, and for many years past had wandered about South and Eastern Africa, collecting butterflies and flowers.

By the natives, and I might add by white people also, he was universally supposed to be mad. This reputation, coupled with his medical skill, enabled him to travel wherever he would without the slightest fear of molestation, since the Kaffirs look upon the mad as inspired by God. Their name for him was "Dogeetah," a ludicrous corruption of the English word "doctor," whereas white folk called him indifferently "Brother John," "Uncle Jonathan," or "Saint John." The second appellation he got from his extraordinary likeness (when cleaned up and nicely dressed) to the figure by which the great American nation is typified in comic papers, as England is typified by John Bull. The first and third arose in the well-known goodness of his character and a taste he was supposed to possess for living on locusts and wild honey, or their local equivalents. Personally, however, he preferred to be addressed as "Brother John."

Oh! who can tell the relief with which I saw him; an angel from heaven could scarcely have been more welcome. As he came I poured out a second jorum of coffee, and remembering that he liked it sweet, put in plenty of sugar.

"How do you do, Brother John?" I said, proffering him the coffee.

"Greeting, Brother Allan," he answered—in those days he affected a kind of old Roman way of speaking, as I imagine it. Then he took the coffee, put his long finger into it to test the temperature and stir up the sugar, drank it off as though it were a dose of medicine, and handed back the tin to be refilled.

"Bug-hunting?" I queried.

He nodded. "That and flowers and observing human nature and the wonderful works of God. Wandering around generally."

"Where from last?" I asked.

"Those hills nearly twenty miles away. Left them at eight in the evening; walked all night."

"Why?" I said, looking at him.

"Because it seemed as though someone were calling me. To be plain, you, Allan."

"Oh! you heard about my being here and the trouble?"

"No, heard nothing. Meant to strike out for the coast this morning. Just as I was turning in, at 8.5 exactly, got your message and started. That's all."

"My message—" I began, then stopped, and asking to see his watch, compared it with mine. Oddly enough, they showed the same time to within two minutes.

"It is a strange thing," I said slowly, "but at 8.5 last night I did try to send a message for some help because I thought my mate was dying," and I jerked my thumb towards the tent. "Only it wasn't to you or any other man, Brother John. Understand?"

"Quite. Message was expressed on, that's all. Expressed and I guess registered as well."

I looked at Brother John and Brother John looked at me, but at the time we made no further remark. The thing was too curious, that is, unless he lied. But nobody had ever known him to lie. He was a truthful person, painfully truthful at times. And yet there are people who do not believe in prayer.

"What is it?" he asked.

"Mauled by leopard. Wounds won't heal, and fever. I don't think he can last long."

"What do you know about it? Let me see him."

Well, he saw him and did wonderful things. That tin box of his was full of medicines and surgical instruments, which latter he boiled before he used them. Also he washed his hands till I thought the skin would come off them, using up more soap than I could spare. First he gave poor Charlie a dose of something that seemed to kill him; he said he had that drug from the Kaffirs. Then he opened up those wounds upon his thigh and cleaned them out and bandaged them with boiled herbs. Afterwards, when Scroope came to again, he gave him a drink that threw him into a sweat and took away the fever. The end of it was that in two days' time his patient sat up and asked for a square meal, and in a week we were able to begin to carry him to the coast.

"Guess that message of yours saved Brother Scroope's life," said old John, as he watched him start.

I made no answer. Here I may state, however, that through my own men I inquired a little as to Brother John's movements at the time of what he called the message. It seemed that he *had* arranged to march towards the coast on the next morning, but that about two hours after sunset suddenly he ordered them to pack up everything and follow him. This they did and to their intense disgust those Kaffirs were forced to trudge all night at the heels of Dogeetah, as they called him. Indeed, so weary did they become, that had they not been afraid of being left alone in an unknown country in the darkness, they said they would have thrown down their loads and refused to go any further.

That is as far as I was able to take the matter, which may be explained by telepathy, inspiration, instinct, or coincidence. It is one as to which the reader must form his own opinion.

During our week together in camp and our subsequent journey to Delagoa Bay and thence by ship to Durban, Brother John and I grew very intimate, with limitations. Of his past, as I have said, he never talked, or of the real object of his wanderings which I learned afterwards, but of his natural history and ethnological (I believe that is the word) studies he spoke a good deal. As, in my humble way, I also am an observer of such matters and know something about African natives and their habits from practical experience, these subjects interested me.

Amongst other things, he showed me many of the specimens that he had collected during his recent journey; insects and beautiful butterflies neatly pinned into boxes, also a quantity of dried flowers pressed between sheets of blotting paper, amongst them some which he told me were orchids. Observing that these attracted me, he asked me if I would like to see the most wonderful orchid in the whole world. Of course I said yes, whereon he produced out of one of his cases a flat package about two feet six square. He undid the grass mats in which it was wrapped, striped, delicately woven mats such as they make in the neighbourhood of Zanzibar. Within these was the lid of a packing-case. Then came more mats and some copies of *The Cape Journal* spread out flat. Then sheets of blotting paper, and last of all between two pieces of cardboard, a flower and one leaf of the plant on which it grew.

Even in its dried state it was a wondrous thing, measuring twenty-four inches from the tip of one wing or petal to the tip of the other, by twenty inches from the top of the back sheath to the bottom of the pouch. The measurement of the back sheath itself I forget, but it must have been quite a foot across. In colour it was, or had been, bright golden, but the back sheath was white, barred with lines of black, and in the exact centre of the pouch was a single black spot shaped like the head of a great ape. There were the overhanging brows, the deep recessed eyes, the surly mouth, the massive jaws—everything.

Although at that time I had never seen a gorilla in the flesh, I had seen a coloured picture of the brute, and if that picture had been photographed on the flower the likeness could not have been more perfect.

"What is it?" I asked, amazed.

"Sir," said Brother John, sometimes he used this formal term when excited, "it is the most marvellous Cypripedium in the whole earth, and, sir, I have discovered it. A healthy root of that plant will be worth £20,000."

"That's better than gold mining," I said. "Well, have you got the root?"

Brother John shook his head sadly as he answered:

"No such luck."

"How's that as you have the flower?"

"I'll tell you, Allan. For a year past and more I have been collecting in the district back of Kilwa and found some wonderful things, yes, wonderful. At last, about three hundred miles inland, I came to a tribe, or rather, a people, that no white man had ever visited. They are called the Mazitu, a numerous and warlike people of bastard Zulu blood."

"I have heard of them," I interrupted. "They broke north before the days of Senzangakona, two hundred years or more ago."

"Well, I could make myself understood among them because they still talk a corrupt Zulu, as do all the tribes in those parts. At first they wanted to kill me, but let me go because they thought that I was mad. Everyone thinks that I am mad, Allan; it is a kind of public delusion, whereas I think that I am sane and that most other people are mad."

"A private delusion," I suggested hurriedly, as I did not wish to discuss Brother John's sanity. "Well, go on about the Mazitu."

"Later they discovered that I had skill in medicine, and their king, Bausi, came to me to be treated for a great external tumour. I risked an operation and cured him. It was anxious work, for if he had died I should have died too, though that would not have troubled me very much," and he sighed. "Of course, from that moment I was supposed to be a great magician. Also Bausi made a blood brotherhood with me, transfusing some of his blood into my veins and some of mine into his. I only hope he has not inoculated me with his tumours, which are congenital. So I became Bausi and Bausi became me. In other words, I was as much chief of the Mazitu as he was, and shall remain so all my life."

"That might be useful," I said, reflectively, "but go on."

"I learned that on the western boundary of the Mazitu territory were great swamps; that beyond these swamps was a lake called Kirua, and beyond that a large and fertile land supposed to be an island, with a mountain in its centre. This land is known as Pongo, and so are the people who live there."

"That is a native name for the gorilla, isn't it?" I asked. "At least so a fellow who had been on the West Coast told me."

"Indeed, then that's strange, as you will see. Now these Pongo are supposed to be great magicians, and the god they worship is said to be a gorilla, which, if you are right, accounts for their name. Or rather," he went on, "they have two gods. The other is that flower you see there. Whether the flower with the monkey's head on it was the first god and suggested the worship of the beast itself, or *vice versa*, I don't know. Indeed I know very little, just what I was told by the Mazitu and a man who called himself a Pongo chief, no more."

"What did they say?"

"The Mazitu said that the Pongo people are devils who came by the secret channels through the reeds in canoes and stole their children and women, whom they sacrificed to their gods. Sometimes, too, they made raids upon them at night, 'howling like hyenas.' The men they killed and the women and children they took away. The Mazitu want to attack them but cannot do so, because they are not water people and have no canoes, and therefore are unable to reach the island, if it is an island. Also they told me about the wonderful flower which grows in the place where the ape-god lives, and is worshipped like the god. They had the story of it from some of their people who had been enslaved and escaped."

"Did you try to get to the island?" I asked.

"Yes, Allan. That is, I went to the edge of the reeds which lie at the end of a long slope of plain, where the lake begins. Here I stopped for some time catching butterflies and collecting plants. One night when I was camped there by myself, for none of my men would remain so near the Pongo country after sunset, I woke up with a sense that I was no longer alone. I crept out of my tent and by the light of the moon, which was setting, for dawn drew near, I saw a man who leant upon the handle of a very wide-bladed spear which was taller than himself, a big man over six feet two high, I should say, and broad in proportion. He wore a long, white cloak reaching from his shoulders almost to the ground. On his head was a tight-fitting cap with lappets, also white. In his ears were rings of copper or gold, and on his wrists bracelets of the same metal. His skin was intensely black, but the features were not at all negroid. They were prominent and finely-cut, the nose being sharp and the lips quite thin; indeed of an Arab type. His left hand was bandaged, and on his face was an expression of great anxiety. Lastly, he appeared to be about fifty years of age. So still did he stand that I began to wonder whether he were one of those ghosts which the Mazitu swore the Pongo wizards send out to haunt their country.

"For a long while we stared at each other, for I was determined that I would not speak first or show any concern. At last he spoke in a low, deep voice and in Mazitu, or a language so similar that I found it easy to understand.

"'Is not your name Dogeetah, O White Lord, and are you not a master of medicine?'

"'Yes,' I answered, 'but who are you who dare to wake me from my sleep?'

"'Lord, I am the Kalubi, the Chief of the Pongo, a great man in my own land yonder.'

"'Then why do you come here alone at night, Kalubi, Chief of the Pongo?'

"'Why do *you* come here alone, White Lord?' he answered evasively.

"'What do you want, anyway?' I asked.

"'O! Dogeetah, I have been hurt, I want you to cure me,' and he looked at his bandaged hand.

"'Lay down that spear and open your robe that I may see you have no knife.'

"He obeyed, throwing the spear to some distance.

"'Now unwrap the hand.'

"He did so. I lit a match, the sight of which seemed to frighten him greatly, although he asked no questions about it, and by its light examined the hand. The first joint of the second finger was gone. From the appearance of the stump which had been cauterized and was tied tightly with a piece of flexible grass, I judged that it had been bitten off.

"'What did this?' I asked.

"'Monkey,' he answered, 'poisonous monkey. Cut off the finger, O Dogeetah, or tomorrow I die.'

"'Why do you not tell your own doctors to cut off the finger, you who are Kalubi, Chief of the Pongo?'

"'No, no,' he replied, shaking his head. 'They cannot do it. It is not lawful. And I, I cannot do it, for if the flesh is black the hand must come off too, and if the flesh is black at the wrist, then the arm must be cut off.'

"I sat down on my camp stool and reflected. Really I was waiting for the sun to rise, since it was useless to attempt an operation in that light. The man, Kalubi, thought that I had refused his petition and became terribly agitated.

"'Be merciful, White Lord,' he prayed, 'do not let me die. I am afraid to die. Life is bad, but death is worse. O! If you refuse me, I will kill myself here before you and then my ghost will haunt you till you die also of fear and come to join me. What fee do you ask? Gold or ivory or slaves? Say and I will give it.'

"'Be silent,' I said, for I saw that if he went on thus he would throw himself into a fever, which might cause the operation to prove fatal. For the same reason I did not question him about many things I should have liked to learn. I lit my fire and boiled the instruments—he thought I was making magic. By the time that everything was ready the sun was up.

"'Now,' I said, 'let me see how brave you are.'

"Well, Allan, I performed that operation, removing the finger at the base where it joins the hand, as I thought there might be something in his story of the poison. Indeed, as I found afterwards on dissection, and can show you, for I have the thing in spirits, there was, for the blackness of which he spoke, a kind of mortification, I presume, had crept almost to the joint, though the flesh beyond was healthy enough. Certainly that Kalubi was a plucky fellow. He sat like a rock and never even winced. Indeed, when he saw that the flesh was sound he uttered a great sigh of relief. After it was all over he turned a little faint, so I gave him some spirits of wine mixed with water which revived him.

"'O Lord Dogeetah,' he said, as I was bandaging his hand, 'while I live I am your slave. Yet, do me one more service. In my land there is a terrible wild beast, that which bit off my finger. It is a devil; it kills us and we fear it. I have heard that you white men have magic weapons which slay with a noise. Come to my land and kill me that wild beast with your magic weapon. I say, Come, Come, for I am terribly afraid,' and indeed he looked it.

"'No,' I answered, 'I shed no blood; I kill nothing except butterflies, and of these only a few. But if you fear this brute why do you not poison it? You black people have many drugs.'

"'No use, no use,' he replied in a kind of wail. 'The beast knows poisons, some it swallows and they do not harm it. Others it will not touch. Moreover, no black man can do it hurt. It is white, and it has been known from of old that if it dies at all, it must be by the hand of one who is white.'

"'A very strange animal,' I began, suspiciously, for I felt sure that he was lying to me. But just at that moment I heard the sound of my men's voices. They were advancing towards me through the giant grass, singing as they came, but as yet a long way off. The Kalubi heard it also and sprang up.

H. RIDER HAGGARD

"'I must be gone,' he said. 'None must see me here. What fee, O Lord of medicine, what fee?'

"'I take no payment for my medicine,' I said. 'Yet—stay. A wonderful flower grows in your country, does it not? A flower with wings and a cup beneath. I would have that flower.'

"'Who told you of the Flower?' he asked. 'The Flower is holy. Still, O White Lord, still for you it shall be risked. Oh, return and bring with you one who can kill the beast and I will make you rich. Return and call to the reeds for the Kalubi, and the Kalubi will hear and come to you.'

"Then he ran to his spear, snatched it from the ground and vanished among the reeds. That was the last I saw, or am ever likely to see, of him."

"But, Brother John, you got the flower somehow."

"Yes, Allan. About a week later when I came out of my tent one morning, there it was standing in a narrow-mouthed, earthenware pot filled with water. Of course I meant that he was to send me the plant, roots and all, but I suppose he understood that I wanted a bloom. Or perhaps he dared not send the plant. Anyhow, it is better than nothing."

"Why did you not go into the country and get it for yourself?"

"For several reasons, Allan, of which the best is that it was impossible. The Mazitu swear that if anyone sees that flower he is put to death. Indeed, when they found that I had a bloom of it, they forced me to move to the other side of the country seventy miles away. So I thought that I would wait till I met with some companions who would accompany me. Indeed, to be frank, Allan, it occurred to me that you were the sort of man who would like to interview this wonderful beast that bites off people's fingers and frightens them to death," and Brother John stroked his long, white beard and smiled, adding, "Odd that we should have met so soon afterwards, isn't it?"

"Did you?" I replied, "now did you indeed? Brother John, people say all sorts of things about you, but I have come to the conclusion that there's nothing the matter with your wits."

Again he smiled and stroked his long, white beard.

II

The Auction Room

I do not think that this conversion about the Pongo savages who were said to worship a Gorilla and a Golden Flower was renewed until we reached my house at Durban. Thither of course I took Mr. Charles Scroope, and thither also came Brother John who, as bedroom accommodation was lacking, pitched his tent in the garden.

One night we sat on the step smoking; Brother John's only concession to human weakness was that he smoked. He drank no wine or spirits; he never ate meat unless he was obliged, but I rejoice to say that he smoked cigars, like most Americans, when he could get them.

"John," said I, "I have been thinking over that yarn of yours and have come to one or two conclusions."

"What may they be, Allan?"

"The first is that you were a great donkey not to get more out of the Kalubi when you had the chance."

"Agreed, Allan, but, amongst other things, I am a doctor and the operation was uppermost in my mind."

"The second is that I believe this Kalubi had charge of the gorilla-god, as no doubt you've guessed; also that it was the gorilla which bit off his finger."

"Why so?"

"Because I have heard of great monkeys called *sokos* that live in Central East Africa which are said to bite off men's toes and fingers. I have heard too that they are very like gorillas."

"Now you mention it, so have I, Allan. Indeed, once I saw a *soko*, though some way off, a huge, brown ape which stood on its hind legs and drummed upon its chest with its fists. I didn't see it for long because I ran away."

"The third is that this yellow orchid would be worth a great deal of money if one could dig it up and take it to England."

"I think I told you, Allan, that I valued it at £20,000, so that conclusion of yours is not original."

"The fourth is that I should like to dig up that orchid and get a share of the £20,000."

Brother John became intensely interested.

"Ah!" he said, "now we are getting to the point. I have been wondering how long it would take you to see it, Allan, but if you are slow, you are sure."

"The fifth is," I went on, "that such an expedition to succeed would need a great deal of money, more than you or I could find. Partners would be wanted, active or sleeping, but partners with cash."

Brother John looked towards the window of the room in which Charlie Scroope was in bed, for being still weak he went to rest early.

"No," I said, "he's had enough of Africa, and you told me yourself that it will be two years before he is really strong again. Also there's a lady in this case. Now listen. I have taken it on myself to write to that lady, whose address I found out while he didn't know what he was saying. I have said that he was dying, but that I hoped he might live. Meanwhile, I added, I thought she would like to know that he did nothing but rave of her; also that he was a hero, with a big H twice underlined. My word! I did lay it on about the hero business with a spoon, a real hotel gravy spoon. If Charlie Scroope knows himself again when he sees my description of him, well, I'm a Dutchman, that's all. The letter caught the last mail and will, I hope, reach the lady in due course. Now listen again. Scroope wants me to go to England with him to look after him on the voyage—that's what he says. What he means is that he hopes I might put in a word for him with the lady, if I should chance to be introduced to her. He offers to pay all my expenses and to give me something for my loss of time. So, as I haven't seen England since I was three years old, I think I'll take the chance."

Brother John's face fell. "Then how about the expedition, Allan?" he asked.

"This is the first of November," I answered, "and the wet season in those parts begins about now and lasts till April. So it would be no use trying to visit your Pongo friends till then, which gives me plenty of time to go to England and come out again. If you'll trust that flower to me I'll take it with me. Perhaps I might be able to find someone who would be willing to put down money on the chance of getting the plant on which it grew. Meanwhile, you are welcome to this house if you care to stay here."

"Thank you, Allan, but I can't sit still for so many months. I'll go somewhere and come back." He paused and a dreamy look came into his dark eyes, then went on, "You see, Brother, it is laid on me to wander and wander through all this great land until—I know."

"Until you know what?" I asked, sharply.

He pulled himself together with a jerk, as it were, and answered with a kind of forced carelessness.

"Until I know every inch of it, of course. There are lots of tribes I have not yet visited."

"Including the Pongo," I said. "By the way, if I can get the money together for a trip up there, I suppose you mean to come too, don't you? If not, the thing's off so far as I am concerned. You see, I am reckoning on you to get us through the Mazitu and into Pongo-land by the help of your friends."

"Certainly I mean to come. In fact, if you don't go, I shall start alone. I intend to explore Pongo-land even if I never come out of it again."

Once more I looked at him as I answered:

"You are ready to risk a great deal for a flower, John. Or are you looking for more than a flower? If so, I hope you will tell me the truth."

This I said as I was aware that Brother John had a foolish objection to uttering, or even acting lies.

"Well, Allan, as you put it like that, the truth is that I heard something more about the Pongo than I told you up country. It was after I had operated on that Kalubi, or I would have tried to get in alone. But this I could not do then as I have said."

"And what did you hear?"

"I heard that they had a white goddess as well as a white god."

"Well, what of it? A female gorilla, I suppose."

"Nothing, except that goddesses have always interested me. Good night."

"You are an odd old fish," I remarked after him, "and what is more you have got something up your sleeve. Well, I'll have it down one day. Meanwhile, I wonder whether the whole thing is a lie, no; not a lie, an hallucination. It can't be—because of that orchid. No one can explain away the orchid. A queer people, these Pongo, with their white god and goddess and their Holy Flower. But after all Africa is a land of queer people, and of queer gods too."

AND NOW THE STORY SHIFTS away to England. (Don't be afraid, my adventurous reader, if ever I have one, it is coming back to Africa again in a very few pages.)

Mr. Charles Scroope and I left Durban a day or two after my last conversation with Brother John. At Cape Town we caught the mail, a wretched little boat you would think it now, which after a long and wearisome journey at length landed us safe at Plymouth. Our companions on that voyage were very dull. I have forgotten most of them, but one lady I do remember. I imagine that she must have commenced life as a barmaid, for she had the orthodox tow hair and blowsy appearance. At any rate, she was the wife of a wine-merchant who had made a fortune at the Cape. Unhappily, however, she had contracted too great a liking for her husband's wares, and after dinner was apt to become talkative. For some reason or other she took a particular aversion to me. Oh! I can see her now, seated in that saloon with the oil lamp swinging over her head (she always chose the position under the oil lamp because it showed off her diamonds). And I can hear her too. "Don't bring any of your elephant-hunting manners here, Mr. Allan" (with an emphasis on the Allan) "Quatermain, they are not fit for polite society. You should go and brush your hair, Mr. Quatermain." (I may explain that my hair sticks up naturally.)

Then would come her little husband's horrified "Hush! hush! you are quite insulting, my dear."

Oh! why do I remember it all after so many years when I have even forgotten the people's names? One of those little things that stick in the mind, I suppose. The Island of Ascension, where we called, sticks also with its long swinging rollers breaking in white foam, its bare mountain peak capped with green, and the turtles in the ponds. Those poor turtles. We brought two of them home, and I used to look at them lying on their backs in the forecastle flapping their fins feebly. One of them died, and I got the butcher to save me the shell. Afterwards I gave it as a wedding present to Mr. and Mrs. Scroope, nicely polished and lined. I meant it for a work-basket, and was overwhelmed with confusion when some silly lady said at the marriage, and in the hearing of the bride and bridegroom, that it was the most beautiful cradle she had ever seen. Of course, like a fool, I tried to explain, whereon everybody tittered.

But why do I write of such trifles that have nothing to do with my story?

I mentioned that I had ventured to send a letter to Miss Margaret Manners about Mr. Charles Scroope, in which I said incidentally that if the hero should happen to live I should probably bring him home by the next mail. Well, we got into Plymouth about eight o'clock in the morning, on a mild, November day, and shortly afterwards a tug arrived to take off the passengers and mails; also some cargo. I, being an early riser, watched it come and saw upon the deck a stout lady wrapped in furs, and by her side a very pretty, fair-haired young woman clad in a neat serge dress and a pork-pie hat. Presently a steward told me that someone wished to speak to me in the saloon. I went and found these two standing side by side.

"I believe you are Mr. Allan Quatermain," said the stout lady. "Where is Mr. Scroope whom I understand you have brought home? Tell me at once."

Something about her appearance and fierce manner of address alarmed me so much that I could only answer feebly:

"Below, madam, below."

"There, my dear," said the stout lady to her companion, "I warned you to be prepared for the worst. Bear up; do not make a scene before all these people. The ways of Providence are just and inscrutable. It is your own temper that was to blame. You should never have sent the poor man off to these heathen countries."

Then, turning to me, she added sharply: "I suppose he is embalmed; we should like to bury him in Essex."

"Embalmed!" I gasped. "Embalmed! Why, the man is in his bath, or was a few minutes ago."

In another second that pretty young lady who had been addressed was weeping with her head upon my shoulder.

"Margaret!" exclaimed her companion (she was a kind of heavy aunt), "I told you not to make a scene in public. Mr. Quatermain, as Mr. Scroope is alive, would you ask him to be so good as to come here."

Well, I fetched him, half-shaved, and the rest of the business may be imagined. It is a very fine thing to be a hero with a big H. Henceforth (thanks to me) that was Charlie Scroope's lot in life. He has grandchildren now, and they all think him a hero. What is more, he does not contradict them. I went down to the lady's place in Essex, a fine property with a beautiful old house. On the night I arrived there was a dinner-party of twenty-four people. I had to make a speech about Charlie Scroope and the leopard. I think it was a good speech. At any rate everybody cheered, including the servants, who had gathered at the back of the big hall.

I remember that to complete the story I introduced several other leopards, a mother and two three-part-grown cubs, also a wounded buffalo, and told how Mr. Scroope finished them off one after the other with a hunting knife. The thing was to watch his face as the history proceeded. Luckily he was sitting next to me and I could kick him under the table. It was all very amusing, and very happy also, for these two really loved each other. Thank God that I, or rather Brother John, was able to bring them together again.

It was during that stay of mine in Essex, by the way, that I first met Lord Ragnall and the beautiful Miss Holmes with whom I was destined to experience some very strange adventures in the after years.

AFTER THIS INTERLUDE I GOT to work. Someone told me that there was a firm in the City that made a business of selling orchids by auction, flowers which at this time were beginning to be very fashionable among rich horticulturists. This, thought I, would be the place for me to show my treasure. Doubtless Messrs. May and Primrose—that was their world-famed style—would be able to put me in touch with opulent orchidists who would not mind venturing a couple of thousands on the chance of receiving a share in a flower that, according to Brother John, should be worth untold gold. At any rate, I would try.

So on a certain Friday, about half-past twelve, I sought out the place of business of Messrs. May and Primrose, bearing with me the golden Cypripedium, which was now enclosed in a flat tin case.

As it happened I chose an unlucky day and hour, for on arriving at the office and asking for Mr. May, I was informed that he was away in the country valuing.

"Then I would like to see Mr. Primrose," I said.

"Mr. Primrose is round at the Rooms selling," replied the clerk, who appeared to be very busy.

"Where are the Rooms?" I asked.

"Out of the door, turn to the left, turn to the left again and under the clock," said the clerk, and closed the shutter.

So disgusted was I with his rudeness that I nearly gave up the enterprise. Thinking better of it, however, I followed the directions given, and in a minute or two found myself in a narrow passage that led to a large room. To one who had never seen anything of the sort before, this room offered a curious sight. The first thing I observed was a notice on the wall to the effect that customers were not allowed to smoke pipes. I thought to myself that orchids must be curious flowers if they could distinguish between the smoke of a cigar and a pipe, and stepped into the room. To my left was a long table covered with pots of the most beautiful flowers that I had ever seen; all of them orchids. Along the wall and opposite were other tables closely packed with withered roots which I concluded were also those of orchids. To my inexperienced eye the whole lot did not look worth five shillings, for they seemed to be dead.

At the head of the room stood the rostrum, where sat a gentleman with an extremely charming face. He was engaged in selling by auction so rapidly that the clerk at his side must have had difficulty in keeping a record of the lots and their purchasers. In front of him was a horseshoe table, round which sat buyers. The end of this table was left unoccupied so that the porters might exhibit each lot before it was put up for sale. Standing under the rostrum was yet another table, a small one, upon which were about twenty pots of flowers, even more wonderful than those on the large table. A notice stated that these would be sold at one-thirty precisely. All about the room stood knots of men (such ladies as were present sat at the table), many of whom had lovely orchids in their buttonholes. These, I found out afterwards, were dealers and amateurs. They were a kindly-faced set of people, and I took a liking to them.

The whole place was quaint and pleasant, especially by contrast with the horrible London fog outside. Squeezing my small person into a corner where I was in nobody's way, I watched the proceedings for a while. Suddenly an agreeable voice at my side asked me if I would like a look at the catalogue. I glanced at the speaker, and in a sense fell in love with him at once—as I have explained before, I am one of those to whom a first impression means a great deal. He was not very tall, though strong-looking and well-made enough. He was not very handsome, though none so ill-favoured. He was just an ordinary fair young Englishman, four or five-and-twenty years of age, with merry blue eyes and one of the pleasantest expressions that I ever saw. At once I felt that he was a sympathetic soul and full of the milk of human kindness. He was dressed in a rough tweed suit rather worn, with the orchid that seemed to be the badge of all this tribe in his buttonhole. Somehow the costume suited his rather pink and white complexion and rumpled fair hair, which I could see as he was sitting on his cloth hat.

"Thank you, no," I answered, "I did not come here to buy. I know nothing about orchids," I added by way of explanation, "except a few

I have seen growing in Africa, and this one," and I tapped the tin case which I held under my arm.

"Indeed," he said. "I should like to hear about the African orchids. What is it you have in the case, a plant or flowers?"

"One flower only. It is not mine. A friend in Africa asked me to— well, that is a long story which might not interest you."

"I'm not sure. I suppose it must be a Cymbidium scape from the size."

I shook my head. "That's not the name my friend mentioned. He called it a Cypripedium."

The young man began to grow curious. "One Cypripedium in all that large case? It must be a big flower."

"Yes, my friend said it is the biggest ever found. It measures twenty-four inches across the wings, petals I think he called them, and about a foot across the back part."

"Twenty-four inches across the petals and a foot across the dorsal sepal!" said the young man in a kind of gasp, "and a Cypripedium! Sir, surely you are joking?"

"Sir," I answered indignantly, "I am doing nothing of the sort. Your remark is tantamount to telling me that I am speaking a falsehood. But, of course, for all I know, the thing may be some other kind of flower."

"Let me see it. In the name of the goddess Flora let me see it!"

I began to undo the case. Indeed it was already half-open when two other gentlemen, who had either overheard some of our conversation or noted my companion's excited look, edged up to us. I observed that they also wore orchids in their buttonholes.

"Hullo! Somers," said one of them in a tone of false geniality, "what have you got there?"

"What has your friend got there?" asked the other.

"Nothing," replied the young man who had been addressed as Somers, "nothing at all; that is—only a case of tropical butterflies."

"Oh! butterflies," said No. 1 and sauntered away. But No. 2, a keen-looking person with the eye of a hawk, was not so easily satisfied.

"Let us see these butterflies," he said to me.

"You can't," exclaimed the young man. "My friend is afraid lest the damp should injure their colours. Ain't you, Brown?"

"Yes, I am, Somers," I replied, taking his cue and shutting the tin case with a snap.

Then the hawk-eyed person departed, also grumbling, for that story about the damp stuck in his throat.

"Orchidist!" whispered the young man. "Dreadful people, orchidists, so jealous. Very rich, too, both of them. Mr. Brown—I hope that is your name, though I admit the chances are against it."

"They are," I replied, "my name is Allan Quatermain."

"Ah! much better than Brown. Well, Mr. Allan Quatermain, there's a private room in this place to which I have admittance. Would you mind coming with that—" here the hawk-eyed gentleman strolled past again, "that case of butterflies?"

"With pleasure," I answered, and followed him out of the auction chamber down some steps through the door to the left, and ultimately into a little cupboard-like room lined with shelves full of books and ledgers.

He closed the door and locked it.

"Now," he said in a tone of the villain in a novel who at last has come face to face with the virtuous heroine, "now we are alone. Mr. Quatermain, let me see—those butterflies."

I placed the case on a deal table which stood under a skylight in the room. I opened it; I removed the cover of wadding, and there, pressed between two sheets of glass and quite uninjured after all its journeyings, appeared the golden flower, glorious even in death, and by its side the broad green leaf.

The young gentleman called Somers looked at it till I thought his eyes would really start out of his head. He turned away muttering something and looked again.

"Oh! Heavens," he said at last, "oh! Heavens, is it possible that such a thing can exist in this imperfect world? You haven't faked it, Mr. Half—I mean Quatermain, have you?"

"Sir," I said, "for the second time you are making insinuations. Good morning," and I began to shut up the case.

"Don't be offhanded," he exclaimed. "Pity the weaknesses of a poor sinner. You don't understand. If only you understood, you would understand."

"No," I said, "I am bothered if I do."

"Well, you will when you begin to collect orchids. I'm not mad, really, except perhaps on this point, Mr. Quatermain,"—this in a low and thrilling voice—"that marvellous Cypripedium—your friend is right, it is a Cypripedium—is worth a gold mine."

"From my experience of gold mines I can well believe that," I said tartly, and, I may add, prophetically.

"Oh! I mean a gold mine in the figurative and colloquial sense, not as the investor knows it," he answered. "That is, the plant on which it grew is priceless. Where is the plant, Mr. Quatermain?"

"In a rather indefinite locality in Africa east by south," I replied. "I can't place it to within three hundred miles."

"That's vague, Mr. Quatermain. I have no right to ask it, seeing that you know nothing of me, but I assure you I am respectable, and in short, would you mind telling me the story of this flower?"

"I don't think I should," I replied, a little doubtfully. Then, after another good look at him, suppressing all names and exact localities, I gave him the outline of the tale, explaining that I wanted to find someone who would finance an expedition to the remote and romantic spot where this particular Cypripedium was believed to grow.

Just as I finished my narrative, and before he had time to comment on it, there came a violent knocking at the door.

"Mr. Stephen," said a voice, "are you there, Mr. Stephen?"

"By Jove! that's Briggs," exclaimed the young man. "Briggs is my father's manager. Shut up the case, Mr. Quatermain. Come in, Briggs," he went on, unlocking the door slowly. "What is it?"

"It is a good deal," replied a thin and agitated person who thrust himself through the opening door. "Your father, I mean Sir Alexander, has come to the office unexpectedly and is in a nice taking because he didn't find you there, sir. When he discovered that you had gone to the orchid sale he grew furious, sir, furious, and sent me to fetch you."

"Did he?" replied Mr. Somers in an easy and unruffled tone. "Well, tell Sir Alexander I am coming at once. Now please go, Briggs, and tell him I am coming at once."

Briggs departed not too willingly.

"I must leave you, Mr. Quatermain," said Mr. Somers as he shut the door behind him. "But will you promise me not to show that flower to anyone until I return? I'll be back within half an hour."

"Yes, Mr. Somers. I'll wait half an hour for you in the sale room, and I promise that no one shall see that flower till you return."

"Thank you. You are a good fellow, and I promise you shall lose nothing by your kindness if I can help it."

We went together into the sale room, where some thought suddenly struck Mr. Somers.

"By Jove!" he said, "I nearly forgot about that Odontoglossum. Where's Woodden? Oh! come here, Woodden, I want to speak to you."

The person called Woodden obeyed. He was a man of about fifty, indefinite in colouring, for his eyes were very light-blue or grey and his hair was sandy, tough-looking and strongly made, with big hands that showed signs of work, for the palms were horny and the nails worn down. He was clad in a suit of shiny black, such as folk of the labouring class wear at a funeral. I made up my mind at once that he was a gardener.

"Woodden," said Mr. Somers, "this gentleman here has got the most wonderful orchid in the whole world. Keep your eye on him and see that he isn't robbed. There are people in this room, Mr. Quatermain, who would murder you and throw your body into the Thames for that flower," he added, darkly.

On receipt of this information Woodden rocked a little on his feet as though he felt the premonitory movements of an earthquake. It was a habit of his whenever anything astonished him. Then, fixing his pale eye upon me in a way which showed that my appearance surprised him, he pulled a lock of his sandy hair with his thumb and finger and said:

"'Servant, sir, and where might this horchid be?"

I pointed to the tin case.

"Yes, it's there," went on Mr. Somers, "and that's what you've got to watch. Mr. Quatermain, if anyone attempts to rob you, call for Woodden and he will knock them down. He's my gardener, you know, and entirely to be trusted, especially if it is a matter of knocking anyone down."

"Aye, I'll knock him down surely," said Woodden, doubling his great fist and looking round him with a suspicious eye.

"Now listen, Woodden. Have you looked at that Odontoglossum Pavo, and if so, what do you think of it?" and he nodded towards a plant which stood in the centre of the little group that was placed on the small table beneath the auctioneer's desk. It bore a spray of the most lovely white flowers. On the top petal (if it is a petal), and also on the lip of each of these rounded flowers was a blotch or spot of which the general effect was similar to the iridescent eye on the tail feathers of a peacock, whence, I suppose, the flower was named "Pavo," or Peacock.

"Yes, master, and I think it the beautifullest thing that ever I saw. There isn't a 'glossum in England like that there 'glossum Paving," he added with conviction, and rocked again as he said the word. "But there's plenty after it. I say they're a-smelling round that blossom like,

like—dawgs round a rat hole. And" (this triumphantly) "they don't do that for nothing."

"Quite so, Woodden, you have got a logical mind. But, look here, we must have that 'Pavo' whatever it costs. Now the Governor has sent for me. I'll be back presently, but I might be detained. If so, you've got to bid on my behalf, for I daren't trust any of these agents. Here's your authority," and he scribbled on a card, "Woodden, my gardener, has directions to bid for me.—S.S." "Now, Woodden," he went on, when he had given the card to an attendant who passed it up to the auctioneer, "don't you make a fool of yourself and let that 'Pavo' slip through your fingers."

In another instant he was gone.

"What did the master say, sir?" asked Woodden of me. "That I was to get that there 'Paving' whatever it cost?"

"Yes," I said, "that's what he said. I suppose it will fetch a good deal—several pounds."

"Maybe, sir, can't tell. All I know is that I've got to buy it as you can bear me witness. Master, he ain't one to be crossed for money. What he wants, he'll have, that is if it be in the orchid line."

"I suppose you are fond of orchids, too, Mr. Woodden?"

"Fond of them, sir? Why, I loves 'em!" (Here he rocked.) "Don't feel for nothing else in the same way; not even for my old woman" (then with a burst of enthusiasm) "no, not even for the master himself, and I'm fond enough of him, God knows! But, begging your pardon, sir" (with a pull at his forelock), "would you mind holding that tin of yours a little tighter? I've got to keep an eye on that as well as on 'O. Paving,' and I just see'd that chap with the tall hat alooking at it suspicious."

After this we separated. I retired into my corner, while Woodden took his stand by the table, with one eye fixed on what he called the "O. Paving" and the other on me and my tin case.

An odd fish truly, I thought to myself. Positive, the old woman; Comparative, his master; Superlative, the orchid tribe. Those were his degrees of affection. Honest and brave and a good fellow though, I bet.

The sale languished. There were so many lots of one particular sort of dried orchid that buyers could not be found for them at a reasonable price, and many had to be bought in. At length the genial Mr. Primrose in the rostrum addressed the audience.

"Gentlemen," he said, "I quite understand that you didn't come here to-day to buy a rather poor lot of Cattleya Mossiæ. You came to buy, or to bid for, or to see sold the most wonderful Odontoglossum that has ever been flowered in this country, the property of a famous firm of importers whom I congratulate upon their good fortune in having obtained such a gem. Gentlemen, this miraculous flower ought to adorn a royal greenhouse. But there it is, to be taken away by whoever will pay the most for it, for I am directed to see that it will be sold without reserve. Now, I think," he added, running his eye over the company, "that most of our great collectors are represented in this room to-day. It is true that I do not see that spirited and liberal young orchidist, Mr. Somers, but he has left his worthy head-gardener, Mr. Woodden, than whom there is no finer judge of an orchid in England" (here Woodden rocked violently) "to bid for him, as I hope, for the glorious flower of which I have been speaking. Now, as it is exactly half-past one, we will proceed to business. Smith, hand the 'Odontoglossum Pavo' round, that everyone may inspect its beauties, and be careful you don't let it fall. Gentlemen, I must ask you not to touch it or to defile its purity with tobacco smoke. Eight perfect flowers in bloom, gentlemen, and four—no, five more to open. A strong plant in perfect health, six pseudo-bulbs with leaves, and three without. Two black leads which I am advised can be separated off at the proper time. Now, what bids for the 'Odontoglossum Pavo.' Ah! I wonder who will have the honour of becoming the owner of this perfect, this unmatched production of Nature. Thank you, sir—three hundred. Four. Five. Six. Seven in three places. Eight. Nine. Ten. Oh! gentlemen, let us get on a little faster. Thank you, sir—fifteen. Sixteen. It is against you, Mr. Woodden. Ah! thank you, seventeen."

There came a pause in the fierce race for "O. Pavo," which I occupied in reducing seventeen hundred shillings to pounds sterling.

My word! I thought to myself, £85 is a goodish price to pay for one plant, however rare. Woodden is acting up to his instructions with a vengeance.

The pleading voice of Mr. Primrose broke in upon my meditations.

"Gentlemen, gentlemen!" he said, "surely you are not going to allow the most wondrous production of the floral world, on which I repeat there is no reserve, to be knocked down at this miserable figure. Come, come. Well, if I must, I must, though after such a disgrace I shall get no sleep to-night. One," and his hammer fell for the first time. "Think, gentlemen, upon my position, think what the eminent owners, who with their usual delicacy have stayed away, will say to me when I am obliged to tell them the disgraceful truth. Two," and his hammer fell a second time. "Smith, hold up that flower. Let the company see it. Let them know what they are losing."

Smith held up the flower at which everybody glared. The little ivory hammer circled round Mr. Primrose's head. It was about to fall, when a quiet man with a long beard who hitherto had not joined in the bidding, lifted his head and said softly:

"Eighteen hundred."

"Ah!" exclaimed Mr. Primrose, "I thought so. I thought that the owner of the greatest collection in England would not see this treasure slip from his grasp without a struggle. Against you, Mr. Woodden."

"Nineteen, sir," said Woodden in a stony voice.

"Two thousand," echoed the gentleman with the long beard.

"Twenty-one hundred," said Woodden.

"That's right, Mr. Woodden," cried Mr. Primrose, "you are indeed representing your principal worthily. I feel sure that you do not mean to stop for a few miserable pounds."

"Not if I knows it," exclaimed Woodden. "I has my orders and I acts up to them."

"Twenty-two hundred," said Long-beard.

"Twenty-three," echoed Woodden.

"Oh, damn!" shouted Long-beard and rushed from the room.

"'Odontoglossum Pavo' is going for twenty-three hundred, only twenty-tree hundred," cried the auctioneer. "Any advance on twenty-three hundred? What? None? Then I must do my duty. One. Two. For the last time—no advance? Three. Gone to Mr. Woodden, bidding for his principal, Mr. Somers."

The hammer fell with a sharp tap, and at this moment my young friend sauntered into the room.

"Well, Woodden," he said, "have they put the 'Pavo' up yet?"

"It's up and it's down, sir. I've bought him right enough."

"The deuce you have! What did it fetch?"

Woodden scratched his head.

"I don't rightly know, sir, never was good at figures, not having much book learning, but it's twenty-three something."

"£23? No, it would have brought more than that. By Jingo! it must be £230. That's pretty stiff, but still, it may be worth it."

At this moment Mr. Primrose, who, leaning over his desk, was engaged in animated conversation with an excited knot of orchid fanciers, looked up:

"Oh! there you are, Mr. Somers," he said. "In the name of all this company let me congratulate you on having become the owner of the matchless 'Odontoglossum Pavo' for what, under all the circumstances, I consider the quite moderate price of £2,300."

Really that young man took it very well. He shivered slightly and turned a little pale, that is all. Woodden rocked to and fro like a tree about to fall. I and my tin box collapsed together in the corner. Yes, I was so surprised that my legs seemed to give way under me. People began to talk, but above the hum of the conversation I heard young Somers say in a low voice:

"Woodden, you're a born fool." Also the answer: "That's what my mother always told me, master, and she ought to know if anyone did. But what's wrong now? I obeyed orders and bought 'O. Paving.'"

"Yes. Don't bother, my good fellow, it's my fault, not yours. I'm the born fool. But heavens above! how am I to face this?" Then, recovering himself, he strolled up to the rostrum and said a few words to the auctioneer. Mr. Primrose nodded, and I heard him answer:

"Oh, that will be all right, sir, don't bother. We can't expect an account like this to be settled in a minute. A month hence will do."

Then he went on with the sale.

III

Sir Alexander and Stephen

It was just at this moment that I saw standing by me a fine-looking, stout man with a square, grey beard and a handsome, but not very good-tempered face. He was looking about him as one does who finds himself in a place to which he is not accustomed.

"Perhaps you could tell me, sir," he said to me, "whether a gentleman called Mr. Somers is in this room. I am rather short-sighted and there are a great many people."

"Yes," I answered, "he has just bought the wonderful orchid called 'Odontoglossum Pavo.' That is what they are all talking about."

"Oh, has he? Has he indeed? And pray what did he pay for the article?"

"A huge sum," I answered. "I thought it was two thousand three hundred shillings, but it appears it was £2,300."

The handsome, elderly gentleman grew very red in the face, so red that I thought he was going to have a fit. For a few moments he breathed heavily.

"A rival collector," I thought to myself, and went on with the story which, it occurred to me, might interest him.

"You see, the young gentleman was called away to an interview with his father. I heard him instruct his gardener, a man named Woodden, to buy the plant at any price."

"At any price! Indeed. Very interesting; continue, sir."

"Well, the gardener bought it, that's all, after tremendous competition. Look, there he is packing it up. Whether his master meant him to go as far as he did I rather doubt. But here he comes. If you know him—"

The youthful Mr. Somers, looking a little pale and *distrait*, strolled up apparently to speak to me; his hands were in his pockets and an unlighted cigar was in his mouth. His eyes fell upon the elderly gentleman, a sight that caused him to shape his lips as though to whistle and drop the cigar.

"Hullo, father," he said in his pleasant voice. "I got your message and have been looking for you, but never thought that I should find you here. Orchids aren't much in your line, are they?"

"Didn't you, indeed!" replied his parent in a choked voice. "No, I haven't much use for—this stinking rubbish," and he waved his umbrella at the beautiful flowers. "But it seems that you have, Stephen. This little gentlemen here tells me you have just bought a very fine specimen."

"I must apologize," I broke in, addressing Mr. Somers. "I had not the slightest idea that this—big gentleman," here the son smiled faintly, "was your intimate relation."

"Oh! pray don't, Mr. Quatermain. Why should you not speak of what will be in all the papers. Yes, father, I have bought a very fine specimen, the finest known, or at least Woodden has on my behalf, while I was hunting for you, which comes to the same thing."

"Indeed, Stephen, and what did you pay for this flower? I have heard a figure, but think that there must be some mistake."

"I don't know what you heard, father, but it seems to have been knocked down to me at £2,300. It's a lot more than I can find, indeed, and I was going to ask you to lend me the money for the sake of the family credit, if not for my own. But we can talk about that afterwards."

"Yes, Stephen, we can talk of that afterwards. In fact, as there is no time like the present, we will talk of it now. Come to my office. And, sir" (this was to me) "as you seem to know something of the circumstances, I will ask you to come also; and you too, Blockhead" (this was to Woodden, who just then approached with the plant).

Now, of course, I might have refused an invitation conveyed in such a manner. But, as a matter of fact, I didn't. I wanted to see the thing out; also to put in a word for young Somers, if I got the chance. So we all departed from that room, followed by a titter of amusement from those of the company who had overheard the conversation. In the street stood a splendid carriage and pair; a powdered footman opened its door. With a ferocious bow Sir Alexander motioned to me to enter, which I did, taking one of the back seats as it gave more room for my tin case. Then came Mr. Stephen, then Woodden bundled in holding the precious plant in front of him like a wand of office, and last of all, Sir Alexander, having seen us safe, entered also.

"Where to, sir?" asked the footman.

"Office," he snapped, and we started.

Four disappointed relatives in a funeral coach could not have been more silent. Our feelings seemed to be too deep for words. Sir Alexander, however, did make one remark and to me. It was:

"If you will remove the corner of that infernal tin box of yours from my ribs I shall be obliged to you, sir."

"Your pardon," I exclaimed, and in my efforts to be accommodating, dropped it on his toe. I will not repeat the remark he made, but I may explain that he was gouty. His son suddenly became afflicted with a sense of the absurdity of the situation. He kicked me on the shin, he even dared to wink, and then began to swell visibly with suppressed laughter. I was in agony, for if he had exploded I do not know what would have happened. Fortunately, at this moment the carriage stopped at the door of a fine office. Without waiting for the footman Mr. Stephen bundled out and vanished into the building—I suppose to laugh in safety. Then I descended with the tin case; then, by command, followed Woodden with the flower, and lastly came Sir Alexander.

"Stop here," he said to the coachman; "I shan't be long. Be so good as to follow me, Mr. What's-your-name, and you, too, Gardener."

We followed, and found ourselves in a big room luxuriously furnished in a heavy kind of way. Sir Alexander Somers, I should explain, was an enormously opulent bullion-broker, whatever a bullion-broker may be. In this room Mr. Stephen was already established; indeed, he was seated on the window-sill swinging his leg.

"Now we are alone and comfortable," growled Sir Alexander with sarcastic ferocity.

"As the boa-constrictor said to the rabbit in the cage," I remarked.

I did not mean to say it, but I had grown nervous, and the thought leapt from my lips in words. Again Mr. Stephen began to swell. He turned his face to the window as though to contemplate the wall beyond, but I could see his shoulders shaking. A dim light of intelligence shone in Woodden's pale eyes. About three minutes later the joke got home. He gurgled something about boa-constrictors and rabbits and gave a short, loud laugh. As for Sir Alexander, he merely said:

"I did not catch your remark, sir, would you be so good as to repeat it?"

As I appeared unwilling to accept the invitation, he went on:

"Perhaps, then, you would repeat what you told me in that sale-room?"

"Why should I?" I asked. "I spoke quite clearly and you seemed to understand."

"You are right," replied Sir Alexander; "to waste time is useless." He wheeled round on Woodden, who was standing near the door still holding the paper-wrapped plant in front of him. "Now, Blockhead," he shouted, "tell me why you brought that thing."

Woodden made no answer, only rocked a little. Sir Alexander reiterated his command. This time Woodden set the plant upon a table and replied:

"If you're aspeaking to me, sir, that baint my name, and what's more, if you calls me so again, I'll punch your head, whoever you be," and very deliberately he rolled up the sleeves on his brawny arms, a sight at which I too began to swell with inward merriment.

"Look here, father," said Mr. Stephen, stepping forward. "What's the use of all this? The thing's perfectly plain. I did tell Woodden to buy the plant at any price. What is more I gave him a written authority which was passed up to the auctioneer. There's no getting out of it. It is true it never occurred to me that it would go for anything like £2,300— the odd £300 was more my idea, but Woodden only obeyed his orders, and ought not to be abused for doing so."

"There's what I call a master worth serving," remarked Woodden.

"Very well, young man," said Sir Alexander, "you have purchased this article. Will you be so good as to tell me how you propose it should be paid for."

"I propose, father, that you should pay for it," replied Mr. Stephen sweetly. "Two thousand three hundred pounds, or ten times that amount, would not make you appreciably poorer. But if, as is probable, you take a different view, then I propose to pay for it myself. As you know a certain sum of money came to me under my mother's will in which you have only a life interest. I shall raise the amount upon that security—or otherwise."

If Sir Alexander had been angry before, now he became like a mad bull in a china shop. He pranced round the room; he used language that should not pass the lips of any respectable merchant of bullion; in short, he did everything that a person in his position ought not to do. When he was tired he rushed to a desk, tore a cheque from a book and filled it in for a sum of £2,300 to bearer, which cheque he blotted, crumpled up and literally threw at the head of his son.

"You worthless, idle young scoundrel," he bellowed. "I put you in this office here that you may learn respectable and orderly habits and in due course succeed to a very comfortable business. What happens? You don't take a ha'porth of interest in bullion-broking, a subject of which I believe you to remain profoundly ignorant. You don't even spend your money, or rather my money, upon any gentleman-like vice, such as horse-racing, or cards, or even—well, never mind. No, you take to flowers, miserable, beastly flowers, things that a cow eats and clerks grow in back gardens."

"An ancient and Arcadian taste. Adam is supposed to have lived in a garden," I ventured to interpolate.

"Perhaps you would ask your friend with the stubbly hair to remain quiet," snorted Sir Alexander. "I was about to add, although for the sake of my name I meet your debts, that I have had enough of this kind of thing. I disinherit you, or will do if I live till 4 P.M. when the lawyer's office shuts, for thank God! there are no entailed estates, and I dismiss you from the firm. You can go and earn your living in any way you please, by orchid-hunting if you like." He paused, gasping for breath.

"Is that all, father?" asked Mr. Stephen, producing a cigar from his pocket.

"No, it isn't, you cold-blooded young beggar. That house you occupy at Twickenham is mine. You will be good enough to clear out of it; I wish to take possession."

"I suppose, father, I am entitled to a week's notice like any other tenant," said Mr. Stephen, lighting the cigar. "In fact," he added, "if you answer no, I think I shall ask you to apply for an ejection order. You will understand that I have arrangements to make before taking a fresh start in life."

"Oh! curse your cheek, you—you—cucumber!" raged the infuriated merchant prince. Then an inspiration came to him. "You think more of an ugly flower than of your father, do you? Well, at least I'll put an end to that," and he made a dash at the plant on the table with the evident intention of destroying the same.

But the watching Woodden saw. With a kind of lurch he interposed his big frame between Sir Alexander and the object of his wrath.

"Touch 'O. Paving' and I knocks yer down," he drawled out.

Sir Alexander looked at "O. Paving," then he looked at Woodden's leg-of-mutton fist, and—changed his mind.

"Curse 'O. Paving,'" he said, "and everyone who has to do with it," and swung out of the room, banging the door behind him.

"Well, that's over," said Mr. Stephen gently, as he fanned himself with a pocket-handkerchief. "Quite exciting while it lasted, wasn't it, Mr. Quatermain—but I have been there before, so to speak. And now what do you say to some luncheon? Pym's is close by, and they have very good oysters. Only I think we'll drive round by the bank and hand in this cheque. When he's angry my parent is capable of anything. He might even stop it. Woodden, get off down to Twickenham with 'O. Pavo.' Keep it warm, for it feels rather like frost. Put it in the stove for to-night and give it a little, just a little tepid water, but be careful not to touch the flower. Take a four-wheeled cab, it's slow but safe, and mind you keep the windows up and don't smoke. I shall be home for dinner."

Woodden pulled his forelock, seized the pot in his left hand, and departed with his right fist raised—I suppose in case Sir Alexander should be waiting for him round the corner.

Then we departed also and, after stopping for a minute at the bank to pay in the cheque, which I noted, notwithstanding its amount, was accepted without comment, ate oysters in a place too crowded to allow of conversation.

"Mr. Quatermain," said my host, "it is obvious that we cannot talk here, and much less look at that orchid of yours, which I want to study at leisure. Now, for a week or so at any rate I have a roof over my head, and in short, will you be my guest for a night or two? I know nothing about you, and of me you only know that I am the disinherited son of a father, to whom I have failed to give satisfaction. Still it is possible that we might pass a few pleasant hours together talking of flowers and other things; that is, if you have no previous engagement."

"I have none," I answered. "I am only a stranger from South Africa lodging at an hotel. If you will give me time to call for my bag, I will pass the night at your house with pleasure."

By the aid of Mr. Somers' smart dog-cart, which was waiting at a city mews, we reached Twickenham while there was still half an hour of daylight. The house, which was called Verbena Lodge, was small, a square, red-brick building of the early Georgian period, but the gardens covered quite an acre of ground and were very beautiful, or must have been so in summer. Into the greenhouse we did not enter, because it was too late to see the flowers. Also, just when we came to them, Woodden arrived in his four-wheeled cab and departed with his master to see to the housing of "O. Pavo."

Then came dinner, a very pleasant meal. My host had that day been turned out upon the world, but he did not allow this circumstance to interfere with his spirits in the least. Also he was evidently determined to enjoy its good things while they lasted, for his champagne and port were excellent.

"You see, Mr. Quatermain," he said, "it's just as well we had the row which has been boiling up for a long while. My respected father has made so much money that he thinks I should go and do likewise. Now I don't see it. I like flowers, especially orchids, and I hate bullion-broking. To me the only decent places in London are that sale-room where we met and the Horticultural Gardens."

"Yes," I answered rather doubtfully, "but the matter seems a little serious. Your parent was very emphatic as to his intentions, and after this kind of thing," and I pointed to the beautiful silver and the port, "how will you like roughing it in a hard world?"

"Don't think I shall mind a bit; it would be rather a pleasant change. Also, even if my father doesn't alter his mind, as he may, for he likes me at bottom because I resemble my dear mother, things ain't so very bad. I have got some money that she left me, £6,000 or £7,000, and I'll sell that 'Odontoglossum Pavo' for what it will fetch to Sir Joshua Tredgold—he was the man with the long beard who you tell me ran up Woodden to over £2,000—or failing him to someone else. I'll write about it to-night. I don't think I have any debts to speak of, for the Governor has been allowing me £3,000 a year, at least that is my share of the profits paid to me in return for my bullion-broking labours, and except flowers, I have no expensive tastes. So the devil take the past, here's to the future and whatever it may bring," and he polished off the glass of port he held and laughed in his jolly fashion.

Really he was a most attractive young man, a little reckless, it is true, but then recklessness and youth mix well, like brandy and soda.

I echoed the toast and drank off my port, for I like a good glass of wine when I can get it, as would anyone who has had to live for months on rotten water, although I admit that agrees with me better than the port.

"Now, Mr. Quatermain," he went on, "if you have done, light your pipe and let's go into the other room and study that Cypripedium of yours. I shan't sleep to-night unless I see it again first. Stop a bit, though, we'll get hold of that old ass, Woodden, before he turns in."

"Woodden," said his master, when the gardener had arrived, "this gentleman, Mr. Quatermain, is going to show you an orchid that is ten times finer than 'O. Pavo!'"

"Beg pardon, sir," answered Woodden, "but if Mr. Quatermain says that, he lies. It ain't in Nature; it don't bloom nowhere."

I opened the case and revealed the golden Cypripedium. Woodden stared at it and rocked. Then he stared again and felt his head as though to make sure it was on his shoulders. Then he gasped.

"Well, if that there flower baint made up, it's a MASTER ONE! If I could see that there flower ablowing on the plant I'd die happy."

"Woodden, stop talking, and sit down," exclaimed his master. "Yes, there, where you can look at the flower. Now, Mr. Quatermain, will you tell us the story of that orchid from beginning to end. Of course omitting its habitat if you like, for it isn't fair to ask that secret. Woodden can be trusted to hold his tongue, and so can I."

I remarked that I was sure they could, and for the next half-hour talked almost without interruption, keeping nothing back and explaining that I was anxious to find someone who would finance an expedition to search for this particular plant; as I believed, the only one of its sort that existed in the world.

"How much will it cost?" asked Mr. Somers.

"I lay it at £2,000," I answered. "You see, we must have plenty of men and guns and stores, also trade goods and presents."

"I call that cheap. But supposing, Mr. Quatermain, that the expedition proves successful and the plant is secured, what then?"

"Then I propose that Brother John, who found it and of whom I have told you, should take one-third of whatever it might sell for, that I as captain of the expedition should take one-third, and that whoever finds the necessary money should take the remaining third."

"Good! That's settled."

"What's settled?" I asked.

"Why, that we should divide in the proportions you named, only I bargain to be allowed to take my whack in kind—I mean in plant, and to have the first option of purchasing the rest of the plant at whatever value may be agreed upon."

"But, Mr. Somers, do you mean that you wish to find £2,000 and make this expedition in person?"

"Of course I do. I thought you understood that. That is, if you will have me. Your old friend, the lunatic, you and I will together seek for and find this golden flower. I say that's settled."

On the morrow accordingly, it was settled with the help of a document, signed in duplicate by both of us.

Before these arrangements were finally concluded, however, I insisted that Mr. Somers should meet my late companion, Charlie

Scroope, when I was not present, in order that the latter might give him a full and particular report concerning myself. Apparently the interview was satisfactory, at least so I judged from the very cordial and even respectful manner in which young Somers met me after it was over. Also I thought it my duty to explain to him with much clearness in the presence of Scroope as a witness, the great dangers of such an enterprise as that on which he proposed to embark. I told him straight out that he must be prepared to find his death in it from starvation, fever, wild beasts or at the hands of savages, while success was quite problematical and very likely would not be attained.

"*You* are taking these risks," he said.

"Yes," I answered, "but they are incident to the rough trade I follow, which is that of a hunter and explorer. Moreover, my youth is past, and I have gone through experiences and bereavements of which you know nothing, that cause me to set a very slight value on life. I care little whether I die or continue in the world for some few added years. Lastly, the excitement of adventure has become a kind of necessity for me. I do not think that I could live in England for very long. Also I'm a fatalist. I believe that when my time comes I must go, that this hour is foreordained and that nothing I can do will either hasten or postpone it by one moment. Your circumstances are different. You are quite young. If you stay here and approach your father in a proper spirit, I have no doubt but that he will forget all the rough words he said to you the other day, for which indeed you know you gave him some provocation. Is it worth while throwing up such prospects and undertaking such dangers for the chance of finding a rare flower? I say this to my own disadvantage, since I might find it hard to discover anyone else who would risk £2,000 upon such a venture, but I do urge you to weigh my words."

Young Somers looked at me for a little while, then he broke into one of his hearty laughs and exclaimed, "Whatever else you may be, Mr. Allan Quatermain, you are a gentleman. No bullion-broker in the City could have put the matter more fairly in the teeth of his own interests."

"Thank you," I said.

"For the rest," he went on, "I too am tired of England and want to see the world. It isn't the golden Cypripedium that I seek, although I should like to win it well enough. That's only a symbol. What I seek are adventure and romance. Also, like you I am a fatalist. God chose

His own time to send us here, and I presume that He will choose His own time to take us away again. So I leave the matter of risks to Him."

"Yes, Mr. Somers," I replied rather solemnly. "You may find adventure and romance, there are plenty of both in Africa. Or you may find a nameless grave in some fever-haunted swamp. Well, you have chosen, and I like your spirit."

Still I was so little satisfied about this business, that a week or so before we sailed, after much consideration, I took it upon myself to write a letter to Sir Alexander Somers, in which I set forth the whole matter as clearly as I could, not blinking the dangerous nature of our undertaking. In conclusion, I asked him whether he thought it wise to allow his only son to accompany such an expedition, mainly because of a not very serious quarrel with himself.

As no answer came to this letter I went on with our preparations. There was money in plenty, since the re-sale of "O. Pavo" to Sir Joshua Tredgold, at some loss, had been satisfactorily carried out, which enabled me to invest in all things needful with a cheerful heart. Never before had I been provided with such an outfit as that which preceded us to the ship.

At length the day of departure came. We stood on the platform at Paddington waiting for the Dartmouth train to start, for in those days the African mail sailed from that port. A minute or two before the train left, as we were preparing to enter our carriage I caught sight of a face that I seemed to recognise, the owner of which was evidently searching for someone in the crowd. It was that of Briggs, Sir Alexander's clerk, whom I had met in the sale-room.

"Mr. Briggs," I said as he passed me, "are you looking for Mr. Somers? If so, he is in here."

The clerk jumped into the compartment and handed a letter to Mr. Somers. Then he emerged again and waited. Somers read the letter and tore off a blank sheet from the end of it, on which he hastily wrote some words. He passed it to me to give to Briggs, and I could not help seeing what was written. It was: "Too late now. God bless you, my dear father. I hope we may meet again. If not, try to think kindly of your troublesome and foolish son, Stephen."

In another minute the train had started.

"By the way," he said, as we steamed out of the station, "I have heard from my father, who enclosed this for you."

I opened the envelope, which was addressed in a bold, round hand that seemed to me typical of the writer, and read as follows:

My Dear Sir,

I appreciate the motives which caused you to write to me and I thank you very heartily for your letter, which shows me that you are a man of discretion and strict honour. As you surmise, the expedition on which my son has entered is not one that commends itself to me as prudent. Of the differences between him and myself you are aware, for they came to a climax in your presence. Indeed, I feel that I owe you an apology for having dragged you into an unpleasant family quarrel. Your letter only reached me to-day having been forwarded to my place in the country from my office. I should have at once come to town, but unfortunately I am laid up with an attack of gout which makes it impossible for me to stir. Therefore, the only thing I can do is to write to my son hoping that the letter which I send by a special messenger will reach him in time and avail to alter his determination to undertake this journey. Here I may add that although I have differed and do differ from him on various points, I still have a deep affection for my son and earnestly desire his welfare. The prospect of any harm coming to him is one upon which I cannot bear to dwell.

"Now I am aware that any change of his plans at this eleventh hour would involve you in serious loss and inconvenience. I beg to inform you formally, therefore, that in this event I will make good everything and will in addition write off the £2,000 which I understand he has invested in your joint venture. It may be, however, that my son, who has in him a vein of my own obstinacy, will refuse to change his mind. In that event, under a Higher Power I can only commend him to your care and beg that you will look after him as though he were your own child. I can ask and you can do no more. Tell him to write me as opportunity offers, as perhaps you will too; also that, although I hate the sight of them, I will look after the flowers which he has left at the house at Twickenham.

Your obliged servant,
ALEXANDER SOMERS

This letter touched me much, and indeed made me feel very uncomfortable. Without a word I handed it to my companion, who read it through carefully.

"Nice of him about the orchids," he said. "My dad has a good heart, although he lets his temper get the better of him, having had his own way all his life."

"Well, what will you do?" I asked.

"Go on, of course. I've put my hand to the plough and I am not going to turn back. I should be a cur if I did, and what's more, whatever he might say he'd think none the better of me. So please don't try to persuade me, it would be no good."

For quite a while afterwards young Somers seemed to be comparatively depressed, a state of mind that in his case was rare indeed. At last, he studied the wintry landscape through the carriage window and said nothing. By degrees, however, he recovered, and when we reached Dartmouth was as cheerful as ever, a mood that I could not altogether share.

Before we sailed I wrote to Sir Alexander telling him exactly how things stood, and so I think did his son, though he never showed me the letter.

At Durban, just as we were about to start up country, I received an answer from him, sent by some boat that followed us very closely. In it he said that he quite understood the position, and whatever happened would attribute no blame to me, whom he should always regard with friendly feelings. He told me that, in the event of any difficulty or want of money, I was to draw on him for whatever might be required, and that he had advised the African Bank to that effect. Further, he added, that at least his son had shown grit in this matter, for which he respected him.

And now for a long while I must bid good-bye to Sir Alexander Somers and all that has to do with England.

IV

Mavovo and Hans

We arrived safely at Durban at the beginning of March and took up our quarters at my house on the Berea, where I expected that Brother John would be awaiting us. But no Brother John was to be found. The old, lame Griqua, Jack, who looked after the place for me and once had been one of my hunters, said that shortly after I went away in the ship, Dogeetah, as he called him, had taken his tin box and his net and walked off inland, he knew not where, leaving, as he declared, no message or letter behind him. The cases full of butterflies and dried plants were also gone, but these, I found he had shipped to some port in America, by a sailing vessel bound for the United States which chanced to put in at Durban for food and water. As to what had become of the man himself I could get no clue. He had been seen at Maritzburg and, according to some Kaffirs whom I knew, afterwards on the borders of Zululand, where, so far as I could learn, he vanished into space.

This, to say the least of it, was disconcerting, and a question arose as to what was to be done. Brother John was to have been our guide. He alone knew the Mazitu people; he alone had visited the borders of the mysterious Pongo-land, I scarcely felt inclined to attempt to reach that country without his aid.

When a fortnight had gone by and still there were no signs of him, Stephen and I held a solemn conference. I pointed out the difficulties and dangers of the situation to him and suggested that, under the circumstances, it might be wise to give up this wild orchid-chase and go elephant-hunting instead in a certain part of Zululand, where in those days these animals were still abundant.

He was inclined to agree with me, since the prospect of killing elephants had attractions for him.

"And yet," I said, after reflection, "it's curious, but I never remember making a successful trip after altering plans at the last moment, that is, unless one was driven to it."

"I vote we toss up," said Somers; "it gives Providence a chance. Now then, heads for the Golden Cyp, and tails for the elephants."

He spun a half-crown into the air. It fell and rolled under a great, yellow-wood chest full of curiosities that I had collected, which it took all our united strength to move. We dragged it aside and not without some excitement, for really a good deal hung upon the chance, I lit a match and peered into the shadow. There in the dust lay the coin.

"What is it?" I asked of Somers, who was stretched on his stomach on the chest.

"Orchid—I mean head," he answered. "Well, that's settled, so we needn't bother any more."

The next fortnight was a busy time for me. As it happened there was a schooner in the bay of about one hundred tons burden which belonged to a Portuguese trader named Delgado, who dealt in goods that he carried to the various East African ports and Madagascar. He was a villainous-looking person whom I suspected of having dealings with the slave traders, who were very numerous and a great power in those days, if indeed he were not one himself. But as he was going to Kilwa whence we proposed to start inland, I arranged to make use of him to carry our party and the baggage. The bargain was not altogether easy to strike for two reasons. First, he did not appear to be anxious that we should hunt in the districts at the back of Kilwa, where he assured me there was no game, and secondly, he said that he wanted to sail at once. However, I overcame his objections with an argument he could not resist—namely, money, and in the end he agreed to postpone his departure for fourteen days.

Then I set about collecting our men, of whom I had made up my mind there must not be less than twenty. Already I had sent messengers summoning to Durban from Zululand and the upper districts of Natal various hunters who had accompanied me on other expeditions. To the number of a dozen or so they arrived in due course. I have always had the good fortune to be on the best of terms with my Kaffirs, and where I went they were ready to go without asking any questions. The man whom I had selected to be their captain under me was a Zulu of the name of Mavovo. He was a short fellow, past middle age, with an enormous chest. His strength was proverbial; indeed, it was said that he could throw an ox by the horns, and myself I have seen him hold down the head of a wounded buffalo that had fallen, until I could come up and shoot it.

When I first knew Mavovo he was a petty chief and witch doctor in Zululand. Like myself, he had fought for the Prince Umbelazi in the great battle of the Tugela, a crime which Cetewayo never forgave him. About a year afterwards he got warning that he had been smelt out as a wizard and was going to be killed. He fled with two of his wives and a child. The slayers overtook them before he could reach the Natal border, and stabbed the elder wife and the child of the second wife. They were four men, but, made mad by the sight, Mavovo turned on them and killed them all. Then, with the remaining wife, cut to pieces as he was, he crept to the river and through it to Natal. Not long after this wife died also; it was said from grief at the loss of her child. Mavovo did not marry again, perhaps because he was now a man without means, for Cetewayo had taken all his cattle; also he was made ugly by an assegai wound which had cut off his right nostril. Shortly after the death of his second wife he sought me out and told me he was a chief without a kraal and wished to become my hunter. So I took him on, a step which I never had any cause to regret, since although morose and at times given to the practice of uncanny arts, he was a most faithful servant and brave as a lion, or rather as a buffalo, for a lion is not always brave.

Another man whom I did not send for, but who came, was an old Hottentot named Hans, with whom I had been more or less mixed up all my life. When I was a boy he was my father's servant in the Cape Colony and my companion in some of those early wars. Also he shared some very terrible adventures with me which I have detailed in the history I have written of my first wife, Marie Marais. For instance, he and I were the only persons who escaped from the massacre of Retief and his companions by the Zulu king, Dingaan. In the subsequence campaigns, including the Battle of the Blood River, he fought at my side and ultimately received a good share of captured cattle. After this he retired and set up a native store at a place called Pinetown, about fifteen miles out of Durban. Here I am afraid he got into bad ways and took to drink more or less; also to gambling. At any rate, he lost most of his property, so much of it indeed that he scarcely knew which way to turn. Thus it happened that one evening when I went out of the house where I had been making up my accounts, I saw a yellow-faced white-haired old fellow squatted on the verandah smoking a pipe made out of a corn-cob.

"Good day, Baas," he said, "here am I, Hans."

"So I see," I answered, rather coldly. "And what are you doing here, Hans? How can you spare time from your drinking and gambling at Pinetown to visit me here, Hans, after I have not seen you for three years?"

"Baas, the gambling is finished, because I have nothing more to stake, and the drinking is done too, because but one bottle of Cape Smoke makes me feel quite ill next morning. So now I only take water and as little of that as I can, water and some tobacco to cover up its taste."

"I am glad to hear it, Hans. If my father, the Predikant who baptised you, were alive now, he would have much to say about your conduct as indeed I have no doubt he will presently when you have gone into a hole (i.e., a grave). For there in the hole he will be waiting for you, Hans."

"I know, I know, Baas. I have been thinking of that and it troubles me. Your reverend father, the Predikant, will be very cross indeed with me when I join him in the Place of Fires where he sits awaiting me. So I wish to make my peace with him by dying well, and in your service, Baas. I hear that the Baas is going on an expedition. I have come to accompany the Baas."

"To accompany me! Why, you are old, you are not worth five shillings a month and your *scoff* (food). You are a shrunken old brandy cask that will not even hold water."

Hans grinned right across his ugly face.

"Oh! Baas, I am old, but I am clever. All these years I have been gathering wisdom. I am as full of it as a bee's nest is with honey when the summer is done. And, Baas, I can stop those leaks in the cask."

"Hans, it is no good, I don't want you. I am going into great danger. I must have those about me whom I can trust."

"Well, Baas, and who can be better trusted than Hans? Who warned you of the attack of the Quabies on Maraisfontein, and so saved the life of—"

"Hush!" I said.

"I understand. I will not speak the name. It is holy not to be mentioned. It is the name of one who stands with the white angels before God; not to be mentioned by poor drunken Hans. Still, who stood at your side in that great fight? Ah! it makes me young again to think of it, when the roof burned; when the door was broken down; when we met the Quabies on the spears; when you held the pistol to the head of the Holy One whose name must not be mentioned, the Great One who knew how to die. Oh! Baas, our lives are twisted up together like the creeper and the tree, and where you go, there I must go also. Do not turn me away. I ask no wages, only a bit of food and a handful of tobacco, and the light of your face and a word now and

H. RIDER HAGGARD

again of the memories that belong to both of us. I am still very strong. I can shoot well—well, Baas, who was it that put it into your mind to aim at the tails of the vultures on the Hill of Slaughter yonder in Zululand, and so saved the lives of all the Boer people, and of her whose holy name must not be mentioned? Baas, you will not turn me away?"

"No," I answered, "you can come. But you will swear by the spirit of my father, the Predikant, to touch no liquor on this journey."

"I swear by his spirit and by that of the Holy One," and he flung himself forward on to his knees, took my hand and kissed it. Then he rose and said in a matter-of-fact tone, "If the Baas can give me two blankets, I shall thank him, also five shillings to buy some tobacco and a new knife. Where are the Baas's guns? I must go to oil them. I beg that the Baas will take with him that little rifle which is named *Intombi* (Maiden), the one with which he shot the vultures on the Hill of Slaughter, the one that killed the geese in the Goose Kloof when I loaded for him and he won the great match against the Boer whom Dingaan called Two-faces."

"Good," I said. "Here are the five shillings. You shall have the blankets and a new gun and all things needful. You will find the guns in the little back room and with them those of the Baas, my companion, who also is your master. Go see to them."

At length all was ready, the cases of guns, ammunition, medicines, presents and food were on board the *Maria*. So were four donkeys that I had bought in the hope that they would prove useful, either to ride or as pack beasts. The donkey, be it remembered, and man are the only animals which are said to be immune from the poisonous effects of the bite of tsetse fly, except, of course, the wild game. It was our last night at Durban, a very beautiful night of full moon at the end of March, for the Portugee Delgado had announced his intention of sailing on the following afternoon. Stephen Somers and I were seated on the stoep smoking and talking things over.

"It is a strange thing," I said, "that Brother John should never have turned up. I know that he was set upon making this expedition, not only for the sake of the orchid, but also for some other reason of which he would not speak. I think that the old fellow must be dead."

"Very likely," answered Stephen (we had become intimate and I called him Stephen now), "a man alone among savages might easily come to grief and never be heard of again. Hark! What's that?" and he pointed to some gardenia bushes in the shadow of the house near by, whence came a sound of something that moved.

"A dog, I expect, or perhaps it is Hans. He curls up in all sorts of places near to where I may be. Hans, are you there?"

A figure arose from the gardenia bushes.

"*Ja*, I am here, Baas."

"What are you doing, Hans?"

"I am doing what the dog does, Baas—watching my master."

"Good," I answered. Then an idea struck me. "Hans, you have heard of the white Baas with the long beard whom the Kaffirs call Dogeetah?"

"I have heard of him and once I saw him, a few moons ago passing through Pinetown. A Kaffir with him told me that he was going over the Drakensberg to hunt for things that crawl and fly, being quite mad, Baas."

"Well, where is he now, Hans? He should have been here to travel with us."

"Am I a spirit that I can tell the Baas whither a white man has wandered. Yet, stay. Mavovo may be able to tell. He is a great doctor, he can see through distance, and even now, this very night his Snake of divination has entered into him and he is looking into the future, yonder, behind the house. I saw him form the circle."

I translated what Hans said to Stephen, for he had been talking in Dutch, then asked him if he would like to see some Kaffir magic.

"Of course," he answered, "but it's all bosh, isn't it?"

"Oh, yes, all bosh, or so most people say," I answered evasively. "Still, sometimes these *Inyangas* tell one strange things."

Then, led by Hans, we crept round the house to where there was a five-foot stone wall at the back of the stable. Beyond this wall, within the circle of some huts where my Kaffirs lived, was an open space with an ant-heap floor where they did their cooking. Here, facing us, sat Mavovo, while in a ring around him were all the hunters who were to accompany us; also Jack, the lame Griqua, and the two house-boys. In front of Mavovo burned a number of little wood fires. I counted them and found that there were fourteen, which, I reflected, was the exact number of our hunters, plus ourselves. One of the hunters was engaged in feeding these fires with little bits of stick and handfuls of dried grass so as to keep them burning brightly. The others sat round perfectly silent and watched with rapt attention. Mavovo himself looked like a man who is asleep. He was crouched on his haunches with his big head resting almost upon his knees. About his middle was a snake-skin, and round his neck an ornament that appeared to be made of human teeth. On his right side lay a pile of feathers from the wings of vultures, and on his left a little heap of silver money—I suppose the fees paid by the hunters for whom he was divining.

After we had watched him for some while from our shelter behind the wall he appeared to wake out of his sleep. First he muttered; then he looked up to the moon and seemed to say a prayer of which I could not catch the words. Next he shuddered three times convulsively and exclaimed in a clear voice:

"My Snake has come. It is within me. Now I can hear, now I can see."

Three of the little fires, those immediately in front of him, were larger than the others. He took up his bundle of vultures' feathers, selected one with care, held it towards the sky, then passed it through the flame of the centre one of the three fires, uttering as he did so, my native name, Macumazana. Withdrawing it from the flame he examined the charred edges of the feather very carefully, a proceeding that caused a cold shiver to go down my back, for I knew well that he was inquiring of his "Spirit" what would be my fate upon this expedition. How it answered, I cannot tell, for he laid the feather down and took another, with which he went through the same process. This time, however, the name he called out was Mwamwazela, which in its shortened form of Wazela, was the Kaffir appellation that the natives had given to Stephen Somers. It means a Smile, and no doubt was selected for him because of his pleasant, smiling countenance.

Having passed it through the right-hand fire of the three, he examined it and laid it down.

So it went on. One after another he called out the names of the hunters, beginning with his own as captain; passed the feather which represented each of them through the particular fire of his destiny, examined and laid it down. After this he seemed to go to sleep again for a few minutes, then woke up as a man does from a natural slumber, yawned and stretched himself.

"Speak," said his audience, with great anxiety. "Have you seen? Have you heard? What does your Snake tell you of me? Of me? Of me? Of me?"

"I have seen, I have heard," he answered. "My Snake tells me that this will be a very dangerous journey. Of those who go on it six will die by the bullet, by the spear or by sickness, and others will be hurt."

"*Ow?*" said one of them, "but which will die and which will come out safe? Does not your Snake tell you that, O Doctor?"

"Yes, of course my Snake tells me that. But my Snake tells me also to hold my tongue on the matter, lest some of us should be turned to cowards. It tells me further that the first who should ask me more, will be one of those who must die. Now do you ask? Or you? Or you? Or you? Ask if you will."

Strange to say no one accepted the invitation. Never have I seen a body of men so indifferent to the future, at least to every appearance. One and all they seemed to come to the conclusion that so far as they were concerned it might be left to look after itself.

"My Snake told me something else," went on Mavovo. "It is that if among this company there is any jackal of a man who, thinking that he might be one of the six to die, dreams to avoid his fate by deserting, it will be of no use. For then my Snake will point him out and show me how to deal with him."

Now with one voice each man present there declared that desertion from the lord Macumazana was the last thing that could possibly occur to him. Indeed, I believe that those brave fellows spoke truth. No doubt they put faith in Mavovo's magic after the fashion of their race. Still the death he promised was some way off, and each hoped he would be one of the six to escape. Moreover, the Zulu of those days was too accustomed to death to fear its terrors over much.

One of them did, however, venture to advance the argument, which Mavovo treated with proper contempt, that the shillings paid for this divination should be returned by him to the next heirs of such of them as happened to decease. Why, he asked, should these pay a shilling in order to be told that they must die? It seemed unreasonable.

Certainly the Zulu Kaffirs have a queer way of looking at things.

"Hans," I whispered, "is your fire among those that burn yonder?"

"Not so, Baas," he wheezed back into my ear. "Does the Baas think me a fool? If I must die, I must die; if I am to live, I shall live. Why then should I pay a shilling to learn what time will declare? Moreover, yonder Mavovo takes the shillings and frightens everybody, but tells nobody anything. *I* call it cheating. But, Baas, do you and the Baas Wazela have no fear. You did not pay shillings, and therefore Mavovo, though without doubt he is a great *Inyanga*, cannot really prophesy concerning you, since his Snake will not work without a fee."

The argument seems remarkably absurd. Yet it must be common, for now that I come to think of it, no gipsy will tell a "true fortune" unless her hand is crossed with silver.

"I say, Quatermain," said Stephen idly, "since our friend Mavovo seems to know so much, ask him what has become of Brother John, as Hans suggested. Tell me what he says afterwards, for I want to see something."

So I went through the little gate in the wall in a natural kind of way, as though I had seen nothing, and appeared to be struck by the sight of the little fires.

"Well, Mavovo," I said, "are you doing doctor's work? I thought that it had brought you into enough trouble in Zululand."

"That is so, *Baba*," replied Mavovo, who had a habit of calling me "father," though he was older than I. "It cost me my chieftainship and my cattle and my two wives and my son. It made of me a wanderer who is glad to accompany a certain Macumazana to strange lands where many things may befall me, yes," he added with meaning, "even the last of all things. And yet a gift is a gift and must be used. You, *Baba*, have a gift of shooting and do you cease to shoot? You have a gift of wandering and can you cease to wander?"

He picked up one of the burnt feathers from the little pile by his side and looked at it attentively. "Perhaps, *Baba*, you have been told—my ears are very sharp, and I thought I heard some such words floating through the air just now—that we poor Kaffir *Inyangas* can prophesy nothing true unless we are paid, and perhaps that is a fact so far as something of the moment is concerned. And yet the Snake in the *Inyanga*, jumping over the little rock which hides the present from it, may see the path that winds far and far away through the valleys, across the streams, up the mountains, till it is lost in the 'heaven above.' Thus on this feather, burnt in my magic fire, I seem to see something of your future, O my father Macumazana. Far and far your road runs," and he drew his finger along the feather. "Here is a journey," and he flicked away a carbonised flake, "here is another, and another, and another," and he flicked off flake after flake. "Here is one that is very successful, it leaves you rich; and here is yet one more, a wonderful journey this in which you see strange things and meet strange people. Then"—and he blew on the feather in such a fashion that all the charred filaments (Brother John says that *laminae* is the right word for them) fell away from it—"then, there is nothing left save such a pole as some of my people stick upright on a grave, the Shaft of Memory they call it. O, my father, you will die in a distant land, but you will leave a great memory behind you that will live for hundreds of years, for see how strong is this quill over which the fire has had no power. With some of these others it is quite different," he added.

"I daresay," I broke in, "but, Mavovo, be so good as to leave me out of your magic, for I don't at all want to know what is going to happen to me. To-day is enough for me without studying next month and next year. There is a saying in our holy book which runs: 'Sufficient to the day is its evil.'"

"Quite so, O Macumazana. Also that is a very good saying as some of those hunters of yours are thinking now. Yet an hour ago they were forcing their shillings on me that I might tell them of the future. And *you*, too, want to know something. You did not come through that gate to quote to me the wisdom of your holy book. What is it, *Baba*? Be quick, for my Snake is getting very tired. He wishes to go back to his hole in the world beneath."

"Well, then," I answered in rather a shamefaced fashion, for Mavovo had an uncanny way of seeing into one's secret motives, "I should like to know, if you can tell me, which you can't, what has become of the white man with the long beard whom you black people call Dogeetah? He should have been here to go on this journey with us; indeed, he was to be our guide and we cannot find him. Where is he and why is he not here?"

"Have you anything about you that belonged to Dogeetah, Macumazana?"

"No," I answered; "that is, yes," and from my pocket I produced the stump of pencil that Brother John had given me, which, being economical, I had saved up ever since. Mavovo took it, and after considering it carefully as he had done in the case of the feathers, swept up a pile of ashes with his horny hand from the edge of the largest of the little fires, that indeed which had represented myself. These ashes he patted flat. Then he drew on them with the point of the pencil, tracing what seemed to me to be the rough image of a man, such as children scratch upon whitewashed walls. When he had finished he sat up and contemplated his handiwork with all the satisfaction of an artist. A breeze had risen from the sea and was blowing in little gusts, so that the fine ashes were disturbed, some of the lines of the picture being filled in and others altered or enlarged.

For a while Mavovo sat with his eyes shut. Then he opened them, studied the ashes and what remained of the picture, and taking a blanket that lay near by, threw it over his own head and over the ashes. Withdrawing it again presently he cast it aside and pointed to the picture which was now quite changed. Indeed, in the moonlight, it looked more like a landscape than anything else.

"All is clear, my father," he said in a matter-of-fact voice. "The white wanderer, Dogeetah, is not dead. He lives, but he is sick. Something is the matter with one of his legs so that he cannot walk. Perhaps a bone is broken or some beast has bitten him. He lies in a hut such as Kaffirs make, only this hut has a verandah round it like your stoep, and there are drawings on the wall. The hut is a long way off, I don't know where."

"Is that all?" I asked, for he paused.

"No, not all. Dogeetah is recovering. He will join us in that country whither we journey, at a time of trouble. That is all, and the fee is half-a-crown."

"You mean one shilling," I suggested.

"No, my father Macumazana. One shilling for simple magic such as foretelling the fate of common black people. Half-a-crown for very difficult magic that has to do with white people, magic of which only great doctors, like me, Mavovo, are the masters."

I gave him the half-crown and said:

"Look here, friend Mavovo, I believe in you as a fighter and a hunter, but as a magician I think you are a humbug. Indeed, I am so sure of it that if ever Dogeetah turns up at a time of trouble in that land whither we are journeying, I will make you a present of that double-barrelled rifle of mine which you admired so much."

One of his rare smiles appeared upon Mavovo's ugly face.

"Then give it to me now, *Baba*," he said, "for it is already earned. My Snake cannot lie—especially when the fee is half-a-crown."

I shook my head and declined, politely but with firmness.

"Ah!" said Mavovo, "you white men are very clever and think that you know everything. But it is not so, for in learning so much that is new, you have forgotten more that is old. When the Snake that is in you, Macumazana, dwelt in a black savage like me a thousand thousand years ago, you could have done and did what I do. But now you can only mock and say, 'Mavovo the brave in battle, the great hunter, the loyal man, becomes a liar when he blows the burnt feather, or reads what the wind writes upon the charmed ashes.'"

"I do not say that you are a liar, Mavovo, I say that you are deceived by your own imaginings. It is not possible that man can know what is hidden from man."

"Is it indeed so, O Macumazana, Watcher by Night? Am I, Mavovo, the pupil of Zikali, the Opener of Roads, the greatest of wizards, indeed deceived by my own imaginings? And has man no other eyes but those in his head, that he cannot see what is hidden from man? Well, you say so and all we black people know that you are very clever, and why should I, a poor Zulu, be able to see what you cannot see? Yet when to-morrow one sends you a message from the ship in which we are to sail, begging you to come fast because there is trouble on the ship, then bethink you of your words and my words, and whether or no man can see what is hidden from man in the blackness of the future. Oh! that rifle of yours is mine already, though you will not give it to me now, you who think that I am a cheat. Well, my father Macumazana, because you think I am a cheat, never again will I blow the feather or read what the wind writes upon the ashes for you or any who eat your food."

Then he rose, saluted me with uplifted right hand, collected his little pile of money and bag of medicines and marched off to the sleeping hut.

On our way round the house we met my old lame caretaker, Jack.

"*Inkoosi*," he said, "the white chief Wazela bade me say that he and the cook, Sam, have gone to sleep on board the ship to look after the goods. Sam came up just now and fetched him away; he says he will show you why to-morrow."

I nodded and passed on, wondering to myself why Stephen had suddenly determined to stay the night on the *Maria*.

V

HASSAN

I suppose it must have been two hours after dawn on the following morning that I was awakened by knocks upon the door and the voice of Jack saying that Sam, the cook, wanted to speak to me.

Wondering what he could be doing there, as I understood he was sleeping on the ship, I called out that he was to come in. Now this Sam, I should say, hailed from the Cape, and was a person of mixed blood. The original stock, I imagine, was Malay which had been crossed with Indian coolie. Also, somewhere or other, there was a dash of white and possibly, but of this I am not sure, a little Hottentot. The result was a person of few vices and many virtues. Sammy, I may say at once, was perhaps the biggest coward I ever met. He could not help it, it was congenital, though, curiously enough, this cowardice of his never prevented him from rushing into fresh danger. Thus he knew that the expedition upon which I was engaged would be most hazardous; remembering his weakness I explained this to him very clearly. Yet that knowledge did not deter him from imploring that he might be allowed to accompany me. Perhaps this was because there was some mutual attachment between us, as in the case of Hans. Once, a good many years before, I had rescued Sammy from a somewhat serious scrape by declining to give evidence against him. I need not enter into the details, but a certain sum of money over which he had control had disappeared. I will merely say, therefore, that at the time he was engaged to a coloured lady of very expensive tastes, whom in the end he never married.

After this, as it chanced, he nursed me through an illness. Hence the attachment of which I have spoken.

Sammy was the son of a native Christian preacher, and brought up upon what he called "The Word." He had received an excellent education for a person of his class, and in addition to many native dialects with which a varied career had made him acquainted, spoke English perfectly, though in the most bombastic style. Never would he use a short word if a long one came to his hand, or rather to his tongue. For several years of his life he was, I believe, a teacher in a school at Capetown where coloured persons received their education; his "department," as he called it, being "English Language and Literature."

Wearying of or being dismissed from his employment for some reason that he never specified, he had drifted up the coast to Zanzibar, where he turned his linguistic abilities to the study of Arabic and became the manager or head cook of an hotel. After a few years he lost this billet, I know not how or why, and appeared at Durban in what he called a "reversed position." Here it was that we met again, just before my expedition to Pongo-land.

In manners he was most polite, in disposition most religious; I believe he was a Baptist by faith, and in appearance a small, brown dandy of a man of uncertain age, who wore his hair parted in the middle and, whatever the circumstances, was always tidy in his garments.

I took him on because he was in great distress, an excellent cook, the best of nurses, and above all for the reason that, as I have said, we were in a way attached to each other. Also, he always amused me intensely, which goes for something on a long journey of the sort that I contemplated.

Such in brief was Sammy.

As he entered the room I saw that his clothes were very wet and asked him at once if it were raining, or whether he had got drunk and been sleeping in the damp grass.

"No, Mr. Quatermain," he answered, "the morning is extremely fine, and like the poor Hottentot, Hans, I have abjured the use of intoxicants. Though we differ on much else, in this matter we agree."

"Then what the deuce is up?" I interrupted, to cut short his flow of fine language.

"Sir, there is trouble on the ship" (remembering Mavovo I started at these words) "where I passed the night in the company of Mr. Somers at his special request." (It was the other way about really.) "This morning before the dawn, when he thought that everybody was asleep, the Portuguese captain and some of his Arabs began to weigh the anchor quite quietly; also to hoist the sails. But Mr. Somers and I, being very much awake, came out of the cabin and he sat upon the capstan with a revolver in his hand, saying—well, sir, I will not repeat what he said."

"No, don't. What happened then?"

"Then, sir, there followed much noise and confusion. The Portugee and the Arabs threatened Mr. Somers, but he, sir, continued to sit upon the capstan with the stern courage of a rock in a rushing stream, and remarked that he would see them all somewhere before they touched it. After this, sir, I do not know what occurred, since while I watched from the bulwarks someone knocked me head over heels into the sea and being fortunately, a good swimmer, I gained the shore and hurried here to advise you."

"And did you advise anyone else, you idiot?" I asked.

"Yes, sir. As I sped along I communicated to an officer of the port that there was the devil of a mess upon the *Maria* which he would do well to investigate."

By this time I was in my shirt and trousers and shouting to Mavovo and the others. Soon they arrived, for as the costume of Mavovo and his company consisted only of a moocha and a blanket, it did not take them long to dress.

"Mavovo," I began, "there is trouble on the ship—"

"O *Baba*," he interrupted with something resembling a grin, "it is very strange, but last night I dreamed that I told you—"

"Curse your dreams," I said. "Gather the men and go down—no, that won't work, there would be murder done. Either it is all over now or it is all right. Get the hunters ready; I come with them. The luggage can be fetched afterwards."

Within less than an hour we were at that wharf off which the *Maria* lay in what one day will be the splendid port of Durban, though in those times its shipping arrangements were exceedingly primitive. A strange-looking band we must have been. I, who was completely dressed, and I trust tidy, marched ahead. Next came Hans in the filthy wide-awake hat which he usually wore and greasy corduroys and after him the oleaginous Sammy arrayed in European reach-me-downs, a billy-cock and a bright blue tie striped with red, garments that would have looked very smart had it not been for his recent immersion. After him followed the fierce-looking Mavovo and his squad of hunters, all of whom wore the "ring" or *isicoco*, as the Zulus call it; that is, a circle of polished black wax sewn into their short hair. They were a grim set of fellows, but as, according to a recent law it was not allowable for them to appear armed in the town, their guns had already been shipped, while their broad stabbing spears were rolled up in their sleeping mats, the blades wrapped round with dried grass.

Each of them, however, bore in his hand a large knobkerry of red-wood, and they marched four by four in martial fashion. It is true that when we embarked on the big boat to go to the ship much of their warlike ardour evaporated, since these men, who feared nothing on the land, were terribly afraid of that unfamiliar element, the water.

We reached the *Maria*, an unimposing kind of tub, and climbed aboard. On looking aft the first thing that I saw was Stephen seated on the capstan with a pistol in his hand, as Sammy had said. Near by, leaning on the bulwark was the villainous-looking Portugee, Delgado, apparently in the worst of tempers and surrounded by a number of equally villainous-looking Arab sailors clad in dirty white. In front was the Captain of the port, a well-known and esteemed gentleman of the name of Cato, like myself a small man who had gone through many adventures. Accompanied by some attendants, he was seated on the after-skylight, smoking, with his eyes fixed upon Stephen and the Portugee.

"Glad to see you, Quatermain," he said. "There's some row on here, but I have only just arrived and don't understand Portuguese, and the gentleman on the capstan won't leave it to explain."

"What's up, Stephen?" I asked, after shaking Mr. Cato by the hand.

"What's up?" replied Somers. "This man," and he pointed to Delgado, "wanted to sneak out to sea with all our goods, that's all, to say nothing of me and Sammy, whom, no doubt, he'd have chucked overboard, as soon as he was out of sight of land. However, Sammy, who knows Portuguese, overheard his little plans and, as you see, I objected."

Well, Delgado was asked for his version of the affair, and, as I expected, explained that he only intended to get a little nearer to the bar and there wait till we arrived. Of course he lied and knew that we were aware of the fact and that his intention had been to slip out to sea with all our valuable property, which he would sell after having murdered or marooned Stephen and the poor cook. But as nothing could be proved, and we were now in strong enough force to look after ourselves and our belongings, I did not see the use of pursuing the argument. So I accepted the explanation with a smile, and asked everybody to join in a morning nip.

Afterwards Stephen told me that while I was engaged with Mavovo on the previous night, a message had reached him from Sammy who was on board the ship in charge of our belongings, saying that he would be glad of some company. Knowing the cook's nervous nature, fortunately enough he made up his mind at once to go and sleep upon the *Maria*. In the morning trouble arose as Sammy had told me. What he did not tell me was that he was not knocked overboard, as he said, but took to the water of his own accord, when complications with Delgado appeared imminent.

"I understand the position," I said, "and all's well that ends well. But it's lucky you thought of coming on board to sleep."

After this everything went right. I sent some of the men back in the charge of Stephen for our remaining effects, which they brought safely aboard, and in the evening we sailed. Our voyage up to Kilwa was beautiful, a gentle breeze driving us forward over a sea so calm that not even Hans, who I think was one of the worst sailors in the world, or the Zulu hunters were really sick, though as Sammy put it, they "declined their food."

I think it was on the fifth night of our voyage, or it may have been the seventh, that we anchored one afternoon off the island of Kilwa, not very far from the old Portuguese fort. Delgado, with whom we had little to do during the passage, hoisted some queer sort of signal. In response a boat came off containing what he called the Port officials, a band of cut-throat, desperate-looking, black fellows in charge of a pock-marked, elderly half-breed who was introduced to us as the Bey Hassan-ben-Mohammed. That Mr. Hassan-ben-Mohammed entirely disapproved of our presence on the ship, and especially of our proposed landing at Kilwa, was evident to me from the moment that I set eyes upon his ill-favoured countenance. After a hurried conference with Delgado, he came forward and addressed me in Arabic, of which I could not understand a word. Luckily, however, Sam the cook, who, as I think I said, was a great linguist, had a fair acquaintance with this tongue, acquired, it appears, while at the Zanzibar hotel; so, not trusting Delgado, I called on him to interpret.

"What is he saying, Sammy?" I asked.

He began to talk to Hassan and replied presently:

"Sir, he makes you many compliments. He says that he has heard what a great man who are from his friend, Delgado, also that you and Mr. Somers are English, a nation which he adores."

"Does he?" I exclaimed. "I should never have thought it from his looks. Thank him for his kind remarks and tell him that we are going to land here and march up country to shoot."

Sammy obeyed, and the conversation went on somewhat as follows:

"With all humility I (i.e. Hassan) request you not to land. This country is not a fit place for such noble gentlemen. There is nothing to eat and no head of game has been seen for years. The people in the interior are savages of the worst sort, whom hunger has driven to take to cannibalism. I would not have your blood upon my head. I beg of you, therefore, to go on in this ship to Delagoa Bay, where you will find a good hotel, or to any other place you may select."

A.Q.: "Might I ask you, noble sir, what is your position at Kilwa, that you consider yourself responsible for our safety?"

H.: "Honoured English lord, I am a trader here of Portuguese nationality, but born of an Arab mother of high birth and brought up among that people. I have gardens on the mainland, tended by my native servants who are as children to me, where I grow palms and cassava and ground nuts and plantains and many other kinds of produce. All the tribes in this district look upon me as their chief and venerated father."

A.Q.: "Then, noble Hassan, you will be able to pass us through them, seeing that we are peaceful hunters who wish to harm no one."

(A long consultation between Hassan and Delgado, during which I ordered Mavovo to bring his Zulus on deck with their guns.)

H.: "Honoured English lord, I cannot allow you to land."

A.Q.: "Noble son of the Prophet, I intend to land with my friend, my followers, my donkeys and my goods early to-morrow morning. If I can do so with your leave I shall be glad. If not—" and I glanced at the fierce group of hunters behind me.

H.: "Honoured English lord, I shall be grieved to use force, but let me tell you that in my peaceful village ashore I have at least a hundred men armed with rifles, whereas here I see under twenty."

A.Q., AFTER REFLECTION AND A FEW WORDS WITH STEPHEN SOMERS: "Can you tell me, noble sir, if from your peaceful village you have yet sighted the English man-of-war, *Crocodile*; I mean the steamer that is engaged in watching for the dhows of wicked slavers? A letter from her captain informed me that he would be in these waters by yesterday. Perhaps, however, he has been delayed for a day or two."

If I had exploded a bomb at the feet of the excellent Hassan its effect could scarcely have been more remarkable than that of this question. He turned—not pale, but a horrible yellow, and exclaimed:

"English man-of-war! *Crocodile*! I thought she had gone to Aden to refit and would not be back at Zanzibar for four months."

A.Q.: "You have been misinformed, noble Hassan. She will not refit till October. Shall I read you the letter?" and I produced a piece of paper from my pocket. "It may be interesting since my friend, the captain, whom you remember is named Flowers, mentions you in it. He says—"

Hassan waved his hand. "It is enough. I see, honoured lord, that you are a man of mettle not easily to be turned from your purpose. In the name of God the Compassionate, land and go wheresoever you like."

A.Q.: "I think that I had almost rather wait until the *Crocodile* comes in."

H.: "Land! Land! Captain Delgado, get up the cargo and man your boat. Mine too is at the service of these lords. You, Captain, will like to get away by this night's tide. There is still light, Lord Quatermain, and such hospitality as I can offer is at your service."

A.Q.: "Ah! I knew Bey Hassan, that you were only joking with me when you said that you wished us to go elsewhere. An excellent jest, truly, from one whose hospitality is so famous. Well, to fall in with your wishes, we will come ashore this evening, and if the Captain Delgado chances to sight the Queen's ship *Crocodile* before he sails, perhaps he will be so good as to signal to us with a rocket."

"Certainly, certainly," interrupted Delgado, who up to this time had pretended that he understood no English, the tongue in which I was speaking to the interpreter, Sammy.

Then he turned and gave orders to his Arab crew to bring up our belongings from the hold and to lower the *Maria's* boat.

Never did I see goods transferred in quicker time. Within half an hour every one of our packages was off that ship, for Stephen Somers kept a count of them. Our personal baggage went into the *Maria's* boat, and the goods together with the four donkeys which were lowered on to the top of them, were rumbled pell-mell into the barge-like punt belonging to Hassan. Here also I was accommodated, with about half of our people, the rest taking their seats in the smaller boat under the charge of Stephen.

At length all was ready and we cast off.

"Farewell, Captain," I cried to Delgado. "If you should sight the *Crocodile*—"

At this point Delgado broke into such a torrent of bad language in Portuguese, Arabic and English that I fear the rest of my remarks never reached him.

As we rowed shorewards I observed that Hans, who was seated near to me under the stomach of a jackass, was engaged in sniffing at the sides and bottom of the barge, as a dog might do, and asked him what he was about.

"Very odd smell in this boat," he whispered back in Dutch. "It stinks of Kaffir man, just like the hold of the *Maria*. I think this boat is used to carry slaves."

"Be quiet," I whispered back, "and stop nosing at those planks." But to myself I thought, Hans is right, we are in a nest of slave-traders, and this Hassan is their leader.

We rowed past the island, on which I observed the ruins of an old Portuguese fort and some long grass-roofed huts, where, I reflected, the slaves were probably kept until they could be shipped away. Observing my glance fixed upon these, Hassan hastened to explain, through Sammy, that they were storehouses in which he dried fish and hides, and kept goods.

"How interesting!" I answered. "Further south we dry hides in the sun."

Crossing a narrow channel we arrived at a rough jetty where we disembarked, whence we were led by Hassan not to the village which I now saw upon our left, but to a pleasant-looking, though dilapidated house that stood a hundred yards from the shore. Something about the appearance of this house impressed me with the idea that it was never built by slavers; the whole look of the place with its verandah and garden suggested taste and civilisation. Evidently educated people had designed it and resided here. I glanced about me and saw, amidst a grove of neglected orange trees that were surrounded with palms of some age, the ruins of a church. About this there was no doubt, for there, surmounted by a stone cross, was a little pent-house in which still hung the bell that once summoned the worshippers to prayer.

"Tell the English lord," said Hassan to Sammy, "that these buildings were a mission station of the Christians, who abandoned them more than twenty years ago. When I came here I found them empty."

"Indeed," I answered, "and what were the names of those who dwelt in them?"

"I never heard," said Hassan; "they had been gone a long while when I came."

Then we went up to the house, and for the next hour and more were engaged with our baggage which was piled in a heap in what had been the garden and in unpacking and pitching two tents for the hunters which I caused to be placed immediately in front of the rooms that were assigned to us. Those rooms were remarkable in their way. Mine had evidently been a sitting chamber, as I judged from some such broken articles of furniture, that appeared to be of American make. That which Stephen occupied had once served as a sleeping-place, for the bedstead of iron still remained there. Also there were a hanging bookcase, now fallen, and some tattered remnants of books. One of these, that oddly enough was well-preserved, perhaps because the white ants or other creatures did not like the taste of its morocco binding, was a Keble's *Christian Year*, on the title-page of which was written, "To my dearest Elizabeth on her birthday, from her husband." I took the liberty to put it in my pocket. On the wall, moreover, still hung the small watercolour picture of a very pretty young woman with fair hair and blue eyes, in the corner of which picture was written in the same handwriting as that in the book, "Elizabeth, aged twenty." This also I annexed, thinking that it might come in useful as a piece of evidence.

"Looks as if the owners of this place had left it in a hurry, Quatermain," said Stephen.

"That's it, my boy. Or perhaps they didn't leave; perhaps they stopped here."

"Murdered?"

I nodded and said, "I dare say friend Hassan could tell us something about the matter. Meanwhile as supper isn't ready yet, let us have a look at that church while it is light."

We walked through the palm and orange grove to where the building stood finely placed upon a mound. It was well-constructed of a kind of coral rock, and a glance showed us that it had been gutted by fire; the discoloured walls told their own tale. The interior was now full of shrubs and creepers, and an ugly, yellowish snake glided from what had been the stone altar. Without, the graveyard was enclosed by a broken wall, only we could see no trace of graves. Near the gateway, however, was a rough mound.

"If we could dig into that," I said, "I expect we should find the bones of the people who inhabited this place. Does that suggest anything to you, Stephen?"

"Nothing, except that they were probably killed."

"You should learn to draw inferences. It is a useful art, especially in Africa. It suggests to me that, if you are right, the deed was not done by natives, who would never take the trouble to bury the dead. Arabs, on the contrary, might do so, especially if there were any bastard Portuguese among them who called themselves Christians. But whatever happened must have been a long while ago," and I pointed to a self-sown hardwood tree growing from the mound which could scarcely have been less than twenty years old.

We returned to the house to find that our meal was ready. Hassan had asked us to dine with him, but for obvious reasons I preferred that Sammy should cook our food and that he should dine with us. He appeared full of compliments, though I could see hate and suspicion in his eye, and we fell to on the kid that we had bought from him, for I did not wish to accept any gifts from this fellow. Our drink was square-face gin, mixed with water that I sent Hans to fetch with his own hands from the stream that ran by the house, lest otherwise it should be drugged.

At first Hassan, like a good Mohammedan, refused to touch any spirits, but as the meal went on he politely relented upon this point, and I poured him out a liberal tot. The appetite comes in eating, as the Frenchman said, and the same thing applies to drinking. So at least it was in Hassan's case, who probably thought that the quantity swallowed made no difference to his sin. After the third dose of square-face he grew quite amiable and talkative. Thinking the opportunity a good one, I sent for Sammy, and through him told our host that we were anxious to hire twenty porters to carry our packages. He declared that there was not such a thing as a porter within a hundred miles, whereon I gave him some more gin. The end of it was that we struck a bargain, I forget for how much, he promising to find us twenty good men who were to stay with us for as long as we wanted them.

Then I asked him about the destruction of the mission station, but although he was half-drunk, on this point he remained very close. All he would say was that he had heard that twenty years ago the people called the Mazitu, who were very fierce, had raided right down to the coast and killed those who dwelt there, except a white man and his wife who had fled inland and never been seen again.

"How many of them were buried in that mound by the church?" I asked quickly.

"Who told you they were buried there?" he replied, with a start, but seeing his mistake, went on, "I do not know what you mean. I never heard of anyone being buried. Sleep well, honoured lords, I must go and see to the loading of my goods upon the *Maria*." Then rising, he salaamed and walked, or rather rolled, away.

"So the *Maria* hasn't sailed after all," I said, and whistled in a certain fashion. Instantly Hans crept into the room out of the darkness, for this was my signal to him.

"Hans," I said, "I hear sounds upon that island. Slip down to the shore and spy out what is happening. No one will see you if you are careful."

"No, Baas," he answered with a grin, "I do not think that anyone will see Hans if he is careful, especially at night," and he slid away as quietly as he had come.

Now I went out and spoke to Mavovo, telling him to keep a good watch and to be sure that every man had his gun ready, as I thought that these people were slave-traders and might attack us in the night.

In that event, I said, they were to fall back upon the stoep, but not to fire until I gave the word.

"Good, my father," he answered. "This is a lucky journey; I never thought there would be hope of war so soon. My Snake forgot to mention it the other night. Sleep safe, Macumazana. Nothing that walks shall reach you while we live."

"Don't be so sure," I answered, and we lay down in the bedroom with our clothes on and our rifles by our sides.

The next thing I remember was someone shaking me by the shoulder. I thought it was Stephen, who had agreed to keep awake for the first part of the night and to call me at one in the morning. Indeed, he was awake, for I could see the glow from the pipe he smoked.

"Baas," whispered the voice of Hans, "I have found out everything. They are loading the *Maria* with slaves, taking them in big boats from the island."

"So," I answered. "But how did you get here? Are the hunters asleep without?"

He chuckled. "No, they are not asleep; they look with all their eyes and listen with all their ears, yet old Hans passed through them; even the Baas Somers did not hear him."

"That I didn't," said Stephen; "thought a rat was moving, no more."

I stepped through the place where the door had been on to the stoep. By the light of the fire which the hunters had lit without I could see Mavovo sitting wide awake, his gun upon his knees, and beyond him two sentries. I called him and pointed to Hans.

"See," I said, "what good watchmen you are when one can step over your heads and enter my room without your knowing it!"

Mavovo looked at the Hottentot and felt his clothes and boots to see whether they were wet with the night dew.

"*Ow!*" he exclaimed in a surly voice, "I said that nothing which walks could reach you, Macumazana, but this yellow snake has crawled between us on his belly. Look at the new mud that stains his waistcoat."

"Yet snakes can bite and kill," answered Hans with a snigger. "Oh! you Zulus think that you are very brave, and shout and flourish spears and battleaxes. One poor Hottentot dog is worth a whole impi of you after all. No, don't try to strike me, Mavovo the warrior, since we both serve the same master in our separate ways. When it comes to fighting I will leave the matter to you, but when it is a case of watching or spying, do you leave it to Hans. Look here, Mavovo," and he opened his hand in which was a horn snuff-box such as Zulus sometimes carry in their ears. "To whom does this belong?"

"It is mine," said Mavovo, "and you have stolen it."

"Yes," jeered Hans, "it is yours. Also I stole it from your ear as I passed you in the dark. Don't you remember that you thought a gnat had tickled you and hit up at your face?"

"It is true," growled Mavovo, "and you, snake of a Hottentot, are great in your own low way. Yet next time anything tickles me, I shall strike, not with my hand, but with a spear."

Then I turned them both out, remarking to Stephen that this was a good example of the eternal fight between courage and cunning. After this, as I was sure that Hassan and his friends were too busy to interfere with us that night, we went to bed and slept the sleep of the just.

When I got up the next morning I found that Stephen Somers had already risen and gone out, nor did he appear until I was half through my breakfast.

"Where on earth have you been?" I asked, noting that his clothes were torn and covered with wet moss.

"Up the tallest of those palm trees, Quatermain. Saw an Arab climbing one of them with a rope and got another Arab to teach me the trick. It isn't really difficult, though it looks alarming."

"What in the name of goodness—" I began.

"Oh!" he interrupted, "my ruling passion. Looking through the glasses I thought I caught sight of an orchid growing near the crown, so went up. It wasn't an orchid after all, only a mass of yellow pollen. But I learned something for my pains. Sitting in the top of that palm I saw the *Maria* working out from under the lee of the island. Also, far away, I noted a streak of smoke, and watching it through the glasses, made out what looked to me uncommonly like a man-of-war steaming slowly along the coast. In fact, I am sure it was, and English too. Then the mist came up and I lost sight of them."

"My word!" I said, "that will be the *Crocodile*. What I told our host, Hassan, was not altogether bunkum. Mr. Cato, the port officer at Durban, mentioned to me that the *Crocodile* was expected to call there within the next fortnight to take in stores after a slave-hunting cruise down the coast. Now it would be odd if she chanced to meet the *Maria* and asked to have a look at her cargo, wouldn't it?"

"Not at all, Quatermain, for unless one or the other of them changes her course that is just what she must do within the next hour or so, and I jolly well hope she will. I haven't forgiven that beast, Delgado, the trick he tried to play on us by slipping away with our goods, to say nothing of those poor devils of slaves. Pass the coffee, will you?"

For the next ten minutes we ate in silence, for Stephen had an excellent appetite and was hungry after his morning climb.

Just as we finished our meal Hassan appeared, looking even more villainous than he had done the previous day. I saw also that he was in a truculent mood, induced perhaps by the headache from which he was evidently suffering as a result of his potations. Or perhaps the fact that the *Maria* had got safe away with the slaves, as he imagined unobserved by us, was the cause of the change of his demeanour. A third alternative may have been that he intended to murder us during the previous night and found no safe opportunity of carrying out his amiable scheme.

We saluted him courteously, but without salaaming in reply he asked me bluntly through Sammy when we intended to be gone, as such "Christian dogs defiled his house," which he wanted for himself.

I answered, as soon as the twenty bearers whom he had promised us appeared, but not before.

"You lie," he said. "I never promised you bearers; I have none here."

"Do you mean that you shipped them all away in the *Maria* with the slaves last night?" I asked, sweetly.

My reader, have you ever taken note of the appearance and proceedings of a tom-cat of established age and morose disposition when a little dog suddenly disturbs it on the prowl? Have you observed how it contorts itself into arched but unnatural shapes, how it swells visibly to almost twice its normal size, how its hair stands up and its eyes flash, and the stream of unmentionable language that proceeds from its open mouth? If so, you will have a very good idea of the effect produced upon Hassan by this remark of mine. The fellow looked as though he were going to burst with rage. He rolled about, his bloodshot eyes seemed to protrude, he cursed us horribly, he put his hand upon the hilt of the great knife he wore, and finally he did what the tom-cat does, he spat.

Now, Stephen was standing with me, looking as cool as a cucumber and very much amused, and being, as it chanced, a little nearer to Hassan than I was, received the full benefit of this rude proceeding. My word! didn't it wake him up. He said something strong, and the next second flew at the half-breed like a tiger, landing him a beauty straight upon the nose. Back staggered Hassan, drawing his knife as he did so, but Stephen's left in the eye caused him to drop it, as he dropped himself. I pounced upon the knife, and since it was too late to interfere, for the mischief had been done, let things take their course and held back the Zulus who had rushed up at the noise.

Hassan rose and, to do him credit, came on like a man, head down. His great skull caught Stephen, who was the lighter of the two, in the chest and knocked him over, but before the Arab could follow up the advantage, he was on his feet again. Then ensued a really glorious mill. Hassan fought with head and fists and feet, Stephen with fists alone. Dodging his opponent's rushes, he gave it to him as he passed, and soon his coolness and silence began to tell. Once he was knocked over by a hooked one under the jaw, but in the next round he sent the Arab literally flying head over heels. Oh! how those Zulus cheered, and I, too, danced with delight. Up Hassan came again, spitting out several teeth and, adopting new tactics, grabbed Stephen round the middle. To and fro they swung, the Arab trying to kick the Englishman with his knees and to bite him also, till the pain reminded him of the absence of his front teeth. Once he nearly got him down—nearly, but not quite, for the collar by which he had gripped him (his object was to strangle) burst and, at that juncture, Hassan's turban fell over his face, blinding him for a moment.

Then Stephen gripped him round the middle with his left arm and with his right pommelled him unmercifully till he sank in a sitting position to the ground and held up his hand in token of surrender.

"The noble English lord has beaten me," he gasped.

"Apologise!" yelled Stephen, picking up a handful of mud, "or I shove this down your dirty throat."

He seemed to understand. At any rate, he bowed till his forehead touched the ground, and apologised very thoroughly.

"Now that is over," I said cheerfully to him, "so how about those bearers?"

"I have no bearers," he answered.

"You dirty liar," I exclaimed; "one of my people has been down to your village there and says it is full of men."

"Then go and take them for yourself," he replied, viciously, for he knew that the place was stockaded.

Now I was in a fix. It was all very well to give a slave-dealer the thrashing he deserved, but if he chose to attack us with his Arabs we should be in a poor way. Watching me with the eye that was not bunged up, Hassan guessed my perplexity.

"I have been beaten like a dog," he said, his rage returning to him with his breath, "but God is compassionate and just, He will avenge in due time."

The words had not left his lips for one second when from somewhere out at sea there floated the sullen boom of a great gun. At this moment, too, an Arab rushed up from the shore, crying:

"Where is the Bey Hassan?"

"Here," I said, pointing at him.

The Arab stared until I thought his eyes would drop out, for the Bey Hassan was indeed a sight to see. Then he gabbled in a frightened voice:

"Captain, an English man-of-war is chasing the *Maria*."

Boom went the great gun for the second time. Hassan said nothing, but his jaw dropped, and I saw that he had lost exactly three teeth.

"That is the *Crocodile*," I remarked slowly, causing Sammy to translate, and as I spoke, produced from my inner pocket a Union Jack which

I had placed there after I heard that the ship was sighted. "Stephen," I went on as I shook it out, "if you have got your wind, would you mind climbing up that palm tree again and signalling with this to the *Crocodile* out at sea?"

"By George! that's a good idea," said Stephen, whose jovial face, although swollen, was now again wreathed in smiles. "Hans, bring me a long stick and a bit of string."

But Hassan did not think it at all a good idea.

"English lord," he gasped, "you shall have the bearers. I will go to fetch them."

"No, you won't," I said, "you will stop here as a hostage. Send that man."

Hassan uttered some rapid orders and the messenger sped away, this time towards the stockaded village on the right.

As he went another messenger arrived, who also stared amazedly at the condition of his chief.

"Bey—if you are the Bey," he said, in a doubtful voice, for by now the amiable face of Hassan had begun to swell and colour, "with the telescope we have seen that the English man-of-war has sent a boat and boarded the *Maria*."

"God is great!" muttered the discomfited Hassan, "and Delgado, who is a thief and a traitor from his mother's breast, will tell the truth. The English sons of Satan will land here. All is finished; nothing is left but flight. Bid the people fly into the bush and take the slaves—I mean their servants. I will join them."

"No, you won't," I interrupted, through Sammy; "at any rate, not at present. You will come with us."

The miserable Hassan reflected, then he asked:

"Lord Quatermain" (I remember the title, because it is the nearest I ever got, or am likely to get, to the peerage), "if I furnish you with the twenty bearers and accompany you for some days on your journey inland, will you promise not to signal to your countrymen on the ship and bring them ashore?"

"What do you think?" I asked of Stephen.

"Oh!" he answered, "I think I'd agree. This scoundrel has had a pretty good dusting, and if once the *Crocodile* people land, there'll be an end of our expedition. As sure as eggs are eggs they will carry us off to Zanzibar or somewhere to give evidence before a slave court. Also nothing will be gained, for by the time the sailors get here, all these rascals will have bolted, except our friend, Hassan. You see it isn't as though we were sure he would be hung. He'd probably escape after all. International law, subject of a foreign Power, no direct proof—that kind of thing, you know."

"Give me a minute or two," I said, and began to reflect very deeply.

Whilst I was thus engaged several things happened. I saw twenty natives being escorted towards us, doubtless the bearers who had been promised; also I saw many others, accompanied by other natives, flying from the village into the bush. Lastly, a third messenger arrived, who announced that the *Maria* was sailing away, apparently in charge of a prize-crew, and that the man-of-war was putting about as though to accompany her. Evidently she had no intention of effecting a landing upon what was, nominally at any rate, Portuguese territory. Therefore, if anything was to be done, we must act at once.

Well, the end of it was that, like a fool, I accepted Stephen's advice and did nothing, always the easiest course and generally that which leads to most trouble. Ten minutes afterwards I changed my mind, but then it was too late; the *Crocodile* was out of signalling distance. This was subsequent to a conversation with Hans.

"Baas," said that worthy, in his leery fashion, "I think you have made a mistake. You forget that these yellow devils in white robes who have run away will come back again, and that when you return from up country, they may be waiting for you. Now if the English man-of-war had destroyed their town, and their slave-sheds, they might have gone somewhere else. However," he added, as an afterthought, glancing at the disfigured Hassan, "we have their captain, and of course you mean to hang him, Baas. Or if you don't like to, leave it to me. I can hang men very well. Once, when I was young, I helped the executioner at Cape Town."

"Get out," I said, but, nevertheless, I knew that Hans was right.

VI

THE SLAVE ROAD

The twenty bearers having arrived, in charge of five or six Arabs armed with guns, we went to inspect them, taking Hassan with us, also the hunters. They were a likely lot of men, though rather thin and scared-looking, and evidently, as I could see from their physical appearance and varying methods of dressing the hair, members of different tribes. Having delivered them, the Arabs, or rather one of them, entered into excited conversation with Hassan. As Sammy was not at hand I do not know what was said, although I gathered that they were contemplating his rescue. If so, they gave up the idea and began to run away as their companions had done. One of them, however, a bolder fellow than the rest, turned and fired at me. He missed by some yards, as I could tell from the sing of the bullet, for these Arabs are execrable shots. Still his attempt at murder irritated me so much that I determined he should not go scot-free. I was carrying the little rifle called "Intombi," that with which, as Hans had reminded me, I shot the vultures at Dingaan's kraal many years before. Of course, I could have killed the man, but this I did not wish to do. Or I could have shot him through the leg, but then we should have had to nurse him or leave him to die! So I selected his right arm, which was outstretched as he fled, and at about fifty paces put a bullet through it just above the elbow.

"There," I said to the Zulus as I saw it double up, "that low fellow will never shoot at anyone again."

"Pretty, Macumazana, very pretty!" said Mavovo, "but as you can aim so well, why not have chosen his head? That bullet is half-wasted."

Next I set to work to get into communication with the bearers, who thought, poor devils, that they had been but sold to a new master. Here I may explain that they were slaves not meant for exportation, but men kept to cultivate Hassan's gardens. Fortunately I found that two of them belonged to the Mazitu people, who it may be remembered are of the same blood as the Zulus, although they separated from the parent stock generations ago. These men talked a dialect that I could understand, though at first not very easily. The foundation of it was Zulu, but it had become much mixed with the languages of other tribes whose women the Mazitu had taken to wife.

Also there was a man who could speak some bastard Arabic, sufficiently well for Sammy to converse with him.

I asked the Mazitus if they knew the way back to their country. They answered yes, but it was far off, a full month's journey. I told them that if they would guide us thither, they should receive their freedom and good pay, adding that if the other men served us well, they also should be set free when we had done with them. On receiving this information the poor wretches smiled in a sickly fashion and looked at Hassan-ben-Mohammed, who glowered at them and us from the box on which he was seated in charge of Mavovo.

How can we be free while that man lives, their look seemed to say. As though to confirm their doubts Hassan, who understood or guessed what was passing, asked by what right we were promising freedom to his slaves.

"By right of that," I answered, pointing to the Union Jack which Stephen still had in his hand. "Also we will pay you for them when we return, according as they have served us."

"Yes," he muttered, "you will pay me for them when you return, or perhaps before that, Englishman."

It was three o'clock in the afternoon before we were able to make a start. There was so much to be arranged that it might have been wiser to wait till the morrow, had we not determined that if we could help it nothing would induce us to spend another night in that place. Blankets were served out to each of the bearers who, poor naked creatures, seemed quite touched at the gift of them; the loads were apportioned, having already been packed at Durban in cases such as one man could carry. The pack saddles were put upon the four donkeys which proved to be none the worse for their journey, and burdens to a weight of about 100 lbs. each fixed on them in waterproof hide bags, besides cooking calabashes and sleeping mats which Hans produced from somewhere. Probably he stole them out of the deserted village, but as they were necessary to us I confess I asked no questions. Lastly, six or eight goats which were wandering about were captured to take with us for food till we could find game. For these I offered to pay Hassan, but when I handed him the money he threw it down in a rage, so I picked it up and put it in my pocket again with a clear conscience.

At length everything was more or less ready, and the question arose as to what was to be done with Hassan. The Zulus, like Hans, wished to kill him, as Sammy explained to him in his best Arabic. Then this murderous fellow showed what a coward he was at heart. He flung himself upon his knees, he wept, he invoked us in the name of the Compassionate Allah who, he explained, was after all the same God that we worshipped, till Mavovo, growing impatient of the noise, threatened him with his kerry, whereon he became silent. The easy-natured Stephen was for letting him go, a plan that seemed to have advantages, for then at least we should be rid of his abominable company. After reflection, however, I decided that we had better take him along with us, at any rate for a day or so, to hold as a hostage in case the Arabs should follow and attack us. At first he refused to stir, but the assegai of one of the Zulu hunters pressed gently against what remained of his robe, furnished an argument that he could not resist.

At length we were off. I with the two guides went ahead. Then came the bearers, then half of the hunters, then the four donkeys in charge of Hans and Sammy, then Hassan and the rest of the hunters, except Mavovo, who brought up the rear with Stephen. Needless to say, all our rifles were loaded, and generally we were prepared for any emergency. The only path, that which the guides said we must follow, ran by the seashore for a few hundred yards and then turned inland through Hassan's village where he lived, for it seemed that the old mission house was not used by him. As we marched along a little rocky cliff—it was not more than ten feet high—where a deep-water channel perhaps fifty yards in breadth separated the mainland from the island whence the slaves had been loaded on to the *Maria*, some difficulty arose about the donkeys. One of these slipped its load and another began to buck and evinced an inclination to leap into the sea with its precious burden. The rearguard of hunters ran to get hold of it, when suddenly there was a splash.

The brute's in! I thought to myself, till a shout told me that not the ass, but Hassan had departed over the cliff's edge. Watching his opportunity and being, it was clear, a first-rate swimmer, he had flung himself backwards in the midst of the confusion and falling into deep water, promptly dived. About twenty yards from the shore he came up for a moment, then dived again heading for the island. I dare say I could have potted him through the head with a snap shot, but somehow I did not like to kill a man swimming for his life as though he were a hippopotamus or a crocodile. Moreover, the boldness of the manoeuvre appealed to me. So I refrained from firing and called to the others to do likewise.

As our late host approached the shore of the island I saw Arabs running down the rocks to help him out of the water. Either they had not left the place, or had re-occupied it as soon as H.M.S. *Crocodile* had vanished with her prize. As it was clear that to recapture Hassan would involve an attack upon the garrison of the island which we were in no position to carry out, I gave orders for the march to be resumed. These, the difficulty with the donkey having been overcome, were obeyed at once.

It was fortunate that we did not delay, for scarcely had the caravan got into motion when the Arabs on the island began to fire at us. Luckily no one was hit, and we were soon round a point and under cover; also their shooting was as bad as usual. One missile, however, it was a pot-leg, struck a donkey-load and smashed a bottle of good brandy and a tin of preserved butter. This made me angry, so motioning to the others to proceed I took shelter behind a tree and waited till a torn and dirty turban, which I recognised as that of Hassan, poked up above a rock. Well, I put a bullet through that turban, for I saw the thing fly, but unfortunately, not through the head beneath it. Having left this P.P.C. card on our host, I bolted from the rock and caught up the others.

Presently we passed round the village; through it I would not go for fear of an ambuscade. It was quite a big place, enclosed with a strong fence, but hidden from the sea by a rise in the intervening land. In the centre was a large eastern-looking house, where doubtless Hassan dwelt with his harem. After we had gone a little way further, to my astonishment I saw flames breaking out from the palm-leaf roof of this house. At the time I could not imagine how this happened, but when, a day or two later, I observed Hans wearing a pair of large and very handsome gold pendants in his ears and a gold bracelet on his wrist, and found that he and one of the hunters were extremely well set up in the matter of British sovereigns—well, I had my doubts. In due course the truth came out. He and the hunter, an adventurous spirit, slipped through a gate in the fence without being observed, ran across the deserted village to the house, stole the ornaments and money from the women's apartments and as they departed, fired the place "in exchange for the bottle of good brandy," as Hans explained.

I was inclined to be angry, but after all, as we had been fired on, Hans's exploit became an act of war rather than a theft. So I made him and his companion divide the gold equally with the rest of the hunters, who no doubt had kept their eyes conveniently shut, not forgetting Sammy, and said no more. They netted £8 apiece, which pleased them very much. In addition to this I gave £1 each, or rather goods to that value, to the bearers as their share of the loot.

Hassan, I remarked, was evidently a great agriculturist, for the gardens which he worked by slave labour were beautiful, and must have brought him in a large revenue.

Passing through these gardens we came to sloping land covered with bush. Here the track was not too good, for the creepers hampered our progress. Indeed, I was very glad when towards sunset we reached the crest of a hill and emerged upon a tableland which was almost clear of trees and rose gradually till it met the horizon. In that bush we might easily have been attacked, but in this open country I was not so much afraid, since the loss to the Arabs would have been great before we were overpowered. As a matter of fact, although spies dogged us for days no assault was ever attempted.

Finding a convenient place by a stream we camped for the night, but as it was so fine, did not pitch the tents. Afterwards I was sorry that we had not gone further from the water, since the mosquitoes bred by millions in the marshes bordering the stream gave us a dreadful time. On poor Stephen, fresh from England, they fell with peculiar ferocity, with the result that in the morning what between the bruises left by Hassan and their bites, he was a spectacle for men and angels. Another thing that broke our rest was the necessity of keeping a strict watch in case the slave-traders should elect to attack us in the hours of darkness; also to guard against the possibility of our bearers running away and perhaps stealing the goods. It is true that before they went to sleep I explained to them very clearly that any of them who attempted to give us the slip would certainly be seen and shot, whereas if they remained with us they would be treated with every kindness. They answered through the two Mazitu that they had nowhere to go, and did not wish to fall again into the power of Hassan, of whom they spoke literally with shudders, pointing the while to their scarred backs and the marks of the slave yokes upon their necks. Their protestations seemed and indeed proved to be sincere, but of this of course we could not then be sure.

As I was engaged at sunrise in making certain that the donkeys had not strayed and generally that all was well, I noted through the thin mist a little white object, which at first I thought was a small bird sitting on an upright stick about fifty yards from the camp. I went towards it and discovered that it was not a bird but a folded piece of paper stuck in a cleft wand, such as natives often use for the carrying of letters. I opened the paper and with great difficulty, for the writing within was bad Portuguese, read as follows:

"English Devils.—Do not think that you have escaped me. I know where you are going, and if you live through the journey it will be but to die at my hands after all. I tell you that I have at my command three hundred brave men armed with guns who worship Allah and thirst for the blood of Christian dogs. With these I will follow, and if you fall into my hands alive, you shall learn what it is to die by fire or pinned over ant-heaps in the sun. Let us see if your English man-of-war will help you then, or your false God either. Misfortune go with you, white-skinned robbers of honest men!"

This pleasing epistle was unsigned, but its anonymous author was not hard to identify. I showed it to Stephen who was so infuriated at its contents that he managed to dab some ammonia with which he was treating his mosquito bites into his eye. When at length the pain was soothed by bathing, we concocted this answer:

"Murderer, known among men as Hassan-ben-Mohammed— Truly we sinned in not hanging you when you were in our power. Oh! wolf who grows fat upon the blood of the innocent, this is a fault that we shall not commit again. Your death is near to you and we believe at our hands. Come with all your villains whenever you will. The more there are of them the better we shall be pleased, who would rather rid the world of many fiends than of a few,
                              Till we meet again, Allan Quatermain,
                                                  Stephen Somers

"Neat, if not Christian," I said when I had read the letter over.
"Yes," replied Stephen, "but perhaps just a little bombastic in tone. If that gentleman did arrive with three hundred armed men—eh?"

"Then, my boy," I answered, "in this way or in that we shall thrash him. I don't often have an inspiration, but I've got one now, and it is to the effect that Mr. Hassan has not very long to live and that we shall be intimately connected with his end. Wait till you have seen a slave caravan and you will understand my feelings. Also I know these gentry. That little prophecy of ours will get upon his nerves and give him a foretaste of things. Hans, go and set this letter in that cleft stick. The postman will call for it before long."

As it happened, within a few days we did see a slave caravan, some of the merchandise of the estimable Hassan.

We had been making good progress through a beautiful and healthy country, steering almost due west, or rather a little to the north of west. The land was undulating and rich, well-watered and only bush-clad in the neighbourhood of the streams, the higher ground being open, of a park-like character, and dotted here and there with trees. It was evident that once, and not very long ago, the population had been dense, for we came to the remains of many villages, or rather towns with large market-places. Now, however, these were burned with fire, or deserted, or occupied only by a few old bodies who got a living from the overgrown gardens. These poor people, who sat desolate and crooning in the sun, or perhaps worked feebly at the once fertile fields, would fly screaming at our approach, for to them men armed with guns must of necessity be slave-traders.

Still from time to time we contrived to catch some of them, and through one member of our party or the other to get at their stories. Really it was all one story. The slaving Arabs, on this pretext or on that, had set tribe against tribe. Then they sided with the stronger and conquered the weaker by aid of their terrible guns, killing out the old folk and taking the young men, women and children (except the infants whom they butchered) to be sold as slaves. It seemed that the business had begun about twenty years before, when Hassan-ben-Mohammed and his companions arrived at Kilwa and drove away the missionary who had built a station there.

At first this trade was extremely easy and profitable, since the raw material lay near at hand in plenty. By degrees, however, the neighbouring communities had been worked out. Countless numbers of them were killed, while the pick of the population passed under the slave yoke, and those of them who survived, vanished in ships to unknown lands.

Thus it came about that the slavers were obliged to go further afield and even to conduct their raids upon the borders of the territory of the great Mazitu people, the inland race of Zulu origin of whom I have spoken. According to our informants, it was even rumoured that they proposed shortly to attack these Mazitus in force, relying on their guns to give them the victory and open to them a new and almost inexhaustible store of splendid human merchandise. Meanwhile they were cleaning out certain small tribes which hitherto had escaped them, owing to the fact that they had their residence in bush or among difficult hills.

The track we followed was the recognised slave road. Of this we soon became aware by the numbers of skeletons which we found lying in the tall grass at its side, some of them with heavy slave-sticks still upon their wrists. These, I suppose, had died from exhaustion, but others, as their split skulls showed had been disposed of by their captors.

On the eighth day of our march we struck the track of a slave caravan. It had been travelling towards the coast, but for some reason or other had turned back. This may have been because its leaders had been warned of the approach of our party. Or perhaps they had heard that another caravan, which was at work in a different district, was drawing near, bringing its slaves with it, and wished to wait for its arrival in order that they might join forces.

The spoor of these people was easy to follow. First we found the body of a boy of about ten. Then vultures revealed to us the remains of two young men, one of whom had been shot and the other killed by a blow from an axe. Their corpses were roughly hidden beneath some grass, I know not why. A mile or two further on we heard a child wailing and found it by following its cries. It was a little girl of about four who had been pretty, though now she was but a living skeleton. When she saw us she scrambled away on all fours like a monkey. Stephen followed her, while I, sick at heart, went to get a tin of preserved milk from our stores. Presently I heard him call to me in a horrified voice. Rather reluctantly, for I knew that he must have found something dreadful, I pushed my way through the bush to where he was. There, bound to the trunk of a tree, sat a young woman, evidently the mother of the child, for it clung to her leg.

Thank God she was still living, though she must have died before another day dawned. We cut her loose, and the Zulu hunters, who are kind folk enough when they are not at war, carried her to camp. In the end with much trouble we saved the lives of that mother and child. I sent for the two Mazitus, with whom I could by now talk fairly well, and asked them why the slavers did these things.

They shrugged their shoulders and one of them answered with a rather dreadful laugh:

"Because, Chief, these Arabs, being black-hearted, kill those who can walk no more, or tie them up to die. If they let them go they might recover and escape, and it makes the Arabs sad that those who have been their slaves should live to be free and happy."

"Does it? Does it indeed?" exclaimed Stephen with a snort of rage that reminded me of his father. "Well, if ever I get a chance I'll make them sad with a vengeance."

Stephen was a tender-hearted young man, and for all his soft and indolent ways, an awkward customer when roused.

Within forty-eight hours he got his chance, thus: That day we camped early for two reasons. The first was that the woman and child we had rescued wee so weak they could not walk without rest, and we had no men to spare to carry them; the second that we came to an ideal spot to pass the night. It was, as usual, a deserted village through which ran a beautiful stream of water. Here we took possession of some outlying huts with a fence round them, and as Mavovo had managed to shoot a fat eland cow and her half-grown calf, we prepared to have a regular feast. Whilst Sammy was making some broth for the rescued woman, and Stephen and I smoked our pipes and watched him, Hans slipped through the broken gate of the thorn fence, or *boma*, and announced that Arabs were coming, two lots of them with many slaves.

We ran out to look and saw that, as he had said, two caravans were approaching, or rather had reached the village, but at some distance from us, and were now camping on what had once been the market-place. One of these was that whose track we had followed, although during the last few hours of our march we had struck away from it, chiefly because we could not bear such sights as I have described. It seemed to comprise about two hundred and fifty slaves and over forty guards, all black men carrying guns, and most of them by their dress Arabs, or bastard Arabs. In the second caravan, which approached from another direction, were not more than one hundred slaves and about twenty or thirty captors.

"Now," I said, "let us eat our dinner and then, if you like, we will go to call upon those gentlemen, just to show that we are not afraid of them. Hans, get the flag and tie it to the top of that tree; it will show them to what country we belong."

Up went the Union Jack duly, and presently through our glasses we saw the slavers running about in a state of excitement; also we saw the poor slaves turn and stare at the bit of flapping bunting and then begin to talk to each other. It struck me as possible that someone among their number had seen a Union Jack in the hands of an English traveller, or had heard of it as flying upon ships or at points on the coast, and what it meant to slaves. Or they may have understood some of the remarks of the Arabs, which no doubt were pointed and explanatory. At any rate, they turned and stared till the Arabs ran among them with sjambocks, that is, whips of hippopotamus hide, and suppressed their animated conversation with many blows.

At first I thought that they would break camp and march away; indeed, they began to make preparations to do this, then abandoned the idea, probably because the slaves were exhausted and there was no other water they could reach before nightfall. In the end they settled down and lit cooking fires. Also, as I observed, they took precautions against attack by stationing sentries and forcing the slaves to construct a *boma* of thorns about their camp.

"Well," said Stephen, when we had finished our dinner, "are you ready for that call?"

"No!" I answered, "I do not think that I am. I have been considering things, and concluded that we had better leave well alone. By this time those Arabs will know all the story of our dealings with their worthy master, Hassan, for no doubt he has sent messengers to them. Therefore, if we go to their camp, they may shoot us at sight. Or, if they receive us well, they may offer hospitality and poison us, or cut our throats suddenly. Our position might be better, still it is one that I believe they would find difficult to take. So, in my opinion, we had better stop still and await developments."

Stephen grumbled something about my being over-cautious, but I took no heed of him. One thing I did do, however. Sending for Hans, I told him to take one of the Mazitu—I dared not risk them both for they were our guides—and another of the natives whom we had borrowed from Hassan, a bold fellow who knew all the local languages, and creep down to the slavers' camp as soon as it was quite dark. There I ordered him to find out what he could, and if possible to mix with the slaves and explain that we were their friends. Hans nodded, for this was exactly the kind of task that appealed to him, and went off to make his preparations.

Stephen and I also made some preparations in the way of strengthening our defences, building large watch-fires and setting sentries.

The night fell, and Hans with his companions departed stealthily as snakes. The silence was intense, save for the occasional wailings of the slaves, which now and again broke out in bursts of melancholy sound, "*La-lu-La-lua!*" and then died away, to be followed by horrid screams as the Arabs laid their lashes upon some poor wretch. Once too, a shot was fired.

"They have seen Hans," said Stephen.

"I think not," I answered, "for if so there would have been more than one shot. Either it was an accident or they were murdering a slave."

After this nothing more happened for a long while, till at length Hans seemed to rise out of the ground in front of me, and behind him I saw the figures of the Mazitu and the other man.

"Tell your story," I said.

"Baas, it is this. Between us we have learned everything. The Arabs know all about you and what men you have. Hassan has sent them orders to kill you. It is well that you did not go to visit them, for certainly you would have been murdered. We crept near and overheard their talk. They purpose to attack us at dawn to-morrow morning unless we leave this place before, which they will know of as we are being watched."

"And if so, what then?" I asked.

"Then, Baas, they will attack as we are making up the caravan, or immediately afterwards as we begin to march."

"Indeed. Anything more, Hans?"

"Yes, Baas. These two men crept among the slaves and spoke with them. They are very sad, those slaves, and many of them have died of heart-pain because they have been taken from their homes and do not know where they are going. I saw one die just now; a young woman. She was talking to another woman and seemed quite well, only tired, till suddenly she said in a loud voice, 'I am going to die, that I may come back as a spirit and bewitch these devils till they are spirits too.' Then she called upon the fetish of her tribe, put her hands to her breast and fell down dead. At least," added Hans, spitting reflectively, "she did not fall quite down because the slave-stick held her head off the ground. The Arabs were very angry, both because she had cursed them and was dead. One of them came and kicked her body and afterwards shot her little boy who was sick, because the mother had cursed them. But fortunately he did not see us, because we were in the dark far from the fire."

"Anything more, Hans?"

"One thing, Baas. These two men lent the knives you gave them to two of the boldest among the slaves that they might cut the cords of the slave-sticks and the other cords with which they were tied, and then pass them down the lines, that their brothers might do the same. But perhaps the Arabs will find it out, and then the Mazitu and the other must lose their knives. That is all. Has the Baas a little tobacco?"

"Now, Stephen," I said when Hans had gone and I had explained everything, "there are two courses open to us. Either we can try to give these gentlemen the slip at once, in which case we must leave the woman and child to their fate, or we can stop where we are and wait to be attacked."

"I won't run," said Stephen sullenly; "it would be cowardly to desert that poor creature. Also we should have a worse chance marching. Remember Hans said that they are watching us."

"Then you would wait to be attacked?"

"Isn't there a third alternative, Quatermain? To attack them?"

"That's the idea," I said. "Let us send for Mavovo."

Presently he came and sat down in front of us, while I set out the case to him.

"It is the fashion of my people to attack rather than to be attacked, and yet, my father, in this case my heart is against it. Hans" (he called him *Inblatu*, a Zulu word which means Spotted Snake, that was the Hottentot's Kaffir name) "says that there are quite sixty of the yellow dogs, all armed with guns, whereas we have not more than fifteen, for we cannot trust the slave men. Also he says that they are within a strong fence and awake, with spies out, so that it will be difficult to surprise them. But here, father, we are in a strong fence and cannot be surprised. Also men who torture and kill women and children, except in war must, I think, be cowards, and will come on faintly against good shooting, if indeed they come at all. Therefore, I say, 'Wait till the buffalo shall either charge or run.' But the word is with you, Macumazana, wise Watcher-by-Night, not with me, your hunter. Speak, you who are old in war, and I will obey."

"You argue well," I answered; "also another reason comes to my mind. Those Arab brutes may get behind the slaves, of whom we should butcher a lot without hurting them. Stephen, I think we had better see the thing through here."

"All right, Quatermain. Only I hope that Mavovo is wrong in thinking that those blackguards may change their minds and run away."

"Really, young man, you are becoming very blood-thirsty—for an orchid grower," I remarked, looking at him. "Now, for my part, I devoutly hope that Mavovo is right, for let me tell you, if he isn't it may be a nasty job."

"I've always been peaceful enough up to the present," replied Stephen. "But the sight of those unhappy wretches of slaves with their heads cut open, and of the woman tied to a tree to starve—"

"Make you wish to usurp the functions of God Almighty," I said. "Well, it is a natural impulse and perhaps, in the circumstances, one that will not displease Him. And now, as we have made up our minds what we are going to do, let's get to business so that these Arab gentlemen may find their breakfast ready when they come to call."

VII

The Rush of the Slaves

W ell, we did all that we could in the way of making ready. After we had strengthened the thorn fence of our *boma* as much as possible and lit several large fires outside of it to give us light, I allotted his place to each of the hunters and saw that their rifles were in order and that they had plenty of ammunition. Then I made Stephen lie down to sleep, telling him that I would wake him to watch later on. This, however, I had no intention of doing as I wanted him to rise fresh and with a steady nerve on the occasion of his first fight.

As soon as I saw that his eyes were shut I sat down on a box to think. To tell the truth, I was not altogether happy in my mind. To begin with I did not know how the twenty bearers would behave under fire. They might be seized with panic and rush about, in which case I determined to let them out of the *boma* to take their chance, for panic is a catching thing.

A worse matter was our rather awkward position. There were a good many trees round the camp among which an attacking force could take cover. But what I feared much more than this, or even than the reedy banks of the stream along which they could creep out of reach of our bullets, was a sloping stretch of land behind us, covered with thick grass and scrub and rising to a crest about two hundred yards away. Now if the Arabs got round to this crest they would fire straight into our *boma* and make it untenable. Also if the wind were in their favour, they might burn us out or attack under the clouds of smoke. As a matter of fact, by the special mercy of Providence, none of these things happened, for a reason which I will explain presently.

In the case of a night, or rather a dawn attack, I have always found that hour before the sky begins to lighten very trying indeed. As a rule everything that can be done is done, so that one must sit idle. Also it is then that both the physical and the moral qualities are at their lowest ebb, as is the mercury in the thermometer. The night is dying, the day is not yet born. All nature feels the influence of that hour. Then bad dreams come, then infants wake and call, then memories of those who are lost to us arise, then the hesitating soul often takes its plunge into the depths of the Unknown. It is not wonderful, therefore, that on this occasion the wheels of Time drave heavily for me. I knew that the morning was at hand by many signs. The sleeping bearers turned and muttered in their sleep, a distant lion ceased its roaring and departed to its own place, an alert-minded cock crew somewhere, and our donkeys rose and began to pull at their tether-ropes. As yet, however, it was quite dark. Hans crept up to me; I saw his wrinkled, yellow face in the light of the watch-fire.

"I smell the dawn," he said and vanished again.

Mavovo appeared, his massive frame silhouetted against the blackness.

"Watcher-by-Night, the night is done," he said. "If they come at all, the enemy should soon be here."

Saluting, he too passed away into the dark, and presently I heard the sounds of spear-blades striking together and of rifles being cocked.

I went to Stephen and woke him. He sat up yawning, muttered something about greenhouses; then remembering, said:

"Are those Arabs coming? We are in for a fight at last. Jolly, old fellow, isn't it?"

"You are a jolly old fool!" I answered inconsequently; and marched off in a rage.

My mind was uneasy about this inexperienced young man. If anything should happen to him, what should I say to his father? Well, in that event, it was probable that something would happen to me too. Very possibly we should both be dead in an hour. Certainly I had no intention of allowing myself to be taken alive by those slaving devils. Hassan's remarks about fires and ant-heaps and the sun were too vividly impressed upon my memory.

In another five minutes everybody was up, though it required kicks to rouse most of the bearers from their slumbers. They, poor men, were accustomed to the presence of Death and did not suffer him to disturb their sleep. Still I noted that they muttered together and seemed alarmed.

"If they show signs of treachery, you must kill them," I said to Mavovo, who nodded in his grave, silent fashion.

Only we left the rescued slave-woman and her child plunged in the stupor of exhaustion in a corner of the camp. What was the use of disturbing her?

Sammy, who seemed far from comfortable, brought two pannikins of coffee to Stephen and myself.

"This is a momentous occasion, Messrs. Quatermain and Somers," he said as he gave us the coffee, and I noted that his hand shook and his teeth chattered. "The cold is extreme," he went on in his copybook English by way of explaining these physical symptoms which he saw I had observed. "Mr. Quatermain, it is all very well for you to paw the ground and smell the battle from afar, as is written in the Book of Job. But I was not brought up to the trade and take it otherwise. Indeed I wish I was back at the Cape, yes, even within the whitewashed walls of the Place of Detention."

"So do I," I muttered, keeping my right foot on the ground with difficulty.

But Stephen laughed outright and asked:

"What will you do, Sammy, when the fighting begins?"

"Mr. Somers," he answered, "I have employed some wakeful hours in making a hole behind that tree-trunk, through which I hope bullets will not pass. There, being a man of peace, I shall pray for our success."

"And if the Arabs get in, Sammy?"

"Then, sir, under Heaven, I shall trust to the fleetness of my legs."

I could stand it no longer, my right foot flew up and caught Sammy in the place at which I had aimed. He vanished, casting a reproachful look behind him.

Just then a terrible clamour arose in the slavers' camp which hitherto had been very silent, and just then also the first light of dawn glinted on the barrels of our guns.

"Look out!" I cried, as I gulped down the last of my coffee, "there's something going on there."

The clamour grew louder and louder till it seemed to fill the skies with a concentrated noise of curses and shrieking. Distinct from it, as it were, I heard shouts of alarm and rage, and then came the sounds of gunshots, yells of agony and the thud of many running feet. By now the light was growing fast, as it does when once it comes in these latitudes. Three more minutes, and through the grey mist of the dawn we saw dozens of black figures struggling up the slope towards us. Some seemed to have logs of wood tied behind them, others crawled along on all fours, others dragged children by the hand, and all yelled at the top of their voices.

"The slaves are attacking us," said Stephen, lifting his rifle.

"Don't shoot," I cried. "I think they have broken loose and are taking refuge with us."

I was right. These unfortunates had used the two knives which our men smuggled to them to good purpose. Having cut their bonds during the night they were running to seek the protection of the Englishmen and their flag. On they surged, a hideous mob, the slave-sticks still fast to the necks of many of them, for they had not found time or opportunity to loose them all, while behind came the Arabs firing. The position was clearly very serious, for if they burst into our camp, we should be overwhelmed by their rush and fall victims to the bullets of their captors.

"Hans," I cried, "take the men who were with you last night and try to lead those slaves round behind us. Quick! Quick now before we are stamped flat."

Hans darted away, and presently I saw him and the two other men running towards the approaching crowd, Hans waving a shirt or some other white object to attract their attention. At the time the foremost of them had halted and were screaming, "Mercy, English! Save us, English!" having caught sight of the muzzles of our guns.

This was a fortunate occurrence indeed, for otherwise Hans and his companions could never have stopped them. The next thing I saw was the white shirt bearing away to the left on a line which led past the fence of our *boma* into the scrub and high grass behind the camp. After it struggled and scrambled the crowd of slaves like a flock of sheep after the bell-wether. To them Hans's shirt was a kind of "white helmet of Navarre."

So that danger passed by. Some of the slaves had been struck by the Arab bullets or trodden down in the rush or collapsed from weakness, and at those of them who still lived the pursuers were firing. One woman, who had fallen under the weight of the great slave-stick which was fastened about her throat, was crawling forward on her hands and knees. An Arab fired at her and the bullet struck the ground under her stomach but without hurting her, for she wriggled forward more quickly. I was sure that he would shoot again, and watched. Presently, for by now the light was good, I saw him, a tall fellow in a white robe, step from behind the shelter of a banana-tree about a hundred and fifty yards away, and take a careful aim at the woman. But I too took aim and—well, I am not bad at this kind of snap-shooting when I try. That Arab's gun never went off. Only he went up two feet or more into the air and fell backwards, shot through the head which was the part of his person that I had covered.

The hunters uttered a low "*Ow!*" of approval, while Stephen, in a sort of ecstasy, exclaimed:

"Oh! what a heavenly shot!"

"Not bad, but I shouldn't have fired it," I answered, "for they haven't attacked us yet. It is a kind of declaration of war, and," I added, as Stephen's sun-helmet leapt from his head, "there's the answer. Down, all of you, and fire through the loopholes."

Then the fight began. Except for its grand finale it wasn't really much of a fight when compared with one or two we had afterwards on this expedition. But, on the other hand, its character was extremely awkward for us. The Arabs made one rush at the beginning, shouting on Allah as they came. But though they were plucky villains they did not repeat that experiment. Either by good luck or good management Stephen knocked over two of them with his double-barrelled rifle, and I also emptied my large-bore breech-loader—the first I ever owned—among them, not without results, while the hunters made a hit or two.

After this the Arabs took cover, getting behind trees and, as I had feared, hiding in the reeds on the banks of the stream. Thence they harassed us a great deal, for amongst them were some very decent shots. Indeed, had we not taken the precaution of lining the thorn fence with a thick bank of earth and sods, we should have fared badly. As it was, one of the hunters was killed, the bullet passing through the loophole and striking him in the throat as he was about to fire, while the unfortunate bearers who were on rather higher ground, suffered a good deal, two of them being dispatched outright and four wounded. After this I made the rest of them lie flat on the ground close against the fence, in such a fashion that we could fire over their bodies.

Soon it became evident that there were more of these Arabs than we had thought, for quite fifty of them were firing from different places. Moreover, by slow degrees they were advancing with the evident object of outflanking us and gaining the high ground behind. Some of them, of course, we stopped as they rushed from cover to cover, but this kind of shooting was as difficult as that at bolting rabbits across a woodland ride, and to be honest, I must say that I alone was much good at the game, for here my quick eye and long practice told.

Within an hour the position had grown very serious indeed, so much so that we found it necessary to consider what should be done. I pointed out that with our small number a charge against the scattered riflemen, who were gradually surrounding us, would be worse than useless, while it was almost hopeless to expect to hold the *boma* till nightfall. Once the Arabs got behind us, they could rake us from the higher ground. Indeed, for the last half-hour we had directed all our efforts to preventing them from passing this *boma*, which, fortunately, the stream on the one side and a stretch of quite open land on the other made it very difficult for them to do without more loss than they cared to face.

"I fear there is only one thing for it," I said at length, during a pause in the attack while the Arabs were either taking counsel or waiting for more ammunition, "to abandon the camp and everything and bolt up the hill. As those fellows must be tired and we are all good runners, we may save our lives in that way."

"How about the wounded," asked Stephen, "and the slave-woman and child?"

"I don't know," I answered, looking down.

Of course I did know very well, but here, in an acute form, arose the ancient question: Were we to perish for the sake of certain individuals in whom we had no great interest and whom we could not save by remaining with them? If we stayed where we were our end seemed fairly certain, whereas if we ran for it, we had a good chance of escape. But this involved the desertion of several injured bearers and a woman and child whom we had picked up starving, all of whom would certainly be massacred, save perhaps the woman and child.

As these reflections flitted through my brain I remembered that a drunken Frenchman named Leblanc, whom I had known in my youth and who had been a friend of Napoleon, or so he said, told me that the great emperor when he was besieging Acre in the Holy Land, was forced to retreat. Being unable to carry off his wounded men, he left them in a monastery on Mount Carmel, each with a dose of poison by his side. Apparently they did not take the poison, for according to Leblanc, who said he was present there (not as a wounded man), the Turks came and butchered them. So Napoleon chose to save his own life and that of his army at the expense of his wounded. But, after all, I reflected, he was no shining example to Christian men and I hadn't time to find any poison. In a few words I explained the situation to Mavovo, leaving out the story of Napoleon, and asked his advice.

"We must run," he answered. "Although I do not like running, life is more than stores, and he who lives may one day pay his debts."

"But the wounded, Mavovo; we cannot carry them."

"I will see to them, Macumazana; it is the fortune of war. Or if they prefer it, we can leave them—to be nursed by the Arabs," which of course was just Napoleon and his poison over again.

I confess that I was about to assent, not wishing that I and Stephen, especially Stephen, should be potted in an obscure engagement with some miserable slave-traders, when something happened.

It will be remembered that shortly after dawn Hans, using a shirt for a flag, had led the fugitive slaves past the camp up to the hill behind. There he and they had vanished, and from that moment to this we had seen nothing of him or them. Now of a sudden he reappeared still waving the shirt. After him rushed a great mob of naked men, two hundred of them perhaps, brandishing slave-sticks, stones and the boughs of trees. When they had almost reached the *boma* whence we watched them amazed, they split into two bodies, half of them passing to our left, apparently under the command of the Mazitu who had accompanied Hans to the slave-camp, and the other half to the right following the old Hottentot himself. I stared at Mavovo, for I was too thunderstruck to speak.

"Ah!" said Mavovo, "that Spotted Snake of yours" (he referred to Hans), "is great in his own way, for he has even been able to put courage into the hearts of slaves. Do you not understand, my father, that they are about to attack those Arabs, yes, and to pull them down, as wild dogs do a buffalo calf?"

It was true: this was the Hottentot's superb design. Moreover, it succeeded. Up on the hillside he had watched the progress of the fight and seen how it must end. Then, through the interpreter who was with him, he harangued those slaves, pointing out to them that we, their white friends, were about to be overwhelmed, and that they must either strike for themselves, or return to the yoke. Among them were some who had been warriors in their own tribes, and through these he stirred the others. They seized the slave-sticks from which they had been freed, pieces of rock, anything that came to their hands, and at a given signal charged, leaving only the women and children behind them.

Seeing them come the scattered Arabs began to fire at them, killing some, but thereby revealing their own hiding-places. At these the slaves rushed. They hurled themselves upon the Arabs; they tore them, they dashed out their brains in such fashion that within another five minutes quite two-thirds of them were dead; and the rest, of whom we took some toll with our rifles as they bolted from cover, were in full flight.

It was a terrible vengeance. Never did I witness a more savage scene than that of these outraged men wreaking their wrongs upon their tormentors. I remember that when most of the Arabs had been killed and a few were escaped, the slaves found one, I think it was the captain of the gang, who had hidden himself in a little patch of dead reeds washed up by the stream. Somehow they managed to fire these; I expect that Hans, who had remained discreetly in the background after the fighting began, emerged when it was over and gave them a match. In due course out came the wretched Arab. Then they flung themselves on him as marching ants do upon a caterpillar, and despite his cries for mercy, tore him to fragments, literally to fragments. Being what they were, it was hard to blame them. If we had seen our parents shot, our infants pitilessly butchered, our homes destroyed and our women and children marched off in the slave-sticks to be sold into bondage, should we not have done the same? I think so, although we are not ignorant savages.

Thus our lives were saved by those whom we had tried to save, and for once justice was done even in those dark parts of Africa, for in that time they were dark indeed. Had it not been for Hans and the courage which he managed to inspire into the hearts of these crushed blacks, I have little doubt but that before nightfall we should have been dead, for I do not think that any attempt at retreat would have proved successful. And if it had, what would have happened to us in that wild country surrounded by enemies and with only the few rounds of ammunition that we could have carried in our flight?

"Ah! Baas," said the Hottentot a little while later, squinting at me with his bead-like eyes, "after all you did well to listen to my prayer and bring me with you. Old Hans is a drunkard, yes, or at least he used to be, and old Hans gambles, yes, and perhaps old Hans will go to hell. But meanwhile old Hans can think, as he thought one day before the attack on Maraisfontein, as he thought one day on the Hill of Slaughter by Dingaan's kraal, and as he thought this morning up there among the bushes. Oh! he knew how it must end. He saw that those dogs of Arabs were cutting down a tree to make a bridge across that deep stream and get round to the high ground at the back of you, whence they would have shot you all in five minutes. And now, Baas, my stomach feels very queer. There was no breakfast on the hillside and the sun was very hot. I think that just one tot of brandy—oh! I know, I promised not to drink, but if *you* give it me the sin is yours, not mine."

Well, I gave him the tot, a stiff one, which he drank quite neat, although it was against my principles, and locked up the bottle afterwards. Also I shook the old fellow's hand and thanked him, which seemed to please him very much, for he muttered something to the effect that it was nothing, since if I had died he would have died too, and therefore he was thinking of himself, not of me. Also two big tears trickled down his snub nose, but these may have been produced by the brandy.

Well, we were the victors and elated as may be imagined, for we knew that the few slavers who had escaped would not attack us again. Our first thought was for food, for it was now past midday and we were starving. But dinner presupposed a cook, which reminded us of Sammy. Stephen, who was in such a state of jubilation that he danced rather than walked, the helmet with a bullet-hole through it stuck ludicrously upon the back of his head, started to look for him, and presently called to me in an alarmed voice. I went to the back of the camp and, staring into a hole like a small grave, that had been hollowed behind a solitary thorn tree, at the bottom of which lay a huddled heap, I found him. It was Sammy to all appearance. We got hold of him, and up he came, limp, senseless, but still holding in his hand a large, thick Bible, bound in boards. Moreover, in the exact centre of this Bible was a bullet-hole, or rather a bullet which had passed through the stout cover and buried itself in the paper behind. I remember that the point of it reached to the First Book of Samuel.

As for Sammy himself, he seemed to be quite uninjured, and indeed after we had poured some water on him—he was never fond of water— he revived quickly enough. Then we found out what had happened.

"Gentlemen," he said, "I was seated in my place of refuge, being as I have told you a man of peace, enjoying the consolation of religion"—he was very pious in times of trouble. "At length the firing slackened, and I ventured to peep out, thinking that perhaps the foe had fled, holding the Book in front of my face in case of accidents. After that I remember no more."

"No," said Stephen, "for the bullet hit the Bible and the Bible hit your head and knocked you silly."

"Ah!" said Sammy, "how true is what I was taught that the Book shall be a shield of defence to the righteous. Now I understand why I was moved to bring the thick old Bible that belonged to my mother in heaven, and not the little thin one given to me by the Sunday school teacher, through which the ball of the enemy would have passed."

Then he went off to cook the dinner.

Certainly it was a wonderful escape, though whether this was a direct reward of his piety, as he thought, is another matter.

As soon as we had eaten, we set to work to consider our position, of which the crux was what to do with the slaves. There they sat in groups outside the fence, many of them showing traces of the recent conflict, and stared at us stupidly. Then of a sudden, as though with one voice, they began to clamour for food.

"How are we to feed several hundred people?" asked Stephen.

"The slavers must have done it somehow," I answered. "Let's go and search their camp."

So we went, followed by our hungry clients, and, in addition to many more things, to our delight found a great store of rice, mealies and other grain, some of which was ground into meal. Of this we served out an ample supply together with salt, and soon the cooking pots were full of porridge. My word! how those poor creatures did eat, nor, although it was necessary to be careful, could we find it in our hearts to stint them of the first full meal that had passed their lips after weeks of starvation. When at length they were satisfied we addressed them, thanking them for their bravery, telling them that they were free and asking what they meant to do.

Upon this point they seemed to have but one idea. They said that they would come with us who were their protectors. Then followed a great *indaba*, or consultation, which really I have not time to set out. The end of it was that we agreed that so many of them as wished should accompany us till they reached country that they knew, when they would be at liberty to depart to their own homes. Meanwhile we divided up the blankets and other stores of the Arabs, such as trade goods and beads, among them, and then left them to their own devices, after placing a guard over the foodstuffs. For my part I hoped devoutly that in the morning we should find them gone.

After this we returned to our *boma* just in time to assist at a sad ceremony, that of the burial of my hunter who had been shot through the head. His companions had dug a deep hole outside the fence and within a few yards of where he fell. In this they placed him in a sitting position with his face turned towards Zululand, setting by his side two gourds that belonged to him, one filled with water and the other with grain. Also they gave him a blanket and his two assegais, tearing the blanket and breaking the handles of the spears, to "kill" them as they said. Then quietly enough they threw in the earth about him and filled the top of the hole with large stones to prevent the hyenas from digging him up. This done, one by one, they walked past the grave, each man stopping to bid him farewell by name. Mavovo, who came last, made a little speech, telling the deceased to *namba kachle*, that is, go comfortably to the land of ghosts, as, he added, no doubt he would do who had died as a man should. He requested him, moreover, if he returned as a spirit, to bring good and not ill-fortune on us, since otherwise when he, Mavovo, became a spirit in his turn, he would have words to say to him on the matter. In conclusion, he remarked that as his, Mavovo's Snake, had foretold this event at Durban, a fact with which the deceased would now be acquainted he, the said deceased, could never complain of not having received value for the shilling he had paid as a divining fee.

"Yes," exclaimed one of the hunters with a note of anxiety in his voice, "but your Snake mentioned six of us to you, O doctor!"

"It did," replied Mavovo, drawing a pinch of snuff up his uninjured nostril, "and our brother there was the first of the six. Be not afraid, the other five will certainly join him in due course, for my Snake must speak the truth. Still, if anyone is in a hurry," and he glared round the little circle, "let him stop and talk with me alone. Perhaps I could arrange that his turn—" here he stopped, for they were all gone.

"Glad *I* didn't pay a shilling to have my fortune told by Mavovo," said Stephen, when we were back in the *boma*, "but why did they bury his pots and spears with him?"

"To be used by the spirit on its journey," I answered. "Although they do not quite know it, these Zulus believe, like all the rest of the world, that man lives on elsewhere."

VIII

The Magic Mirror

I did not sleep very well that night, for now that the danger was over I found that the long strain of it had told upon my nerves. Also there were many noises. Thus, the bearers who were shot had been handed over to their companions, who disposed of them in a simple fashion, namely by throwing them into the bush where they attracted the notice of hyenas. Then the four wounded men who lay near to me groaned a good deal, or when they were not groaning uttered loud prayers to their local gods. We had done the best we could for these unlucky fellows. Indeed, that kind-hearted little coward, Sammy, who at some time in his career served as a dresser in a hospital, had tended their wounds, none of which were mortal, very well indeed, and from time to time rose to minister to them.

But what disturbed me most was the fearful hubbub which came from the camp below. Many of the tropical African tribes are really semi-nocturnal in their habits, I suppose because there the night is cooler than the day, and on any great occasion this tendency asserts itself.

Thus every one of these freed slaves seemed to be howling his loudest to an accompaniment of clashing iron pots or stones, which, lacking their native drums, they beat with sticks.

Moreover, they had lit large fires, about which they flitted in an ominous and unpleasant fashion, that reminded me of some mediaeval pictures of hell, which I had seen in an old book.

At last I could stand it no longer, and kicking Hans who, curled up like a dog, slept at my feet, asked him what was going on. His answer caused me to regret the question.

"Plenty of those slaves cannibal men, Baas. Think they eat the Arabs and like them very much," he said with a yawn, then went to sleep again.

I did not continue the conversation.

When at length we made a start on the following morning the sun was high over us. Indeed, there was a great deal to do. The guns and ammunition of the dead Arabs had to be collected; the ivory, of which they carried a good store, must be buried, for to take it with us was impossible, and the loads apportioned.* Also it was necessary to make litters for the wounded, and to stir up the slaves from their debauch, into the nature of which I made no further inquiries, was no easy task. On mustering them I found that a good number had vanished during the night, where to I do not know. Still a mob of well over two hundred people, a considerable portion of whom were women and children, remained, whose one idea seemed to be to accompany us wherever we might wander. So with this miscellaneous following at length we started.

To describe our adventures during the next month would be too long if not impossible, for to tell the truth, after the lapse of so many years, these have become somewhat entangled in my mind. Our great difficulty was to feed such a multitude, for the store of rice and grain, upon which we were quite unable to keep a strict supervision, they soon devoured. Fortunately the country through which we passed, at this time of the year (the end of the wet season) was full of game, of which, travelling as we did very slowly, we were able to shoot a great deal. But this game killing, delightful as it may be to the sportsman, soon palled on us as a business. To say nothing of the expenditure of ammunition, it meant incessant work.

Against this the Zulu hunters soon began to murmur, for, as Stephen and I could rarely leave the camp, the burden of it fell on them. Ultimately I hit upon this scheme. Picking out thirty or forty of the likeliest men among the slaves, I served out to each of them ammunition and one of the Arab guns, in the use of which we drilled them as best we could. Then I told them that they must provide themselves and their companions with meat. Of course accidents happened. One man was accidentally shot and three others were killed by a cow elephant and a wounded buffalo. But in the end they learned to handle their rifles sufficiently well to supply the camp. Moreover, day by day little parties of the slaves disappeared, I presume to seek their own homes, so that when at last we entered the borders of the Mazitu country there were not more than fifty of them left, including seventeen of those whom we had taught to shoot.

Then it was that our real adventures began.

One evening, after three days' march through some difficult bush in which lions carried off a slave woman, killed one of the donkeys and mauled another so badly that it had to be shot, we found ourselves upon

---

* To my sorrow we never saw this ivory again.—A.Q.

the edge of a great grassy plateau that, according to my aneroid, was 1,640 feet above sea level.

"What place is this?" I asked of the two Mazitu guides, those same men whom we had borrowed from Hassan.

"The land of our people, Chief," they answered, "which is bordered on one side by the bush and on the other by the great lake where live the Pongo wizards."

I looked about me at the bare uplands that already were beginning to turn brown, on which nothing was visible save vast herds of buck such as were common further south. A dreary prospect it was, for a slight rain was falling, accompanied by mist and a cold wind.

"I do not see your people or their kraals," I said; "I only see grass and wild game."

"Our people will come," they replied, rather nervously. "No doubt even now their spies watch us from among the tall grass or out of some hole."

"The deuce they do," I said, or something like it, and thought no more of the matter. When one is in conditions in which anything *may* happen, such as, so far as I am concerned, have prevailed through most of my life, one grows a little careless as to what *will* happen. For my part I have long been a fatalist, to a certain extent. I mean I believe that the individual, or rather the identity which animates him, came out from the Source of all life a long while, perhaps hundreds of thousands or millions of years ago, and when his career is finished, perhaps hundreds of thousands or millions of years hence, or perhaps to-morrow, will return perfected, but still as an individual, to dwell in or with that Source of Life. I believe also that his various existences, here or elsewhere, are fore-known and fore-ordained, although in a sense he may shape them by the action of his free will, and that nothing which he can do will lengthen or shorten one of them by a single hour. Therefore, so far as I am concerned, I have always acted up to the great injunction of our Master and taken no thought for the morrow.

However, in this instance, as in many others of my experience, the morrow took plenty of thought for itself. Indeed, before the dawn, Hans, who never seemed really to sleep any more than a dog does, woke me up with the ominous information that he heard a sound which he thought was caused by the tramp of hundreds of marching men.

"Where?" I asked, after listening without avail—to look was useless, for the night was dark as pitch.

He put his ear to the ground and said:

"There."

I put *my* ear to the ground, but although my senses are fairly acute, could hear nothing.

Then I sent for the sentries, but these, too, could hear nothing. After this I gave the business up and went to sleep again.

However, as it proved, Hans was quite right; in such matters he generally was right, for his senses were as keen as those of any wild beast. At dawn I was once more awakened, this time by Mavovo, who reported that we were being surrounded by a regiment, or regiments. I rose and looked out through the mist. There, sure enough, in dim and solemn outline, though still far off, I perceived rank upon rank of men, armed men, for the light glimmered faintly upon their spears.

"What is to be done, Macumazana?" asked Mavovo.

"Have breakfast, I think," I answered. "If we are going to be killed it may as well be after breakfast as before," and calling the trembling Sammy, I instructed him to make the coffee. Also I awoke Stephen and explained the situation to him.

"Capital!" he answered. "No doubt these are the Mazitu, and we have found them much more easily than we expected. People generally take such a lot of hunting for in this confounded great country."

"That's not such a bad way of looking at things," I answered, "but would you be good enough to go round the camp and make it clear that not on any account is anyone to fire without orders. Stay, collect all the guns from those slaves, for heaven knows what they will do with them if they are frightened!"

Stephen nodded and sauntered off with three or four of the hunters. While he was gone, in consultation with Mavovo, I made certain little arrangements of my own, which need not be detailed. They were designed to enable us to sell our lives as dearly as possible, should things come to the worst. One should always try to make an impression upon the enemy in Africa, for the sake of future travellers if for no other reason.

In due course Stephen and the hunters returned with the guns, or most of them, and reported that the slave people were in great state of terror, and showed a disposition to bolt.

"Let them bolt," I answered. "They would be of no use to us in a row and might even complicate matters. Call in the Zulus who are watching at once."

He nodded, and a few minutes later I heard—for the mist which hung about the bush to the east of the camp was still too dense to allow of my seeing anything—a clamour of voices, followed by the sound of scuttling feet. The slave people, including our bearers, had gone, every one of them. They even carried away the wounded. Just as the soldiers who surrounded us were completing their circle they bolted between the two ends of it and vanished into the bush out of which we had marched on the previous evening. Often since then I have wondered what became of them. Doubtless some perished, and the rest worked their way back to their homes or found new ones among other tribes. The experiences of those who escaped must be interesting to them if they still live. I can well imagine the legends in which these will be embodied two or three generations hence.

Deducting the slave people and the bearers whom we had wrung out of Hassan, we were now a party of seventeen, namely eleven Zulu hunters including Mavovo, two white men, Hans and Sammy, and the two Mazitus who had elected to remain with us, while round us was a great circle of savages which closed in slowly.

As the light grew—it was long in coming on that dull morning—and the mist lifted, I examined these people, without seeming to take any particular notice of them. They were tall, much taller than the average Zulu, and slighter in their build, also lighter in colour. Like the Zulus they carried large hide shields and one very broad-bladed spear. Throwing assegais seemed to be wanting, but in place of them I saw that they were armed with short bows, which, together with a quiver of arrows, were slung upon their backs. The officers wore a short skin cloak or kaross, and the men also had cloaks, which I found out afterwards were made from the inner bark of trees.

They advanced in the most perfect silence and very slowly. Nobody said anything, and if orders were given this must have been done by signs. I could not see that any of them had firearms.

"Now," I said to Stephen, "perhaps if we shot and killed some of those fellows, they might be frightened and run away. Or they might not; or if they did they might return."

"Whatever happened," he remarked sagely, "we should scarcely be welcome in their country afterwards, so I think we had better do nothing unless we are obliged."

I nodded, for it was obvious that we could not fight hundreds of men, and told Sammy, who was perfectly livid with fear, to bring the breakfast. No wonder he was afraid, poor fellow, for we were in great danger. These Mazitu had a bad name, and if they chose to attack us we should all be dead in a few minutes.

The coffee and some cold buck's flesh were put upon our little camp-table in front of the tent which we had pitched because of the rain, and we began to eat. The Zulu hunters also ate from a bowl of mealie porridge which they had cooked on the previous night, each of them with his loaded rifle upon his knees. Our proceedings appeared to puzzle the Mazitu very much indeed. They drew quite near to us, to within about forty yards, and halted there in a dead circle, staring at us with their great round eyes. It was like a scene in a dream; I shall never forget it.

Everything about us appeared to astonish them, our indifference, the colour of Stephen and myself (as a matter of fact at that date Brother John was the only white man they had ever seen), our tent and our two remaining donkeys. Indeed, when one of these beasts broke into a bray, they showed signs of fright, looking at each other and even retreating a few paces.

At length the position got upon my nerves, especially as I saw that some of them were beginning to fiddle with their bows, and that their General, a tall, one-eyed old fellow, was making up his mind to do something. I called to one of the two Mazitus, whom I forgot to say we had named Tom and Jerry, and gave him a pannikin of coffee.

"Take that to the captain there with my good wishes, Jerry, and ask him if he will drink with us," I said.

Jerry, who was a plucky fellow, obeyed. Advancing with the steaming coffee, he held it under the Captain's nose. Evidently he knew the man's name, for I heard him say:

"O Babemba, the white lords, Macumazana and Wazela, ask if you will share their holy drink with them?"

I could perfectly understand the words, for these people spoke a dialect so akin to Zulu that by now it had no difficulty for me.

"Their holy drink!" exclaimed the old fellow, starting back. "Man, it is hot red-water. Would these white wizards poison me with *mwavi*?"

Here I should explain that *mwavi* or *mkasa*, as it is sometimes called, is the liquor distilled from the inner bark of a sort of mimosa tree or sometimes from a root of the strychnos tribe, which is administered by the witch-doctors to persons accused of crime. If it makes them sick they are declared innocent. If they are thrown into convulsions or stupor they are clearly guilty and die, either from the effects of the poison or afterwards by other means.

"This is no *mwavi*, O Babemba," said Jerry. "It is the divine liquor that makes the white lords shoot straight with their wonderful guns which kill at a thousand paces. See, I will swallow some of it," and he did, though it must have burnt his tongue.

Thus encouraged, old Babemba sniffed at the coffee and found it fragrant. Then he called a man, who from his peculiar dress I took to be a doctor, made him drink some, and watched the results, which were that the doctor tried to finish the pannikin. Snatching it away indignantly Babemba drank himself, and as I had half-filled the cup with sugar, found the mixture good.

"It is indeed a holy drink," he said, smacking his lips. "Have you any more of it?"

"The white lords have more," said Jerry. "They invite you to eat with them."

Babemba stuck his finger into the tin, and covering it with the sediment of sugar, sucked and reflected.

"It's all right," I whispered to Stephen. "I don't think he'll kill us after drinking our coffee, and what's more, I believe he is coming to breakfast."

"This may be a snare," said Babemba, who now began to lick the sugar out of the pannikin.

"No," answered Jerry with creditable resource; "though they could easily kill you all, the white lords do not hurt those who have partaken of their holy drink, that is unless anyone tries to harm them."

"Cannot you bring some more of the holy drink here?" he asked, giving a final polish to the pannikin with his tongue.

"No," said Jerry, "if you want it you must go there. Fear nothing. Would I, one of your own people, betray you?"

"True!" exclaimed Babemba. "By your talk and your face you are a Mazitu. How came you—well, we will speak of that afterwards. I am very thirsty. I will come. Soldiers, sit down and watch, and if any harm happens to me, avenge it and report to the king."

Now, while all this was going on, I had made Hans and Sammy open one of the boxes and extract therefrom a good-sized mirror in a wooden frame with a support at the back so that it could be stood anywhere. Fortunately it was unbroken; indeed, our packing had been so careful that none of the looking-glasses or other fragile things were injured. To this mirror I gave a hasty polish, then set it upright upon the table.

Old Babemba came along rather suspiciously, his one eye rolling over us and everything that belonged to us. When he was quite close it fell upon the mirror. He stopped, he stared, he retreated, then drawn by his overmastering curiosity, came on again and again stood still.

"What is the matter?" called his second in command from the ranks.

"The matter is," he answered, "that here is great magic. Here I see myself walking towards myself. There can be no mistake, for one eye is gone in my other self."

"Advance, O Babemba," cried the doctor who had tried to drink all the coffee, "and see what happens. Keep your spear ready, and if your witch-self attempts to harm you, kill it."

Thus encouraged, Babemba lifted his spear and dropped it again in a great hurry.

"That won't do, fool of a doctor," he shouted back. "My other self lifts a spear also, and what is more all of you who should be behind are in front of me. The holy drink has made me drunk; I am bewitched. Save me!"

Now I saw that the joke had gone too far, for the soldiers were beginning to string their bows in confusion. Luckily at this moment, the sun at length came out almost opposite to us.

"O Babemba," I said in a solemn voice, "it is true that this magic shield, which we have brought as a gift to you, gives you another self. Henceforth your labours will be halved, and your pleasures doubled, for when you look into this shield you will be not one but two. Also it has other properties—see," and lifting the mirror I used it as a heliograph, flashing the reflected sunlight into the eyes of the long half-circle of men in front of us. My word! didn't they run.

"Wonderful!" exclaimed old Babemba, "and can I learn to do that also, white lord?"

"Certainly," I answered, "come and try. Now, hold it so while I say the spell," and I muttered some hocus-pocus, then directed it towards certain of the Mazitu who were gathering again. "There! Look! Look! You have hit them in the eye. You are a master of magic. They run, they run!" and run they did indeed. "Is there anyone yonder whom you dislike?"

"Yes, plenty," answered Babemba with emphasis, "especially that witch-doctor who drank nearly all the holy drink."

"Very well; by-and-by I will show you how you can burn a hole in him with this magic. No, not now, not now. For a while this mocker of the sun is dead. Look," and dipping the glass beneath the table I produced it back first. "You cannot see anything, can you?"

"Nothing except wood," replied Babemba, staring at the deal slip with which it was lined.

Then I threw a dish-cloth over it and, to change the subject, offered him another pannikin of the "holy drink" and a stool to sit on.

The old fellow perched himself very gingerly upon the stool, which was of the folding variety, stuck the iron-tipped end of his great spear in the ground between his knees and took hold of the pannikin. Or rather he took hold of a pannikin and not the right one. So ridiculous was his appearance that the light-minded Stephen, who, forgetting the perils of the situation, had for the last minute or two been struggling with inward laughter, clapped down his coffee on the table and retired into the tent, where I heard him gurgling in unseemly merriment. It was this coffee that in the confusion of the moment Sammy gave to old Babemba. Presently Stephen reappeared, and to cover his confusion seized the pannikin meant for Babemba and drank it, or most of it. Then Sammy, seeing his mistake, said:

"Mr. Somers, I regret that there is an error. You are drinking from the cup which that stinking savage has just licked clean."

The effect was dreadful and instantaneous, for then and there Stephen was violently sick.

"Why does the white lord do that?" asked Babemba. "Now I see that you are truly deceiving me, and that what you are giving me to swallow is nothing but hot *mwavi*, which in the innocent causes vomiting, but that in those who mean evil, death."

"Stop that foolery, you idiot," I muttered to Stephen, kicking him on the shins, "or you'll get our throats cut." Then, collecting myself with an effort, I said:

"Oh! not at all, General. This white lord is the priest of the holy drink and—what you see is a religious rite."

"Is it so," said Babemba. "Then I hope that the rite is not catching."

"Never," I replied, proffering him a biscuit. "And now, General Babemba, tell me, why do you come against us with about five hundred armed men?"

"To kill you, white lords—oh! how hot is this holy drink, yet pleasant. You said that it was not catching, did you not? For I feel—"

"Eat the cake," I answered. "And why do you wish to kill us? Be so good as to tell me the truth now, or I shall read it in the magic shield which portrays the inside as well as the out," and lifting the cloth I stared at the glass.

"If you can read my thoughts, white lord, why trouble me to tell them?" asked Babemba sensibly enough, his mouth full of biscuit. "Still, as that bright thing may lie, I will set them out. Bausi, king of our people, has sent me to kill you, because news has reached him that you are great slave dealers who come hither with guns to capture the Mazitus and take them away to the Black Water to be sold and sent across it in big canoes that move of themselves. Of this he has been warned by messengers from the Arab men. Moreover, we know that it is true, for last night you had with you many slaves who, seeing our spears, ran away not an hour ago."

Now I stared hard at the looking-glass and answered coolly:

"This magic shield tells a somewhat different story. It says that your king, Bausi, for whom by the way we have many things as presents, told you to lead us to him with honour, that we might talk over matters with him."

The shot was a good one. Babemba grew confused.

"It is true," he stammered, "that—I mean, the king left it to my judgment. I will consult the witch-doctor."

"If he left it to your judgment, the matter is settled," I said, "since certainly, being so great a noble, you would never try to murder those of whose holy drink you have just partaken. Indeed if you did so," I added in a cold voice, "you would not live long yourself. One secret word and that drink will turn to *mwavi* of the worst sort inside of you."

"Oh! yes, white lord, it is settled," exclaimed Babemba, "it is settled. Do not trouble the secret word. I will lead you to the king and you shall talk with him. By my head and my father's spirit you are safe from me. Still, with your leave, I will call the great doctor, Imbozwi, and ratify the agreement in his presence, and also show him the magic shield."

So Imbozwi was sent for, Jerry taking the message. Presently he arrived. He was a villainous-looking person of uncertain age, humpbacked like the picture of Punch, wizened and squint-eyed. His costume was of the ordinary witch-doctor type being set off with snake skins, fish bladders, baboon's teeth and little bags of medicine. To add to his charms a broad strip of pigment, red ochre probably, ran down his forehead and the nose beneath, across the lips and chin, ending in a red mark the size of a penny where the throat joins the chest. His woolly hair also, in which was twisted a small ring of black gum, was soaked with grease and powdered blue. It was arranged in a kind of horn, coming to a sharp point about five inches above the top of the skull. Altogether he looked extremely like the devil. What was more, he was a devil in a bad temper, for the first words he said embodied a reproach to us for not having asked him to partake of our "holy drink" with Babemba.

We offered to make him some more, but he refused, saying that we should poison him.

Then Babemba set the matter out, rather nervously I thought, for evidently he was afraid of this old wizard, who listened in complete silence. When Babemba explained that without the king's direct order it would be foolish and unjustifiable to put to death such magicians as we were, Imbozwi spoke for the first time, asking why he called us magicians.

Babemba instanced the wonders of the shining shield that showed pictures.

"Pooh!" said Imbozwi, "does not calm water or polished iron show pictures?"

"But this shield will make fire," said Babemba. "The white lords say it can burn a man up."

"Then let it burn me up," replied Imbozwi with ineffable contempt, "and I will believe that these white men are magicians worthy to be kept alive, and not common slave-traders such as we have often heard of."

"Burn him, white lords, and show him that I am right," exclaimed the exasperated Babemba, after which they fell to wrangling. Evidently they were rivals, and by this time both of them had lost their tempers.

The sun was now very hot, quite sufficiently so to enable us to give Mr. Imbozwi a taste of our magic, which I determined he should have. Not being certain whether an ordinary mirror would really reflect enough heat to scorch, I drew from my pocket a very powerful burning-glass which I sometimes used for the lighting of fires in order to save matches, and holding the mirror in one hand and the burning-glass in the other, I worked myself into a suitable position for the experiment. Babemba and the witch-doctor were arguing so fiercely that neither of them seemed to notice what I was doing. Getting the focus right, I directed the concentrated spark straight on to Imbozwi's greased top-knot, where I knew he would feel nothing, my plan being to char a hole in it. But as it happened this top-knot was built up round something of a highly inflammable nature, reed or camphor-wood, I expect. At any rate, about thirty seconds later the top-knot was burning like a beautiful torch.

"*Ow!*" said the Kaffirs who were watching. "My Aunt!" exclaimed Stephen. "Look, look!" shouted Babemba in tones of delight. "Now will you believe, O blown-out bladder of a man, that there are greater magicians than yourself in the world?"

"What is the matter, son of a dog, that you make a mock of me?" screeched the unfuriated Imbozwi, who alone was unaware of anything unusual.

As he spoke some suspicion rose in his mind which caused him to put his hand to his top-knot, and withdraw it with a howl. Then he sprang up and began to dance about, which of course only fanned the fire that had now got hold of the grease and gum. The Zulus applauded; Babemba clapped his hands; Stephen burst into one of his idiotic fits of laughter. For my part I grew frightened. Near at hand stood a large wooden pot such as the Kaffirs make, from which the coffee kettle had been filled, that fortunately was still half-full of water. I seized it and ran to him.

"Save me, white lord!" he howled. "You are the greatest of magicians and I am your slave."

Here I cut him short by clapping the pot bottom upwards on his burning head, into which it vanished as a candle does into an extinguisher. Smoke and a bad smell issued from beneath the pot, the water from which ran all over Imbozwi, who stood quite still. When I was sure the fire was out, I lifted the pot and revealed the discomfited wizard, but without his elaborate head-dress. Beyond a little scorching he was not in the least hurt, for I had acted in time; only he was bald, for when touched the charred hair fell off at the roots.

"It is gone," he said in an amazed voice after feeling at his scalp.

"Yes," I answered, "quite. The magic shield worked very well, did it not?"

"Can you put it back again, white lord?" he asked.

"That will depend upon how you behave," I replied.

Then without another word he turned and walked back to the soldiers, who received him with shouts of laughter. Evidently Imbozwi was not a popular character, and his discomfiture delighted them.

Babemba also was delighted. Indeed, he could not praise our magic enough, and at once began to make arrangements to escort us to the king at his head town, which was called Beza, vowing that we need fear no harm at his hands or those of his soldiers. In fact, the only person who did not appreciate our black arts was Imbozwi himself. I caught a look in his eye as he marched off which told me that he hated us bitterly, and reflected to myself that perhaps I had been foolish to use that burning-glass, although in truth I had not intended to set his head on fire.

"My father," said Mavovo to me afterwards, "it would have been better to let that snake burn to death, for then you would have killed his poison. I am something of a doctor myself, and I tell you there is nothing our brotherhood hates so much as being laughed at. You have made a fool of him before all his people and he will not forget it, Macumazana."

IX

BAUSI THE KING

About midday we made a start for Beza Town where King Bausi lived, which we understood we ought to reach on the following evening. For some hours the regiment marched in front, or rather round us, but as we complained to Babemba of the noise and dust, with a confidence that was quite touching, he sent it on ahead. First, however, he asked us to pass our word "by our mothers," which was the most sacred of oaths among many African peoples, that we would not attempt to escape. I confess that I hesitated before giving an answer, not being entirely enamoured of the Mazitu and of our prospects among them, especially as I had discovered through Jerry that the discomfited Imbozwi had departed from the soldiers on some business of his own. Had the matter been left to me, indeed, I should have tried to slip back into the bush over the border, and there put in a few months shooting during the dry season, while working my way southwards. This, too, was the wish of the Zulu hunters, of Hans, and I need not add of Sammy. But when I mentioned the matter to Stephen, he implored me to abandon the idea.

"Look here, Quatermain," he said, "I have come to this God-forsaken country to get that great Cypripedium, and get it I will or die in the attempt. Still," he added after surveying our rather blank faces, "I have no right to play with your lives, so if you think the thing too dangerous I will go on alone with this old boy, Babemba. Putting everything else aside, I think that one of us ought to visit Bausi's kraal in case the gentleman who you call Brother John should turn up there. In short, I have made up my mind, so it is no use talking."

I lit my pipe, and for quite a time contemplated this obstinate young man while considering the matter from every point of view. Finally, I came to the conclusion that he was right and I was wrong. It was true that by bribing Babemba, or otherwise, there was still an excellent prospect of effecting a masterly retreat and of avoiding many perils. On the other hand, we had not come to this wild place in order to retreat. Further, at whose expense had we come here? At that of Stephen Somers who wished to proceed. Lastly, to say nothing of the chance of meeting Brother John, to whom I felt no obligation since he had given us the slip at Durban, I did not like the idea of being beaten. We had started out to visit some mysterious savages who worshipped a monkey and a flower, and we might as well go on till circumstances were too much for us. After all, dangers are everywhere; those who turn back because of dangers will never succeed in any life that we can imagine.

"Mavovo," I said presently, pointing to Stephen with my pipe, "the *inkoosi* Wazela does not wish to try to escape. He wishes to go on to the country of the Pongo people if we can get there. And, Mavovo, remember that he has paid for everything; we are his hired servants. Also that he says that if we run back he will walk forward alone with these Mazitus. Still, if any of you hunters desire to slip off, he will not look your way, nor shall I. What say you?"

"I say, Macumazana, that, though young, Wazela is a chief with a great heart, and that where you and he go, I shall go also, as I think will the rest of us. I do not like these Mazitu, for if their fathers were Zulus their mothers were low people. They are bastards, and of the Pongo I hear nothing but what is evil. Still, no good ox ever turns in the yoke because of a mud-hole. Let us go on, for if we sink in the swamp what does it matter? Moreover, my Snake tells me that we shall not sink, at least not all of us."

So it was arranged that no effort should be made to return. Sammy, it is true, wished to do so, but when it came to the point and he was offered one of the remaining donkeys and as much food and ammunition as he could carry, he changed his mind.

"I think it better, Mr. Quatermain," he said, "to meet my end in the company of high-born, lofty souls than to pursue a lonely career towards the inevitable in unknown circumstances."

"Very well put, Sammy," I answered; "so while waiting for the inevitable, please go and cook the dinner."

Having laid aside our doubts, we proceeded on the journey comfortably enough, being well provided with bearers to take the place of those who had run away. Babemba, accompanied by a single orderly, travelled with us, and from him we collected much information. It seemed that the Mazitu were a large people who could muster from five to seven thousand spears. Their tradition was that they came from the south and were of the same stock as the Zulus, of whom they had heard vaguely. Indeed, many of their customs, to say nothing of their language, resembled those of that country. Their military organisation, however, was not so thorough, and in other ways they struck me as a lower race. In one particular, it is true, that of their houses, they were more advanced, for these, as we saw in the many kraals that we passed, were better built, with doorways through which one could walk upright, instead of the Kaffir bee-holes.

We slept in one of these houses on our march, and should have found it very comfortable had it not been for the innumerable fleas which at length drove us out into the courtyard. For the rest, these Mazitu much resembled the Zulus. They had kraals and were breeders of cattle; they were ruled by headmen under the command of a supreme chief or king; they believed in witchcraft and offered sacrifice to the spirits of their ancestors, also in some kind of a vague and mighty god who dominated the affairs of the world and declared his will through the doctors. Lastly, they were, and I dare say still are, a race of fighting men who loved war and raided the neighbouring peoples upon any and every pretext, killing their men and stealing their women and cattle. They had their virtues, too, being kindly and hospitable by nature, though cruel enough to their enemies. Moreover, they detested dealing in slaves and those who practised it, saying that it was better to kill a man than to deprive him of his freedom. Also they had a horror of the cannibalism which is so common in the dark regions of Africa, and for this reason, more than any other, loathed the Pongo folk who were supposed to be eaters of men.

On the evening of the second day of our march, during which we had passed through a beautiful and fertile upland country, very well watered, and except in the valleys, free from bush, we arrived at Beza. This town was situated on a wide plain surrounded by low hills and encircled by a belt of cultivated land made beautiful by the crops of maize and other cereals which were then ripe to harvest. It was fortified in a way. That is, a tall, unclimbable palisade of timber surrounded the entire town, which fence was strengthened by prickly pears and cacti planted on its either side.

Within this palisade the town was divided into quarters more or less devoted to various trades. Thus one part of it was called the Ironsmiths' Quarter; another the Soldiers' Quarter; another the Quarter of the Land-tillers; another that of the Skin-dressers, and so on. The king's dwelling and those of his women and dependents were near the North gate, and in front of these, surrounded by semi-circles of huts, was a wide space into which cattle could be driven if necessary. This, however, at the time of our visit, was used as a market and a drilling ground.

We entered the town, that must in all have contained a great number of inhabitants, by the South gate, a strong log structure facing a wooded slope through which ran a road. Just as the sun was setting we marched to the guest-huts up a central street lined with the population of the place who had gathered to stare at us. These huts were situated in the Soldiers' Quarter, not far from the king's house and surrounded by an inner fence to keep them private.

None of the people spoke as we passed them, for the Mazitu are polite by nature; also it seemed to me that they regarded us with awe tempered by curiosity. They only stared, and occasionally those of them who were soldiers saluted us by lifting their spears. The huts into which we were introduced by Babemba, with whom we had grown very friendly, were good and clean.

Here all our belongings, including the guns which we had collected just before the slaves ran away, were placed in one of the huts over which a Mazitu mounted guard, the donkeys being tied to the fence at a little distance. Outside this fence stood another armed Mazitu, also on guard.

"Are we prisoners here?" I asked of Babemba.

"The king watches over his guests," he answered enigmatically. "Have the white lords any message for the king whom I am summoned to see this night?"

"Yes," I answered. "Tell the king that we are the brethren of him who more than a year ago cut a swelling from his body, whom we have arranged to meet here. I mean the white lord with a long beard who among you black people is called Dogeetah."

Babemba started. "You are the brethren of Dogeetah! How comes it then that you never mentioned his name before, and when is he going to meet you here? Know that Dogeetah is a great man among us, for with him alone of all men the king has made blood-brotherhood. As the king is, so is Dogeetah among the Mazitu."

"We never mentioned him because we do not talk about everything at once, Babemba. As to when Dogeetah will meet us I am not sure; I am only sure that he is coming."

"Yes, lord Macumazana, but when, when? That is what the king will want to know and that is what you must tell him. Lord," he added, dropping his voice, "you are in danger here where you have many enemies, since it is not lawful for white men to enter this land. If you would save your lives, be advised by me and be ready to tell the king to-morrow when

Dogeetah, whom he loves, will appear here to vouch for you, and see that he does appear very soon and by the day you name. Since otherwise when he comes, if come he does, he may not find you able to talk to him. Now I, your friend, have spoken and the rest is with you."

Then without another word he rose, slipped through the door of the hut and out by the gateway of the fence from which the sentry moved aside to let him pass. I, too, rose from the stool on which I sat and danced about the hut in a perfect fury.

"Do you understand what that infernal (I am afraid I used a stronger word) old fool told me?" I exclaimed to Stephen. "He says that we must be prepared to state exactly when that other infernal old fool, Brother John, will turn up at Beza Town, and that if we don't we shall have our throats cut as indeed has already been arranged."

"Rather awkward," replied Stephen. "There are no express trains to Beza, and if there were we couldn't be sure that Brother John would take one of them. I suppose there *is* a Brother John?" he added reflectively. "To me he seems to be—intimately connected with Mrs. Harris."

"Oh! there is, or there was," I explained. "Why couldn't the confounded ass wait quietly for us at Durban instead of fooling off butterfly hunting to the north of Zululand and breaking his leg or his neck there if he has done anything of the sort?"

"Don't know, I am sure. It's hard enough to understand one's own motives, let alone Brother John's."

Then we sat down on our stools again and stared at each other. At this moment Hans crept into the hut and squatted down in front of us. He might have walked in as there was a doorway, but he preferred to creep on his hands and knees, I don't know why.

"What is it, you ugly little toad?" I asked viciously, for that was just what he looked like; even the skin under his jaw moved like a toad's.

"The Baas is in trouble?" remarked Hans.

"I should think he was," I answered, "and so will you be presently when you are wriggling on the point of a Mazitu spear."

"They are broad spears that would make a big hole," remarked Hans again, whereupon I rose to kick him out, for his ideas were, as usual, unpleasant.

"Baas," he went on, "I have been listening—there is a very good hole in this hut for listening if one lies against the wall and pretends to be asleep. I have heard all and understood most of your talk with that one-eyed savage and the Baas Stephen."

"Well, you little sneak, what of it?"

"Only, Baas, that if we do not want to be killed in this place from which there is no escape, it is necessary that you should find out exactly on what day and at what hour Dogeetah is going to arrive."

"Look here, you yellow idiot," I exclaimed, "if you are beginning that game too, I'll—" then I stopped, reflecting that my temper was getting the better of me and that I had better hear what Hans had to say before I vented it on him.

"Baas, Mavovo is a great doctor; it is said that his Snake is the straightest and the strongest in all Zululand save that of his master, Zikali, the old slave. He told you that Dogeetah was laid up somewhere with a hurt leg and that he was coming to meet you here; no doubt therefore he can tell you also *when* he is coming. I would ask him, but he won't set his Snake to work for me. So you must ask him, Baas, and perhaps he will forget that you laughed at his magic and that he swore you would never see it again."

"Oh! blind one," I answered, "how do I know that Mavovo's story about Dogeetah was not all nonsense?"

Hans stared at me amazed.

"Mavovo's story nonsense! Mavovo's Snake a liar! Oh! Baas, that is what comes of being too much a Christian. Now, thanks to your father the Predikant, I am a Christian too, but not so much that I have forgotten how to know good magic from bad. Mavovo's Snake a liar, and after he whom we buried yonder was the first of the hunters whom the feathers named to him at Durban!" and he began to chuckle in intense amusement, then added, "Well, Baas, there it is. You must either ask Mavovo, and very nicely, or we shall all be killed. *I* don't mind much, for I should rather like to begin again a little younger somewhere else, but just think what a noise Sammy will make!" and turning he crept out as he had crept in.

"Here's a nice position," I groaned to Stephen when he had gone. "I, a white man, who, in spite of some coincidences with which I am acquainted, know that all this Kaffir magic is bosh am to beg a savage to tell me something of which he *must* be ignorant. That is, unless we educated people have got hold of the wrong end of the stick altogether. It is humiliating; it isn't Christian, and I'm hanged if I'll do it!"

"I dare say you will be—hanged I mean—whether you do it or whether you don't," replied Stephen with his sweet smile. "But I say, old fellow, how do you know it is all bosh? We are told about lots of miracles which weren't bosh, and if miracles ever existed, why can't they exist now? But there, I know what you mean and it is no use arguing. Still, if you're proud, I ain't. I'll try to soften the stony heart of Mavovo—we are rather pals, you know—and get him to unroll the book of his occult wisdom," and he went.

A few minutes later I was called out to receive a sheep which, with milk, native beer, some corn, and other things, including green forage for the donkeys, Bausi had sent for us to eat. Here I may remark that while we were among the Mazitu we lived like fighting cocks. There was none of that starvation which is, or was, so common in East Africa where the traveller often cannot get food for love or money—generally because there is none.

When this business was settled by my sending a message of thanks to the king with an intimation that we hoped to wait upon him on the morrow with a few presents, I went to seek Sammy in order to tell him to kill and cook the sheep. After some search I found, or rather heard him beyond a reed fence which divided two of the huts. He was acting as interpreter between Stephen Somers and Mavovo.

"This Zulu man declares, Mr. Somers," he said, "that he quite understands everything you have been explaining, and that it is probable that we shall all be butchered by this savage Bausi, if we cannot tell him when the white man, Dogeetah, whom he loves, will arrive here. He says also that he thinks that by his magic he could learn when this will happen—if it is to happen at all—(which of course, Mr. Somers, for your private information only, is a mighty lie of the ignorant heathen). He adds, however, that he does not care one brass farthing—his actual expression, Mr. Somers, is 'one grain of corn on a mealie-cob'—about his or anybody else's life, which from all I have heard of his proceedings I can well believe to be true. He says in his vulgar language that there is no difference between the belly of a Mazitu-land hyena and that of any other hyena, and that the earth of Mazitu-land is as welcome to his bones as any other earth, since the earth is the wickedest of all hyenas, in that he has observed that soon or late it devours everlastingly everything which once it bore. You must forgive me for reproducing his empty and childish talk, Mr. Somers, but you bade me to render the words of this savage with exactitude. In fact, Mr. Somers, this reckless person intimates, in short that some power with which he is not acquainted—he calls it the 'Strength that makes the Sun to shine and broiders the blanket of the night with stars' (forgive me for repeating his silly words), caused him 'to be born into this world, and, at an hour already appointed, will draw him from this world back into its dark, eternal bosom, there to be rocked in sleep, or nursed to life again, according to its unknown will'—I translate exactly, Mr. Somers, although I do not know what it all means—and that he does not care a curse when this happens. Still, he says that whereas he is growing old and has known many sorrows—he alludes here, I gather, to some nigger wives of his whom another savage knocked on the head; also to a child to whom he appears to have been attached—you are young with all your days and, he hopes, joys, before you. Therefore he would gladly do anything in his power to save your life, because although you are white and he is black he has conceived an affection for you and looks on you as his child. Yes, Mr. Somers, although I blush to repeat it, this black fellow says he looks upon you as his child. He adds, indeed, that if the opportunity arises, he will gladly give his life to save your life, and that it cuts his heart in two to refuse you anything. Still he must refuse this request of yours, that he will ask the creature he calls his Snake—what he means by that, I don't know, Mr. Somers—to declare when the white man, named Dogeetah, will arrive in this place. For this reason, that he told Mr. Quatermain when he laughed at him about his divinations that he would make no more magic for him or any of you, and that he will die rather than break his word. That's all, Mr. Somers, and I dare say you will think—quite enough, too."

"I understand," replied Stephen. "Tell the chief, Mavovo" (I observed he laid an emphasis on the word, *chief*) "that I *quite* understand, and that I thank him very much for explaining things to me so fully. Then ask him whether, as the matter is so important, there is no way out of this trouble?"

Sammy translated into Zulu, which he spoke perfectly, as I noted without interpolations or additions.

"Only one way," answered Mavovo in the intervals of taking snuff. "It is that Macumazana himself shall ask me to do this thing, Macumazana is my old chief and friend, and for his sake I will forget what in the case of others I should always remember. If he will come and ask me, without mockery, to exercise my skill on behalf of all of us, I will try to exercise it, although I know very well that he believes it to be but as an idle little whirlwind that stirs the dust, that raises the dust and lets it fall again without purpose or meaning, forgetting, as the wise white men forget, that even the wind which blows the dust is the same that breathes in our nostrils, and that to it, we also are as is the dust."

Now I, the listener, thought for a moment or two. The words of this fighting savage, Mavovo, even those of them of which I had heard only the translation, garbled and beslavered by the mean comments of the unutterable Sammy, stirred my imagination. Who was I that I should dare to judge of him and his wild, unknown gifts? Who was I that I should mock at him and by my mockery intimate that I believed him to be a fraud?

Stepping through the gateway of the fence, I confronted him.

"Mavovo," I said, "I have overheard your talk. I am sorry if I laughed at you in Durban. I do not understand what you call your magic. It is beyond me and may be true or may be false. Still, I shall be grateful to you if you will use your power to discover, if you can, whether Dogeetah is coming here, and if so, when. Now, do as it may please you; I have spoken."

"And I have heard, Macumazana, my father. To-night I will call upon my Snake. Whether it will answer or what it will answer, I cannot say."

Well, he did call upon his Snake with due and portentous ceremony and, according to Stephen, who was present, which I declined to be, that mystic reptile declared that Dogeetah, alias Brother John, would arrive in Beza Town precisely at sunset on the third day from that night. Now as he had divined on Friday, according to our almanac, this meant that we might hope to see him—hope exactly described my state of mind on the matter—on the Monday evening in time for supper.

"All right," I said briefly. "Please do not talk to me any more about this impious rubbish, for I want to go to sleep."

Next morning early we unpacked our boxes and made a handsome selection of gifts for the king, Bausi, hoping thus to soften his royal heart. It included a bale of calico, several knives, a musical box, a cheap American revolver, and a bundle of tooth-picks; also several pounds of the best and most fashionable beads for his wives. This truly noble present we sent to the king by our two Mazitu servants, Tom and Jerry, who were marched off in the charge of several sentries, for I hoped that these men would talk to their compatriots and tell them what good fellows we were. Indeed I instructed them to do so.

Imagine our horror, therefore, when about an hour later, just as we were tidying ourselves up after breakfast, there appeared through the gate, not Tom and Jerry, for they had vanished, but a long line of

Mazitu soldiers each of whom carried one of the articles that we had sent. Indeed the last of them held the bundle of toothpicks on his fuzzy head as though it were a huge faggot of wood. One by one they set them down upon the lime flooring of the verandah of the largest hut. Then their captain said solemnly:

"Bausi, the Great Black One, has no need of the white men's gifts."

"Indeed," I replied, for my dander was up. "Then he won't get another chance at them."

The men turned away without more words, and presently Babemba turned up with a company of about fifty soldiers.

"The king is waiting to see you, white lords," he said in a voice of very forced jollity, "and I have come to conduct you to him."

"Why would he not accept our presents?" I asked, pointing to the row of them.

"Oh! that is because of Imbozwi's story of the magic shield. He said he wanted no gifts to burn his hair off. But, come, come. He will explain for himself. If the Elephant is kept waiting he grows angry and trumpets."

"Does he?" I said. "And how many of us are to come?"

"All, all, white lord. He wishes to see every one of you."

"Not me, I suppose?" said Sammy, who was standing close by. "I must stop to make ready the food."

"Yes, you too," replied Babemba. "The king would look on the mixer of the holy drink."

Well, there was no way out of it, so off we marched, all well armed as I need not say, and were instantly surrounded by the soldiers. To give an unusual note to the proceedings I made Hans walk first, carrying on his head the rejected musical box from which flowed the touching melody of "Home, Sweet Home." Then came Stephen bearing the Union Jack on a pole, then I in the midst of the hunters and accompanied by Babemba, then the reluctant Sammy, and last of all the two donkeys led by Mazitus, for it seemed that the king had especially ordered that these should be brought also.

It was a truly striking cavalcade, the sight of which under any other circumstances would have made me laugh. Nor did it fail in its effect, for even the silent Mazitu people through whom we wended our way, were moved to something like enthusiasm. "Home, Sweet Home" they evidently thought heavenly, though perhaps the two donkeys attracted them most, especially when these brayed.

"Where are Tom and Jerry?" I asked of Babemba.

"I don't know," he answered; "I think they have been given leave to go to see their friends."

Imbozwi is suppressing evidence in our favour, I thought to myself, and said no more.

Presently we reached the gate of the royal enclosure. Here to my dismay the soldiers insisted on disarming us, taking away our rifles, our revolvers, and even our sheath knives. In vain did I remonstrate, saying that we were not accustomed to part with these weapons. The answer was that it was not lawful for any man to appear before the king armed even with so much as a dancing-stick. Mavovo and the Zulus showed signs of resisting and for a minute I thought there was going to be a row, which of course would have ended in our massacre, for although the Mazitus feared guns very much, what could we have done against hundreds of them? I ordered him to give way, but for once he was on the point of disobeying me. Then by a happy thought I reminded him that, according to his Snake, Dogeetah was coming, and that therefore all would be well. So he submitted with an ill grace, and we saw our precious guns borne off we knew not where.

Then the Mazitu soldiers piled their spears and bows at the gate of the kraal and we proceeded with only the Union Jack and the musical box, which was now discoursing "Britannia rules the waves."

Across the open space we marched to where several broad-leaved trees grew in front of a large native house. Not far from the door of this house a fat, middle-aged and angry-looking man was seated on a stool, naked except for a moocha of catskins about his loins and a string of large blue beads round his neck.

"Bausi, the King," whispered Babemba.

At his side squatted a little hunchbacked figure, in whom I had no difficulty in recognising Imbozwi, although he had painted his scorched scalp white with vermillion spots and adorned his snub nose with a purple tip, his dress of ceremony I presume. Round and behind there were a number of silent councillors. At some signal or on reaching a given spot, all the soldiers, including old Babemba, fell upon their hands and knees and began to crawl. They wanted us to do the same, but here I drew the line, feeling that if once we crawled we must always crawl.

So at my word we advanced upright, but with slow steps, in the midst of all this wriggling humanity and at length found ourselves in the august presence of Bausi, "the Beautiful Black One," King of the Mazitu.

X

The Sentence

We stared at Bausi and Bausi stared at us.

"I am the Black Elephant Bausi," he exclaimed at last, worn out by our solid silence, "and I trumpet! I trumpet! I trumpet!" (It appeared that this was the ancient and hallowed formula with which a Mazitu king was wont to open a conversation with strangers.)

After a suitable pause I replied in a cold voice:

"We are the white lions, Macumazana and Wazela, and we roar! we roar! we roar!"

"I can trample," said Bausi.

"And we can bite," I said haughtily, though how we were to bite or do anything else effectual with nothing but a Union Jack, I did not in the least know.

"What is that thing?" asked Bausi, pointing to the flag.

"That which shadows the whole earth," I answered proudly, a remark that seemed to impress him, although he did not at all understand it, for he ordered a soldier to hold a palm leaf umbrella over him to prevent it from shadowing *him*.

"And that," he asked again, pointing to the music box, "which is not alive and yet makes a noise?"

"That sings the war-song of our people," I said. "We sent it to you as a present and you returned it. Why do you return our presents, O Bausi?"

Then of a sudden this potentate grew furious.

"Why do you come here, white men," he asked, "uninvited and against the law of my land, where only one white man is welcome, my brother Dogeetah, who cured me of sickness with a knife? I know who you are. You are dealers in men. You come here to steal my people and sell them into slavery. You had many slaves with you on the borders of my country, but you sent them away. You shall die, you shall die, you who call yourselves lions, and the painted rag which you say shadows the world, shall rot with your bones. As for that box which sings a war-song, I will smash it; it shall not bewitch me as your magic shield bewitched my great doctor, Imbozwi, burning off his hair."

Then springing up with wonderful agility for one so fat, he knocked the musical box from Hans' head, so that it fell to the ground and after a little whirring grew silent.

"That is right," squeaked Imbozwi. "Trample on their magic, O Elephant. Kill them, O Black One; burn them as they burned my hair."

Now things were, I felt, very serious, for already Bausi was looking about him as though to order his soldiers to make an end of us. So I said in desperation:

"O King, you mentioned a certain white man, Dogeetah, a doctor of doctors, who cured you of sickness with a knife, and called him your brother. Well, he is our brother also, and it was by his invitation that we have come to visit you here, where he will meet us presently."

"If Dogeetah is your friend, then you are my friends," answered Bausi, "for in this land he rules as I rule, he whose blood flows in my veins, as my blood flows in his veins. But you lie. Dogeetah is no brother of slave-dealers, his heart is good and yours are evil. You say that he will meet you here. When will he meet you? Tell me, and if it is soon, I will hold my hand and wait to hear his report of you before I put you to death, for if he speaks well of you, you shall not die."

Now I hesitated, as well I might, for I felt that looking at our case from his point of view, Bausi, believing us to be slave-traders, was not angry without cause. While I was racking my brains for a reply that might be acceptable to him and would not commit us too deeply, to my astonishment Mavovo stepped forward and confronted the king.

"Who are you, fellow?" shouted Bausi.

"I am a warrior, O King, as my scars show," and he pointed to the assegai wounds upon his breast and to his cut nostril. "I am a chief of a people from whom your people sprang and my name is Mavovo, Mavovo who is ready to fight you or any man whom you may name, and to kill him or you if you will. Is there one here who wishes to be killed?"

No one answered, for the mighty-chested Zulu looked very formidable.

"I am a doctor also," went on Mavovo, "one of the greatest of doctors who can open the 'Gates of Distance' and read that which is hid in the womb of the Future. Therefore I will answer your questions which you put to the lord Macumazana, the great and wise white man whom I serve, because we have fought together in many battles. Yes, I will be his Mouth, I will answer. The white man Dogeetah, who is your blood-brother and whose word is your word among the Mazitu, will arrive here at sunset on the second day from now. I have spoken."

Bausi looked at me in question.

"Yes," I exclaimed, feeling that I must say something and that it did not much matter what I said, "Dogeetah will arrive here on the second day from now within half an hour after sunset."

Something, I know not what, prompted me to allow that extra half-hour, which in the event, saved all our lives. Now Bausi consulted a while with the execrable Imbozwi and also with the old one-eyed General Babemba while we watched, knowing that our fate hung upon the issue.

At length he spoke.

"White men," he said, "Imbozwi, the head of the witch-finders here, whose hair you burnt off by your evil magic, says that it would be better to kill you at once as your hearts are bad and you are planning mischief against my people. So I think also. But Babemba my General, with whom I am angry because he did not obey my orders and put you to death on the borders of my country when he met you there with your caravan of slaves, thinks otherwise. He prays me to hold my hand, first because you have bewitched him into liking you and secondly because if you should happen to be speaking the truth—which we do not believe—and to have come here at the invitation of my brother Dogeetah, he, Dogeetah, would be pained if he arrived and found you dead, nor could even he bring you to life again. This being so, since it matters little whether you die now or later, my command is that you be kept prisoners till sunset of the second day from this, and that then you will be led out and tied to stakes in the market-place, there to wait till the approach of darkness, by when you say Dogeetah will be here. If he arrives and owns you as his brethren, well and good; if he does not arrive, or disowns you—better still, for then you shall be shot to death with arrows as a warning to all other stealers of men not to cross the borders of the Mazitu."

I listened to this atrocious sentence with horror, then gasped out:

"We are not stealers of men, O King, we are freers of men, as Tom and Jerry of your own people could tell you."

"Who are Tom and Jerry?" he asked, indifferently. "Well, it does not matter, for doubtless they are liars like the rest of you. I have spoken. Take them away, feed them well and keep them safe till within an hour of sunset on the second day from this."

Then, without giving us any further opportunity of speaking, Bausi rose, and followed by Imbozwi and his councillors, marched off into his big hut. We too, were marched off, this time under a double guard commanded by someone whom I had not seen before. At the gate of the kraal we halted and asked for the arms that had been taken from us. No answer was given; only the soldiers put their hands upon our shoulders and thrust us along.

"This is a nice business," I whispered to Stephen.

"Oh! it doesn't matter," he answered. "There are lots more guns in the huts. I am told that these Mazitus are dreadfully afraid of bullets. So all we have to do is just to break out and shoot our way through them, for of course they will run when we begin to fire."

I looked at him but did not answer, for to tell the truth I felt in no mood for argument.

Presently we arrived at our quarters, where the soldiers left us, to camp outside. Full of his warlike plan, Stephen went at once to the hut in which the slavers' guns had been stored with our own spare rifles and all the ammunition. I saw him emerge looking very blank indeed and asked him what was the matter.

"Matter!" he answered in a voice that for once really was full of dismay. "The matter is that those Mazitu have stolen all the guns and all the ammunition. There's not enough powder left to make a blue devil."

"Well," I replied, with the kind of joke one perpetrates under such circumstances, "we shall have plenty of blue devils without making any more."

Truly ours was a dreadful situation. Let the reader imagine it. Within a little more than forty-eight hours we were to be shot to death with arrows if an erratic old gentleman who, for aught I knew might be dead, did not turn up at what was then one of the remotest and most inaccessible spots in Central Africa. Moreover, our only hope that such a thing would happen, if hope it could be called, was the prophecy of a Kaffir witch-doctor.

To rely on this in any way was so absurd that I gave up thinking of it and set my mind to considering if there were any possible means of escape. After hours of reflection I could find none. Even Hans, with all his experience and nearly superhuman cunning, could suggest none. We were unarmed and surrounded by thousands of savages, all of whom save perhaps Babemba, believed us to be slave-traders, a race that very properly they held in abhorrence, who had visited the country with the object of stealing their women and children. The king, Bausi, a very prejudiced fellow, was dead against us. Also by a piece of foolishness which I now bitterly regretted, as indeed I regretted the whole expedition, or at any rate entering on it in the absence of Brother John, we had made an implacable enemy of the head medicine-man, who to these folk was a sort of Archbishop of Canterbury. Short of a miracle, there was no hope for us. All that we could do was to say our prayers and prepare for the end.

Mavovo, it is true, remained cheerful. His faith in his "Snake" was really touching. He offered to go through that divination process again in our presence and demonstrate that there was no mistake. I declined because I had no faith in divinations, and Stephen also declined, for another reason, namely that the result might prove to be different, which, he held, would be depressing. The other Zulus oscillated between belief and scepticism, as do the unstable who set to work to study the evidences of Christianity. But Sammy did not oscillate, he literally howled, and prepared the food which poured in upon us so badly that I had to turn on Hans to do the cooking, for however little appetite we might have, it was necessary that we should keep up our strength by eating.

"What, Mr. Quatermain," asked Sammy between his tears, "is the use of dressing viands that our systems will never have time to thoroughly assimilate?"

The first night passed somehow, and so did the next day and the next night which heralded our last morning. I got up quite early and watched the sunrise. Never, I think, had I realised before what a beautiful thing the sunrise is, at least not to the extent I did now when I was saying good-bye to it for ever. Unless indeed there should prove to be still lovelier sunrises beyond the dark of death! Then I went into our hut, and as Stephen, who had the nerves of a rhinoceros, was still sleeping like a tortoise in winter, I said my prayers earnestly enough, mourned over my sins which proved to be so many that at last I gave up the job in despair, and then tried to occupy myself by reading the Old Testament, a book to which I have always been extremely attached.

As a passage that I lit on described how the prophet Samuel for whom I could not help reading "Imbozwi," hewed Agag in pieces after Bausi—I mean Saul—had relented and spared his life, I cannot say that it consoled me very much. Doubtless, I reflected, these people believe that I, like Agag, had "made women childless" by my sword, so there remained nothing save to follow the example of that unhappy king and walk "delicately" to doom.

Then, as Stephen was still sleeping—how *could* he do it, I wondered—I set to work to make up the accounts of the expedition to date. It had already cost £1,423. Just fancy expending £1,423 in order to be tied to a post and shot to death with arrows. And all to get a rare orchid! Oh! I reflected to myself, if by some marvel I should escape, or if I should live again in any land where these particular flowers flourish, I would never even look at them. And as a matter of fact I never have.

At length Stephen did wake up and, as criminals are reported to do in the papers before execution, made an excellent breakfast.

"What's the good of worrying?" he said presently. "I shouldn't if it weren't for my poor old father. It must have come to this one day, and the sooner it is over the sooner to sleep, as the song says. When one comes to think of it there are enormous advantages in sleep, for that's the only time one is quite happy. Still, I should have liked to see that Cypripedium first."

"Oh! drat the Cypripedium!" I exclaimed, and blundered from the hut to tell Sammy that if he didn't stop his groaning I would punch his head.

"Jumps! Regular jumps! Who'd have thought it of Quatermain?" I heard Stephen mutter in the intervals of lighting his pipe.

The morning went "like lightning that is greased," as Sammy remarked. Three o'clock came and Mavovo and his following sacrificed a kid to the spirits of their ancestors, which, as Sammy remarked again, was "a horrible, heathen ceremony much calculated to prejudice our cause with Powers Above."

When it was over, to my delight, Babemba appeared. He looked so pleasant that I jumped to the conclusion that he brought the best of news with him. Perhaps that the king had pardoned us, or perhaps— blessed thought—that Brother John had really arrived before his time.

But not a bit of it! All he had to say was that he had caused inquiries to be made along the route that ran to the coast and that certainly for a hundred miles there was at present no sign of Dogeetah. So as the Black Elephant was growing more and more enraged under the stirrings up of Imbozwi, it was obvious that that evening's ceremony must be performed. Indeed, as it was part of his duty to superintend the erection of the posts to which we were to be tied and the digging of our graves at their bases, he had just come to count us again to be sure that he had not made any mistake as to the number. Also, if there were any articles that we would like buried with us, would we be so kind as to point them out and he would be sure to see to the matter. It would be soon over, and not painful, he added, as he had selected the very best archers in Beza Town who rarely missed and could, most of them, send an arrow up to the feather into a buffalo.

Then he chatted a little about other matters, as to where he should find the magic shield I had given him, which he would always value as a souvenir, etc., took a pinch of snuff with Mavovo and departed, saying that he would be sure to return again at the proper time.

It was now four o'clock, and as Sammy was quite beyond it, Stephen made himself some tea. It was very good tea, especially as we had milk to put in it, although I did not remember what it tasted like till afterwards.

Now, having abandoned hope, I went into a hut alone to compose myself to meet my end like a gentleman, and seated there in silence and semi-darkness my spirit grew much calmer. After all, I reflected, why should I cling to life? In the country whither I travelled, as the reader who has followed my adventures will know, were some whom I clearly longed to see again, notably my father and my mother, and two noble women who were even more to me. My boy, it is true, remained (he was alive then), but I knew that he would find friends, and as I was not so badly off at that time, I had been able to make a proper provision for him. Perhaps it was better that I should go, seeing that if I lived on it would only mean more troubles and more partings.

What was about to befall me of course I could not tell, but I knew then as I know now, that it was not extinction or even that sleep of which Stephen had spoken. Perhaps I was passing to some place where at length the clouds would roll away and I should understand; whence, too, I should see all the landscape of the past and future, as an eagle does watching from the skies, and be no longer like one struggling through dense bush, wild-beast and serpent haunted, beat upon by the storms of heaven and terrified with its lightnings, nor knowing whither I hewed my path. Perhaps in that place there would be no longer what St. Paul describes as another law in my members warring against the law of my mind, and bringing me into captivity to the law of sin. Perhaps there the past would be forgiven by the Power which knows whereof we are made, and I should become what I have always longed to be—good in every sense and even find open to me new and better roads of service. I take these thoughts from a note that I made in my pocket-book at the time.

Thus I reflected and then wrote a few lines of farewell in the fond and foolish hope that somehow they might find those to whom they were addressed (I have those letters still and very oddly they read to-day). This done, I tried to throw out my mind towards Brother John if he still lived, as indeed I had done for days past, so that I might inform him of our plight and, I am afraid, reproach him for having brought us to such an end by his insane carelessness or want of faith.

Whilst I was still engaged thus Babemba arrived with his soldiers to lead us off to execution. It was Hans who came to tell me that he was there. The poor old Hottentot shook me by the hand and wiped his eyes with his ragged coat-sleeve.

"Oh! Baas, this is our last journey," he said, "and you are going to be killed, Baas, and it is all my fault, Baas, because I ought to have found a way out of the trouble which is what I was hired to do. But I can't, my head grows so stupid. Oh! if only I could come even with Imbozwi I shouldn't mind, and I will, I *will*, if I have to return as a ghost to do it. Well, Baas, you know the Predikant, your father, told us that we don't go out like a fire, but burn again for always elsewhere—"

("I hope not," I thought to myself.)

"And that quite easily without anything to pay for the wood. So I hope that we shall always burn together, Baas. And meanwhile, I have brought you a little something," and he produced what looked like a peculiarly obnoxious horseball. "You swallow this now and you will never feel anything; it is a very good medicine that my grandfather's grandfather got from the Spirit of his tribe. You will just go to sleep as nicely as though you were very drunk, and wake up in the beautiful fire which burns without any wood and never goes out for ever and ever, Amen."

"No, Hans," I said, "I prefer to die with my eyes open."

"And so would I, Baas, if I thought there was any good in keeping them open, but I don't, for I can't believe any more in the Snake of that black fool, Mavovo. If it had been a good Snake, it would have told him to keep clear of Beza Town, so I will swallow one of these pills and give the other to the Baas Stephen," and he crammed the filthy mess into his mouth and with an effort got it down, as a young turkey does a ball of meal that is too big for its throat.

Then, as I heard Stephen calling me, I left him invoking a most comprehensive and polyglot curse upon the head of Imbozwi, to whom he rightly attributed all our woes.

"Our friend here says it is time to start," said Stephen, rather shakily, for the situation seemed to have got a hold of him at last, and nodding towards old Babemba, who stood there with a cheerful smile looking as though he were going to conduct us to a wedding.

"Yes, white lord," said Babemba, "it is time, and I have hurried so as not to keep you waiting. It will be a very fine show, for the 'Black Elephant' himself is going to do you the honour to be present, as will all the people of Beza Town and those for many miles round."

"Hold your tongue, you old idiot," I said, "and stop your grinning. If you had been a man and not a false friend you would have got us out of this trouble, knowing as you do very well that we are no sellers of men, but rather the enemy of those who do such things."

"Oh! white lord," said Babemba, in a changed voice, "believe me I only smile to make you happy up to the end. My lips smile, but I am crying inside. I know that you are good and have told Bausi so, but he will not believe me, who thinks that I have been bribed by you. What can I do against that evil-hearted Imbozwi, the head of the witch-doctors, who hates you because he thinks you have better magic than he has and who whispers day and night into the king's ear, telling him that if he does not kill you, all our people will be slain or sold for slaves, as you are only the scouts or a big army that is coming. Only last night Imbozwi held a great divination *indaba*, and read this and a great deal more in the enchanted water, making the king think he saw it in pictures, whereas I, looking over his shoulder, could see nothing at all, except the ugly face of Imbozwi reflected in the water. Also he swore that his spirit told me that Dogeetah, the king's blood-brother, being dead, would never come to Beza Town again. I have done my best. Keep your heart white towards me, O Macumazana, and do not haunt me, for I tell you I have done my best, and if ever I should get a chance against Imbozwi, which I am afraid I shan't, as he will poison me first, I will pay him back. Oh! he shall not die quickly as you will."

"I wish I could get a chance at him," I muttered, for even in this solemn moment I could cultivate no Christian spirit towards Imbozwi.

Feeling that he was honest after all, I shook old Babemba's hand and gave him the letters I had written, asking him to try and get them to the coast. Then we started on our last walk.

The Zulu hunters were already outside the fence, seated on the ground, chatting and taking snuff. I wondered if this was because they really believed in Mavovo's confounded Snake, or from bravado, inspired by the innate courage of their race. When they saw me they sprang to their feet and, lifting their right hands, gave me a loud and hearty salute of "Inkoosi! Baba! Inkoosi! Macumazana!" Then, at a signal from Mavovo, they broke into some Zulu war-chant, which they kept up till we reached the stakes. Sammy, too, broke into a chant, but one of quite a different nature.

"Be quiet!" I said to him. "Can't you die like a man?"

"No, indeed I cannot, Mr. Quatermain," he answered, and went on howling for pity in about twenty different languages.

Stephen and I walked together, he still carrying the Union Jack, of which no one tried to deprive him. I think the Mazitu believed it was his fetish. We didn't talk much, though once he said:

"Well, the love of orchids has brought many a man to a bad end. I wonder whether the Governor will keep my collection or sell it."

After this he relapsed into silence, and not knowing and indeed not caring what would happen to his collection, I made no answer.

We had not far to go; personally I could have preferred a longer walk. Passing with our guards down a kind of by-street, we emerged suddenly at the head of the market-place, to find that it was packed with thousands of people gathered there to see our execution. I noticed that they were arranged in orderly companies and that a broad open roadway was left between them, running to the southern gate of the market, I suppose to facilitate the movements of so large a crowd.

All this multitude received us in respectful silence, though Sammy's howls caused some of them to smile, while the Zulu war-chant appeared to excite their wonder, or admiration. At the head of the market-place, not far from the king's enclosure, fifteen stout posts had been planted on as many mounds. These mounds were provided so that everyone might see the show and, in part at any rate, were made of soil hollowed from fifteen deep graves dug almost at the foot of the mounds. Or rather there were seventeen posts, an extra large one being set at each end of the line in order to accommodate the two donkeys, which it appeared were also to be shot to death. A great number of soldiers kept a space clear in front of the posts. On this space were gathered Bausi, his councillors, some of his head wives, Imbozwi more hideously painted than usual, and perhaps fifty or sixty picked archers with strung bows and an ample supply of arrows, whose part in the ceremony it was not difficult for us to guess.

"King Bausi," I said as I was led past that potentate, "you are a murderer and Heaven Above will be avenged upon you for this crime.

If our blood is shed, soon you shall die and come to meet us where *we* have power, and your people shall be destroyed."

My words seemed to frighten the man, for he answered:

"I am no murderer. I kill you because you are robbers of men. Moreover, it is not I who have passed sentence on you. It is Imbozwi here, the chief of the doctors, who has told me all about you, and whose spirit says you must die unless my brother Dogeetah appears to save you. If Dogeetah comes, which he cannot do because he is dead, and vouches for you, then I shall know that Imbozwi is a wicked liar, and as you were to die, so he shall die."

"Yes, yes," screeched Imbozwi. "If Dogeetah comes, as that false wizard prophesies," and he pointed to Mavovo, "then I shall be ready to die in your place, white slave-dealers. Yes, yes, then you may shoot *me* with arrows."

"King, take note of those words, and people, take note of those words, that they may be fulfilled if Dogeetah comes," said Mavovo in a great, deep voice.

"I take note of them," answered Bausi, "and I swear by my mother on behalf of all the people, that they shall be fulfilled—if Dogeetah comes."

"Good," exclaimed Mavovo, and stalked on to the stake which had been pointed out to him.

As he went he whispered something into Imbozwi's ear that seemed to frighten that limb of Satan, for I saw him start and shiver. However, he soon recovered, for in another minute he was engaged in superintending those whose business it was to lash us to the posts.

This was done simply and effectively by tying our wrists with a grass rope behind these posts, each of which was fitted with two projecting pieces of wood that passed under our arms and practically prevented us from moving. Stephen and I were given the places of honour in the middle, the Union Jack being fixed, by his own request, to the top of Stephen's stake. Mavovo was on my right, and the other Zulus were ranged on either side of us. Hans and Sammy occupied the end posts respectively (except those to which the poor jackasses were bound). I noted that Hans was already very sleepy and that shortly after he was fixed up, his head dropped forward on his breast. Evidently his medicine was working, and almost I regretted that I had not taken some while I had the chance.

When we were all fastened, Imbozwi came round to inspect. Moreover, with a piece of white chalk he made a round mark on the breast of each of us; a kind of bull's eye for the archers to aim at.

"Ah! white man," he said to me as he chalked away at my shooting coat, "you will never burn anyone's hair again with your magic shield. Never, never, for presently I shall be treading down the earth upon you in that hole, and your goods will belong to me."

I did not answer, for what was the use of talking to this vile brute when my time was so short. So he passed on to Stephen and began to chalk him. Stephen, however, in whom the natural man still prevailed, shouted:

"Take your filthy hands off me," and lifting his leg, which was unfettered, gave the painted witch-doctor such an awful kick in the stomach, that he vanished backwards into the grave beneath him.

"*Ow!* Well done, Wazela!" said the Zulus, "we hope that you have killed him."

"I hope so too," said Stephen, and the multitude of spectators gasped to see the sacred person of the head witch-doctor, of whom they evidently went in much fear, treated in such a way. Only Babemba grinned, and even the king Bausi did not seem displeased.

But Imbozwi was not to be disposed of so easily, for presently, with the help of sundry myrmidons, minor witch-doctors, he scrambled out of the grave, cursing and covered with mud, for it was wet down there. After that I took no more heed of him or of much else. Seeing that I had only half an hour to live, as may be imagined, I was otherwise engaged.

XI

The Coming of Dogeetah

The sunset that day was like the sunrise, particularly fine, although as in the case of the tea, I remembered little of it till afterwards. In fact, thunder was about, which always produces grand cloud effects in Africa.

The sun went down like a great red eye, over which there dropped suddenly a black eyelid of cloud with a fringe of purple lashes.

There's the last I shall see of you, my old friend, thought I to myself, unless I catch you up presently.

The gloom began to gather. The king looked about him, also at the sky overhead, as though he feared rain, then whispered something to Babemba, who nodded and strolled up to my post.

"White lord," he said, "the Elephant wishes to know if you are ready, as presently the light will be very bad for shooting?"

"No," I answered with decision, "not till half an hour after sundown as was agreed."

Babemba went to the king and returned to me.

"White lord, the king says that a bargain is a bargain, and he will keep to his word. Only you must not then blame him if the shooting is bad, since of course he did not know that the night would be so cloudy, which is not usual at this time of year."

It grew darker and darker, till at length we might have been lost in a London fog. The dense masses of the people looked like banks, and the archers, flitting to and fro as they made ready, might have been shadows in Hades. Once or twice lightning flashed and was followed after a pause by the distant growling of thunder. The air, too, grew very oppressive. Dense silence reigned. In all those multitudes no one spoke or stirred; even Sammy ceased his howling, I suppose because he had become exhausted and fainted away, as people often do just before they are hanged. It was a most solemn time. Nature seemed to be adapting herself to the mood of sacrifice and making ready for us a mighty pall.

At length I heard the sound of arrows being drawn from their quivers, and then the squeaky voice of Imbozwi, saying:

"Wait a little, the cloud will lift. There is light behind it, and it will be nicer if they can see the arrows coming."

The cloud did begin to lift, very slowly, and from beneath it flowed a green light like that in a cat's eye.

"Shall we shoot, Imbozwi?" asked the voice of the captain of the archers.

"Not yet, not yet. Not till the people can watch them die."

The edge of cloud lifted a little more; the green light turned to a fiery red thrown by the sunk sun and reflected back upon the earth from the dense black cloud above. It was as though all the landscape had burst into flames, while the heaven over us remained of the hue of ink. Again the lightning flashed, showing the faces and staring eyes of the thousands who watched, and even the white teeth of a great bat that flittered past. That flash seemed to burn off an edge of the lowering cloud and the light grew stronger and stronger, and redder and redder.

Imbozwi uttered a hiss like a snake. I heard a bow-string twang, and almost at the same moment the thud of an arrow striking my post just above my head. Indeed, by lifting myself I could touch it. I shut my eyes and began to see all sorts of queer things that I had forgotten for years and years. My brain swam and seemed to melt into a kind of confusion. Through the intense silence I thought I heard the sound of some animal running heavily, much as a fat bull eland does when it is suddenly disturbed. Someone uttered a startled exclamation, which caused me to open my eyes again. The first thing I saw was the squad of savage archers lifting their bows—evidently that first arrow had been a kind of trial shot. The next, looking absolutely unearthly in that terrible and ominous light, was a tall figure seated on a white ox shambling rapidly towards us along the open roadway that ran from the southern gate of the market-place.

Of course, I knew that I dreamed, for this figure exactly resembled Brother John. There was his long, snowy beard. There in his hand was his butterfly net, with the handle of which he seemed to be prodding the ox. Only he was wound about with wreaths of flowers as were the great horns of the ox, and on either side of him and before and behind him ran girls, also wreathed with flowers. It was a vision, nothing else, and I shut my eyes again awaiting the fatal arrow.

"Shoot!" screamed Imbozwi.

"Nay, shoot not!" shouted Babemba. "*Dogeetah is come!*"

A moment's pause, during which I heard arrows falling to the ground; then from all those thousands of throats a roar that shaped itself to the words:

"Dogeetah! Dogeetah is come to save the white lords."

I must confess that after this my nerve, which is generally pretty good, gave out to such an extent that I think I fainted for a few minutes. During that faint I seemed to be carrying on a conversation with Mavovo, though whether it ever took place or I only imagined it I am not sure, since I always forgot to ask him.

He said, or I thought he said, to me:

"And now, Macumazana, my father, what have you to say? Does my Snake stand upon its tail or does it not? Answer, I am listening."

To which I replied, or seemed to reply:

"Mavovo, my child, certainly it appears as though your Snake *does* stand upon its tail. Still, I hold that all this is a phantasy; that we live in a land of dream in which nothing is real except those things which we cannot see or touch or hear. That there is no me and no you and no Snake at all, nothing but a Power in which we move, that shows us pictures and laughs when we think them real."

Whereon Mavovo said, or seemed to say:

"Ah! at last you touch the truth, O Macumazana, my father. All things are a shadow and we are shadows in a shadow. But what throws the shadow, O Macumazana, my father? Why does Dogeetah appear to come hither riding on a white ox and why do all these thousands think that my Snake stands so very stiff upon its tail?"

"I'm hanged if I know," I replied and woke up.

There, without doubt, *was* old Brother John with a wreath of flowers—I noted in disgust that they were orchids—hanging in a bacchanalian fashion from his dinted sun-helmet over his left eye. He was in a furious rage and reviling Bausi, who literally crouched before him, and I was in a furious rage and reviling him. What I said I do not remember, but he said, his white beard bristling with indignation while he threatened Bausi with the handle of the butterfly net:

"You dog! You savage, whom I saved from death and called Brother. What were you doing to these white men who are in truth my brothers, and to their followers? Were you about to kill them? Oh! if so, I will forget my vow, I will forget the bond that binds us and—"

"Don't, pray don't," said Bausi. "It is all a horrible mistake; I am not to be blamed at all. It is that witch-doctor, Imbozwi, whom by the ancient law of the land I must obey in such matters. He consulted his Spirit and declared that you were dead; also that these white lords were the most wicked of men, slave-traders with spotted hearts, who came hither to spy out the Mazitu people and to destroy them with magic and bullets."

"Then he lied," thundered Brother John, "and he knew that he lied."

"Yes, yes, it is evident that he lied," answered Bausi. "Bring him here, and with him those who serve him."

Now by the light of the moon which was shining brightly in the heavens, for the thunder-clouds had departed with the last glow of sunset, soldiers began an active search for Imbozwi and his confederates. Of these they caught eight or ten, all wicked-looking fellows hideously painted and adorned like their master, but Imbozwi himself they could not find.

I began to think that in the confusion he had given us the slip, when presently from the far end of the line, for we were still all tied to our stakes, I heard the voice of Sammy, hoarse, it is true, but quite cheerful now, saying:

"Mr. Quatermain, in the interests of justice, will you inform his Majesty that the treacherous wizard for whom he is seeking, is now peeping and muttering at the bottom of the grave which was dug to receive my mortal remains."

I did inform his Majesty, and in double-quick time our friend Imbozwi was once more fished out of a grave by the strong arms of Babemba and his soldiers, and dragged into the presence of the irate Bausi.

"Loose the white lords and their followers," said Bausi, "and let them come here."

So our bonds were undone and we walked to where the king and Brother John stood, the miserable Imbozwi and his attendant doctors huddled in a heap before them.

"Who is this?" said Bausi to him, pointing at Brother John. "Is it not he whom you vowed was dead?"

Imbozwi did not seem to think that the question required an answer, so Bausi continued:

"What was the song that you sang in our ears just now—that if Dogeetah came you would be ready to be shot to death with arrows in the place of these white lords whose lives you swore away, was it not?"

Again Imbozwi made no answer, although Babemba called his attention to the king's query with a vigorous kick. Then Bausi shouted:

"By your own mouth are you condemned, O liar, and that shall be done to you which you have yourself decreed," adding almost in the words of Elijah after he had triumphed over the priests of Baal, "Take away these false prophets. Let none of them escape. Say you not so, O people?"

"Aye," roared the multitude fiercely, "take them away."

"Not a popular character, Imbozwi," Stephen remarked to me in a reflective voice. "Well, he is going to be served hot on his own toast now, and serve the brute right."

"Who is the false doctor now?" mocked Mavovo in the silence that followed. "Who is about to sup on arrow-heads, O Painter-of-white-spots?" and he pointed to the mark that Imbozwi had so gleefully chalked over his heart as a guide to the arrows of the archers.

Now, seeing that all was lost, the little humpbacked villain with a sudden twist caught me by the legs and began to plead for mercy. So piteously did he plead, that being already softened by the fact of our wonderful escape from those black graves, my heart was melted in me. I turned to ask the king to spare his life, though with little hope that the prayer would be granted, for I saw that Bausi feared and hated the man and was only too glad of the opportunity to be rid of him. Imbozwi, however, interpreted my movement differently, since among savages the turning of the back always means that a petition is refused. Then, in his rage and despair, the venom of his wicked heart boiled over. He leapt to his feet, and drawing a big, carved knife from among his witch-doctor's trappings, sprang at me like a wild cat, shouting:

"At least you shall come too, white dog!"

Most mercifully Mavovo was watching him, for that is a good Zulu saying which declares that "Wizard is Wizard's fate." With one bound he was on him. Just as the knife touched me—it actually pricked my skin though without drawing blood, which was fortunate as probably it was poisoned—he gripped Imbozwi's arm in his grasp of iron and hurled him to the ground as though he were but a child.

After this of course all was over.

"Come away," I said to Stephen and Brother John; "this is no place for us."

So we went and gained our huts without molestation and indeed quite unobserved, for the attention of everyone in Beza Town was fully occupied elsewhere. From the market-place behind us rose so hideous a clamour that we rushed into my hut and shut the door to escape or lessen the sound. It was dark in the hut, for which I was really thankful, for the darkness seemed to soothe my nerves. Especially was this so when Brother John said:

"Friend, Allan Quatermain, and you, young gentleman, whose name I don't know, I will tell you what I think I never mentioned to you before, that, in addition to being a doctor, I am a clergyman of the American Episcopalian Church. Well, as a clergyman, I will ask your leave to return thanks for your very remarkable deliverance from a cruel death."

"By all means," I muttered for both of us, and he did so in a most earnest and beautiful prayer. Brother John may or may not have been a little touched in the head at this time of his life, but he was certainly an able and a good man.

Afterwards, as the shrieks and shouting had now died down to a confused murmur of many voices, we went and sat outside under the projecting eaves of the hut, where I introduced Stephen Somers to Brother John.

"And now," I said, "in the name of goodness, where do you come from tied up in flowers like a Roman priest at sacrifice, and riding on a bull like the lady called Europa? And what on earth do you mean by playing us such a scurvy trick down there in Durban, leaving us without a word after you had agreed to guide us to this hellish hole?"

Brother John stroked his long beard and looked at me reproachfully.

"I guess, Allan," he said in his American fashion, "there is a mistake somewhere. To answer the last part of your question first, I did not leave you without a word; I gave a letter to that lame old Griqua gardener of yours, Jack, to be handed to you when you arrived."

"Then the idiot either lost it and lied to me, as Griquas will, or he forgot all about it."

"That is likely. I ought to have thought of that, Allan, but I didn't. Well, in that letter I said that I would meet you here, where I should have been six weeks ago awaiting you. Also I sent a message to Bausi to warn him of your coming in case I should be delayed, but I suppose that something happened to it on the road."

"Why did you not wait and come with us like a sensible man?"

"Allan, as you ask me straight out, I will tell you, although the subject is one of which I do not care to speak. I knew that you were going to journey by Kilwa; indeed it was your only route with a lot of people and so much baggage, and I did not wish to visit Kilwa." He paused, then went on: "A long while ago, nearly twenty-three years to be accurate, I went to live at Kilwa as a missionary with my young wife. I built a mission station and a church there, and we were happy and fairly successful in our work. Then on one evil day the Swahili and other Arabs came in dhows to establish a slave-dealing station. I resisted them, and the end of it was that they attacked us, killed most of my people and enslaved the rest. In that attack I received a cut from a sword on the head—look, here is the mark of it," and drawing his white hair apart he showed us a long scar that was plainly visible in the moonlight.

"The blow knocked me senseless just about sunset one evening. When I came to myself again it was broad daylight and everybody was gone, except one old woman who was tending me. She was half-crazed with grief because her husband and two sons had been killed, and another son, a boy, and a daughter had been taken away. I asked her where my young wife was. She answered that she, too, had been taken away eight or ten hours before, because the Arabs had seen the lights of a ship out at sea, and thought they might be those of a British man-of-war that was known to be cruising on the coast. On seeing these they had fled inland in a hurry, leaving me for dead, but killing the wounded before they went. The old woman herself had escaped by hiding among some rocks on the seashore, and after the Arabs had gone had crept back to the house and found me still alive.

"I asked her where my wife had been taken. She said she did not know, but some others of our people told her that they had heard the Arabs say they were going to some place a hundred miles inland, to join their leader, a half-bred villain named Hassan-ben-Mohammed, to whom they were carrying my wife as a present.

"Now we knew this wretch, for after the Arabs landed at Kilwa, but before actual hostilities broke out between us, he had fallen sick of smallpox and my wife had helped to nurse him. Had it not been for her, indeed, he would have died. However, although the leader of the band, he was not present at the attack, being engaged in some slave-raiding business in the interior.

"When I learned this terrible news, the shock of it, or the loss of blood, brought on a return of insensibility, from which I only awoke two days later to find myself on board a Dutch trading vessel that was sailing for Zanzibar. It was the lights of this ship that the Arabs had seen and mistaken for those of an English man-of-war. She had put into Kilwa for water, and the sailors, finding me on the verandah of the house and still living, in the goodness of their hearts carried me on board. Of the old woman they had seen nothing; I suppose that at their approach she ran away.

"At Zanzibar, in an almost dying condition, I was handed over to a clergyman of our mission, in whose house I lay desperately ill for a long while. Indeed six months went by before I fully recovered my right mind. Some people say that I have never recovered it; perhaps you are one of them, Allan.

"At last the wound in my skull healed, after a clever English naval surgeon had removed some bits of splintered bone, and my strength came back to me. I was and still am an American subject, and in those days we had no consul at Zanzibar, if there is one there now, of which I am not sure, and of course no warship. The English made what inquiries they could for me, but could find out little or nothing, since all the country about Kilwa was in possession of Arab slave-traders who were supported by a ruffian who called himself the Sultan of Zanzibar."

Again he paused, as though overcome by the sadness of his recollections.

"Did you never hear any more of your wife?" asked Stephen.

"Yes, Mr. Somers; I heard at Zanzibar from a slave whom our mission bought and freed, that he had seen a white woman who answered to her description alive and apparently well, at some place I was unable to identify. He could only tell me that it was fifteen days' journey from the coast. She was then in charge of some black people, he did not know of what tribe, who, he believed, had found her wandering in the bush. He noted that the black people seemed to treat her with the greatest reverence, although they could not understand what she said. On the following day, whilst searching for six lost goats, he was captured by Arabs who, he heard afterwards, were out looking for this white woman. The day after the man had told me this, he was seized with inflammation of the lungs, of which, being in a weak state from his sufferings in the slave gang, he quickly died. Now you will understand why I was not particularly anxious to revisit Kilwa."

"Yes," I said, "we understand that, and a good deal more of which we will talk later. But, to change the subject, where do you come from now, and how did you happen to turn up just in the nick of time?"

"I was journeying here across country by a route I will show you on my map," he answered, "when I met with an accident to my leg" (here Stephen and I looked at each other) "which kept me laid up in a Kaffir hut for six weeks. When I got better, as I could not walk very well I rode upon oxen that I had trained. That white beast you saw is the last of them; the others died of the bite of the tsetse fly. A fear which I could not define caused me to press forward as fast as possible; for the last twenty-four hours I have scarcely stopped to eat or sleep. When I got into the Mazitu country this morning I found the kraals empty, except for some women and girls, who knew me again, and threw these flowers over me. They told me that all the men had gone to Beza Town for a great feast, but what the feast was they either did not know or would not reveal. So I hurried on and arrived in time—thank God in time! It is a long story; I will tell you the details afterwards. Now we are all too tired. What's that noise?"

I listened and recognised the triumphant song of the Zulu hunters, who were returning from the savage scene in the market-place. Presently they arrived, headed by Sammy, a very different Sammy from the wailing creature who had gone out to execution an hour or two before. Now he was the gayest of the gay, and about his neck were strung certain weird ornaments which I identified as the personal property of Imbozwi.

"Virtue is victorious and justice has been done, Mr. Quatermain. These are the spoils of war," he said, pointing to the trappings of the late witch-doctor.

"Oh! get out, you little cur! We want to know nothing more," I said. "Go, cook us some supper," and he went, not in the least abashed.

The hunters were carrying between them what appeared to be the body of Hans. At first I was frightened, thinking that he must be dead, but examination showed that he was only in a state of insensibility such as might be induced by laudanum. Brother John ordered him to be wrapped up in a blanket and laid by the fire, and this was done.

Presently Mavovo approached and squatted down in front of us.

"Macumazana, my father," he said quietly, "what words have you for me?"

"Words of thanks, Mavovo. If you had not been so quick, Imbozwi would have finished me. As it is, the knife only touched my skin without breaking it, for Dogeetah has looked to see."

Mavovo waved his hand as though to sweep this little matter aside, and asked, looking me straight in the eyes:

"And what other words, Macumazana? As to my Snake I mean."

"Only that you were right and I was wrong," I answered shamefacedly. "Things have happened as you foretold, how or why I do not understand."

"No, my father, because you white men are so vain" ("blown out" was his word), "that you think you have all wisdom. Now you have learned that this is not so. I am content. The false doctors are all dead, my father, and I think that Imbozwi—"

I held up my hand, not wishing to hear details. Mavovo rose, and with a little smile, went about his business.

"What does he mean about his Snake?" inquired Brother John curiously.

I told him as briefly as I could, and asked him if he could explain the matter. He shook his head.

"The strangest example of native vision that I have ever heard of," he answered, "and the most useful. Explain! There is no explanation, except the old one that there are more things in heaven and earth, etc., and that God gives different gifts to different men."

Then we ate our supper; I think one of the most joyful meals of which I have ever partaken. It is wonderful how good food tastes when one never expected to swallow another mouthful. After it was finished the others went to bed but, with the still unconscious Hans for my only companion, I sat for a while smoking by the fire, for on this high tableland the air was chilly. I felt that as yet I could not sleep; if for no other reason because of the noise that the Mazitu were making in the town, I suppose in celebration of the execution of the terrible witch-doctors and the return of Dogeetah.

Suddenly Hans awoke, and sitting up, stared at me through the bright flame which I had recently fed with dry wood.

"Baas," he said in a hollow voice, "there you are, here I am, and there is the fire which never goes out, a very good fire. But, Baas, why are we not inside of it as your father the Predikant promised, instead of outside here in the cold?"

"Because you are still in the world, you old fool, and not where you deserve to be," I answered. "Because Mavovo's Snake was a snake with a true tongue after all, and Dogeetah came as it foretold. Because we are all alive and well, and it is Imbozwi with his spawn who are dead upon the posts. That is why, Hans, as you would have seen for yourself if you had kept awake, instead of swallowing filthy medicine like a frightened woman, just because you were afraid of death, which at your age you ought to have welcomed."

"Oh! Baas," broke in Hans, "don't tell me that things are so and that we are really alive in what your honoured father used to call this gourd full of tears. Don't tell me, Baas, that I made a coward of myself and swallowed that beastliness—if you knew what it was made of you would understand, Baas—for nothing but a bad headache. Don't tell me that Dogeetah came when my eyes were not open to see him, and worst of all, that Imbozwi and his children were tied to those poles when I was not able to help them out of the bottle of tears into the fire that burns for ever and ever. Oh! it is too much, and I swear, Baas, that however often I have to die, henceforward it shall always be with my eyes open," and holding his aching head between his hands he rocked himself to and fro in bitter grief.

Well might Hans be sad, seeing that he never heard the last of the incident. The hunters invented a new and gigantic name for him, which meant "The little-yellow-mouse-who-feeds-on-sleep-while-the-black-rats-eat-up-their-enemies." Even Sammy made a mock of him, showing him the spoils which he declared he had wrenched unaided from the mighty master of magic, Imbozwi. As indeed he had—after the said Imbozwi was stone dead at the stake.

It was very amusing until things grew so bad that I feared Hans would kill Sammy, and had to put a stop to the joke.

H. RIDER HAGGARD

XII

Brother John's Story

Although I went to bed late I was up before sunrise. Chiefly because I wished to have some private conversation with Brother John, whom I knew to be a very early riser. Indeed, he slept less than any man I ever met.

As I expected, I found him astir in his hut; he was engaged in pressing flowers by candlelight.

"John," I said, "I have brought you some property which I think you have lost," and I handed him the morocco-bound *Christian Year* and the water-colour drawing which we had found in the sacked mission house at Kilwa.

He looked first at the picture and then at the book; at least, I suppose he did, for I went outside the hut for a while—to observe the sunrise. In a few minutes he called me, and when the door was shut, said in an unsteady voice:

"How did you come by these relics, Allan?"

I told him the story from beginning to end. He listened without a word, and when I had finished said:

"I may as well tell what perhaps you have guessed, that the picture is that of my wife, and the book is her book."

"Is!" I exclaimed.

"Yes, Allan. I say *is* because I do not believe that she is dead. I cannot explain why, any more than I could explain last night how that great Zulu savage was able to prophesy my coming. But sometimes we can wring secrets from the Unknown, and I believe that I have won this truth in answer to my prayers, that my wife still lives."

"After twenty years, John?"

"Yes, after twenty years. Why do you suppose," he asked almost fiercely, "that for two-thirds of a generation I have wandered about among African savages, pretending to be crazy because these wild people revere the mad and always let them pass unharmed?"

"I thought it was to collect butterflies and botanical specimens."

"Butterflies and botanical specimens! These were the pretext. I have been and am searching for my wife. You may think it a folly, especially considering what was her condition when we separated—she was expecting a child, Allan—but I do not. I believe that she is hidden away among some of these wild peoples."

"Then perhaps it would be as well not to find her," I answered, bethinking me of the fate which had overtaken sundry white women in the old days, who had escaped from shipwrecks on the coast and become the wives of Kaffirs.

"Not so, Allan. On that point I fear nothing. If God has preserved my wife, He has also protected her from every harm. And now," he went on, "you will understand why I wish to visit these Pongo—the Pongo who worship a white goddess!"

"I understand," I said and left him, for having learned all there was to know, I thought it best not to prolong a painful conversation. To me it seemed incredible that this lady should still live, and I feared the effect upon him of the discovery that she was no more. How full of romance is this poor little world of ours! Think of Brother John (Eversley was his real name as I discovered afterwards), and what his life had been. A high-minded educated man trying to serve his Faith in the dark places of the earth, and taking his young wife with him, which for my part I have never considered right thing to do. Neither tradition nor Holy Writ record that the Apostles dragged their wives and families into the heathen lands where they went to preach, although I believe that some of them were married. But this is by the way.

Then falls the blow; the mission house is sacked, the husband escapes by a miracle and the poor young lady is torn away to be the prey of a vile slave-trader. Lastly, according to the quite unreliable evidence of some savage already in the shadow of death, she is seen in the charge of other unknown savages. On the strength of this the husband, playing the part of a mad botanist, hunts for her for a score of years, enduring incredible hardships and yet buoyed up by a high and holy trust. To my mind it was a beautiful and pathetic story. Still, for reasons which I have suggested, I confess that I hoped that long ago she had returned into the hands of the Power which made her, for what would be the state of a young white lady who for two decades had been at the mercy of these black brutes?

And yet, and yet, after my experience of Mavovo and his Snake, I did not feel inclined to dogmatise about anything. Who and what was I, that I should venture not only to form opinions, but to thrust them down the throats of others? After all, how narrow are the limits of the knowledge upon which we base our judgments. Perhaps the great sea of intuition that surrounds us is safer to float on than are these little islets of individual experience, whereon we are so wont to take our stand.

Meanwhile my duty was not to speculate on the dreams and mental attitudes of others, but like a practical hunter and trader, to carry to a successful issue an expedition that I was well paid to manage, and to dig up a certain rare flower root, if I could find it, in the marketable value of which I had an interest. I have always prided myself upon my entire lack of imagination and all such mental phantasies, and upon an aptitude for hard business and an appreciation of the facts of life, that after all are the things with which we have to do. This is the truth; at least, I hope it is. For if I were to be *quite* honest, which no one ever has been, except a gentleman named Mr. Pepys, who, I think, lived in the reign of Charles II, and who, to judge from his memoirs, which I have read lately, did not write for publication, I should have to admit that there is another side to my nature. I sternly suppress it, however, at any rate for the present.

While we were at breakfast Hans who, still suffering from headache and remorse, was lurking outside the gateway far from the madding crowd of critics, crept in like a beaten dog and announced that Babemba was approaching followed by a number of laden soldiers. I was about to advance to receive him. Then I remembered that, owing to a queer native custom, such as that which caused Sir Theophilus Shepstone, whom I used to know very well, to be recognised as the holder of the spirit of the great Chaka and therefore as the equal of the Zulu monarchs, Brother John was the really important man in our company. So I gave way and asked him to be good enough to take my place and to live up to that station in savage life to which it had pleased God to call him.

I am bound to say he rose to the occasion very well, being by nature and appearance a dignified old man. Swallowing his coffee in a hurry, he took his place at a little distance from us, and stood there in a statuesque pose. To him entered Babemba crawling on his hands and knees, and other native gentlemen likewise crawling, also the burdened soldiers in as obsequious an attitude as their loads would allow.

"O King Dogeetah," said Babemba, "your brother king, Bausi, returns the guns and fire-goods of the white men, your children, and sends certain gifts."

"Glad to hear it, General Babemba," said Brother John, "although it would be better if he had never taken them away. Put them down and get on to your feet. I do not like to see men wriggling on their stomachs like monkeys."

The order was obeyed, and we checked the guns and ammunition; also our revolvers and the other articles that had been taken away from us. Nothing was missing or damaged; and in addition there were four fine elephant's tusks, an offering to Stephen and myself, which, as a business man, I promptly accepted; some karosses and Mazitu weapons, presents to Mavovo and the hunters, a beautiful native bedstead with ivory legs and mats of finely-woven grass, a gift to Hans in testimony to his powers of sleep under trying circumstances (the Zulus roared when they heard this, and Hans vanished cursing behind the huts), and for Sammy a weird musical instrument with a request that in future he would use it in public instead of his voice.

Sammy, I may add, did not see the joke any more than Hans had done, but the rest of us appreciated the Mazitu sense of humour very much.

"It is very well, Mr. Quatermain," he said, "for these black babes and sucklings to sit in the seat of the scornful. On such an occasion silent prayers would have been of little use, but I am certain that my loud crying to Heaven delivered you all from the bites of the heathen arrows."

"O Dogeetah and white lords," said Babemba, "the king invites your presence that he may ask your forgiveness for what has happened, and this time there will be no need for you to bring arms, since henceforward no hurt can come to you from the Mazitu people."

So presently we set out once more, taking with us the gifts that had been refused. Our march to the royal quarters was a veritable triumphal progress. The people prostrated themselves and clapped their hands slowly in salutation as we passed, while the girls and children pelted us with flowers as though we were brides going to be married. Our road ran by the place of execution where the stakes, at which I confess I looked with a shiver, were still standing, though the graves had been filled in.

On our arrival Bausi and his councillors rose and bowed to us. Indeed, the king did more, for coming forward he seized Brother John by the hand, and insisted upon rubbing his ugly black nose against that of this revered guest. This, it appeared, was the Mazitu method of embracing, an honour which Brother John did not seem at all to appreciate. Then followed long speeches, washed down with draughts of thick native beer. Bausi explained that his evil proceedings were entirely due to the wickedness of the deceased Imbozwi and his disciples, under whose tyranny the land had groaned for long, since the people believed them to speak "with the voice of 'Heaven Above.'"

Brother John, on our behalf, accepted the apology, and then read a lecture, or rather preached a sermon, that took exactly twenty-five minutes to deliver (he is rather long in the wind), in which he demonstrated the evils of superstition and pointed to a higher and a better path. Bausi replied that he would like to hear more of that path another time which, as he presumed that we were going to spend the rest of our lives in his company, could easily be found—say during the next spring when the crops had been sown and the people had leisure on their hands.

After this we presented our gifts, which now were eagerly accepted. Then I took up my parable and explained to Bausi that so far from stopping in Beza Town for the rest of our lives, we were anxious to press forward at once to Pongo-land. The king's face fell, as did those of his councillors.

"Listen, O lord Macumazana, and all of you," he said. "These Pongo are horrible wizards, a great and powerful people who live by themselves amidst the swamps and mix with none. If the Pongo catch Mazitu or folk of any other tribe, either they kill them or take them as prisoners to their own land where they enslave them, or sometimes sacrifice them to the devils they worship."

"That is so," broke in Babemba, "for when I was a lad I was a slave to the Pongo and doomed to be sacrificed to the White Devil. It was in escaping from them that I lost this eye."

Needless to say, I made a note of this remark, though I did not think the moment opportune to follow the matter up. If Babemba has once been to Pongo-land, I reflected to myself, Babemba can go again or show us the way there.

"And if we catch any of the Pongo," went on Bausi, "as sometimes we do when they come to hunt for slaves, we kill them. Ever since the Mazitu have been in this place there has been hate and war between them and the Pongo, and if I could wipe out those evil ones, then I should die happily."

"That you will never do, O King, while the White Devil lives," said Babemba. "Have you not heard the Pongo prophecy, that while the White Devil lives and the Holy Flower blooms, they will live. But when the White Devil dies and the Holy Flower ceases to bloom, then their women will become barren and their end will be upon them."

"Well, I suppose that this White Devil will die some day," I said.

"Not so, Macumazana. It will never die of itself. Like its wicked Priest, it has been there from the beginning and will always be there unless it is killed. But who is there that can kill the White Devil?"

I thought to myself that I would not mind trying, but again I did not pursue the point.

"My brother Dogeetah and lords," exclaimed Bausi, "it is not possible that you should visit these wizards except at the head of an army. But how can I send an army with you, seeing that the Mazitu are a land people and have no canoes in which to cross the great lake, and no trees whereof to make them?"

We answered that we did not know but would think the matter over, as we had come from our own place for this purpose and meant to carry it out.

Then the audience came to an end, and we returned to our huts, leaving Dogeetah to converse with his "brother Bausi" on matters connected with the latter's health. As I passed Babemba I told him that I should like to see him alone, and he said that he would visit me that evening after supper. The rest of the day passed quietly, for we had asked that people might be kept away from our encampment.

We found Hans, who had not accompanied us, being a little shy of appearing in public just then, engaged in cleaning the rifles, and this reminded me of something. Taking the double-barrelled gun of which I have spoken, I called Mavovo and handed it to him, saying:

"It is yours, O true prophet."

"Yes, my father," he answered, "it is mine for a little while, then perhaps it will be yours again."

The words struck me, but I did not care to ask their meaning. Somehow I wanted to hear no more of Mavovo's prophecies.

Then we dined, and for the rest of that afternoon slept, for all of us, including Brother John, needed rest badly. In the evening Babemba came, and we three white men saw him alone.

"Tell us about the Pongo and this white devil they worship," I said.

"Macumazana," he answered, "fifty years have gone by since I was in that land and I see things that happened to me there as through a mist. I went to fish amongst the reeds when I was a boy of twelve, and tall men robed in white came in a canoe and seized me. They led me to a town where there were many other such men, and treated me very well, giving me sweet things to eat till I grew fat and my skin shone. Then in the evening I was taken away, and we marched all night to the mouth of a great cave. In this cave sat a horrible old man about whom danced robed people, performing the rites of the White Devil.

"The old man told me that on the following morning I was to be cooked and eaten, for which reason I had been made so fat. There was a canoe at the mouth of the cave, beyond which lay water. While all were asleep I crept to the canoe. As I loosed the rope one of the priests woke up and ran at me. But I hit him on the head with the paddle, for though only a boy I was bold and strong, and he fell into the water. He came up again and gripped the edge of the canoe, but I struck his fingers with the paddle till he let go. A great wind was blowing that night, tearing off boughs from the trees which grew upon the other shore of the water. It whirled the canoe round and round and one of the boughs struck me in the eye. I scarcely felt it at the time, but afterwards the eye withered. Or perhaps it was a spear or a knife that struck me in the eye, I do not know. I paddled till I lost my senses and always that wind blew. The last thing that I remember was the sound of the canoe being driven by the gale through reeds. When I woke up again I found myself near a shore, to which I waded through the mud, scaring great crocodiles. But this must have been some days later, for now I was quite thin. I fell down upon the shore, and there some of our people found me and nursed me till I recovered. That is all."

"And quite enough too," I said. "Now answer me. How far was the town from the place where you were captured in Mazitu-land?"

"A whole day's journey in the canoe, Macumazana. I was captured in the morning early and we reached the harbour in the evening at a place where many canoes were tied up, perhaps fifty of them, some of which would hold forty men."

"And how far was the town from this harbour?"

"Quite close, Macumazana."

Now Brother John asked a question.

"Did you hear anything about the land beyond the water by the cave?"

"Yes, Dogeetah. I heard then, or afterwards—for from time to time rumours reach us concerning these Pongo—that it is an island where grows the Holy Flower, of which you know, for when last you were here you had one of its blooms. I heard, too, that this Holy Flower was tended by a priestess named Mother of the Flower, and her servants, all of whom were virgins."

"Who was the priestess?"

"I do not know, but I heave heard that she was one of those people who, although their parents are black, are born white, and that if any females among the Pongo are born white, or with pink eyes, or deaf and dumb, they are set apart to be the servants of the priestess. But this priestess must now be dead, seeing that when I was a boy she was already old, very, very old, and the Pongo were much concerned because there was no one of white skin who could be appointed to succeed her. Indeed she *is* dead, since many years ago there was a great feast in Pongo-land and numbers of slaves were eaten, because the priests had found a beautiful new princess who was white with yellow hair and had finger-nails of the right shape."

Now I bethought me that this finding of the priestess named "Mother of the Flower," who must be distinguished by certain personal peculiarities, resembled not a little that of the finding of the Apis bull-god, which also must have certain prescribed and holy markings, by the old Egyptians, as narrated by Herodotus. However, I said nothing about it at the time, because Brother John asked sharply:

"And is this priestess also dead?"

"I do not know, Dogeetah, but I think not. If she were dead I think that we should have heard some rumour of the Feast of the eating of the dead Mother."

"Eating the dead mother!" I exclaimed.

"Yes, Macumazana. It is the law among the Pongo that, for a certain sacred reason, the body of the Mother of the Flower, when she dies, must be partaken of by those who are privileged to the holy food."

"But the White Devil neither dies nor is eaten?" I said.

"No, as I have told you, he never dies. It is he who causes others to die, as if you go to Pongo-land doubtless you will find out," Babemba added grimly.

Upon my word, thought I to myself, as the meeting broke up because Babemba had nothing more to say, if I had my way I would leave Pongo-land and its white devil alone. Then I remembered how Brother John stood in reference to this matter, and with a sigh resigned myself to fate. As it proved it, I mean Fate, was quite equal to the occasion. The very next morning, early, Babemba turned up again.

"Lords, lords," he said, "a wonderful thing has happened! Last night we spoke of the Pongo and now behold! an embassy from the Pongo is here; it arrived at sunrise."

"What for?" I asked.

"To propose peace between their people and the Mazitu. Yes, they ask that Bausi should send envoys to their town to arrange a lasting peace. As if anyone would go!" he added.

"Perhaps some might dare to," I answered, for an idea occurred to me, "but let us go to see Bausi."

Half an hour later we were seated in the king's enclosure, that is, Stephen and I were, for Brother John was already in the royal hut, talking to Bausi. As we went a few words had passed between us.

"Has it occurred to you, John," I asked, "that if you really wish to visit Pongo-land here is perhaps what you would call a providential opportunity. Certainly none of these Mazitu will go, since they fear lest they should find a permanent peace—inside of the Pongo. Well, you are a blood-brother to Bausi and can offer to play the part of Envoy Extraordinary, with us as the members of your staff."

"I have already thought of it, Allan," he replied, stroking his long beard.

We sat down among a few of the leading councillors, and presently Bausi came out of his hut accompanied by Brother John, and having greeted us, ordered the Pongo envoys to be admitted. They were led in at once, tall, light-coloured men with regular and Semitic features, who were clothed in white linen like Arabs, and wore circles of gold or copper upon their necks and wrists.

In short, they were imposing persons, quite different from ordinary Central African natives, though there was something about their appearance which chilled and repelled me. I should add that their spears had been left outside, and that they saluted the king by folding their arms upon their breasts and bowing in a dignified fashion.

"Who are you?" asked Bausi, "and what do you want?"

"I am Komba," answered their spokesman, quite a young man with flashing eyes, "the Accepted-of-the-Gods, who, in a day to come that perhaps is near, will be the Kalubi of the Pongo people, and these are my servants. I have come here bearing gifts of friendship which are without, by the desire of the holy Motombo, the High Priest of the gods—"

"I thought that the Kalubi was the priest of your gods," interrupted Bausi.

"Not so. The Kalubi is the King of the Pongo as you are the King of the Mazitu. The Motombo, who is seldom seen, is King of the spirits and the Mouth of the gods."

Bausi nodded in the African fashion, that is by raising the chin, not depressing it, and Komba went on:

"I have placed myself in your power, trusting to your honour. You can kill me if you wish, though that will avail nothing, since there are others waiting to become Kalubi in my place."

"Am I a Pongo that I should wish to kill messengers and eat them?" asked Bausi, with sarcasm, a speech at which I noticed the Pongo envoys winced a little.

"King, you are mistaken. The Pongo only eat those whom the White God has chosen. It is a religious rite. Why should they who have cattle in plenty desire to devour men?"

"I don't know," grunted Bausi, "but there is one here who can tell a different story," and he looked at Babemba, who wriggled uncomfortably.

Komba also looked at him with his fierce eyes.

"It is not conceivable," he said, "that anybody should wish to eat one so old and bony, but let that pass. I thank you, King, for your promise of safety. I have come here to ask that you should send envoys to confer with the Kalubi and the Motombo, that a lasting peace may be arranged between our peoples."

"Why do not the Kalubi and the Motombo come here to confer?" asked Bausi.

"Because it is not lawful that they should leave their land, O King. Therefore they have sent me who am the Kalubi-to-come. Hearken. There has been war between us for generations. It began so long ago that only the Motombo knows of its beginning which he has from the gods. Once the Pongo people owned all this land and only had their sacred places beyond the water. Then your forefathers came and fell on them, killing many, enslaving many and taking their women to wife. Now, say the Motombo and the Kalubi, in the place of war let there be peace; where there is but barren sand, there let corn and flowers grow; let the darkness, wherein men lose their way and die, be changed to pleasant light in which they can sit in the sun holding each other's hands."

"Hear, hear!" I muttered, quite moved by this eloquence. But Bausi was not at all moved; indeed, he seemed to view these poetic proposals with the darkest suspicion.

"Give up killing our people or capturing them to be sacrificed to your White Devil, and then in a year or two we may listen to your words that are smeared with honey," he said. "As it is, we think that they are but a trap to catch flies. Still, if there are any of our councillors willing to visit your Motombo and your Kalubi and hear what they have to propose, taking the risk of whatever may happen to them there, I do not forbid it. Now, O my Councillors, speak, not altogether, but one by one, and be swift, since to the first that speaks shall be given this honour."

I think I never heard a denser silence than that which followed this invitation. Each of the *indunas* looked at his neighbour, but not one of them uttered a single word.

"What!" exclaimed Bausi, in affected surprise. "Do none speak? Well, well, you are lawyers and men of peace. What says the great general, Babemba?"

"I say, O King, that I went once to Pongo-land when I was young, taken by the hair of my head, to leave an eye there and that I do not wish to visit it again walking on the soles of my feet."

"It seems, O Komba, that since none of my people are willing to act as envoys, if there is to be talk of peace between us, the Motombo and the Kalubi must come here under safe conduct."

"I have said that cannot be, O King."

"If so, all is finished, O Komba. Rest, eat of our food and return to your own land."

Then Brother John rose and said:

"We are blood-brethren, Bausi, and therefore I can speak for you. If you and your councillors are willing, and these Pongos are willing, I and my friends do not fear to visit the Motombo and the Kalubi, to talk with them of peace on behalf of your people, since we love to see new lands and new races of mankind. Say, Komba, if the king allows, will you accept us as ambassadors?"

"It is for the king to name his own ambassadors," answered Komba. "Yet the Kalubi has heard of the presence of you white lords in Mazitu-land and bade me say that if it should be your pleasure to accompany the embassy and visit him, he would give you welcome. Only when the matter was laid before the Motombo, the oracle spoke thus:

"'Let the white men come if come they will, or let them stay away. But if they come, let them bring with them none of those iron tubes, great or small, whereof the land has heard, that vomit smoke with a noise and cause death from afar. They will not need them to kill meat, for meat shall be given to them in plenty; moreover, among the Pongo they will be safe, unless they offer insult to the god.'"

These words Komba spoke very slowly and with much emphasis, his piercing eyes fixed upon my face as though to read the thoughts it hid.

As I heard them my courage sank into my boots. Well, I knew that the Kalubi was asking us to Pongo-land that we might kill this Great White Devil that threatened his life, which, I took it, was a monstrous ape. And how could we face that or some other frightful brute without firearms? My mind was made up in a minute.

"O Komba," I said, "my gun is my father, my mother, my wife and all my other relatives. I do not stir from here without it."

"Then, white lord," answered Komba, "you will do well to stop in this place in the midst of your family, since, if you try to bring it with you to Pongo-land, you will be killed as you set foot upon the shore."

Before I could find an answer Brother John spoke, saying:

"It is natural that the great hunter, Macumazana, should not wish to be parted from what which to him is as a stick to a lame man. But with me it is different. For years I have used no gun, who kill nothing that God made, except a few bright-winged insects. I am ready to visit your country with naught save this in my hand," and he pointed to the butterfly net that leaned against the fence behind him.

"Good, you are welcome," said Komba, and I thought that I saw his eyes gleam with unholy joy. There followed a pause, during which I explained everything to Stephen, showing that the thing was madness. But here, to my horror, that young man's mulish obstinacy came in.

"I say, you know, Quatermain," he said, "we can't let the old boy go alone, or at least I can't. It's another matter for you who have a son dependent on you. But putting aside the fact that I mean to get—" he was about to add, "the orchid," when I nudged him. Of course, it was ridiculous, but an uneasy fear took me lest this Komba should in some mysterious way understand what he was saying. "What's up? Oh! I see, but the beggar can't understand English. Well, putting aside everything else, it isn't the game, and there you are, you know. If Mr. Brother John goes, I'll go too, and indeed if he doesn't go, I'll go alone."

"You unutterable young ass," I muttered in a stage aside.

"What is it the young white lord says he wishes in our country?" asked the cold Komba, who with diabolical acuteness had read some of Stephen's meaning in his face.

"He says that he is a harmless traveller who would like to study the scenery and to find out if you have any gold there," I answered.

"Indeed. Well, he shall study the scenery and we have gold," and he touched the bracelets on his arm, "of which he shall be given as much as he can carry away. But perchance, white lords, you would wish to talk this matter over alone. Have we your leave to withdraw a while, O King?"

Five minutes later we were seated in the king's "great house" with Bausi himself and Babemba. Here there was a mighty argument. Bausi implored Brother John not to go, and so did I. Babemba said that to go would be madness, as he smelt witchcraft and murder in the air, he who knew the Pongo.

Brother John replied sweetly that he certainly intended to avail himself of this heaven-sent opportunity to visit one of the few remaining districts in this part of Africa through which he had not yet wandered. Stephen yawned and fanned himself with a pocket-handkerchief, for the hut was hot, and remarked that having come so far after a certain rare flower he did not mean to return empty-handed.

"I perceive, Dogeetah," said Bausi at last, "that you have some reason for this journey which you are hiding from me. Still, I am minded to hold you here by force."

"If you do, it will break our brotherhood," answered Brother John. "Seek not to know what I would hide, Bausi, but wait till the future shall declare it."

Bausi groaned and gave in. Babemba said that Dogeetah and Wazela were bewitched, and that I, Macumazana, alone retained my senses.

"Then that's settled," exclaimed Stephen. "John and I are to go as envoys to the Pongo, and you, Quatermain, will stop here to look after the hunters and the stores."

"Young man," I replied, "do you wish to insult me? After your father put you in my charge, too! If you two are going, I shall come also, if I have to do so mother-naked. But let me tell you once and for all in the most emphatic language I can command, that I consider you a brace of confounded lunatics, and that if the Pongo don't eat you, it will be more than you deserve. To think that at my age I should be dragged among a lot of cannibal savages without even a pistol, to fight some unknown brute with my bare hands! Well, we can only die once—that is, so far as we know at present."

"How true," remarked Stephen; "how strangely and profoundly true!"

Oh! I could have boxed his ears.

We went into the courtyard again, whither Komba was summoned with his attendants. This time they came bearing gifts, or having them borne for them. These consisted, I remember, of two fine tusks of ivory which suggested to me that their country could not be entirely surrounded by water, since elephants would scarcely live upon an island; gold dust in a gourd and copper bracelets, which showed that it was mineralized; white native linen, very well woven, and some really beautiful decorated pots, indicating that the people had artistic tastes. Where did they get them from, I wonder, and what was the origin of their race? I cannot answer the question, for I never found out with any certainty. Nor do I think they knew themselves.

The *indaba* was resumed. Bausi announced that we three white men with a servant apiece (I stipulated for this) would visit Pongo-land as his envoys, taking no firearms with us, there to discuss terms of peace between the two peoples, and especially the questions of trade and intermarriage. Komba was very insistent that this should be included; at the time I wondered why. He, Komba, on behalf of the Motombo and the Kalubi, the spiritual and temporal rulers of his land, guaranteed us safe conduct on the understanding that we attempted no insult or violence to the gods, a stipulation from which there was no escape, though I liked it little. He swore also that we should be delivered safe and sound in the Mazitu country within six days of our having left its shores.

Bausi said that it was good, adding that he would send five hundred armed men to escort us to the place where we were to embark, and to receive us on our return; also that if any hurt came to us he would wage war upon the Pongo people for ever until he found means to destroy them.

So we parted, it being agreed that we were to start upon our journey on the following morning.

XIII

Rica Town

As a matter of fact we did not leave Beza Town till twenty-four hours later than had been arranged, since it took some time for old Babemba, who was to be in charge of it, to collect and provision our escort of five hundred men.

Here, I may mention, that when we got back to our huts we found the two Mazitu bearers, Tom and Jerry, eating a hearty meal, but looking rather tired. It appeared that in order to get rid of their favourable evidence, the ceased witch-doctor, Imbozwi, who for some reason or other had feared to kill them, caused them to be marched off to a distant part of the land where they were imprisoned. On the arrival of the news of the fall and death of Imbozwi and his subordinates, they were set at liberty, and at once returned to us at Beza Town.

Of course it became necessary to explain to our servants what we were about to do. When they understood the nature of our proposed expedition they shook their heads, and when they learned that we had promised to leave our guns behind us, they were speechless with amazement.

"*Kransick! Kransick!*" which means "ill in the skull," or "mad," exclaimed Hans to the others as he tapped his forehead significantly. "They have caught it from Dogeetah, one who lives on insects which he entangles in a net, and carries no gun to kill game. Well, I knew they would."

The hunters nodded in assent, and Sammy lifted his arms to Heaven as though in prayer. Only Mavovo seemed indifferent. Then came the question of which of them was to accompany us.

"So far as I am concerned that is soon settled," said Mavovo. "I go with my father, Macumazana, seeing that even without a gun I am still strong and can fight as my male ancestors fought with a spear."

"And I, too, go with the Baas Quatermain," grunted Hans, "seeing that even without a gun I am cunning, as *my* female ancestors were before me."

"Except when you take medicine, Spotted Snake, and lose yourself in the mist of sleep," mocked one of the Zulus. "Does that fine bedstead which the king sent you go with you?"

"No, son of a fool!" answered Hans. "I'll lend it to you who do not understand that there is more wisdom within me when I am asleep than there is in you when you are awake."

It remained to be decided who the third man should be. As neither of Brother John's two servants, who had accompanied him on his cross-country journey, was suitable, one being ill and the other afraid, Stephen suggested Sammy as the man, chiefly because he could cook.

"No, Mr. Somers, no," said Sammy, with earnestness. "At this proposal I draw the thick rope. To ask one who can cook to visit a land where he will be cooked, is to seethe the offspring in its parent's milk."

So we gave him up, and after some discussion fixed upon Jerry, a smart and plucky fellow, who was quite willing to accompany us. The rest of that day we spent in making our preparations which, if simple, required a good deal of thought. To my annoyance, at the time I wanted to find Hans to help me, he was not forthcoming. When at length he appeared I asked him where he had been. He answered, to cut himself a stick in the forest, as he understood we should have to walk a long way. Also he showed me the stick, a long, thick staff of a hard and beautiful kind of bamboo which grows in Mazitu-land.

"What do you want that clumsy thing for," I said, "when there are plenty of sticks about?"

"New journey, new stick! Baas. Also this kind of wood is full of air and might help me to float if we are upset into the water."

"What an idea!" I exclaimed, and dismissed the matter from my mind.

At dawn, on the following day, we started, Stephen and I riding on the two donkeys, which were now fat and lusty, and Brother John upon his white ox, a most docile beast that was quite attached to him. All the hunters, fully armed, came with us to the borders of the Mazitu country, where they were to await our return in company with the Mazitu regiment. The king himself went with us to the west gate of the town, where he bade us all, and especially Brother John, an affectionate farewell. Moreover, he sent for Komba and his attendants, and again swore to him that if any harm happened to us, he would not rest till he had found a way to destroy the Pongo, root and branch.

"Have no fear," answered the cold Komba, "in our holy town of Rica we do not tie innocent guests to stakes to be shot to death with arrows."

The repartee, which was undoubtedly neat, irritated Bausi, who was not fond of allusions to this subject.

"If the white men are so safe, why do you not let them take their guns with them?" he asked, somewhat illogically.

"If we meant evil, King, would their guns help them, they being but few among so many. For instance, could we not steal them, as you did when you plotted the murder of these white lords. It is a law among the Pongo that no such magic weapon shall be allowed to enter their land."

"Why?" I asked, to change the conversation, for I saw that Bausi was growing very wrath and feared complications.

"Because, my lord Macumazana, there is a prophecy among us that when a gun is fired in Pongo-land, its gods will desert us, and the Motombo, who is their priest, will die. That saying is very old, but until a little while ago none knew what it meant, since it spoke of 'a hollow spear that smoked,' and such a weapon was not known to us."

"Indeed," I said, mourning within myself that we should not be in a position to bring about the fulfilment of that prophecy, which, as Hans said, shaking his head sadly, "was a great pity, a very great pity!"

Three days' march over country that gradually sloped downwards from the high tableland on which stood Beza Town, brought us to the lake called Kirua, a word which, I believe, means The Place of the Island. Of the lake itself we could see nothing, because of the dense brake of tall reeds which grew out into the shallow water for quite a mile from the shore and was only pierced here and there with paths made by the hippopotami when they came to the mainland at night to feed. From a high mound which looked exactly like a tumulus and, for aught I know, may have been one, however, the blue waters beyond were visible, and in the far distance what, looked at through glasses, appeared to be a tree-clad mountain top. I asked Komba what it might be, and he answered that it was the Home of the gods in Pongo-land.

"What gods?" I asked again, whereon he replied like a black Herodotus, that of these it was not lawful to speak.

I have rarely met anyone more difficult to pump than that frigid and un-African Komba.

On the top of this mound we planted the Union Jack, fixed to the tallest pole that we could find. Komba asked suspiciously why we did so, and as I was determined to show this unsympathetic person that there were others as unpumpable as himself, I replied that it was the god of our tribe, which we set up there to be worshipped, and that anyone who tried to insult or injure it, would certainly die, as the witch-doctor, Imbozwi, and his children had found out. For once Komba seemed a little impressed, and even bowed to the bunting as he passed by.

What I did not inform him was that we had set the flag there to be a sign and a beacon to us in case we should ever be forced to find our way back to this place unguided and in a hurry. As a matter of fact, this piece of forethought, which oddly enough originated with the most reckless of our party, Stephen, proved our salvation, as I shall tell later on. At the foot of the mound we set our camp for the night, the Mazitu soldiers under Babemba, who did not mind mosquitoes, making theirs nearer to the lake, just opposite to where a wide hippopotamus lane pierced the reeds, leaving a little canal of clear water.

I asked Komba when and how we were to cross the lake. He said that we must start at dawn on the following morning when, at this time of the year, the wind generally blew off shore, and that if the weather were favourable, we should reach the Pongo town of Rica by nightfall. As to how we were to do this, he would show me if I cared to follow him. I nodded, and he led me four or five hundred yards along the edge of the reeds in a southerly direction.

As we went, two things happened. The first of these was that a very large, black rhinoceros, which was sleeping in some bushes, suddenly got our wind and, after the fashion of these beasts, charged down on us from about fifty yards away. Now I was carrying a heavy, single-barrelled rifle, for as yet we and our weapons were not parted. On came the rhinoceros, and Komba, small blame to him for he only had a spear, started to run. I cocked the rifle and waited my chance.

When it was not more than fifteen paces away the rhinoceros threw up its head, at which, of course, it was useless to fire because of the horn, and I let drive at the throat. The bullet hit it fair, and I suppose penetrated to the heart. At any rate, it rolled over and over like a shot rabbit, and with a single stretch of its limbs, expired almost at my feet.

Komba was much impressed. He returned; he stared at the dead rhinoceros and at the hole in its throat; he stared at me; he stared at the still smoking rifle.

"The great beast of the plains killed with a noise!" he muttered. "Killed in an instant by this little monkey of a white man" (I thanked him for that and made a note of it) "and his magic. Oh! the Motombo was wise when he commanded—" and with an effort he stopped.

"Well, friend, what is the matter?" I asked. "You see there was no need for you to run. If you had stepped behind me you would have been as safe as you are now—after running."

"It is so, lord Macumazana, but the thing is strange to me. Forgive me if I do not understand."

"Oh! I forgive you, my lord Kalubi—that is—to be. It is clear that you have a good deal to learn in Pongo-land."

"Yes, my lord Macumazana, and so perhaps have you," he replied dryly, having by this time recovered his nerve and sarcastic powers.

Then after telling Mavovo, who appeared mysteriously at the sound of the shot—I think he was stalking us in case of accidents—to fetch men to cut up the rhinoceros, Komba and I proceeded on our walk.

A little further on, just by the edge of the reeds, I caught sight of a narrow, oblong trench dug in a patch of stony soil, and of a rusted mustard tin half-hidden by some scanty vegetation.

"What is that?" I asked, in seeming astonishment, though I knew well what it must be.

"Oh!" replied Komba, who evidently was not yet quite himself, "that is where the white lord Dogeetah, Bausi's blood-brother, set his little canvas house when he was here over twelve moons ago."

"Really!" I exclaimed, "he never told me he was here." (This was a lie, but somehow I was not afraid of lying to Komba.) "How do you know that he was here?"

"One of our people who was fishing in the reeds saw him."

"Oh! that explains it, Komba. But what an odd place for him to fish in; so far from home; and I wonder what he was fishing for. When you have time, Komba, you must explain to me what it is that you catch amidst the roots of thick reeds in such shallow water."

Komba replied that he would do so with pleasure—when he had time. Then, as though to avoid further conversation he ran forward, and thrusting the reeds apart, showed me a great canoe, big enough to hold thirty or forty men, which with infinite labour had been hollowed out of the trunk of a single, huge tree. This canoe differed from the majority of those that personally I have seen used on African lakes and rivers, in that it was fitted for a mast, now unshipped. I looked at it and said it was a fine boat, whereon Komba replied that there were a hundred such at Rica Town, though not all of them were so large.

Ah! thought I to myself as we walked back to the camp. Then, allowing an average of twenty to a canoe, the Pongo tribe number about two thousand males old enough to paddle, an estimate which turned out to be singularly correct.

Next morning at dawn we started, with some difficulty. To begin with, in the middle of the night old Babemba came to the canvas shelter under which I was sleeping, woke me up and in a long speech implored me not to go. He said he was convinced that the Pongo intended foul play of some sort and that all this talk of peace was a mere trick to entrap us white men into the country, probably in order to sacrifice us to its gods for a religious reason.

I answered that I quite agreed with him, but that as my companions insisted upon making this journey, I could not desert them. All that I could do was to beg him to keep a sharp look-out so that he might be able to help us in case we got into trouble.

"Here I will stay and watch for you, lord Macumazana," he answered, "but if you fall into a snare, am I able to swim through the water like a fish, or to fly through the air like a bird to free you?"

After he had gone one of the Zulu hunters arrived, a man named Ganza, a sort of lieutenant to Mavovo, and sang the same song. He said that it was not right that I should go without guns to die among devils and leave him and his companions wandering alone in a strange land.

I answered that I was much of the same opinion, but that Dogeetah insisted upon going and that I had no choice.

"Then let us kill Dogeetah, or at any rate tie him up, so that he can do no more mischief in his madness," Ganza suggested blandly, whereon I turned him out.

Lastly Sammy arrived and said:

"Mr. Quatermain, before you plunge into this deep well of foolishness, I beg that you will consider your responsibilities to God and man, and especially to us, your household, who are now but lost sheep far from home, and further, that you will remember that if anything disagreeable should overtake you, you are indebted to me to the extent of two months' wages which will probably prove unrecoverable."

I produced a little leather bag from a tin box and counted out to Sammy the wages due to him, also those for three months in advance.

To my astonishment he began to weep. "Sir," he said, "I do not seek filthy lucre. What I mean is that I am afraid you will be killed by these Pongo, and, alas! although I love you, sir, I am too great a coward to come and be killed with you, for God made me like that. I pray you not to go, Mr. Quatermain, because I repeat, I love you, sir."

"I believe you do, my good fellow," I answered, "and I also am afraid of being killed, who only seem to be brave because I must. However, I hope we shall come through all right. Meanwhile, I am going to give this box and all the gold in it, of which there is a great deal, into your charge, Sammy, trusting to you, if anything happens to us, to get it safe back to Durban if you can."

"Oh! Mr. Quatermain," he exclaimed, "I am indeed honoured, especially as you know that once I was in jail for—embezzlement—with extenuating circumstances, Mr. Quatermain. I tell you that although I am a coward, I will die before anyone gets his fingers into that box."

"I am sure that you will, Sammy my boy," I said. "But I hope, although things look queer, that none of us will be called upon to die just yet."

THE MORNING CAME AT LAST, and the six of us marched down to the canoe which had been brought round to the open waterway. Here we had to undergo a kind of customs-house examination at the hands of Komba and his companions, who seemed terrified lest we should be smuggling firearms.

"You know what rifles are like," I said indignantly. "Can you see any in our hands? Moreover, I give you my word that we have none."

Komba bowed politely, but suggested that perhaps some "little guns," by which he meant pistols, remained in our baggage—by accident. Komba was a most suspicious person.

"Undo all the loads," I said to Hans, who obeyed with an enthusiasm which I confess struck me as suspicious.

Knowing his secretive and tortuous nature, this sudden zeal for openness seemed almost unnatural. He began by unrolling his own blanket, inside of which appeared a miscellaneous collection of articles. I remember among them a spare pair of very dirty trousers, a battered tin cup, a wooden spoon such as Kaffirs use to eat their *scoff* with, a bottle full of some doubtful compound, sundry roots and other native medicines, an old pipe I had given him, and last but not least, a huge head of yellow tobacco in the leaf, of a kind that the Mazitu, like the Pongos, cultivate to some extent.

"What on earth do you want so much tobacco for, Hans?" I asked.

"For us three black people to smoke, Baas, or to take as snuff, or to chew. Perhaps where we are going we may find little to eat, and then tobacco is a food on which one can live for days. Also it brings sleep at nights."

"Oh! that will do," I said, fearing lest Hans, like a second Walter Raleigh, was about to deliver a long lecture upon the virtue of tobacco.

"There is no need for the yellow man to take this weed to our land," interrupted Komba, "for there we have plenty. Why does he cumber himself with the stuff?" and he stretched out his hand idly as though to take hold of and examine it closely.

At this moment, however, Mavovo called attention to his bundle which he had undone, whether on purpose or by accident, I do not know, and forgetting the tobacco, Komba turned to attend to him. With a marvellous celerity Hans rolled up his blanket again. In less than a minute the lashings were fast and it was hanging on his back. Again suspicion took me, but an argument which had sprung up between Brother John and Komba about the former's butterfly net, which Komba suspected of being a new kind of gun or at least a magical instrument of a dangerous sort, attracted my notice. After this dispute, another arose over a common garden trowel that Stephen had thought fit to bring with him. Komba asked what it was for. Stephen replied through Brother John that it was to dig up flowers.

"Flowers!" said Komba. "One of our gods is a flower. Does the white lord wish to dig up our god?"

Of course this was exactly what Stephen did desire to do, but not unnaturally he kept the fact to himself. The squabble grew so hot that finally I announced that if our little belongings were treated with so much suspicion, it might be better that we should give up the journey altogether.

"We have passed our word that we have no firearms," I said in the most dignified manner that I could command, "and that should be enough for you, O Komba."

Then Komba, after consultation with his companions, gave way. Evidently he was anxious that we should visit Pongo-land.

So at last we started. We three white men and our servants seated ourselves in the stern of the canoe on grass cushions that had been provided. Komba went to the bows and his people, taking the broad paddles, rowed and pushed the boat along the water-way made by the hippopotami through the tall and matted reeds, from which ducks and other fowl rose in multitudes with a sound like thunder. A quarter of an hour or so of paddling through these weed-encumbered shallows brought us to the deep and open lake. Here, on the edge of the reeds a tall pole that served as a mast was shipped, and a square sail, made of closely-woven mats, run up. It filled with the morning off-land breeze and presently we were bowling along at a rate of quite eight miles the hour. The shore grew dim behind us, but for a long while above the clinging mists I could see the flag that we had planted on the mound. By degrees it dwindled till it became a mere speck and vanished. As it grew smaller my spirits sank, and when it was quite gone, I felt very low indeed.

Another of your fool's errands, Allan my boy, I said to myself. I wonder how many more you are destined to survive.

The others, too, did not seem in the best of spirits. Brother John stared at the horizon, his lips moving as though he were engaged in prayer, and even Stephen was temporarily depressed. Jerry had fallen asleep, as a native generally does when it is warm and he has nothing to do. Mavovo looked very thoughtful. I wondered whether he had been consulting his Snake again, but did not ask him. Since the episode of our escape from execution by bow and arrow I had grown somewhat afraid of that unholy reptile. Next time it might foretell our immediate doom, and if it did I knew that I should believe.

As for Hans, he looked much disturbed, and was engaged in wildly hunting for something in the flap pockets of an antique corduroy waistcoat which, from its general appearance, must, I imagine, years ago have adorned the person of a British game-keeper.

"Three," I heard him mutter. "By my great grandfather's spirit! only three left."

"Three what?" I asked in Dutch.

"Three charms, Baas, and there ought to have been quite twenty-four. The rest have fallen out through a hole that the devil himself made in this rotten stuff. Now we shall not die of hunger, and we shall not be shot, and we shall not be drowned, at least none of those things will happen to me. But there are twenty-one other things that may finish us, as I have lost the charms to ward them off. Thus—"

"Oh! stop your rubbish," I said, and fell again into the depths of my uncomfortable reflections. After this I, too, went to sleep. When I woke it was past midday and the wind was falling. However, it held while we ate some food we had brought with us, after which it died away altogether, and the Pongo people took to their paddles. At my suggestion we offered to help them, for it occurred to me that we might just as well learn how to manage these paddles. So six were given to us, and Komba, who now I noted was beginning to speak in a somewhat imperious tone, instructed us in their use. At first we made but a poor hand at the business, but three or four hours' steady practice taught us a good deal. Indeed, before our journey's end, I felt that we should be quite capable of managing a canoe, if ever it became necessary for us to do so.

By three in the afternoon the shores of the island we were approaching—if it really was an island, a point that I never cleared up—were well in sight, the mountain top that stood some miles inland having been visible for hours. In fact, through my glasses, I had been able to make out its configuration almost from the beginning of the voyage. About five we entered the mouth of a deep bay fringed on either side with forests, in which were cultivated clearings with small villages of the ordinary African stamp. I observed from the smaller size of the trees adjacent to these clearings, that much more land had once been under cultivation here, probably within the last century, and asked Komba why this was so.

He answered in an enigmatic sentence which impressed me so much that I find I entered it verbatim in my notebook.

"When man dies, corn dies. Man is corn, and corn is man."

Under this entry I see that I wrote "Compare the saying, 'Bread is the staff of life.'"

I could not get any more out of him. Evidently he referred, however, to a condition of shrinking in the population, a circumstance which he did not care to discuss.

After the first few miles the bay narrowed sharply, and at its end came to a point where a stream of no great breadth fell into it. On either side of this stream that was roughly bridged in many places stood the town of Rica. It consisted of a great number of large huts roofed with palm leaves and constructed apparently of whitewashed clay, or rather, as we discovered afterwards, of lake mud mixed with chopped straw or grass.

Reaching a kind of wharf which was protected from erosion by piles formed of small trees driven into the mud, to which were tied a fleet of canoes, we landed just as the sun was beginning to sink. Our approach had doubtless been observed, for as we drew near the wharf a horn was blown by someone on the shore, whereon a considerable number of men appeared. I suppose out of the huts, and assisted to make the canoe fast. I noted that these all resembled Komba and his companions in build and features; they were so like each other that, except for the difference of their ages, it was difficult to tell them apart. They might all have been members of one family; indeed, this was practically the case, owing to constant intermarriage carried on for generations.

There was something in the appearance of these tall, cold, sharp-featured, white-robed men that chilled my blood, something unnatural and almost inhuman. Here was nothing of the usual African jollity. No one shouted, no one laughed or chattered. No one crowded on us, trying to handle our persons or clothes. No one appeared afraid or even astonished. Except for a word or two they were silent, merely contemplating us in a chilling and distant fashion, as though the arrival of three white men in a country where before no white man had ever set foot were an everyday occurrence.

Moreover, our personal appearance did not seem to impress them, for they smiled faintly at Brother John's long beard and at my stubbly hair, pointing these out to each other with their slender fingers or with the handles of their big spears. I remarked that they never used the blade of the spear for this purpose, perhaps because they thought that we might take this for a hostile or even a warlike demonstration. It is humiliating to have to add that the only one of our company who seemed to move them to wonder or interest was Hans. His extremely ugly and wrinkled countenance, it was clear, did appeal to them to some extent, perhaps because they had never seen anything in the least like it before, or perhaps for another reason which the reader may guess in due course.

At any rate, I heard one of them, pointing to Hans, ask Komba whether the ape-man was our god or only our captain. The compliment seemed to please Hans, who hitherto had never been looked on either as a god or a captain. But the rest of us were not flattered; indeed, Mavovo was indignant, and told Hans outright that if he heard any more such talk he would beat him before these people, to show them that he was neither a captain nor a god.

"Wait till I claim to be either, O butcher of a Zulu, before you threaten to treat me thus!" exclaimed Hans, indignantly. Then he added, with his peculiar Hottentot snigger, "Still, it is true that before all the meat is eaten (i.e. before all is done) you may think me both," a dark saying which at the time we did not understand.

When we had landed and collected our belongings, Komba told us to follow him, and led us up a wide street that was very tidily kept and bordered on either side by the large huts whereof I have spoken.

Each of these huts stood in a fenced garden of its own, a thing I have rarely seen elsewhere in Africa. The result of this arrangement was that although as a matter of fact it had but a comparatively small population, the area covered by Rica was very great. The town, by the way, was not surrounded with any wall or other fortification, which showed that the inhabitants feared no attack. The waters of the lake were their defence.

For the rest, the chief characteristic of this place was the silence that brooded there. Apparently they kept no dogs, for none barked, and no poultry, for I never heard a cock crow in Pongo-land. Cattle and native sheep they had in abundance, but as they did not fear any enemy, these were pastured outside the town, their milk and meat being brought in as required. A considerable number of people were gathered to observe us, not in a crowd, but in little family groups which collected separately at the gates of the gardens.

For the most part these consisted of a man and one or more wives, finely formed and handsome women. Sometimes they had children with them, but these were very few; the most I saw with any one family was three, and many seemed to possess none at all. Both the women and the children, like the men, were decently clothed in long, white garments, another peculiarity which showed that these natives were no ordinary African savages.

Oh! I can see Rica Town now after all these many years: the wide street swept and garnished, the brown-roofed, white-walled huts in their fertile, irrigated gardens, the tall, silent folk, the smoke from the cooking fires rising straight as a line in the still air, the graceful palms and other tropical trees, and at the head of the street, far away to the north, the rounded, towering shape of the forest-clad mountain that was called House of the Gods. Often that vision comes back to me in my sleep, or at times in my waking hours when some heavy odour reminds me of the overpowering scent of the great trumpet-like blooms which hung in profusion upon broad-leaved bushes that were planted in almost every garden.

On we marched till at last we reached a tall, live fence that was covered with brilliant scarlet flowers, arriving at its gate just as the last red glow of day faded from the sky and night began to fall. Komba pushed open the gate, revealing a scene that none of us are likely to forget. The fence enclosed about an acre of ground of which the back part was occupied by two large huts standing in the usual gardens.

In front of these, not more than fifteen paces from the gate, stood another building of a totally different character. It was about fifty feet in length by thirty broad and consisted only of a roof supported upon carved pillars of wood, the spaces between the pillars being filled with grass mats or blinds. Most of these blinds were pulled down, but four exactly opposite the gate were open. Inside the shed forty or fifty men, who wore white robes and peculiar caps and who were engaged in chanting a dreadful, melancholy song, were gathered on three sides of a huge fire that burned in a pit in the ground. On the fourth side, that facing the gate, a man stood alone with his arms outstretched and his back towards us.

Of a sudden he heard our footsteps and turned round, springing to the left, so that the light might fall on us. Now we saw by the glow of the great fire, that over it was an iron grid not unlike a small bedstead, and that on this grid lay some fearful object. Stephen, who was a little ahead, stared, then exclaimed in a horrified voice:

"My God! it is a woman!"

In another second the blinds fell down, hiding everything, and the singing ceased.

XIV

The Kalubi's Oath

B e silent!" I whispered, and all understood my tone if they did not catch the words. Then steadying myself with an effort, for this hideous vision, which might have been a picture from hell, made me feel faint, I glanced at Komba, who was a pace or two in front of us. Evidently he was much disturbed—the motions of his back told me this—by the sense of some terrible mistake that he had made. For a moment he stood still, then wheeled round and asked me if we had seen anything.

"Yes," I answered indifferently, "we saw a number of men gathered round a fire, nothing more."

He tried to search our faces, but luckily the great moon, now almost at her full, was hidden behind a thick cloud, so that he could not read them well. I heard him sigh in relief as he said:

"The Kalubi and the head men are cooking a sheep; it is their custom to feast together on those nights when the moon is about to change. Follow me, white lords."

Then he led us round the end of the long shed at which we did not even look, and through the garden on its farther side to the two fine huts I have mentioned. Here he clapped his hands and a woman appeared, I know not whence. To her he whispered something. She went away and presently returned with four or five other women who carried clay lamps filled with oil in which floated a wick of palm fibre. These lamps were set down in the huts that proved to be very clean and comfortable places, furnished after a fashion with wooden stools and a kind of low table of which the legs were carved to the shape of antelope's feet. Also there was a wooden platform at the end of the hut whereon lay beds covered with mats and stuffed with some soft fibre.

"Here you may rest safe," he said, "for, white lords, are you not the honoured guests of the Pongo people? Presently food" (I shuddered at the word) "will be brought to you, and after you have eaten well, if it is your pleasure, the Kalubi and his councillors will receive you in yonder feast-house and you can talk with them before you sleep. If you need aught, strike upon that jar with a stick," and he pointed to what looked like a copper cauldron that stood in the garden of the hut near the place where the women were already lighting a fire, "and some will wait on you. Look, here are your goods; none are missing, and here comes water in which you may wash. Now I must go to make report to the Kalubi," and with a courteous bow he departed.

So after a while did the silent, handsome women—to fetch our meal, I understood one of them to say, and at length we were alone.

"My aunt!" said Stephen, fanning himself with his pocket-handkerchief, "did you see that lady toasting? I have often heard of cannibals, those slaves, for instance, but the actual business! Oh! my aunt!"

"It is no use addressing your absent aunt—if you have got one. What did you expect if you would insist on coming to a hell like this?" I asked gloomily.

"Can't say, old fellow. Don't trouble myself much with expectations as a rule. That's why I and my poor old father never could get on. I always quoted the text 'Sufficient to the day is the evil thereof' to him, until at length he sent for the family Bible and ruled it out with red ink in a rage. But I say, do you think that we shall be called upon to understudy St. Lawrence on that grid?"

"Certainly, I do," I replied, "and, as old Babemba warned you, you can't complain."

"Oh! but I will and I can. And so will you, won't you, Brother John?"

Brother John woke up from a reverie and stroked his long beard.

"Since you ask me, Mr. Somers," he said, reflectively, "if it were a case of martyrdom for the Faith, like that of the saint to whom you have alluded, I should not object—at any rate in theory. But I confess that, speaking from a secular point of view, I have the strongest dislike to being cooked and eaten by these very disagreeable savages. Still, I see no reason to suppose that we shall fall victims to their domestic customs."

I, being in a depressed mood, was about to argue to the contrary, when Hans poked his head into the hut and said:

"Dinner coming, Baas, very fine dinner!"

So we went out into the garden where the tall, impassive ladies were arranging many wooden dishes on the ground. Now the moon was clear of clouds, and by its brilliant light we examined their contents. Some were cooked meat covered with a kind of sauce that made its nature indistinguishable. As a matter of fact, I believe it was mutton, but—who could say? Others were evidently of a vegetable nature. For instance, there was a whole platter full of roasted mealie cobs and a great boiled pumpkin, to say nothing of some bowls of curdled milk. Regarding this feast I became aware of a sudden and complete conversion to those principles of vegetarianism which Brother John was always preaching to me.

"I am sure you are quite right," I said to him, nervously, "in holding that vegetables are the best diet in a hot climate. At any rate I have made up my mind to try the experiment for a few days," and throwing manners to the winds, I grabbed four of the upper mealie cobs and the top of the pumpkin which I cut off with a knife. Somehow I did not seem to fancy that portion of it which touched the platter, for who knew what those dishes might have contained and how often they were washed.

Stephen also appeared to have found salvation on this point, for he, too, patronized the mealie cobs and the pumpkin; so did Mavovo, and so did even that inveterate meat-eater, Hans. Only the simple Jerry tackled the fleshpots of Egypt, or rather of Pongo-land, with appetite, and declared that they were good. I think that he, being the last of us through the gateway, had not realized what it was which lay upon the grid.

At length we finished our simple meal—when you are very hungry it takes a long time to fill oneself with squashy pumpkin, which is why I suppose ruminants and other grazing animals always seem to be eating—and washed it down with water in preference to the sticky-looking milk which we left to the natives.

"Allan," said Brother John to me in a low voice as we lit our pipes, "that man who stood with his back to us in front of the gridiron was the Kalubi. Against the firelight I saw the gap in his hand where I cut away the finger."

"Well, if we want to get any further, you must cultivate him," I answered. "But the question is, shall we get further than—that grid? I believe we have been trapped here to be eaten."

Before Brother John could reply, Komba arrived, and after inquiring whether our appetites had been good, intimated that the Kalubi and head men were ready to receive us. So off we went with the exception of Jerry, whom we left to watch our things, taking with us the presents we had prepared.

Komba led us to the feast-house, where the fire in the pit was out, or had been covered over, and the grid and its horrible burden had disappeared. Also now all the mats were rolled up, so that the clear moonlight flowed into and illuminated the place. Seated in a semicircle on wooden stools with their faces towards the gateway were the Kalubi, who occupied the centre, and eight councillors, all of them grey-haired men. This Kalubi was a tall, thin individual of middle age with, I think, the most nervous countenance that I ever saw. His features twitched continually and his hands were never still. The eyes, too, as far as I could see them in that light, were full of terrors.

He rose and bowed, but the councillors remained seated, greeting us with a long-continued and soft clapping of the hands, which, it seemed, was the Pongo method of salute.

We bowed in answer, then seated ourselves on three stools that had been placed for us, Brother John occupying the middle stool. Mavovo and Hans stood behind us, the latter supporting himself with his large bamboo stick. As soon as these preliminaries were over the Kalubi called upon Komba, whom he addressed in formal language as "You-who-have-passed-the-god," and "You-the-Kalubi-to-be" (I thought I saw him wince as he said these words), to give an account of his mission and of how it came about that they had the honour of seeing the white lords there.

Komba obeyed. After addressing the Kalubi with every possible title of honour, such as "Absolute Monarch," "Master whose feet I kiss," "He whose eyes are fire and whose tongue is a sword," "He at whose nod people die," "Lord of the Sacrifice, first Taster of the Sacred meat," "Beloved of the gods" (here the Kalubi shrank as though he had been pricked with a spear), "Second to none on earth save the Motombo the most holy, the most ancient, who comes from heaven and speaks with the voice of heaven," etc., etc., he gave a clear but brief account of all that had happened in the course of his mission to Beza Town.

Especially did he narrate how, in obedience to a message which he had received from the Motombo, he had invited the white lords to Pongo-land, and even accepted them as envoys from the Mazitu when none would respond to King Bausi's invitation to fill that office. Only he had stipulated that they should bring with them none of their magic weapons which vomited out smoke and death, as the Motombo had commanded. At this information the expressive countenance of the Kalubi once more betrayed mental disturbance that I think Komba noted as much as we did. However, he said nothing, and after a pause, Komba went on to explain that no such weapons had been brought, since, not satisfied with our word that this was so, he and his companions had searched our baggage before we left Mazitu-land.

Therefore, he added, there was no cause to fear that we should bring about the fulfilment of the old prophecy that when a gun was fired among the Pongo the gods would desert the land and the people cease to be a people.

Having finished his speech, he sat down in a humble place behind us. Then the Kalubi, after formally accepting us as ambassadors from Bausi, King of the Mazitu, discoursed at length upon the advantages which would result to both peoples from a lasting peace between them. Finally he propounded the articles of such a peace. These, it was clear, had been carefully prepared, but to set them out would be useless, since they never came to anything, and I doubt whether it was intended that they should. Suffice it to say that they provided for intermarriage, free trade between the countries, blood-brotherhood, and other things that I have forgotten, all of which was to be ratified by Bausi taking a daughter of the Kalubi to wife, and the Kalubi taking a daughter of Bausi.

We listened in silence, and when he had finished, after a pretended consultation between us, I spoke as the Mouth of Brother John, who, I explained, was too grand a person to talk himself, saying that the proposals seemed fair and reasonable, and that we should be happy to submit them to Bausi and his council on our return.

The Kalubi expressed great satisfaction at this statement, but remarked incidentally that first of all the whole matter must be laid before the Motombo for his opinion, without which no State transaction had legal weight among the Pongo. He added that with our approval he proposed that we should visit his Holiness on the morrow, starting when the sun was three hours old, as he lived at a distance of a day's journey from Rica. After further consultation we replied that although we had little time to spare, as we understood that the Motombo was old and could not visit us, we, the white lords, would stretch a point and call on him. Meanwhile we were tired and wished to go to bed. Then we presented our gifts, which were gracefully accepted, with an intimation that return presents would be made to us before we left Pongo-land.

After this the Kalubi took a little stick and broke it, to intimate that the conference was at an end, and having bade him and his councillors good night we retired to our huts.

I should add, because it has a bearing on subsequent events, that on this occasion we were escorted, not by Komba, but by two of the

H. RIDER HAGGARD

councillors. Komba, as I noted for the first time when we rose to say good-bye, was no longer present at the council. When he left it I cannot say, since it will be remembered that his seat was behind us in the shadow, and none of us saw him go.

"WHAT DO YOU MAKE OF all that?" I asked the others when the door was shut.

Brother John merely shook his head and said nothing, for in those days he seemed to be living in a kind of dreamland.

Stephen answered. "Bosh! Tommy rot! All my eye and my elbow! Those man-eating Johnnies have some game up their wide sleeves, and whatever it may be, it isn't peace with the Mazitu."

"I agree," I said. "If the real object were peace they would have haggled more, stood out for better terms, or hostages, or something. Also they would have got the consent of this Motombo beforehand. Clearly he is the master of the situation, not the Kalubi, who is only his tool; if business were meant he should have spoken first, always supposing that he exists and isn't a myth. However, if we live we shall learn, and if we don't, it doesn't matter, though personally I think we should be wise to leave Motombo alone and to clear out to Mazitu-land by the first canoe to-morrow morning."

"I intend to visit this Motombo," broke in Brother John with decision.

"Ditto, ditto," exclaimed Stephen, "but it's no use arguing that all over again."

"No," I replied with irritation. "It is, as you remark, of no use arguing with lunatics. So let's go to bed, and as it will probably be our last, have a good night's sleep."

"Hear, hear!" said Stephen, taking off his coat and placing it doubled up on the bed to serve as a pillow. "I say," he added, "stand clear a minute while I shake this blanket. It's covered with bits of something," and he suited the action to the word.

"Bits of something?" I said suspiciously. "Why didn't you wait a minute to let me see them. I didn't notice any bits before."

"Rats running about the roof, I expect," said Stephen carelessly.

Not being satisfied, I began to examine this roof and the clay walls, which I forgot to mention were painted over in a kind of pattern with whorls in it, by the feeble light of the primitive lamps. While I was thus engaged there was a knock on the door. Forgetting all about the dust, I opened it and Hans appeared.

"One of these man-eating devils wants to speak to you, Baas. Mavovo keeps him without."

"Let him in," I said, since in this place fearlessness seemed our best game, "but watch well while he is with us."

Hans whispered a word over his shoulder, and next moment a tall man wrapped from head to foot in white cloth, so that he looked like a ghost, came or rather shot into the hut and closed the door behind him.

"Who are you?" I asked.

By way of answer he lifted or unwrapped the cloth from about his face, and I saw that the Kalubi himself stood before us.

"I wish to speak alone with the white lord, Dogeetah," he said in a hoarse voice, "and it must be now, since afterwards it will be impossible."

Brother John rose and looked at him.

"How are you, Kalubi, my friend?" he asked. "I see that your wound has healed well."

"Yes, yes, but I would speak with you alone."

"Not so," replied Brother John. "If you have anything to say, you must say it to all of us, or leave it unsaid, since these lords and I are one, and that which I hear, they hear."

"Can I trust them?" muttered the Kalubi.

"As you can trust me. Therefore speak, or go. Yet, first, can we be overheard in this hut?"

"No, Dogeetah. The walls are thick. There is no one on the roof, for I have looked all round, and if any strove to climb there, we should hear. Also your men who watch the door would see him. None can hear us save perhaps the gods."

"Then we will risk the gods, Kalubi. Go on; my brothers know your story."

"My lords," he began, rolling his eyes about him like a hunted creature, "I am in a terrible pass. Once, since I saw you, Dogeetah, I should have visited the White God that dwells in the forest on the mountain yonder, to scatter the sacred seed. But I feigned to be sick, and Komba, the Kalubi-to-be, 'who has passed the god,' went in my place and returned unharmed. Now to-morrow, the night of the full moon, as Kalubi, I must visit the god again and once more scatter the seed and—Dogeetah, he will kill me whom he has once bitten. He will certainly kill me unless I can kill him. Then Komba will rule as Kalubi in my stead, and he will kill you in a way you can guess, by the 'Hot death,' as a sacrifice to the gods, that the women of the Pongo may once more become the mothers of many children. Yes, yes, unless we can kill the god who dwells in the forest, we all must die," and he paused, trembling, while the sweat dropped from him to the floor.

"That's pleasant," said Brother John, "but supposing that we kill the god how would that help us or you to escape from the Motombo and these murdering people of yours? Surely they would slay us for the sacrilege."

"Not so, Dogeetah. If the god dies, the Motombo dies. It is known from of old, and therefore the Motombo watches over the god as a mother over her child. Then, until a new god is found, the Mother of the Holy Flower rules, she who is merciful and will harm none, and I rule under her and will certainly put my enemies to death, especially that wizard Komba."

Here I thought I heard a faint sound in the air like the hiss of a snake, but as it was not repeated and I could see nothing, concluded that I was mistaken.

"Moreover," he went on, "I will load you with gold dust and any gifts you may desire, and set you safe across the water among your friends, the Mazitu."

"Look here," I broke in, "let us understand matters clearly, and, John, do you translate to Stephen. Now, friend Kalubi, first of all, who and what is this god you talk of?"

"Lord Macumazana, he is a huge ape white with age, or born white, I know not which. He is twice as big as any man, and stronger than twenty men, whom he can break in his hands, as I break a reed, or whose heads he can bite off in his mouth, as he bit off my finger for a warning. For that is how he treats the Kalubis when he wearies of them. First he bites off a finger and lets them go, and next he breaks them like a reed, as also he breaks those who are doomed to sacrifice before the fire."

"Ah!" I said, "a great ape! I thought as much. Well, and how long has this brute been a god among you?"

"I do not know how long. From the beginning. He was always there, as the Motombo was always there, for they are one."

"That's a lie any way," I said in English, then went on. "And who is this Mother of the Holy Flower? Is she also always there, and does she live in the same place as the ape god?"

"Not so, lord Macumazana. She dies like other mortals, and is succeeded by one who takes her place. Thus the present Mother is a white woman of your race, now of middle age. When she dies she will be succeeded by her daughter, who also is a white woman and very beautiful. After she dies another who is white will be found, perhaps one who is of black parents but born white."

"How old is this daughter?" interrupted Brother John in a curiously intent voice, "and who is her father?"

"The daughter was born over twenty years ago, Dogeetah, after the Mother of the Flower was captured and brought here. She says that the father was a white man to whom she was married, but who is dead."

Brother John's head dropped upon his chest, and his eyes shut as though he had gone to sleep.

"As for where the Mother lives," went on the Kalubi, "it is on the island in the lake at the top of the mountain that is surrounded by water. She has nothing to do with the White God, but those women who serve her go across the lake at times to tend the fields where grows the seed that the Kalubi sows, of which the corn is the White God's food."

"Good," I said, "now we understand—not much, but a little. Tell us next what is your plan? How are we to come into the place where this great ape lives? And if we come there, how are we to kill the beast, seeing that your successor, Komba, was careful to prevent us from bringing our firearms to your land?"

"Aye, lord Macumazana, may the teeth of the god meet in his brain for that trick; yes, may he die as I know how to make him die. That prophecy of which he told you is no prophecy from of old. It arose in the land within the last moon only, though whether it came from Komba or from the Motombo I know not. None save myself, or at least very few here, had heard of the iron tubes that throw out death, so how should there be a prophecy concerning them?"

"I am sure I don't know, Kalubi, but answer the rest of the question."

"As to your coming into the forest—for the White God lives in a forest on the slopes of the mountain, lords—that will be easy since the Motombo and the people will believe that I am trapping you there to be a sacrifice, such as they desire for sundry reasons," and he looked at the plump Stephen in a very suggestive way. "As to how you are to kill the god without your tubes of iron, that I do not know. But you are very brave and great magicians. Surely you can find a way."

Here Brother John seemed to wake up again.

"Yes," he said, "we shall find a way. Have no fear of that, O Kalubi.

We are not afraid of the big ape whom you call a god. Yet it must be at a price. We will not kill this beast and try to save your life, save at a price."

"What price?" asked the Kalubi nervously. "There are wives and cattle—no, you do not want the wives, and the cattle cannot be taken across the lake. There are gold dust and ivory. I have already promised these, and there is nothing more that I can give."

"The price is, O Kalubi, that you hand over to us to be taken away the white woman who is called Mother of the Holy Flower, with her daughter—"

"And," interrupted Stephen, to whom I had been interpreting, "the Holy Flower itself, all of it dug up by the roots."

When he heard these modest requests the poor Kalubi became like one upon the verge of madness.

"Do you understand," he gasped, "do you understand that you are asking for the gods of my country?"

"Quite," replied Brother John with calmness; "for the gods of your country—nothing more nor less."

The Kalubi made as though he would fly from the hut, but I caught him by the arm and said:

"See, friend, things are thus. You ask us, at great danger to ourselves, to kill one of the gods of your country, the highest of them, in order to save your life. Well, in payment we ask you to make a present of the remaining gods of your country, and to see us and them safe across the lake. Do you accept or refuse?"

"I refuse," answered the Kalubi sullenly. "To accept would mean the last curse upon my spirit; that is too horrible to tell."

"And to refuse means the first curse upon your body; namely, that in a few hours it must be broken and chewed by a great monkey which you call a god. Yes, broken and chewed, and afterwards, I think, cooked and eaten as a sacrifice. Is it not so?"

The Kalubi nodded his head and groaned.

"Yet," I went on, "for our part we are glad that you have refused, since now we shall be rid of a troublesome and dangerous business and return in safety to Mazitu land."

"How will you return in safety, O lord Macumazana, you who are doomed to the 'Hot Death' if you escape the fangs of the god?"

"Very easily, O Kalubi, by telling Komba, the Kalubi-to-be, of your plots against this god of yours, and how we have refused to listen to your wickedness. In fact, I think this may be done at once while you are here with us, O Kalubi, where perhaps you do not expect to be found. I will go strike upon the pot without the door; doubtless though it is late, some will hear. Nay, man, stand you still; we have knives and our servants have spears," and I made as though to pass him.

"Lord," he said, "I will give you the Mother of the Holy Flower and her daughter; aye, and the Holy Flower itself dug up by the roots, and I swear that if I can, I will set you and them safe across the lake, only asking that I may come with you, since here I dare not stay. Yet the curse will come too, but if so, it is better to die of a curse in a day to be, than to-morrow at the fangs of the god. Oh! why was I born! Why was I born!" and he began to weep.

"That is a question many have asked and none have been able to answer, O friend Kalubi, though mayhap there is an answer somewhere," I replied in a kind voice.

For my heart was stirred with pity of this poor wretch mazed and lost in his hell of superstition; this potentate who could not escape from the trappings of a hateful power, save by the door of a death too horrible to contemplate; this priest whose doom it was to be slain by the very hands of his god, as those who went before him had been slain, and as those who came after him would be slain.

"Yet," I went on, "I think you have chosen wisely, and we hold you to your word. While you are faithful to us, we will say nothing. But of this be sure—that if you attempt to betray us, we who are not so helpless as we seem, will betray you, and it shall be you who die, not us. Is it a bargain?"

"It is a bargain, white lord, although blame me not if things go wrong, since the gods know all, and they are devils who delight in human woe and mock at bargains and torment those who would injure them. Yet, come what will, I swear to keep faith with you thus, by the oath that may not be broken," and drawing a knife from his girdle, he thrust out the tip of his tongue and pricked it. From the puncture a drop of blood fell to the floor.

"If I break my oath," he said, "may my flesh grow cold as that blood grows cold, and may it rot as that blood rots! Aye, and may my spirit waste and be lost in the world of ghosts as that blood wastes into the air and is lost in the dust of the world!"

It was a horrible scene and one that impressed me very much, especially as even then there fell upon me a conviction that this unfortunate man was doomed, that a fate which he could not escape was upon him.

We said nothing, and in another moment he had thrown his white wrappings over his face and slipped through the door.

"I am afraid we are playing it rather low down on that jumpy old boy," said Stephen remorsefully.

"The white woman, the white woman and her daughter," muttered Brother John.

"Yes," reflected Stephen aloud. "One is justified in doing anything to get two white women out of this hell, if they exist. So one may as well have the orchid also, for they'd be lonely without it, poor things, wouldn't they? Glad I thought of that, it's soothing to the conscience."

"I hope you'll find it so when we are all on that iron grid which I noticed is wide enough for three," I remarked sarcastically. "Now be quiet, I want to go to sleep."

I am sorry to have to add that for the most of that night Want remained my master. But if I couldn't sleep, I could, or rather was obliged to, think, and I thought very hard indeed.

First I reflected on the Pongo and their gods. What were these and why did they worship them? Soon I gave it up, remembering that the problem was one which applied equally to dozens of the dark religions of this vast African continent, to which none could give an answer, and least of all their votaries. That answer indeed must be sought in the horrible fears of the unenlightened human heart, which sees death and terror and evil around it everywhere and, in this grotesque form or in that, personifies them in gods, or rather in devils who must be propitiated. For always the fetish or the beast, or whatever it may be, is not the real object of worship. It is only the thing or creature which is inhabited by the spirit of the god or devil, the temple, as it were, that furnishes it with a home, which temple is therefore holy. And these spirits are diverse, representing sundry attributes or qualities.

Thus the great ape might be Satan, a prince of evil and blood. The Holy Flower might symbolise fertility and the growth of the food of man from the bosom of the earth. The Mother of the Flower might represent mercy and goodness, for which reason it was necessary that she should be white in colour, and dwell, not in the shadowed forest, but on a soaring mountain, a figure of light, in short, as opposed to darkness. Or she might be a kind of African Ceres, a goddess of the corn and harvest which were symbolised in the beauteous bloom she tended. Who could tell? Not I, either then or afterwards, for I never found out.

As for the Pongo themselves, their case was obvious. They were a dying tribe, the last descendants of some higher race, grown barren from intermarriage. Probably, too, they were at first only cannibals occasionally and from religious reasons. Then in some time of dearth they became very religious in that respect, and the habit overpowered them. Among cannibals, at any rate in Africa, as I knew, this dreadful food is much preferred to any other meat. I had not the slightest doubt that although the Kalubi himself had brought us here in the wild hope that we might save him from a terrible death at the hands of the Beelzebub he served, Komba and the councillors, inspired thereto by the prophet called Motombo, designed that we should be murdered and eaten as an offering to the gods. How we were to escape this fate, being unarmed, I could not imagine, unless some special protection were vouchsafed to us. Meanwhile, we must go on to the end, whatever it might be.

Brother John, or to give him his right name, the Reverend John Eversley, was convinced that the white woman imprisoned in the mountain was none other than the lost wife for whom he had searched for twenty weary years, and that the second white woman of whom we had heard that night was, strange as it might seem, her daughter and his own. Perhaps he was right and perhaps he was wrong. But even in the latter case, if two white persons were really languishing in this dreadful land, our path was clear. We must go on in faith until we saved them or until we died.

> "Our life is granted, not in Pleasure's round,
> Or even Love's sweet dream, to lapse, content;
> Duty and Faith are words of solemn sound,
> And to their echoes must the soul be bent,"

as some one or other once wrote, very nobly I think. Well, there was but little of "Pleasure's round" about the present entertainment, and any hope of "Love's sweet dream" seemed to be limited to Brother John (here I was quite mistaken, as I so often am). Probably the "echoes" would be my share; indeed, already I seemed to hear their ominous thunder.

At last I did go to sleep and dreamed a very curious dream. It seemed to me that I was disembodied, although I retained all my powers of thought and observation; in fact, dead and yet alive. In this state I hovered over the people of the Pongo who were gathered together on a great plain under an inky sky. They were going about their business as usual, and very unpleasant business it often was. Some of them were worshipping a dim form that I knew was the devil; some were committing murders; some were feasting—at that on which they feasted I would not look; some were labouring or engaged in barter; some were thinking. But I, who had the power of looking into them, saw within the breast of each a tiny likeness of the man or woman or child as it might be, humbly bent upon its knees with hands together in an attitude of prayer, and with imploring, tear-stained face looking upwards to the black heaven.

Then in that heaven there appeared a single star of light, and from this star flowed lines of gentle fire that spread and widened till all the immense arc was one flame of glory. And now from the pulsing heart of the Glory, which somehow reminded me of moving lips, fell countless flakes of snow, each of which followed an appointed path till it lit upon the forehead of one of the tiny, imploring figures hidden within those savage breasts, and made it white and clean.

Then the Glory shrank and faded till there remained of it only the similitude of two transparent hands stretched out as though in blessing—and I woke up wondering how on earth I found the fancy to invent such a vision, and whether it meant anything or nothing.

Afterwards I repeated it to Brother John, who was a very spiritually minded as well as a good man—the two things are often quite different—and asked him to be kind enough to explain. At the time he shook his head, but some days later he said to me:

"I think I have read your riddle, Allan; the answer came to me quite of a sudden. In all those sin-stained hearts there is a seed of good and an aspiration towards the right. For every one of them also there is at last mercy and forgiveness, since how could they learn who never had a teacher? Your dream, Allan, was one of the ultimate redemption of even the most evil of mankind, by gift of the Grace that shall one day glow through the blackness of the night in which they wander."

That is what he said, and I only hope that he was right, since at present there is something very wrong with the world, especially in Africa.

Also we blame the blind savage for many things, but on the balance are we so much better, considering our lights and opportunities? Oh! the truth is that the devil—a very convenient word that—is a good fisherman. He has a large book full of flies of different sizes and colours, and well he knows how to suit them to each particular fish. But white or black, every fish takes one fly or the other, and then comes the question—is the fish that has swallowed the big gaudy lure so much worse or more foolish than that which has fallen to the delicate white moth with the same sharp barb in its tail?

In short, are we not all miserable sinners as the Prayer Book says, and in the eye of any judge who can average up the elemental differences of those waters wherein we were bred and are called upon to swim, is there so much to choose between us? Do we not all need those outstretched Hands of Mercy which I saw in my dream?

But there, there! What right has a poor old hunter to discuss things that are too high for him?

XV

The Motombo

After my dream I went to sleep again, till I was finally aroused by a strong ray of light hitting me straight in the eye.

Where the dickens does that come from? thought I to myself, for these huts had no windows.

Then I followed the ray to its source, which I perceived was a small hole in the mud wall some five feet above the floor. I rose and examined the said hole, and noted that it appeared to have been freshly made, for the clay at the sides of it was in no way discoloured. I reflected that if anyone wanted to eavesdrop, such an aperture would be convenient, and went outside the hut to pursue my investigations. Its wall, I found, was situated about four feet from the eastern part of the encircling reed fence, which showed no signs of disturbance, although there, in the outer face of the wall, was the hole, and beneath it on the lime flooring lay some broken fragments of plaster. I called Hans and asked him if he had kept watch round the hut when the wrapped-up man visited us during the night. He answered yes, and that he could swear that no one had come near it, since several times he had walked to the back and looked.

Somewhat comforted, though not satisfied, I went in to wake up the others, to whom I said nothing of this matter since it seemed foolish to alarm them for no good purpose. A few minutes later the tall, silent women arrived with our hot water. It seemed curious to have hot water brought to us in such a place by these very queer kind of housemaids, but so it was. The Pongo, I may add, were, like the Zulus, very clean in their persons, though whether they all used hot water, I cannot say. At any rate, it was provided for us.

Half an hour later they returned with breakfast, consisting chiefly of a roasted kid, of which, as it was whole, and therefore unmistakable, we partook thankfully. A little later the Majestic Komba appeared. After many compliments and inquiries as to our general health, he asked whether we were ready to start on our visit to the Motombo who, he added, was expecting us with much eagerness. I inquired how he knew that, since we had only arranged to call on him late on the previous night, and I understood that he lived a day's journey away. But Komba put the matter by with a smile and a wave of his hand.

So in due course off we went, taking with us all our baggage, which now that it had been lightened by the delivery of the presents, was of no great weight.

Five minutes' walk along the wide, main street led us to the northern gate of Rica Town. Here we found the Kalubi himself with an escort of thirty men armed with spears; I noted that unlike the Mazitu they had no bows and arrows. He announced in a loud voice that he proposed to do us the special honour of conducting us to the sanctuary of the Holy One, by which we understood him to mean the Motombo. When we politely begged him not to trouble, being in an irritable mood, or assuming it, he told us rudely to mind our own business. Indeed, I think this irritability was real enough, which, in the circumstances known to the reader, was not strange. At any rate, an hour or so later it declared itself in an act of great cruelty which showed us how absolute was this man's power in all temporal matters.

Passing through a little clump of bush we came to some gardens surrounded by a light fence through which a number of cattle of a small and delicate breed—they were not unlike Jerseys in appearance—had broken to enjoy themselves by devouring the crops. This garden, it appeared, belonged to the Kalubi for the time being, who was furious at the destruction of its produce by the cattle which also belonged to him.

"Where is the herd?" he shouted.

A hunt began—and presently the poor fellow—he was no more than a lad, was discovered asleep behind a bush. When he was dragged before him the Kalubi pointed, first to the cattle, then to the broken fence and the devastated garden. The lad began to mutter excuses and pray for mercy.

"Kill him!" said the Kalubi, whereon the herd flung himself to the ground, and clutching him by the ankles, began to kiss his feet, crying out that he was afraid to die. The Kalubi tried to kick himself free, and failing in this, lifted his big spear and made an end of the poor boy's prayers and life at a single stroke.

The escort clapped their hands in salute or approval, after which four of them, at a sign, took up the body and started with it at a trot for Rica Town, where probably that night it appeared upon the grid. Brother John saw, and his big white beard bristled with indignation like the hair on the back of an angry cat, while Stephen spluttered something

H. RIDER HAGGARD

beginning with "You brute," and lifted his fist as though to knock the Kalubi down. This, had I not caught hold of him, I have no doubt he would have done.

"O Kalubi!" gasped Brother John, "do you not know that blood calls for blood? In the hour of your own death remember this death."

"Would you bewitch me, white man?" said the Kalubi, glaring at him angrily. "If so——" and once more he lifted the spear, but as John never stirred, held it poised irresolutely. Komba thrust himself between them, crying:

"Back, Dogeetah, who dare to meddle with our customs! Is not the Kalubi Lord of life and death?"

Brother John was about to answer, but I called to him in English:

"For Heaven's sake be silent, unless you want to follow the boy. We are in these men's power."

Then he remembered and walked away, and presently we marched forward as though nothing had happened. Only from that moment I do not think that any of us worried ourselves about the Kalubi and what might befall him. Still, looking back on the thing, I think that there was this excuse to be made for the man. He was mad with the fear of death and knew not what he did.

All that day we travelled on through a rich, flat country that, as we could tell from various indications, had once been widely cultivated. Now the fields were few and far between, and bush, for the most part a kind of bamboo scrub, was reoccupying the land. About midday we halted by a water-pool to eat and rest, for the sun was hot, and here the four men who had carried off the boy's body rejoined us and made some report. Then we went forward once more towards what seemed to be a curious and precipitous wall of black cliff, beyond which the volcanic-looking mountain towered in stately grandeur. By three o'clock we were near enough to this cliff, which ran east and west as far as the eye could reach, to see a hole in it, apparently where the road terminated, that appeared to be the mouth of a cave.

The Kalubi came up to us, and in a shy kind of way tried to make conversation. I think that the sight of this mountain, drawing ever nearer, vividly recalled his terrors and caused him to desire to efface the bad impression he knew he had made on us, to whom he looked for safety. Among other things he told us that the hole we saw was the door of the House of the Motombo.

I nodded my head, but did not answer, for the presence of this murderous king made me feel sick. So he went away again, looking at us in a humble and deprecatory manner.

Nothing further happened until we reached the remarkable wall of rock that I have mentioned, which I suppose is composed of some very hard stone that remained when the softer rock in which it lay was disintegrated by millions of years of weather or washings by the water of the lake. Or perhaps its substance was thrown out of the bowels of the volcano when this was active. I am no geologist, and cannot say, especially as I lacked time to examine the place. At any rate there it was, and there in it appeared the mouth of a great cave that I presume was natural, having once formed a kind of drain through which the lake overflowed when Pongo-land was under water.

We halted, staring dubiously at this darksome hole, which no doubt was the same that Babemba had explored in his youth. Then the Kalubi gave an order, and some of the soldiers went to huts that were built near the mouth of the cave, where I suppose guardians or attendants lived, though of these we saw nothing. Presently they returned with a number of lighted torches that were distributed among us. This done, we plunged, shivering (at least, I shivered), into the gloomy recesses of that great cavern, the Kalubi going before us with half of our escort, and Komba following behind us with the remainder.

The floor of the place was made quite smooth, doubtless by the action of water, as were the walls and roof, so far as we could see them, for it was very wide and lofty. It did not run straight, but curved about in the thickness of the cliff. At the first turn the Pongo soldiers set up a low and eerie chant which they continued during its whole length, that according to my pacings was something over three hundred yards. On we wound, the torches making stars of light in the intense blackness, till at length we rounded a last corner where a great curtain of woven grass, now drawn, was stretched across the cave. Here we saw a very strange sight.

On either side of it, near to the walls, burned a large wood fire that gave light to the place. Also more light flowed into it from its further mouth that was not more than twenty paces from the fires. Beyond the mouth was water which seemed to be about two hundred yards wide, and beyond the water rose the slopes of the mountain that was covered with huge trees. Moreover, a little bay penetrated into the cavern, the point of which bay ended between the two fires. Here the water, which was not more than six or eight feet wide, and shallow, formed the berthing place of a good-sized canoe that lay there. The walls of the cavern, from the turn to the point of the tongue of water, were pierced with four doorways, two on either side, which led, I presume, to chambers hewn in the rock. At each of these doorways stood a tall woman clothed in white, who held in her hand a burning torch. I concluded that these were attendants set there to guide and welcome us, for after we had passed, they vanished into the chambers.

But this was not all. Set across the little bay of water just above the canoe that floated there was a wooden platform, eight feet or so square, on either side of which stood an enormous elephant's tusk, bigger indeed than any I have seen in all my experience, which tusks seemed to be black with age. Between the tusks, squatted upon rugs of some kind of rich fur, was what from its shape and attitude I at first took to be a huge toad. In truth, it had all the appearance of a very bloated toad. There was the rough corrugated skin, there the prominent backbone (for its back was towards us), and there were the thin, splayed-out legs.

We stared at this strange object for quite a long while, unable to make it out in that uncertain light, for so long indeed, that I grew nervous and was about to ask the Kalubi what it might be. As my lips opened, however, it stirred, and with a slow, groping, circular movement turned itself towards us very slowly. At length it was round, and as the head came in view all the Pongo from the Kalubi down ceased their low, weird chant and flung themselves upon their faces, those who had torches still holding them up in their right hands.

Oh! what a thing appeared! It was not a toad, but a man that moved upon all fours. The large, bald head was sunk deep between the shoulders, either through deformity or from age, for this creature was undoubtedly very old. Looking at it, I wondered how old, but could form no answer in my mind. The great, broad face was sunken and withered, like to leather dried in the sun; the lower lip hung pendulously upon the prominent and bony jaw. Two yellow, tusk-like teeth projected one at each corner of the great mouth; all the rest were gone, and from time to time it licked the white gums with a red-pointed tongue as a snake might do. But the chief wonder of the Thing lay in its eyes that were large and round, perhaps because the flesh had shrunk away from them, which gave them the appearance of being set in the hollow orbits of a skull. These eyes literally shone like fire; indeed, at times they seemed positively to blaze, as I have seen a lion's eyes do in the dark. I confess that the aspect of the creature terrified and for a while paralysed me; to think that it was human was awful.

I glanced at the others and saw that they, too, were frightened. Stephen turned very white. I thought that he was going to be sick again, as he was after he drank the coffee out of the wrong bowl on the day we entered Mazitu-land. Brother John stroked his white beard and muttered some invocation to Heaven to protect him. Hans exclaimed in his abominable Dutch:

"*Oh! keek, Baas, da is je lelicher oud deel!*" ("Oh! look, Baas, there is the ugly old devil himself!")

Jerry went flat on his face among the Pongo, muttering that he saw Death before him. Only Mavovo stood firm; perhaps because as a witch-doctor of repute he felt that it did not become him to show the white feather in the presence of an evil spirit.

The toad-like creature on the platform swayed its great head slowly as a tortoise does, and contemplated us with its flaming eyes. At length it spoke in a thick, guttural voice, using the tongue that seemed to be common to this part of Africa and indeed to that branch of the Bantu people to which the Zulus belong, but, as I thought, with a foreign accent.

"So *you* are the white men come back," it said slowly. "Let me count!" and lifting one skinny hand from the ground, it pointed with the forefinger and counted. "One. Tall, with a white beard. Yes, that is right. Two. Short, nimble like a monkey, with hair that wants no comb; clever, too, like a father of monkeys. Yes, that is right. Three. Smooth-faced, young and stupid, like a fat baby that laughs at the sky because he is full of milk, and thinks that the sky is laughing at him. Yes, that is right. All three of you are just the same as you used to be. Do you remember, White Beard, how, while we killed you, you said prayers to One Who sits above the world, and held up a cross of bone to which a man was tied who wore a cap of thorns? Do you remember how you kissed the man with the cap of thorns as the spear went into you? You shake your head—oh! you are a clever liar, but I will show you that you are a liar, for I have the thing yet," and snatching up a horn which lay on the kaross beneath him, he blew.

As the peculiar, wailing note that the horn made died away, a woman dashed out of one of the doorways that I have described and flung herself on her knees before him. He muttered something to her and she dashed back again to re-appear in an instant holding in her hand a yellow ivory crucifix.

"Here it is, here it is," he said. "Take it, White Beard, and kiss it once more, perhaps for the last time," and he threw the crucifix to Brother John, who caught it and stared at it amazed. "And do you remember, Fat Baby, how we caught you? You fought well, very well, but we killed you at last, and you were good, very good; we got much strength from you.

"And do you remember, Father of Monkeys, how you escaped from us by your cleverness? I wonder where you went to and how you died. I shall not forget you, for you gave me this," and he pointed to a big white scar upon his shoulder. "You would have killed me, but the stuff in that iron tube of yours burned slowly when you held the fire to it, so that I had time to jump aside and the iron ball did not strike me in the heart as you meant that it should. Yet, it is still here; oh! yes, I carry it with me to this day, and now that I have grown thin I can feel it with my finger."

I listened astonished to this harangue, which if it meant anything, meant that we had all met before, in Africa at some time when men used matchlocks that were fired with a fuse—that is to say, about the year 1700, or earlier. Reflection, however, showed me the interpretation of this nonsense. Obviously this old priest's forefather, or, if one put him at a hundred and twenty years of age, and I am sure that he was not a day less, perhaps his father, as a young man, was mixed up with some of the first Europeans who penetrated to the interior of Africa. Probably these were Portuguese, of whom one may have been a priest and the other two an elderly man and his son, or young brother, or companion. The manner of the deaths of these people and of what happened to them generally would of course be remembered by the descendants of the chief or head medicine-man of the tribe.

"Where did we meet, and when, O Motombo?" I asked.

"Not in this land, not in this land, Father of Monkeys," he replied in his low rumbling voice, "but far, far away towards the west where the sun sinks in the water; and not in this day, but long, long ago. Twenty Kalubis have ruled the Pongo since that day; some have ruled for many years and some have ruled for a few years—that depends upon the will of my brother, the god yonder," and he chuckled horribly and jerked his thumb backwards over his shoulder towards the forest on the mountain. "Yes, twenty have ruled, some for thirty years and none for less than four."

"Well, you *are* a large old liar," I thought to myself, for, taking the average rule of the Kalubis at ten years, this would mean that we met him two centuries ago at least.

"You were clothed otherwise then," he went on, "and two of you wore hats of iron on the head, but that of White Beard was shaven. I caused a picture of you to be beaten by the master-smith upon a plate of copper. I have it yet."

Again he blew upon his horn; again a woman darted out, to whom he whispered; again she went to one of the chambers and returned bearing an object which he cast to us.

We looked at it. It was a copper or bronze plaque, black, apparently with age, which once had been nailed on something for there were the holes. It represented a tall man with a long beard and a tonsured head who held a cross in his hand; and two other men, both short, who wore round metal caps and were dressed in queer-looking garments and boots with square toes. These man carried big and heavy matchlocks, and in the hand of one of them was a smoking fuse. That was all we could make out of the thing.

"Why did you leave the far country and come to this land, O Motombo?" I asked.

"Because we were afraid that other white men would follow on your steps and avenge you. The Kalubi of that day ordered it, though I said No, who knew that none can escape by flight from what must come when it must come. So we travelled and travelled till we found this place, and here we have dwelt from generation to generation. The gods came with us also; my brother that dwells in the forest came, though we never saw him on the journey, yet he was here before us. The Holy Flower came too, and the white Mother of the Flower—she was the wife of one of you, I know not which."

"Your brother the god?" I said. "If the god is an ape as we have heard, how can he be the brother of a man?"

"Oh! you white men do not understand, but we black people understand. In the beginning the ape killed my brother who was Kalubi, and his spirit entered into the ape, making him as a god, and so he kills every other Kalubi and their spirits enter also into him. Is it not so, O Kalubi of to-day, you without a finger?" and he laughed mockingly.

The Kalubi, who was lying on his stomach, groaned and trembled, but made no other answer.

"So all has come about as I foresaw," went on the toad-like creature. "You have returned, as I knew you would, and now we shall learn whether White Beard yonder spoke true words when he said that his god would be avenged upon our god. You shall go to be avenged on him if you can, and then we shall learn. But this time you have none of your iron tubes which alone we fear. For did not the god declare to us through me that when the white men came back with an iron tube, then he, the god, would die, and I, the Motombo, the god's Mouth, would die, and the Holy Flower would be torn up, and the Mother of the Flower would pass away, and the people of the Pongo would be dispersed and become wanderers and slaves? And did he not declare that if the white men came again without their iron tubes, then certain secret things would happen—oh! ask them not, in time they shall be known to you, and the people of the Pongo who were dwindling would again become fruitful and very great? And that is why we welcome you, white men, who arise again from the land of ghosts, because through you we, the Pongo, shall become fruitful and very great."

Of a sudden he ceased his rumbling talk, his head sank back between his shoulders and he sat silent for a long while, his fierce, sparkling eyes playing on us as though he would read our very thoughts. If he succeeded, I hope that mine pleased him. To tell the truth, I was filled with mixed fear, fury and loathing. Although, of course, I did not believe a word of all the rubbish he had been saying, which was akin to much that is evolved by these black-hearted African wizards, I hated the creature whom I felt to be only half-human. My whole nature sickened at his aspect and talk. And yet I was dreadfully afraid of him. I felt as a man might who wakes up to find himself alone with some peculiarly disgusting Christmas-story kind of ghost. Moreover I was quite sure that he meant us ill, fearful and imminent ill. Suddenly he spoke again:

"Who is that little yellow one," he said, "that old one with a face like a skull," and he pointed to Hans, who had kept as much out of sight as possible behind Mavovo, "that wizened, snub-nosed one who might be a child of my brother the god, if ever he had a child? And why, being so small, does he need so large a staff?" Here he pointed again to Hans's big bamboo stick. "I think he is as full of guile as a new-filled gourd with water. The big black one," and he looked at Mavovo, "I do not fear, for his magic is less than my magic," (he seemed to recognise a brother doctor in Mavovo) "but the little yellow one with the big stick and the pack upon his back, I fear him. I think he should be killed."

He paused and we trembled, for if he chose to kill the poor Hottentot, how could we prevent him? But Hans, who saw the great danger, called his cunning to his aid.

"O Motombo," he squeaked, "you must not kill me for I am the servant of an ambassador. You know well that all the gods of every land hate and will be revenged upon those who touch ambassadors or their servants, whom they, the gods, alone may harm. If you kill me I shall haunt you. Yes, I shall sit on your shoulder at night and jibber into your ear so that you cannot sleep, until you die. For though you are old you must die at last, Motombo."

"It is true," said the Motombo. "Did I not tell you that he was full of cunning? All the gods will be avenged upon those who kill ambassadors or their servants. That"—here he laughed again in his dreadful way—"is the rights of the gods alone. Let the gods of the Pongo settle it."

I uttered a sigh of relief, and he went on in a new voice, a dull, business-like voice if I may so describe it:

"Say, O Kalubi, on what matter have you brought these white men to speak with me, the Mouth of the god? Did I dream that it was a matter of a treaty with the King of the Mazitu? Rise and speak."

So the Kalubi rose and with a humble air set out briefly and clearly the reason of our visit to Pongo-land as the envoys of Bausi and the heads of the treaty that had been arranged subject to the approval of the Motombo and Bausi. We noted that the affair did not seem to interest the Motombo at all. Indeed, he appeared to go to sleep while the speech was being delivered, perhaps because he was exhausted with the invention of his outrageous falsehoods, or perhaps for other reasons. When it was finished he opened his eyes and pointed to Komba, saying:

"Arise, Kalubi-that-is-to-be."

So Komba rose, and in his cold, precise voice narrated his share in the transaction, telling how he had visited Bausi, and all that had happened in connection with the embassy. Again the Motombo appeared to go to sleep, only opening his eyes once as Komba described how we had been searched for firearms, whereon he nodded his great head in approval and licked his lips with his thin red tongue. When Komba had done, he said:

"The gods tell me that the plan is wise and good, since without new blood the people of the Pongo will die, but of the end of the matter the god knows alone, if even he can read the future."

He paused, then asked sharply:

"Have you anything more to say, O Kalubi-that-is-to-be? Now of a sudden the god puts it into my mouth to ask if you have anything more to say?"

"Something, O Motombo. Many moons ago the god bit *off* the finger of our High Lord, the Kalubi. The Kalubi, having heard that a white man skilled in medicine who could cut off limbs with knives, was in the country of the Mazitu and camped on the borders of the great lake, took a canoe and rowed to where the white man was camped, he with the beard, who is named Dogeetah, and who stands before you. I followed him in another canoe, because I wished to know what he was doing, also to see a white man. I hid my canoe and those who went with me in the reeds far from the Kalubi's canoe. I waded through the shallow water and concealed myself in some thick reeds quite near to the white man's linen house. I saw the white man cut off the Kalubi's finger and I heard the Kalubi pray the white man to come to our country with the iron tubes that smoke, and to kill the god of whom he was afraid."

Now from all the company went up a great gasp, and the Kalubi fell down upon his face again, and lay still. Only the Motombo seemed to show no surprise, perhaps because he already knew the story.

"Is that all?" he asked.

"No, O Mouth of the god. Last night, after the council of which you have heard, the Kalubi wrapped himself up like a corpse and visited the white men in their hut. I thought that he would do so, and had made ready. With a sharp spear I bored a hole in the wall of the hut, working from outside the fence. Then I thrust a reed through from the fence across the passage between the fence and the wall, and through the hole in the hut, and setting my ear to the end of the reed, I listened."

"Oh! clever, clever!" muttered Hans in involuntary admiration, "and to think that I looked and looked too low, beneath the reed. Oh! Hans, though you are old, you have much to learn."

"Among much else I heard this," went on Komba in sentences so clear and cold that they reminded me of the tinkle of falling ice, "which I think is enough, though I can tell you the rest if you wish, O Mouth. I heard," he said, in the midst of a silence that was positively awful, "our lord, the Kalubi, whose name is Child of the god, agree with the white men that they should kill the god—how I do not know, for it was not said—and that in return they should receive the persons of the Mother of the Holy Flower and of her daughter, the Mother-that-is-to-be, and should dig up the Holy Flower itself by the roots and take it away across the water, together with the Mother and the Mother-that-is-to-be. That is all, O Motombo."

Still in the midst of an intense silence, the Motombo glared at the prostrate figure of the Kalubi. For a long while he glared. Then the silence was broken, for the wretched Kalubi sprang from the floor, seized a spear and tried to kill himself. Before the blade touched him it was snatched from his hand, so that he remained standing, but weaponless.

Again there was silence and again it was broken, this time by the Motombo, who rose from his seat before which he stood, a huge, bloated object, and roared aloud in his rage. Yes, he roared like a wounded buffalo. Never would I have believed that such a vast volume of sound could have proceeded from the lungs of a single aged man. For fully a minute his furious bellowings echoed down that great cave, while all the Pongo soldiers, rising from their recumbent position, pointed their hands, in some of which torches still burned, at the miserable Kalubi on whom their wrath seemed to be concentrated, rather than on us, and hissed like snakes.

Really it might have been a scene in hell with the Motombo playing the part of Satan. Indeed, his swollen, diabolical figure supported on the thin, toad-like legs, the great fires burning on either side, the lurid lights of evening reflected from the still water beyond and glowering among the tree tops of the mountain, the white-robed forms of the tall Pongo, bending, every one of them, towards the wretched culprit and hissing like so many fierce serpents, all suggested some uttermost deep in the infernal regions as one might conceive them in a nightmare.

It went on for some time, I don't know how long, till at length the Motombo picked up his fantastically shaped horn and blew. Thereon the women darted from the various doorways, but seeing that they were not wanted, checked themselves in their stride and remained standing so, in the very attitude of runners about to start upon a race. As the blast of the horn died away the turmoil was suddenly succeeded by an utter stillness, broken only by the crackling of the fires whose flames, of all the living things in that place, alone seemed heedless of the tragedy which was being played.

"All up now, old fellow!" whispered Stephen to me in a shaky voice.

"Yes," I answered, "all up high as heaven, where I hope we are going. Now back to back, and let's make the best fight we can. We've got the spears."

While we were closing in the Motombo began to speak.

"So you plotted to kill the god, Kalubi-who-*was*," he screamed, "with these white ones whom you would pay with the Holy Flower and her who guards it. Good! You shall go, all of you, and talk with the god. And I, watching here, will learn who dies—you or the god. Away with them!"

XVI

THE GODS

With a roar the Pongo soldiers leapt on us. I think that Mavovo managed to get his spear up and kill a man, for I saw one of them fall backwards and lie still. But they were too quick for the rest of us. In half a minute we were seized, the spears were wrenched from our hands and we were thrown headlong into the canoe, all six of us, or rather seven including the Kalubi. A number of the soldiers, including Komba, who acted as steersman, also sprang into the canoe that was instantly pushed out from beneath the bridge or platform on which the Motombo sat and down the little creek into the still water of the canal or estuary, or whatever it may be, that separates the wall of rock which the cave pierces from the base of the mountain.

As we floated out of the mouth of the cave the toad-like Motombo, who had wheeled round upon his stool, shouted an order to Komba.

"O Kalubi," he said, "set the Kalubi-who-*was* and the three white men and their three servants on the borders of the forest that is named House-of-the-god and leave them there. Then return and depart, for here I would watch alone. When all is finished I will summon you."

Komba bowed his handsome head and at a sign two of the men got out paddles, for more were not needed, and with slow and gentle strokes rowed us across the water. The first thing I noted about this water at the time was that its blackness was inky, owing, I suppose, to its depth and the shadows of the towering cliff on one side and of the tall trees on the other. Also I observed—for in this emergency, or perhaps because of it, I managed to keep my wits about me—that its banks on either side were the home of great numbers of crocodiles which lay there like logs. I saw, further, that a little lower down where the water seemed to narrow, jagged boughs projected from its surface as though great trees had fallen, or been thrown into it. I recalled in a numb sort of way that old Babemba had told us that when he was a boy he had escaped in a canoe down this estuary, and reflected that it would not be possible for him to do so now because of those snags. Unless, indeed, he had floated over them in a time of great flood.

A couple of minutes or so of paddling brought us to the further shore which, as I think I have said, was only about two hundred yards from the mouth of the cave. The bow of the canoe grated on the bank, disturbing a huge crocodile that vanished into the depths with an angry plunge.

"Land, white lords, land," said Komba with the utmost politeness, "and go, visit the god who doubtless is waiting for you. And now, as we shall meet no more—farewell. You are wise and I am foolish, yet hearken to my counsel. If ever you should return to the Earth again, be advised by me. Cling to your own god if you have one, and do not meddle with those of other peoples. Again farewell."

The advice was excellent, but at that moment I felt a hate for Komba which was really superhuman. To me even the Motombo seemed an angel of light as compared with him. If wishes could have killed, our farewell would indeed have been complete.

Then, admonished by the spear points of the Pongo, we landed in the slimy mud. Brother John went first with a smile upon his handsome countenance that I thought idiotic under the circumstances, though doubtless he knew best when he ought to smile, and the wretched Kalubi came last. Indeed, so great was his shrinking from that ominous shore, that I believe he was ultimately propelled from the boat by his successor in power, Komba. Once he had trodden it, however, a spark of spirit returned to him, for he wheeled round and said to Komba,

"Remember, O Kalubi, that my fate to-day will be yours also in a day to come. The god wearies of his priests. This year, next year, or the year after; he always wearies of his priests."

"Then, O Kalubi-that-was," answered Komba in a mocking voice as the canoe was pushed off, "pray to the god for me, that it may be the year after; pray it as your bones break in his embrace."

While we watched that craft depart there came into my mind the memory of a picture in an old Latin book of my father's, which represented the souls of the dead being paddled by a person named Charon across a river called the Styx. The scene before us bore a great resemblance to that picture. There was Charon's boat floating on the dreadful Styx. Yonder glowed the lights of the world, here was the gloomy, unknown shore. And we, we were the souls of the dead awaiting the last destruction at the teeth and claws of some unknown monster, such as that which haunts the recesses of the Egyptian hell. Oh! the parallel was painfully exact. And yet, what do you think was the remark of that irrepressible young man Stephen?

"Here we are at last, Allan, my boy," he said, "and after all without any trouble on our own part. I call it downright providential. Oh! isn't it jolly! Hip, hip, hooray!"

Yes, he danced about in that filthy mud, threw up his cap and cheered!

I withered, or rather tried to wither him with a look, muttering the single word: "Lunatic."

Providential! Jolly! Well, it's fortunate that some people's madness takes a cheerful turn. Then I asked the Kalubi where the god was.

"Everywhere," he replied, waving his trembling hand at the illimitable forest. "Perhaps behind this tree, perhaps behind that, perhaps a long way off. Before morning we shall know."

"What are you going to do?" I inquired savagely.

"Die," he answered.

"Look here, fool," I exclaimed, shaking him, "you can die if you like, but we don't mean to. Take us to some place where we shall be safe from this god."

"One is never safe from the god, lord, especially in his own House," and he shook his silly head and went on, "How can we be safe when there is nowhere to go and even the trees are too big to climb?"

I looked at them, it was true. They were huge and ran up for fifty or sixty feet without a bough. Moreover, it was probable that the god climbed better than we could. The Kalubi began to move inland in an indeterminate fashion, and I asked him where he was going.

"To the burying-place," he answered. "There are spears yonder with the bones."

I pricked up my ears at this—for when one has nothing but some clasp knives, spears are not to be despised—and ordered him to lead on. In another minute we were walking uphill through the awful wood where the gloom at this hour of approaching night was that of an English fog.

Three or four hundred paces brought us to a kind of clearing, where I suppose some of the monster trees had fallen down in past years and never been allowed to grow up again. Here, placed upon the ground, were a number of boxes made of imperishable ironwood, and on the top of each box sat, or rather lay, a mouldering and broken skull.

"Kalubi-that-were!" murmured our guide in explanation. "Look, Komba has made my box ready," and he pointed to a new case with the lid off.

"How thoughtful of him!" I said. "But show us the spears before it gets quite dark." He went to one of the newer coffins and intimated that we should lift off the lid as he was afraid to do so.

I shoved it aside. There within lay the bones, each of them separate and wrapped up in something, except of course the skull. With these were some pots filled apparently with gold dust, and alongside of the pots two good spears that, being made of copper, had not rusted much. We went on to other coffins and extracted from them more of these weapons that were laid there for the dead man to use upon his journey through the Shades, until we had enough. The shafts of most of them were somewhat rotten from the damp, but luckily they were furnished with copper sockets from two and a half to three feet long, into which the wood of the shaft fitted, so that they were still serviceable.

"Poor things these to fight a devil with," I said.

"Yes, Baas," said Hans in a cheerful voice, "very poor. It is lucky that I have got a better."

I stared at him; we all stared at him.

"What do you mean, Spotted Snake?" asked Mavovo.

"What do you mean, child of a hundred idiots? Is this a time to jest? Is not one joker enough among us?" I asked, and looked at Stephen.

"Mean, Baas? Don't you know that I have the little rifle with me, that which is called *Intombi*, that with which you shot the vultures at Dingaan's kraal? I never told you because I was sure you knew; also because if you didn't know it was better that you should not know, for if *you* had known, those Pongo *skellums* (that is, vicious ones) might have come to know also. And if *they* had known—"

"Mad!" interrupted Brother John, tapping his forehead, "quite mad, poor fellow! Well, in these depressing circumstances it is not wonderful."

I inspected Hans again, for I agreed with John. Yet he did not look mad, only rather more cunning than usual.

"Hans," I said, "tell us where this rifle is, or I will knock you down and Mavovo shall flog you."

"Where, Baas! Why, cannot you see it when it is before your eyes?"

"You are right, John," I said, "he's off it"; but Stephen sprang at Hans and began to shake him.

"Leave go, Baas," he said, "or you may hurt the rifle."

Stephen obeyed in sheer astonishment. Then, oh! then Hans did something to the end of his great bamboo stick, turned it gently upside down and out of it slid the barrel of a rifle neatly tied round with greased cloth and stoppered at the muzzle with a piece of tow!

I could have kissed him. Yes, such was my joy that I could have kissed that hideous, smelly old Hottentot.

"The stock?" I panted. "The barrel isn't any use without the stock, Hans."

"Oh! Baas," he answered, grinning, "do you think that I have shot with you all these years without knowing that a rifle must have a stock to hold it by?"

Then he slipped off the bundle from his back, undid the lashings of the blanket, revealing the great yellow head of tobacco that had excited my own and Komba's interest on the shores of the lake. This head he tore apart and produced the stock of the rifle nicely cleaned, a cap set ready on the nipple, on to which the hammer was let down, with a little piece of wad between to prevent the cap from being fired by any sudden jar.

"Hans," I exclaimed, "Hans, you are a hero and worth your weight in gold!"

"Yes, Baas, though you never told me so before. Oh! I made up my mind that I wouldn't go to sleep in the face of the Old Man (death). Oh! which of you ought to sleep now upon that bed that Bausi sent me?" he asked as he put the gun together. "*You*, I think, you great stupid Mavovo. *You* never brought a gun. If you were a wizard worth the name you would have sent the rifles on and had them ready to meet us here. Oh! will you laugh at me any more, you thick-head of a Zulu?"

"No," answered Mavovo candidly. "I will give you *sibonga*. Yes, I will make for you Titles of Praise, O clever Spotted Snake."

"And yet," went on Hans, "I am not all a hero; I am worth but half my weight in gold. For, Baas, although I have plenty of powder and bullets in my pocket, I lost the caps out of a hole in my waistcoat. You remember, Baas, I told you it was charms I lost. But three remain; no, four, for there is one on the nipple. There, Baas, there is *Intombi* all ready and loaded. And now when the white devil comes you can shoot him in the eye, as you how to do up to a hundred yards, and send him to the other devils down in hell. Oh! won't your holy father the Predikant be glad to see him there."

Then with a self-satisfied smirk he half-cocked the rifle and handed it to me ready for action.

"I thank God!" said Brother John solemnly, "who has taught this poor Hottentot how to save us."

"No, Baas John, God never taught me, I taught myself. But, see, it grows dark. Had we not better light a fire," and forgetting the rifle he began to look about for wood.

"Hans," called Stephen after him, "if ever we get out of this, I will give you £500, or at least my father will, which is the same thing."

"Thank you, Baas, thank you, though just now I'd rather have a drop of brandy and—I don't see any wood."

He was right. Outside of the graveyard clearing lay, it is true, some huge fallen boughs. But these were too big for us to move or cut. Moreover, they were so soaked with damp, like everything in this forest, that it would be impossible to fire them.

The darkness closed in. It was not absolute blackness, because presently the moon rose, but the sky was rainy and obscured it; moreover, the huge trees all about seemed to suck up whatever light there was. We crouched ourselves upon the ground back to back as near as possible to the centre of the place, unrolled such blankets as we had to protect us from the damp and cold, and ate some biltong or dried game flesh and parched corn, of which fortunately the boy Jerry carried a bagful that had remained upon his shoulders when he was thrown into the canoe. Luckily I had thought of bringing this food with us; also a flask of spirits.

Then it was that the first thing happened. Far away in the forest resounded a most awful roar, followed by a drumming noise, such a roar as none of us had ever heard before, for it was quite unlike that of a lion or any other beast.

"What is that?" I asked.

"The god," groaned the Kalubi, "the god praying to the moon with which he always rises."

I said nothing, for I was reflecting that four shots, which was all we had, was not many, and that nothing should tempt me to waste one of them. Oh! why had Hans put on that rotten old waistcoat instead of the new one I gave him in Durban?

Since we heard no more roars Brother John began to question the Kalubi as to where the Mother of the Flower lived.

"Lord," answered the man in a distracted way, "there, towards the East. You walk for a quarter of the sun's journey up the hill, following a path that is marked by notches cut upon the trees, till beyond the garden of the god at the top of the mountain more water is found surrounding an island. There on the banks of the water a canoe is hidden in the bushes, by which the water may be crossed to the island, where dwells the Mother of the Holy Flower."

Brother John did not seem to be quite satisfied with the information, and remarked that he, the Kalubi, would be able to show us the road on the morrow.

"I do not think that I shall ever show you the road," groaned the shivering wretch.

At that moment the god roared again much nearer. Now the Kalubi's nerve gave out altogether, and quickened by some presentiment, he began to question Brother John, whom he had learned was a priest of an unknown sort, as to the possibility of another life after death.

Brother John, who, be it remembered, was a very earnest missionary by calling, proceeded to administer some compressed religious consolations, when, quite near to us, the god began to beat upon some kind of very large and deep drum. He didn't roar this time, he only worked away at a massed-band military drum. At least that is what it sounded like, and very unpleasant it was to hear in that awful forest with skulls arranged on boxes all round us, I can assure you, my reader.

The drumming ceased, and pulling himself together, Brother John continued his pious demonstrations. Also just at that time a thick rain-cloud quite obscured the moon, so that the darkness grew dense. I heard John explaining to the Kalubi that he was not really a Kalubi, but an immortal soul (I wonder whether he understood him). Then I became aware of a horrible shadow—I cannot describe it in any other way—that was blacker than the blackness, which advanced towards us at extraordinary speed from the edge of the clearing.

Next second there was a kind of scuffle a few feet from me, followed by a stifled yell, and I saw the shadow retreating in the direction from which it had come.

"What's the matter?" I asked.

"Strike a match," answered Brother John; "I think something has happened."

I struck a match, which burnt up very well, for the air was quite still. In the light of it I saw first the anxious faces of our party—how ghastly they looked!—and next the Kalubi who had risen and was waving his right arm in the air, a right arm that was bloody and *lacked the hand*.

"The god has visited me and taken away my hand!" he moaned in a wailing voice.

I don't think anybody spoke; the thing was beyond words, but we tried to bind the poor fellow's arm up by the light of matches. Then we sat down again and watched.

The darkness grew still denser as the thick of the cloud passed over the moon, and for a while the silence, that utter silence of the tropical forest at night, was broken only by the sound of our breathing, the buzz of a few mosquitoes, the distant splash of a plunging crocodile and the stifled groans of the mutilated man.

Again I saw, or thought I saw—this may have been half an hour later—that black shadow dart towards us, as a pike darts at a fish in a pond. There was another scuffle, just to my left—Hans sat between me and the Kalubi—followed by a single prolonged wail.

"The king-man has gone," whispered Hans. "I felt him go as though a wind had blown him away. Where he was there is nothing but a hole."

Of a sudden the moon shone out from behind the clouds. In its sickly light about half-way between us and the edge of the clearing, say thirty yards off, I saw—oh! what did I see! The devil destroying a lost soul. At least, that is what it looked like. A huge, grey-black creature, grotesquely human in its shape, had the thin Kalubi in its grip. The Kalubi's head had vanished in its maw and its vast black arms seemed to be employed in breaking him to pieces.

Apparently he was already dead, though his feet, that were lifted off the ground, still moved feebly.

I sprang up and covered the beast with the rifle which was cocked, getting full on to its head which showed the clearest, though this was rather guesswork, since I could not see distinctly the fore-sight. I pulled, but either the cap or the powder had got a little damp on the journey and hung fire for the fraction of a second. In that infinitesimal time the devil—it is the best name I can give the thing—saw me, or perhaps it only saw the light gleaming on the barrel. At any rate it dropped the Kalubi, and as though some intelligence warned it what to expect, threw up its massive right arm—I remember how extraordinarily long the limb seemed and that it looked thick as a man's thigh—in such a fashion as to cover its head.

Then the rifle exploded and I heard the bullet strike. By the light of the flash I saw the great arm tumble down in a dead, helpless kind of way, and next instant the whole forest began to echo with peal upon peal of those awful roarings that I have described, each of which ended with a dog-like *yowp* of pain.

"You have hit him, Baas," said Hans, "and he isn't a ghost, for he doesn't like it. But he's still very lively."

"Close up," I answered, "and hold out the spears while I reload."

My fear was that the brute would rush on us. But it did not. For all that dreadful night we saw or heard it no more. Indeed, I began to hope that after all the bullet had reached some mortal part and that the great ape was dead.

At length, it seemed to be weeks afterwards, the dawn broke and revealed us sitting white and shivering in the grey mist; that is, all except Stephen, who had gone comfortably to sleep with his head resting on Mavovo's shoulder. He is a man so equably minded and so devoid of nerves, that I feel sure he will be one of the last to be disturbed by the trump of the archangel. At least, so I told him indignantly when at length we roused him from his indecent slumbers.

"You should judge things by results, Allan," he said with a yawn. "I'm as fresh as a pippin while you all look as though you had been to a ball with twelve extras. Have you retrieved the Kalubi yet?"

Shortly afterwards, when the mist lifted a little, we went out in a line to "retrieve the Kalubi," and found—well, I won't describe what we found. He was a cruel wretch, as the incident of the herd-boy had told us, but I felt sorry for him. Still, his terrors were over, or at least I hope so.

We deposited him in the box that Komba had kindly provided in preparation for this inevitable event, and Brother John said a prayer over his miscellaneous remains. Then, after consultation and in the very worst of spirits, we set out to seek the way to the home of the Mother of the Flower. The start was easy enough, for a distinct, though very faint path led from the clearing up the slope of the hill. Afterwards it became more difficult for the denser forest began. Fortunately very few creepers grew in this forest, but the flat tops of the huge trees meeting high above entirely shut out the sky, so that the gloom was great, in places almost that of night.

Oh! it was a melancholy journey as, filled with fears, we stole, a pallid throng, from trunk to trunk, searching them for the notches that indicated our road, and speaking only in whispers, lest the sound of our voices should attract the notice of the dreadful god. After a mile or two of this we became aware that its notice was attracted despite our precautions, for at times we caught glimpses of some huge grey thing slipping along parallel to us between the boles of the trees. Hans wanted me to try a shot, but I would not, knowing that the chances of hitting it were small indeed. With only three charges, or rather three caps left, it was necessary to be saving.

We halted and held a consultation, as a result of which we decided that there was no more danger in going on than in standing still or attempting to return. So we went on, keeping close together. To me, as I was the only one with a rifle, was accorded what I did not at all appreciate, the honour of heading the procession.

Another half-mile and again we heard that strange rolling sound which was produced, I believe, by the great brute beating upon its breast, but noted that it was not so continuous as on the previous night.

"Ha!" said Hans, "he can only strike his drum with one stick now. Your bullet broke the other, Baas."

A little farther and the god roared quite close, so loudly that the air seemed to tremble.

"The drum is all right, whatever may have happened to the sticks," I said.

A hundred yards or so more and the catastrophe occurred. We had reached a spot in the forest where one of the great trees had fallen down, letting in a little light. I can see it to this hour. There lay the enormous tree, its bark covered with grey mosses and clumps of a giant species of maidenhair fern. On our side of it was the open space which may have measured forty feet across, where the light fell in a perpendicular ray, as it does through the smoke-hole of a hut. Looking at this prostrate trunk, I saw first two lurid and fiery eyes that glowed red in the shadow; and then, almost in the same instant, made out what looked like the head of a fiend enclosed in a wreath of the delicate green ferns. I can't describe it, I can only repeat that it looked like the head of a very large fiend with a pallid face, huge overhanging eyebrows and great yellow tushes on either side of the mouth.

Before I had even time to get the rifle up, with one terrific roar the brute was on us. I saw its enormous grey shape on the top of the trunk, I saw it pass me like a flash, running upright as a man does, but with the head held forward, and noted that the arm nearest to me was swinging as though broken. Then as I turned I heard a scream of terror and perceived that it had gripped the poor Mazitu, Jerry, who walked last but one of our line which was ended by Mavovo. Yes, it had gripped him and was carrying him off, clasped to its breast with its sound arm. When I say that Jerry, although a full-grown man and rather inclined to stoutness, looked like a child in that fell embrace, it will give some idea of the creature's size.

Mavovo, who had the courage of a buffalo, charged at it and drove the copper spear he carried into its side. They all charged like berserkers, except myself, for even then, thank Heaven! I knew a trick worth two of that. In three seconds there was a struggling mass in the centre of the clearing. Brother John, Stephen, Mavovo and Hans were all stabbing at the enormous gorilla, for it was a gorilla, although their blows seemed to do it no more harm than pinpricks. Fortunately for them, for its part, the beast would not let go of Jerry, and having only one sound arm, could but snap at its assailants, for if it had lifted a foot to rend them, its top-heavy bulk would have caused it to tumble over.

At length it seemed to realise this, and hurled Jerry away, knocking down Brother John and Hans with his body. Then it leapt on Mavovo, who, seeing it come, placed the copper socket of the spear against his own breast, with the result that when the gorilla tried to crush him, the point of the spear was driven into its carcase. Feeling the pain, it unwound its arm from about Mavovo, knocking Stephen over with the backward sweep. Then it raised its great hand to crush Mavovo with a blow, as I believe gorillas are wont to do.

This was the chance for which I was waiting. Up till that moment I had not dared to fire, fearing lest I should kill one of my companions. Now for an instant it was clear of them all, and steadying myself, I aimed at the huge head and let drive. The smoke thinned, and through it I saw the gigantic ape standing quite still, like a creature lost in meditation.

Then it threw up its sound arm, turned its fierce eyes to the sky, and uttering one pitiful and hideous howl, sank down dead. The bullet had entered just behind the ear and buried itself in the brain.

The great silence of the forest flowed in over us, as it were; for quite a while no one did or said anything. Then from somewhere down amidst the mosses I heard a thin voice, the sound of which reminded me of air being squeezed out of an indiarubber cushion.

"Very good shot, Baas," it piped up, "as good as that which killed the king-vulture at Dingaan's kraal, and more difficult. But if the Baas could pull the god off me I should say—Thank you."

The "thank you" was almost inaudible, and no wonder, for poor Hans had fainted. There he lay under the huge bulk of the gorilla, just his nose and mouth appearing between the brute's body and its arm.

Had it not been for the soft cushion of wet moss in which he reclined, I think that he would have been crushed flat.

We rolled the creature off him somehow and poured a little brandy down his throat, which had a wonderful effect, for in less than a minute he sat up, grasping like a dying fish, and asked for more.

Leaving Brother John to examine Hans to see if he was really injured, I bethought me of poor Jerry and went to look at him. One glance was enough. He was quite dead. Indeed, he seemed to be crushed out of shape like a buck that has been enveloped in the coils of a boa-constrictor. Brother John told me afterwards that both his arms and nearly all his ribs had been broken in that terrible embrace. Even his spine was dislocated.

I have often wondered why the gorilla ran down the line without touching me or the others, to vent his rage upon Jerry. I can only suggest that it was because the unlucky Mazitu had sat next to the Kalubi on the previous night, which may have caused the brute to identify him by smell with the priest whom he had learned to hate and killed. It is true that Hans had sat on the other side of the Kalubi, but perhaps the odour of the Pongo had not clung to him so much, or perhaps it meant to deal with him after it had done with Jerry.

When we knew that the Mazitu was past human help and had discovered to our joy that, save for a few bruises, no one else was really hurt, although Stephen's clothes were half-torn off him, we made an examination of the dead god. Truly it was a fearful creature.

What its exact weight or size may have been we had no means of ascertaining, but I never saw or heard of such an enormous ape, if a gorilla is really an ape. It needed the united strength of the five of us to lift the carcase with a great effort off the fainting Hans and even to roll it from side to side when subsequently we removed the skin. I would never have believed that so ancient an animal of its stature, which could not have been more than seven feet when it stood erect, could have been so heavy. For ancient undoubtedly it was. The long, yellow, canine tusks were worn half-away with use; the eyes were sunken far into the skull; the hair of the head, which I am told is generally red or brown, was quite white, and even the bare breast, which should be black, was grey in hue. Of course, it was impossible to say, but one might easily have imagined that this creature was two hundred years or more old, as the Motombo had declared it to be.

Stephen suggested that it should be skinned, and although I saw little prospect of our being able to carry away the hide, I assented and helped in the operation on the mere chance of saving so great a curiosity. Also, although Brother John was restless and murmured something about wasting time, I thought it necessary that we should have a rest after our fearful anxieties and still more fearful encounter with this consecrated monster. So we set to work, and as a result of more than an hour's toil, dragged off the hide, which was so tough and thick that, as we found, the copper spears had scarcely penetrated to the flesh. The bullet that I had put into it on the previous night struck, we discovered, upon the bone of the upper arm, which it shattered sufficiently to render that limb useless, if it did not break it altogether. This, indeed, was fortunate for us, for had the creature retained both its arms uninjured, it would certainly have killed more of us in its attack. We were saved only by the fact that when it was hugging Jerry it had no limb left with which it could strike, and luckily did not succeed in its attempts to get hold with its tremendous jaws that had nipped off the Kalubi's hand as easily as a pair of scissors severs the stalk of a flower.

When the skin was removed, except that of the hands, which we did not attempt to touch, we pegged it out, raw side uppermost, to dry in the centre of the open place where the sun struck. Then, having buried poor Jerry in the hollow trunk of the great fallen tree, we washed ourselves with the wet mosses and ate some of the food that remained to us.

After this we started forward again in much better spirits. Jerry, it was true, was dead, but so was the god, leaving us happily still alive and practically untouched. Never more would the Kalubis of Pongo-land shiver out their lives at the feet of this dreadful divinity who soon or late must become their executioner, for I believe, with the exception of two who committed suicide through fear, that no Kalubi was ever known to have died except by the hand—or teeth—of the god.

What would I not give to know that brute's history? Could it possibly, as the Motombo said, have accompanied the Pongo people from their home in Western or Central Africa, or perhaps have been brought here by them in a state of captivity? I am unable to answer the question, but it should be noted that none of the Mazitu or other natives had ever heard of the existence of more true gorillas in this part of Africa. The creature, if it had its origin in the locality, must either have been solitary in its habits or driven away from its fellows, as sometimes happens to old elephants, which then, like this gorilla, become fearfully ferocious.

H. RIDER HAGGARD

That is all I can say about the brute, though of course the Pongo had their own story. According to them it was an evil spirit in the shape of an ape, which evil spirit had once inhabited the body of an early Kalubi, and had been annexed by the ape when it killed the said Kalubi. Also they declared that the reason the creature put all the Kalubis to death, as well as a number of other people who were offered up to it, was that it needed "to refresh itself with the spirits of men," by which means it was enabled to avoid the effects of age. It will be remembered that the Motombo referred to this belief, of which afterwards I heard in more detail from Babemba. But if this god had anything supernatural about it, at least its magic was no shield against a bullet from a Purdey rifle.

Only a little way from the fallen tree we came suddenly upon a large clearing, which we guessed at once must be that "Garden of the god" where twice a year the unfortunate Kalubis were doomed to scatter the "sacred seed." It was a large garden, several acres of it, lying on a shelf, as it were, of the mountain and watered by a stream. Maize grew in it, also other sorts of corn, while all round was a thick belt of plantain trees. Of course these crops had formed the food of the god who, whenever it was hungry, came to this place and helped itself, as we could see by many signs. The garden was well kept and comparatively free from weeds. At first we wondered how this could be, till I remembered that the Kalubi, or someone, had told me that it was tended by the servants of the Mother of the Flower, who were generally albinos or mutes.

We crossed it and pushed on rapidly up the mountain, once more following an easy and well-beaten path, for now we saw that we were approaching what we thought must be the edge of a crater. Indeed, our excitement was so extreme that we did not speak, only scrambled forward, Brother John, notwithstanding his lame leg, leading at a greater pace than we could equal. He was the first to reach our goal, closely followed by Stephen. Watching, I saw him sink down as though in a swoon. Stephen also appeared astonished, for he threw up his hands.

I rushed to them, and this was what I saw. Beneath us was a steep slope quite bare of forest, which ceased at its crest. This slope stretched downwards for half a mile or more to the lip of a beautiful lake, of which the area was perhaps two hundred acres. Set in the centre of the deep blue water of this lake, which we discovered afterwards to be unfathomable, was an island not more than five and twenty or thirty acres in extent, that seemed to be cultivated, for on it we could see fields, palms and other fruit-bearing trees. In the middle of the island stood a small, near house thatched after the fashion of the country, but civilized in its appearance, for it was oblong, not round, and encircled by a verandah and a reed fence. At a distance from this house were a number of native huts, and in front of it a small enclosure surrounded by a high wall, on the top of which mats were fixed on poles as though to screen something from wind or sun.

"The Holy Flower lives there, you bet," gasped Stephen excitedly— he could think of nothing but that confounded orchid. "Look, the mats are up on the sunny side to prevent its scorching, and those palms are planted round to give it shade."

"The Mother of the Flower lives there," whispered Brother John, pointing to the house. "Who is she? Who is she? Suppose I should be mistaken after all. God, let me not be mistaken, for it would be more than I can bear."

"We had better try to find out," I remarked practically, though I am sure I sympathised with his suspense, and started down the slope at a run.

In five minutes or less we reached the foot of it, and, breathless and perspiring though we were, began to search amongst the reeds and bushes growing at the edge of the lake for the canoe of which we had been told by the Kalubi. What if there were none? How could we cross that wide stretch of deep water? Presently Hans, who, following certain indications which caught his practised eye, had cast away to the left, held up his hand and whistled. We ran to him.

"Here it is, Baas," he said, and pointed to something in a tiny bush-fringed inlet, that at first sight looked like a heap of dead reeds. We tore away at the reeds, and there, sure enough, was a canoe of sufficient size to hold twelve or fourteen people, and in it a number of paddles.

Another two minutes and we were rowing across that lake.

We came safely to the other side, where we found a little landing-stage made of poles sunk into the lake. We tied up the canoe, or rather I did, for nobody else remembered to take that precaution, and presently were on a path which led through the cultivated fields to the house. Here I insisted upon going first with the rifle, in case we should be suddenly attacked. The silence and the absence of any human beings suggested to me that this might very well happen, since it would be strange if we had not been seen crossing the lake.

Afterwards I discovered why the place seemed so deserted. It was owing to two reasons. First, it was now noontime, an hour at which these poor slaves retired to their huts to eat and sleep through the heat of the day. Secondly, although the "Watcher," as she was called, had seen the canoe on the water, she concluded that the Kalubi was visiting the Mother of the Flower and, according to practice on these occasions, withdrew herself and everybody else, since the rare meetings of the Kalubi and the Mother of the Flower partook of the nature of a religious ceremony and must be held in private.

First we came to the little enclosure that was planted about with palms and, as I have described, screened with mats. Stephen ran at it and, scrambling up the wall, peeped over the top.

Next instant he was sitting on the ground, having descended from the wall with the rapidity of one shot through the head.

"Oh! by Jingo!" he exclaimed, "oh! by Jingo!" and that was all I could get out of him, though it is true I did not try very hard at the time.

Not five paces from this enclosure stood a tall reed fence that surrounded the house. It had a gate also of reeds, which was a little ajar. Creeping up to it very cautiously, for I thought I heard a voice within, I peeped through the half-opened gate. Four or five feet away was the verandah from which a doorway led into one of the rooms of the house where stood a table on which was food.

Kneeling on mats upon this verandah were—*two white women*—clothed in garments of the purest white adorned with a purple fringe, and wearing bracelets and other ornaments of red native gold. One of these appeared to be about forty years of age. She was rather stout, fair in colouring, with blue eyes and golden hair that hung down her back. The other might have been about twenty. She also was fair, but her eyes were grey and her long hair was of a chestnut hue. I saw at once that she was tall and very beautiful. The elder woman was praying, while the other, who knelt by her side, listened and looked up vacantly at the sky.

"O God," prayed the woman, "for Christ's sake look in pity upon us two poor captives, and if it be possible, send us deliverance from this savage land. We thank Thee Who hast protected us unharmed and in health for so many years, and we put our trust in Thy mercy, for Thou alone canst help us. Grant, O God, that our dear husband and father may still live, and that in Thy good time we may be reunited to him. Or if he be dead and there is no hope for us upon the earth, grant that we, too, may die and find him in Thy Heaven."

Thus she prayed in a clear, deliberate voice, and I noticed that as she did so the tears ran down her cheeks. "Amen," she said at last, and the girl by her side, speaking with a strange little accent, echoed the "Amen."

I looked round at Brother John. He had heard something and was utterly overcome. Fortunately enough he could not move or even speak.

"Hold him," I whispered to Stephen and Mavovo, "while I go in and talk to these ladies."

Then, handing the rifle to Hans, I took off my hat, pushed the gate a little wider open, slipped through it and called attention to my presence by coughing.

The two women, who had risen from their knees, stared at me as though they saw a ghost.

"Ladies," I said, bowing, "pray do not be alarmed. You see God Almighty sometimes answers prayers. In short, I am one of—a party—of white people who, with some trouble, have succeeded in getting to this place and—and—would you allow us to call on you?"

Still they stared. At length the elder woman opened her lips.

"Here I am called the Mother of the Holy Flower, and for a stranger to speak with the Mother is death. Also if you are a man, how did you reach us alive?"

"That's a long story," I answered cheerfully. "May we come in? We will take the risks, we are accustomed to them and hope to be able to do you a service. I should explain that three of us are white men, two English and one—American."

"American!" she gasped, "American! What is he like, and how is he named?"

"Oh!" I replied, for my nerve was giving out and I grew confused, "he is oldish, with a white beard, rather like Father Christmas in short, and his Christian name (I didn't dare to give it all at once) is—er—John, Brother John, we call him. Now I think of it," I added, "he has some resemblance to your companion there."

I thought that the lady was going to die, and cursed myself for my awkwardness. She flung her arm about the girl to save herself from falling—a poor prop, for she, too, looked as though she were going to die, having understood some, if not all, of my talk. It must be remembered that this poor young thing had never even seen a white man before.

"Madam, madam," I expostulated, "I pray you to bear up. After living through so much sorrow it would be foolish to decease of—joy. May I call in Brother John? He is a clergyman and might be able to say something appropriate, which I, who am only a hunter, cannot do."

She gathered herself together, opened her eyes and whispered:

"Send him here."

I pushed open the gate behind which the others were clustered. Catching Brother John, who by now had recovered somewhat, by the arm, I dragged him forward. The two stood staring at each other, and the young lady also looked with wide eyes and open mouth.

"Elizabeth!" said John.

She uttered a faint scream, then with a cry of "*Husband!*" flung herself upon his breast.

I slipped through the gate and shut it fast.

"I say, Allan," said Stephen, when we had retreated to a little distance, "did you see her?"

"Her? Who? Which?" I asked.

"The young lady in the white clothes. She is lovely."

"Hold your tongue, you donkey!" I answered. "Is this a time to talk of female looks?"

Then I went away behind the wall and literally wept for joy. It was one of the happiest moments of my life, for how seldom things happen as they should!

Also I wanted to put up a little prayer of my own, a prayer of thankfulness and for strength and wit to overcome the many dangers that yet awaited us.

XVII

The Home of the Holy Flower

Half an hour or so passed, during which I was engaged alternately in thinking over our position and in listening to Stephen's rhapsodies. First he dilated on the loveliness of the Holy Flower that he had caught a glimpse of when he climbed the wall, and secondly, on the beauty of the eyes of the young lady in white. Only by telling him that he might offend her did I persuade him not to attempt to break into the sacred enclosure where the orchid grew. As we were discussing the point, the gate opened and she appeared.

"Sirs," she said, with a reverential bow, speaking slowly and in the drollest halting English, "the mother and the father—yes, the father—ask, will you feed?"

We intimated that we would "feed" with much pleasure, and she led the way to the house, saying:

"Be not astonished at them, for they are very happy too, and please forgive our unleavened bread."

Then in the politest way possible she took me by the hand, and followed by Stephen, we entered the house, leaving Mavovo and Hans to watch outside.

It consisted of but two rooms, one for living and one for sleeping. In the former we found Brother John and his wife seated on a kind of couch gazing at each other in a rapt way. I noted that they both looked as though they had been crying—with happiness, I suppose.

"Elizabeth," said John as we entered, "this is Mr. Allan Quatermain, through whose resource and courage we have come together again, and this young gentleman is his companion, Mr. Stephen Somers."

She bowed, for she seemed unable to speak, and held out her hand, which we shook.

"What be 'resource and courage'?" I heard her daughter whisper to Stephen, "and why have you none, O Stephen Somers?"

"It would take a long time to explain," he said with his jolly laugh, after which I listened to no more of their nonsense.

Then we sat down to the meal, which consisted of vegetables and a large bowl of hard-boiled ducks' eggs, of which eatables an ample supply was carried out to Hans and Mavovo by Stephen and Hope. This, it seemed, was the name that her mother had given to the girl when she was born in the hour of her black despair.

It was an extraordinary story that Mrs. Eversley had to tell, and yet a short one.

She *had* escaped from Hassan-ben-Mohammed and the slave-traders, as the rescued slave told her husband at Zanzibar before he died, and, after days of wandering, been captured by some of the Pongo who were scouring the country upon dark business of their own, probably in search of captives. They brought her across the lake to Pongo-land and, the former Mother of the Flower, an albino, having died at a great age, installed her in the office on this island, which from that day she had never left. Hither she was led by the Kalubi of the time and some others who had "passed the god." This brute, however, she had never seen, although once she heard him roar, for it did not molest them or even appear upon their journey.

Shortly after her arrival on the island her daughter was born, on which occasion some of the women "servants of the Flower" nursed her. From that moment both she and the child were treated with the utmost care and veneration, since the Mother of the Flower and the Flower itself being in some strange way looked upon as embodiments of the natural forces of fertility, this birth was held to be the best of omens for the dwindling Pongo race. Also it was hoped that in due course the "Child of the Flower" would succeed the Mother in her office. So here they dwelt absolutely helpless and alone, occupying themselves with superintending the agriculture of the island. Most fortunately also when she was captured, Mrs. Eversley had a small Bible in her possession which she had never lost. From this she was able to teach her child to read and all that is to be learned in the pages of Holy Writ.

Often I have thought that if I were doomed to solitary confinement for life and allowed but one book, I would choose the Bible, since, in addition to all its history and the splendour of its language, it contains the record of the hope of man, and therefore should be sufficient for him. So at least it had proved to be in this case.

Oddly enough, as she told us, like her husband, Mrs. Eversley during all those endless years had never lost some kind of belief that she would one day be saved otherwise than by death.

"I always thought that you still lived and that we should meet again, John," I heard her say to him.

Also her own and her daughter's spirits were mysteriously supported, for after the first shock and disturbance of our arrival we found them cheerful people; indeed, Miss Hope was quite a merry soul. But then she had never known any other life, and human nature is very adaptable. Further, if I may say so, she had grown up a lady in the true sense of the word. After all, why should she not, seeing that her mother, the Bible and Nature had been her only associates and sources of information, if we except the poor slaves who waited on them, most of whom were mutes.

When Mrs. Eversley's story was done, we told ours, in a compressed form. It was strange to see the wonder with which these two ladies listened to its outlines, but on that I need not dwell. When it was finished I heard Miss Hope say:

"So it would seem, O Stephen Somers, that it is you who are saviour to us."

"Certainly," answered Stephen, "but why?"

"Because you see the dry Holy Flower far away in England, and you say, 'I must be Holy Father to that Flower.' Then you pay down shekels (here her Bible reading came in) for the cost of journey and hire brave hunter to kill devil-god and bring my old white-head parent with you. Oh yes, you are saviour," and she nodded her head at him very prettily.

"Of course," replied Stephen with enthusiasm; "that is, not exactly, but it is all the same thing, as I will explain later. But, Miss Hope, meanwhile could you show us the Flower?"

"Oh! Holy Mother must do that. If you look thereon without her, you die."

"Really!" said Stephen, without alluding to his little feat of wall climbing.

Well, the end of it was that after a good deal of hesitation, the Holy Mother obliged, saying that as the god was dead she supposed nothing else mattered. First, however, she went to the back of the house and clapped her hands, whereon an old woman, a mute and a very perfect specimen of an albino native, appeared and stared at us wonderingly. To her Mrs. Eversley talked upon her fingers, so rapidly that I could scarcely follow her movements. The woman bowed till her forehead nearly touched the ground, then rose and ran towards the water.

"I have sent her to fetch the paddles from the canoe," said Mrs. Eversley, "and to put my mark upon it. Now none will dare to use it to cross the lake."

"That is very wise," I replied, "as we don't want news of our whereabouts to get to the Motombo."

Next we went to the enclosure, where Mrs. Eversley with a native knife cut a string of palm fibres that was sealed with clay on to the door and one of its uprights in such a fashion that none could enter without breaking the string. The impression was made with a rude seal that she wore round her neck as a badge of office. It was a very curious object fashioned of gold and having deeply cut upon its face a rough image of an ape holding a flower in its right paw. As it was also ancient, this seemed to show that the monkey god and the orchid had been from the beginning jointly worshipped by the Pongo.

When she had opened the door, there appeared, growing in the centre of the enclosure, the most lovely plant, I should imagine, that man ever saw. It measured some eight feet across, and the leaves were dark green, long and narrow. From its various crowns rose the scapes of bloom. And oh! those blooms, of which there were about twelve, expanded now in the flowering season. The measurements made from the dried specimen I have given already, so I need not repeat them. I may say here, however, that the Pongo augured the fertility or otherwise of each succeeding year from the number of the blooms on the Holy Flower. If these were many the season would prove very fruitful; if few, less so; while if, as sometimes happened, the plant failed to flower, draught and famine were always said to follow. Truly those were glorious blossoms, standing as high as a man, with their back sheaths of vivid white barred with black, their great pouches of burnished gold and their wide wings also of gold. Then in the centre of each pouch appeared the ink-mark that did indeed exactly resemble the head of a monkey. But if this orchid astonished me, its effect upon Stephen, with whom this class of flower was a mania, may be imagined. Really he went almost mad. For a long while he glared at the plant, and finally flung himself upon his knees, causing Miss Hope to exclaim:

"What, O Stephen Somers! do you also make sacrifice to the Holy Flower?"

"Rather," he answered; "I'd—I'd—die for it!"

"You are likely to before all is done," I remarked with energy, for I hate to see a grown man make a fool of himself. There's only one thing in the world which justifies *that*, and it isn't a flower.

Mavovo and Hans had followed us into the enclosure, and I overheard a conversation between them which amused me. The gist of it was that Hans explained to Mavovo that the white people admired this weed—he called it a weed—because it was like gold, which was the god they really worshipped, although that god was known among them by many names. Mavovo, who was not at all interested in the affair, replied with a shrug that it might be so, though for his part he believed the true reason to be that the plant produced some medicine which gave courage or strength. Zulus, I may say, do not care for flowers unless they bear a fruit that is good to eat.

When I had satisfied myself with the splendour of these magnificent blooms, I asked Mrs. Eversley what certain little mounds might be that were dotted about the enclosure, beyond the circle of cultivated peaty soil which surrounded the orchid's roots.

"They are the graves of the Mothers of the Holy Flower," she answered. "There are twelve of them, and here is the spot chosen for the thirteenth, which was to have been mine."

To change the subject I asked another question, namely: If there were more such orchids growing in the country?

"No," she replied, "or at least I never heard of any. Indeed, I have always been told that this one was brought from far away generations ago. Also, under an ancient law, it is never allowed to increase. Any shoots it sends up beyond this ring must be cut off by me and destroyed with certain ceremonies. You see that seed-pod which has been left to grow on the stalk of one of last year's blooms. It is now ripe, and on the night of the next new moon, when the Kalubi comes to visit me, I must with much ritual burn it in his presence, unless it has burst before he arrives, in which case I must burn any seedlings that may spring up with almost the same ritual."

"I don't think the Kalubi will come any more; at least, not while you are here. Indeed, I am sure of it," I said.

As we were leaving the place, acting on my general principle of making sure of anything of value when I get the chance, I broke off that ripe seed-pod, which was of the size of an orange. No one was looking at the time, and as it went straight into my pocket, no one missed it.

Then, leaving Stephen and the young lady to admire this Cypripedium—or each other—in the enclosure, we three elders returned to the house to discuss matters.

"John and Mrs. Eversley," I said, "by Heaven's mercy you are reunited after a terrible separation of over twenty years. But what is to be done now? The god, it is true, is dead, and therefore the passage of the forest will be easy. But beyond it is the water which we have no means of crossing and beyond the water that old wizard, the Motombo, sits in the mouth of his cave watching like a spider in its web. And beyond the Motombo and his cave are Komba, the new Kalubi and his tribe of cannibals—"

"Cannibals!" interrupted Mrs. Eversley, "I never knew that they were cannibals. Indeed, I know little about the Pongo, whom I scarcely ever see."

"Then, madam, you must take my word for it that they are; also, as I believe, that they have every expectation of eating *us*. Now, as I presume that you do not wish to spend the rest of your lives, which would probably be short, upon this island, I want to ask how you propose to escape safely out of the Pongo country?"

They shook their heads, which were evidently empty of ideas. Only John stroked his white beard, and inquired mildly:

"What have you arranged, Allan? My dear wife and I are quite willing to leave the matter to you, who are so resourceful."

"Arranged!" I stuttered. "Really, John, under any other circumstances—" Then after a moment's reflection I called to Hans and Mavovo, who came and squatted down upon the verandah.

"Now," I said, after I had put the case to them, "what have *you* arranged?" Being devoid of any feasible suggestions, I wished to pass on that intolerable responsibility.

"My father makes a mock of us," said Mavovo solemnly. "Can a rat in a pit arrange how it is to get out with the dog that is waiting at the top? So far we have come in safety, as the rat does into the pit. Now I see nothing but death."

"That's cheerful," I said. "Your turn, Hans."

"Oh! Baas," replied the Hottentot, "for a while I grew clever again when I thought of putting the gun *Intombi* into the bamboo. But now my head is like a rotten egg, and when I try to shake wisdom out of it my brain melts and washes from side to side like the stuff in the rotten egg. Yet, yet, I have a thought—let us ask the Missie. Her brain is young and not tired, it may hit on something: to ask the Baas Stephen is no good, for already he is lost in other things," and Hans grinned feebly.

More to give myself time than for any other reason I called to Miss Hope, who had just emerged from the sacred enclosure with Stephen, and put the riddle to her, speaking very slowly and clearly, so that she might understand me. To my surprise she answered at once.

"What is a god, O Mr. Allen? Is it not more than man? Can a god be bound in a pit for a thousand years, like Satan in Bible? If a god want to move, see new country and so on, who can say no?"

"I don't quite understand," I said, to draw her out further, although, in fact, I had more than a glimmering of what she meant.

"O Allan, Holy Flower there a god, and my mother priestess. If Holy Flower tired of this land, and want to grow somewhere else, why priestess not carry it and go too?"

"Capital idea," I said, "but you see, Miss Hope, there are, or were, two gods, one of which cannot travel."

"Oh! that very easy, too. Put skin of god of the woods on to this man," and she pointed to Hans, "and who know difference? They like as two brothers already, only he smaller."

"She's got it! By Jingo, she's got it!" exclaimed Stephen in admiration.

"What Missie say?" asked Hans, suspiciously.

I told him.

"Oh! Baas," exclaimed Hans, "think of the smell inside of that god's skin when the sun shines on it. Also the god was a very big god, and I am small."

Then he turned and made a proposal to Mavovo, explaining that his stature was much better suited to the job.

"First will I die," answered the great Zulu. "Am I, who have high blood in my veins and who am a warrior, to defile myself by wrapping the skin of a dead brute about me and appear as an ape before men? Propose it to me again, Spotted Snake, and we shall quarrel."

"See here, Hans," I said. "Mavovo is right. He is a soldier and very strong in battle. You also are very strong in your wits, and by doing this you will make fools of all the Pongo. Also, Hans, it is better that you should wear the skin of a gorilla for a few hours than that I, your master, and all these should be killed."

"Yes, Baas, it is true, Baas; though for myself I almost think that, like Mavovo, I would rather die. Yet it would be sweet to deceive those Pongo once again, and, Baas, I won't see you killed just to save myself another bad smell or two. So, if you wish it, I will become a god."

Thus through the self-sacrifice of that good fellow, Hans, who is the real hero of this history, that matter was settled, if anything could be looked on as settled in our circumstances. Then we arranged that we would start upon our desperate adventure at dawn on the following morning.

Meanwhile, much remained to be done. First, Mrs. Eversley summoned her attendants, who, to the number of twelve, soon appeared in front of the verandah. It was very sad to see these poor women, all of whom were albinos and unpleasant to look on, while quite half appeared to be deaf and dumb. To these, speaking as a priestess, she explained that the god who dwelt in the woods was dead, and that therefore she must take the Holy Flower, which was called "Wife of the god" and make report to the Motombo of this dreadful catastrophe. Meanwhile, they must remain on the island and continue to cultivate the fields.

This order threw the poor creatures, who were evidently much attached to their mistress and her daughter, into a great state of consternation. The eldest of them all, a tall, thin old lady with white wool and pink eyes who looked, as Stephen said, like an Angora rabbit, prostrated herself and kissing the Mother's foot, asked when she would return, since she and the "Daughter of the Flower" were all they had to love, and without them they would die of grief.

Suppressing her evident emotion as best she could, the Mother replied that she did not know; it depended on the will of Heaven and the Motombo. Then to prevent further argument she bade them bring their picks with which they worked the land; also poles, mats, and palmstring, and help to dig up the Holy Flower. This was done under the superintendence of Stephen, who here was thoroughly in his element, although the job proved far from easy. Also it was sad, for all these women wept as they worked, while some of them who were not dumb, wailed aloud.

Even Miss Hope cried, and I could see that her mother was affected with a kind of awe. For twenty years she had been guardian of this plant, which I think she had at last not unnaturally come to look upon with some of the same veneration that was felt for it by the whole Pongo people.

"I fear," she said, "lest this sacrilege should bring misfortune upon us."

But Brother John, who held very definite views upon African superstitions, quoted the second commandment to her, and she became silent.

We got the thing up at last, or most of it, with a sufficiency of earth to keep it alive, injuring the roots as little as possible in the process. Underneath it, at a depth of about three feet, we found several things. One of these was an ancient stone fetish that was rudely shaped to the likeness of a monkey and wore a gold crown.

This object, which was small, I still have. Another was a bed of charcoal, and amongst the charcoal were some partially burnt bones, including a skull that was very little injured. This may have belonged to a woman of a low type, perhaps the first Mother of the Flower, but its general appearance reminded me of that of a gorilla. I regret that there was neither time nor light to enable me to make a proper examination of these remains, which we found it impossible to bring away.

Mrs. Eversley told me afterwards, however, that the Kalubis had a tradition that the god once possessed a wife which died before the Pongo migrated to their present home. If so, these may have been the bones of that wife. When it was finally clear of the ground on which it had grown for so many generations, the great plant was lifted on to a large mat, and after it had been packed with wet moss by Stephen in a most skilful way, for he was a perfect artist at this kind of work, the mat was bound round the roots in such a fashion that none of the contents could escape. Also each flower scape was lashed to a thin bamboo so as to prevent it from breaking on the journey. Then the whole bundle was lifted on to a kind of bamboo stretcher that we made and firmly secured to it with palm-fibre ropes.

By this time it was growing dark and all of us were tired.

"Baas," said Hans to me, as we were returning to the house, "would it not be well that Mavovo and I should take some food and go sleep in the canoe? These women will not hurt us there, but if we do not, I, who have been watching them, fear lest in the night they should make paddles of sticks and row across the lake to warn the Pongo."

Although I did not like separating our small party, I thought the idea so good that I consented to it, and presently Hans and Mavovo, armed with spears and carrying an ample supply of food, departed to the lake side.

One more incident has impressed itself upon my memory in connection with that night. It was the formal baptism of Hope by her father. I never saw a more touching ceremony, but it is one that I need not describe.

Stephen and I slept in the enclosure by the packed flower, which he would not leave out of his sight. It was as well that we did so, since about twelve o'clock by the light of the moon I saw the door in the wall open gently and the heads of some of the albino women appear through the aperture. Doubtless, they had come to steal away the holy plant they worshipped. I sat up, coughed, and lifted the rifle, whereon they fled and returned no more.

Long before dawn Brother John, his wife and daughter were up and making preparations for the march, packing a supply of food and so forth. Indeed, we breakfasted by moonlight, and at the first break of day, after Brother John had first offered up a prayer for protection, departed on our journey.

It was a strange out-setting, and I noted that both Mrs. Eversley and her daughter seemed sad at bidding good-bye to the spot where they had dwelt in utter solitude and peace for so many years; where one of them, indeed, had been born and grown up to womanhood. However, I kept on talking to distract their thoughts, and at last we were off.

I arranged that, although it was heavy for them, the two ladies, whose white robes were covered with curious cloaks made of soft prepared bark, should carry the plant as far as the canoe, thinking it was better that the Holy Flower should appear to depart in charge of its consecrated guardians. I went ahead with the rifle, then came the stretcher and the flower, while Brother John and Stephen, carrying the paddles, brought up the rear. We reached the canoe without accident, and to our great relief found Mavovo and Hans awaiting us. I learned, however, that it was fortunate they had slept in the boat, since during the night the albino women arrived with the evident object of possessing themselves of it, and only ran away when they saw that it was guarded. As we were making ready the canoe those unhappy slaves appeared in a body and throwing themselves upon their faces with piteous words, or those of them who could not speak, by signs, implored the Mother not to desert them, till both she and Hope began to cry. But there was no help for it, so we pushed off as quickly as we could, leaving the albinos weeping and wailing upon the bank.

I confess that I, too, felt compunction at abandoning them thus, but what could we do? I only trust that no harm came to them, but of course we never heard anything as to their fate.

On the further side of the lake we hid away the canoe in the bushes where we had found it, and began our march. Stephen and Mavovo, being the two strongest among us, now carried the plant, and although Stephen never murmured at its weight, how the Zulu did swear after the first few hours! I could fill a page with his objurgations at what he considered an act of insanity, and if I had space, should like to do so, for really some of them were most amusing. Had it not been for his friendship for Stephen I think that he would have thrown it down.

We crossed the Garden of the god, where Mrs. Eversley told me the Kalubi must scatter the sacred seed twice a year, thus confirming the story that we had heard. It seems that it was then, as he made his long journey through the forest, that the treacherous and horrid brute which we had killed, would attack the priest of whom it had grown weary. But, and this shows the animal's cunning, the onslaught always took place *after* he had sown the seed which would in due season produce the food it ate. Our Kalubi, it is true, was killed before we had reached the Garden, which seems an exception to the rule. Perhaps, however, the gorilla knew that his object in visiting it was not to provide for its needs. Or perhaps our presence excited it to immediate action.

Who can analyse the motives of a gorilla?

These attacks were generally spread over a year and a half. On the first occasion the god which always accompanied the priest to the garden and back again, would show animosity by roaring at him. On the second he would seize his hand and bite off one of the fingers, as happened to our Kalubi, a wound that generally caused death from blood poisoning. If, however, the priest survived, on the third visit it killed him, for the most part by crushing his head in its mighty jaws. When making these visits the Kalubi was accompanied by certain dedicated youths, some of whom the god always put to death. Those who had made the journey six times without molestation were selected for further special trials, until at last only two remained who were declared to have "passed" or "been accepted by" the god. These youths were treated with great honour, as in the instance of Komba and on the destruction of the Kalubi, one of them took his office, which he generally filled without much accident, for a minimum of ten years, and perhaps much longer.

Mrs. Eversley knew nothing of the sacramental eating of the remains of the Kalubi, or of the final burial of his bones in the wooden coffins that we had seen, for such things, although they undoubtedly happened, were kept from her. She added, that each of the three Kalubis whom she had known, ultimately went almost mad through terror at his approaching end, especially after the preliminary roarings and the biting off of the finger. In truth uneasy lay the head that wore a crown in Pongo-land, a crown that, mind you, might not be refused upon pain of death by torture. Personally, I can imagine nothing more terrible than the haunted existence of these poor kings whose pomp and power must terminate in such a fashion.

I asked her whether the Motombo ever visited the god. She answered, Yes, once in every five years. Then after many mystic ceremonies he spent a week in the forest at a time of full moon. One of the Kalubis had told her that on this occasion he had seen the Motombo and the god sitting together under a tree, each with his arm round the other's neck and apparently talking "like brothers." With the exception of certain tales of its almost supernatural cunning, this was all that I could learn about the god of the Pongos which I have sometimes been tempted to believe was really a devil hid in the body of a huge and ancient ape.

No, there was one more thing which I quote because it bears out Babemba's story. It seems that captives from other tribes were sometimes turned into the forest that the god might amuse itself by killing them. This, indeed, was the fate to which we ourselves had been doomed in accordance with the hateful Pongo custom.

Certainly, thought I to myself when she had done, I did a good deed in sending that monster to whatever dim region it was destined to inhabit, where I sincerely trust it found all the dead Kalubis and its other victims ready to give it an appropriate welcome.

AFTER CROSSING THE GOD'S GARDEN, we came to the clearing of the Fallen Tree, and found the brute's skin pegged out as we had left it, though shrunken in size. Only it had evidently been visited by a horde of the forest ants which, fortunately for Hans, had eaten away every particle of flesh, while leaving the hide itself absolutely untouched, I suppose because it was too tough for them. I never saw a neater job. Moreover, these industrious little creatures had devoured the beast itself. Nothing remained of it except the clean, white bones lying in the exact position in which we had left the carcase. Atom by atom that marching myriad army had eaten all and departed on its way into the depths of the forest, leaving this sign of their passage.

How I wished that we could carry off the huge skeleton to add to my collection of trophies, but this was impossible. As Brother John said, any museum would have been glad to purchase it for hundreds of pounds, for I do not suppose that its like exists in the world. But it was too heavy; all I could do was to impress its peculiarities upon my mind by a close study of the mighty bones. Also I picked out of the upper right arm, and kept the bullet I had fired when it carried off the Kalubi. This I found had sunk into and shattered the bone, but without absolutely breaking it.

On we went again bearing with us the god's skin, having first stuffed the head, hands and feet (these, I mean the hands and feet, had been cleaned out by the ants) with wet moss in order to preserve their shape. It was no light burden, at least so declared Brother John and Hans, who bore it between them upon a dead bough from the fallen tree.

Of the rest of our journey to the water's edge there is nothing to tell, except that notwithstanding our loads, we found it easier to walk down that steep mountain side than it had been to ascend the same. Still our progress was but slow, and when at length we reached the burying-place only about an hour remained to sunset. There we sat down to rest and eat, also to discuss the situation.

What was to be done? The arm of stagnant water lay near to us, but we had no boat with which to cross to the further shore. And what was that shore? A cave where a creature who seemed to be but half-human, sat watching like a spider in its web. Do not let it be supposed that this question of escape had been absent from our minds. On the contrary, we had even thought of trying to drag the canoe in which we crossed to and from the island of the Flower through the forest. The idea was abandoned, however, because we found that being hollowed from a single log with a bottom four or five inches thick, it was impossible for us to carry it so much as fifty yards. What then could we do without a boat? Swimming seemed to be out of the question because of the crocodiles. Also on inquiry I discovered that of the whole party Stephen and I alone could swim. Further there was no wood of which to make a raft.

I called to Hans and leaving the rest in the graveyard where we knew that they were safe, we went down to the edge of the water to study the situation, being careful to keep ourselves hidden behind the reeds and bushes of the mangrove tribe with which it was fringed. Not that there was much fear of our being seen, for the day, which had been very hot, was closing in and a great storm, heralded by black and bellying clouds, was gathering fast, conditions which must render us practically invisible at a distance.

We looked at the dark, slimy water—also at the crocodiles which sat upon its edge in dozens waiting, eternally waiting, for what, I wondered. We looked at the sheer opposing cliff, but save where a black hole marked the cave mouth, far as the eye could see, the water came up against it, as that of a moat does against the wall of a castle. Obviously, therefore, the only line of escape ran through this cave, for, as I have explained, the channel by which I presume Babemba reached the open lake, was now impracticable. Lastly, we searched to see if there was any fallen log upon which we could possibly propel ourselves to the other side, and found—nothing that could be made to serve, no, nor, as I have said, any dry reeds or brushwood out of which we might fashion a raft.

"Unless we can get a boat, here we must stay," I remarked to Hans, who was seated with me behind a screen of rushes at the water's edge.

He made no answer, and as I thought, in a sort of subconscious way, I engaged myself in watching a certain tragedy of the insect world. Between two stout reeds a forest spider of the very largest sort had spun a web as big as a lady's open parasol. There in the midst of this web of which the bottom strands almost touched the water, sat the spider waiting for its prey, as the crocodiles were waiting on the banks, as the great ape had waited for the Kalubis, as Death waits for Life, as the Motombo was waiting for God knows what.

It rather resembled the Motombo in his cave, did that huge, black spider with just a little patch of white upon its head, or so I thought fancifully enough. Then came the tragedy. A great, white moth of the Hawk species began to dart to and fro between the reeds, and presently struck the web on its lower side some three inches above the water. Like a flash that spider was upon it. It embraced the victim with its long legs to still its tremendous battlings. Next, descending below, it began to make the body fast, when something happened. From the still surface of the water beneath poked up the mouth of a very large fish which quite quietly closed upon the spider and sank again into the depths, taking with it a portion of the web and thereby setting the big moth free. With a struggle it loosed itself, fell on to a piece of wood and floated away, apparently little the worse for the encounter.

"Did you see that, Baas?" said Hans, pointing to the broken and empty web. "While you were thinking, I was praying to your reverend father the Predikant, who taught me how to do it, and he has sent us a sign from the Place of Fire."

Even then I could not help laughing to myself as I pictured what my dear father's face would be like if he were able to hear his convert's remarks. An analysis of Hans's religious views would be really interesting, and I only regret that I never made one. But sticking to business I merely asked:

"What sign?"

"Baas, this sign: That web is the Motombo's cave. The big spider is the Motombo. The white moth is us, Baas, who are caught in the web and going to be eaten."

"Very pretty, Hans," I said, "but what is the fish that came up and swallowed the spider so that the moth fell on the wood and floated away?"

"Baas, *you* are the fish, who come up softly, softly out of the water in the dark, and shoot the Motombo with the little rifle, and then the rest of us, who are the moth, fall into the canoe and float away. There is a storm about to break, Baas, and who will see you swim the stream in the storm and the night?"

"The crocodiles," I suggested.

"Baas, I didn't see a crocodile eat the fish. I think the fish is laughing down there with the fat spider in its stomach. Also when there is a storm crocodiles go to bed because they are afraid lest the lightning should kill them for their sins."

Now I remembered that I had often heard, and indeed to some extent noted, that these great reptiles do vanish in disturbed weather, probably because their food hides away. However that might be, in an instant I made up my mind.

As soon as it was quite dark I would swim the water, holding the little rifle, *Intombi*, above my head, and try to steal the canoe. If the old wizard was watching, which I hoped might not be the case, well, I must deal with him as best I could. I knew the desperate nature of the expedient, but there was no other way. If we could not get a boat we must remain in that foodless forest until we starved. Or if we returned to the island of the Flower, there ere long we should certainly be attacked and destroyed by Komba and the Pongos when they came to look for our bodies.

"I'll try it, Hans," I said.

"Yes, Baas, I thought you would. I'd come, too, only I can't swim and when I was drowning I might make a noise, because one forgets oneself then, Baas. But it will be all right, for if it were otherwise I am sure that your reverend father would have shown us so in the sign. The moth floated off quite comfortably on the wood, and just now I saw it spread its wings and fly away. And the fish, ah! how he laughs with that fat old spider in his stomach!"

XVIII

Fate Stabs

We went back to the others whom we found crouched on the ground among the coffins, looking distinctly depressed. No wonder; night was closing in, the thunder was beginning to growl and echo through the forest and rain to fall in big drops. In short, although Stephen remarked that every cloud has a silver lining, a proverb which, as I told him, I seemed to have heard before, in no sense could the outlook be considered bright.

"Well, Allan, what have you arranged?" asked Brother John, with a faint attempt at cheerfulness as he let go of his wife's hand. In those days he always seemed to be holding his wife's hand.

"Oh!" I answered, "I am going to get the canoe so that we can all row over comfortably."

They stared at me, and Miss Hope, who was seated by Stephen, asked in her usual Biblical language:

"Have you the wings of a dove that you can fly, O Mr. Allan?"

"No," I answered, "but I have the fins of a fish, or something like them, and I can swim."

Now there arose a chorus of expostulation.

"You shan't risk it," said Stephen, "I can swim as well as you and I'm younger. I'll go, I want a bath."

"That you will have, O Stephen," interrupted Miss Hope, as I thought in some alarm. "The latter rain from heaven will make you clean." (By now it was pouring.)

"Yes, Stephen, you can swim," I said, "but you will forgive me for saying that you are not particularly deadly with a rifle, and clean shooting may be the essence of this business. Now listen to me, all of you. I am going. I hope that I shall succeed, but if I fail it does not so very much matter, for you will be no worse off than you were before. There are three pairs of you. John and his wife; Stephen and Miss Hope; Mavovo and Hans. If the odd man of the party comes to grief, you will have to choose a new captain, that is all, but while I lead I mean to be obeyed."

Then Mavovo, to whom Hans had been talking, spoke.

"My father Macumazana is a brave man. If he lives he will have done his duty. If he dies he will have done his duty still better, and, on the earth or in the under-world among the spirits of our fathers, his name shall be great for ever; yes, his name shall be a song."

When Brother John had translated these words, which I thought fine, there was silence.

"Now," I said, "come with me to the water's edge, all of you. You will be in less danger from the lightning there, where are no tall trees. And while I am gone, do you ladies dress up Hans in that gorilla-skin as best you can, lacing it on to him with some of that palm-fibre string which we brought with us, and filling out the hollows and the head with leaves or reeds. I want him to be ready when I come back with the canoe."

Hans groaned audibly, but made no objection and we started with our impedimenta down to the edge of the estuary where we hid behind a clump of mangrove bushes and tall, feathery reeds. Then I took off some of my clothes, stripping in fact to my flannel shirt and the cotton pants I wore, both of which were grey in colour and therefore almost invisible at night.

Now I was ready and Hans handed me the little rifle.

"It is at full cock, Baas, with the catch on," he said, "and carefully loaded. Also I have wrapped the lining of my hat, which is very full of grease, for the hair makes grease especially in hot weather, Baas, round the lock to keep away the wet from the cap and powder. It is not tied, Baas, only twisted. Give the rifle a shake and it will fall off."

"I understand," I said, and gripped the gun with my left hand by the tongue just forward of the hammer, in such a fashion that the horrid greased rag from Hans's hat was held tight over the lock and cap. Then I shook hands with the others and when I came to Miss Hope I am proud to add that she spontaneously and of her own accord imprinted a kiss upon my mediaeval brow. I felt inclined to return it, but did not.

"It is the kiss of peace, O Allan," she said. "May you go and return in peace."

"Thank you," I said, "but get on with dressing Hans in his new clothes."

Stephen muttered something about feeling ashamed of himself. Brother John put up a vigorous and well-directed prayer. Mavovo saluted with the copper assegai and began to give me *sibonga* or Zulu titles of praise beneath his breath, and Mrs. Eversley said:

"Oh! I thank God that I have lived to see a brave English gentleman again," which I thought a great compliment to my nation and myself, though when I afterwards discovered that she herself was English by birth, it took off some of the polish.

Next, just after a vivid flash of lightning, for the storm had broken in earnest now, I ran swiftly to the water's edge, accompanied by Hans, who was determined to see the last of me.

"Get back, Hans, before the lightning shows you," I said, as I slid gently from a mangrove-root into that filthy stream, "and tell them to keep my coat and trousers dry if they can."

"Good-bye, Baas," he murmured, and I heard that he was sobbing. "Keep a good heart, O Baas of Baases. After all, this is nothing to the vultures of the Hill of Slaughter. *Intombi* pulled us through then, and so she will again, for she knows who can hold her straight!"

That was the last I heard of Hans, for if he said any more, the hiss of the torrential rain smothered his words.

Oh! I had tried to "keep a good heart" before the others, but it is beyond my powers to describe the deadly fright I felt, perhaps the worst of all my life, which is saying a great deal. Here I was starting on one of the maddest ventures that was ever undertaken by man. I needn't put its points again, but that which appealed to me most at the moment was the crocodiles. I have always hated crocodiles since—well, never mind—and the place was as full of them as the ponds at Ascension are of turtles.

Still I swam on. The estuary was perhaps two hundred yards wide, not more, no great distance for a good swimmer as I was in those days. But then I had to hold the rifle above the water with my left hand at all cost, for if once it went beneath it would be useless. Also I was desperately afraid of being seen in the lightning flashes, although to minimise this risk I had kept my dark-coloured cloth hat upon my head. Lastly there was the lightning itself to fear, for it was fearful and continuous and seemed to be striking along the water. It was a fact that a fire-ball or something of the sort hit the surface within a few yards of me, as though it had aimed at the rifle-barrel and just missed. Or so I thought, though it may have been a crocodile rising at the moment.

In one way, or rather, in two, however, I was lucky. The first was the complete absence of wind which must have raised waves that might have swamped me and would at any rate have wetted the rifle. The second was that there was no fear of my losing my path for in the mouth of the cave I could see the glow of the fires which burned on either side of the Motombo's seat. They served the same purpose to me as did the lamp of the lady called Hero to her lover Leander when he swam the Hellespont to pay her clandestine visits at night. But he had something pleasant to look forward to, whereas I—! Still, there was another point in common between us. Hero, if I remember right, was a priestess of the Greek goddess of love, whereas the party who waited me was also in a religious line of business. Only, as I firmly believe, he was a priest of the devil.

I suppose that swim took me about a quarter-of-an-hour, for I went slowly to save my strength, although the crocodiles suggested haste. But thank Heaven they never appeared to complicate matters. Now I was quite near the cave, and now I was beneath the overhanging roof and in the shallow water of the little bay that formed a harbour for the canoe. I stood upon my feet on the rock bottom, the water coming up to my breast, and peered about me, while I rested and worked my left arm, stiff with the up-holding of the gun, to and fro. The fires had burnt somewhat low and until my eyes were freed from the raindrops and grew accustomed to the light of the place I could not see clearly.

I took the rag from round the lock of the rifle, wiped the wet off the barrel with it and let it fall. Then I loosed the catch and by touching a certain mechanism, made the rifle hair-triggered. Now I looked again and began to make out things. There was the platform and there, alas! on it sat the toad-like Motombo. But his back was to me; he was gazing not towards the water, but down the cave. I hesitated for one fateful moment. Perhaps the priest was asleep, perhaps I could get the canoe away without shooting. I did not like the job; moreover, his head was held forward and invisible, and how was I to make certain of killing him with a shot in the back? Lastly, if possible, I wished to avoid firing because of the report.

At that instant the Motombo wheeled round. Some instinct must have warned him of my presence, for the silence was gravelike save for the soft splash of the rain without. As he turned the lightning blazed and he saw me.

"It is the white man," he muttered to himself in his hissing whisper, while I waited through the following darkness with the rifle at my shoulder, "the white man who shot me long, long ago, and again he has a gun! Oh! Fate stabs, doubtless the god is dead and I too must die!"

Then as if some doubt struck him he lifted the horn to summon help.

Again the lightning flashed and was accompanied by a fearful crack of thunder. With a prayer for skill, I covered his head and fired by the glare of it just as the trumpet touched his lips. It fell from his hand. He seemed to shrink together, and moved no more.

Oh! thank God, thank God! in this supreme moment of trial the art of which I am a master had not failed me. If my hand had shaken ever so little, if my nerves, strained to breaking point, had played me false in the least degree, if the rag from Hans's hat had not sufficed to keep away the damp from the cap and powder! Well, this history would never have been written and there would have been some more bones in the graveyard of the Kalubis, that is all!

For a moment I waited, expecting to see the women attendants dart from the doorways in the sides of the cave, and to hear them sound a shrill alarm. None appeared, and I guessed that the rattle of the thunder had swallowed up the crack of the rifle, a noise, be it remembered, that none of them had ever heard. For an unknown number of years this ancient creature, I suppose, had squatted day and night upon that platform, whence, I daresay, it was difficult for him to move. So after they had wrapped his furs round him at sunset and made up the fires to keep him warm, why should his women come to disturb him unless he called them with his horn? Probably it was not even lawful that they should do so.

Somewhat reassured I waded forward a few paces and loosed the canoe which was tied by the prow. Then I scrambled into it, and laying down the rifle, took one of the paddles and began to push out of the creek. Just then the lightning flared once more, and by it I caught sight of the Motombo's face that was now within a few feet of my own. It seemed to be resting almost on his knees, and its appearance was dreadful. In the centre of the forehead was a blue mark where the bullet had entered, for I had made no mistake in that matter. The deep-set round eyes were open and, all their fire gone, seemed to stare at me from beneath the overhanging brows. The massive jaw had fallen and the red tongue hung out upon the pendulous lip. The leather-like skin of the bloated cheeks had assumed an ashen hue still streaked and mottled with brown.

Oh! the thing was horrible, and sometimes when I am out of sorts, it haunts me to this day. Yet that creature's blood does not lie heavy on my mind, of it my conscience is not afraid. His end was necessary to save the innocent and I am sure that it was well deserved. For he was a devil, akin to the great god ape I had slain in the forest, to whom, by the way, he bore a most remarkable resemblance in death. Indeed if their heads had been laid side by side at a little distance, it would not have been too easy to tell them apart with their projecting brows, beardless, retreating chins and yellow tushes at the corners of the mouth.

Presently I was clear of the cave. Still for a while I lay to at one side of it against the towering cliff, both to listen in case what I had done should be discovered, and for fear lest the lightning which was still bright, although the storm centre was rapidly passing away, should reveal me to any watchers.

For quite ten minutes I hid thus, and then, determining to risk it, paddled softly towards the opposite bank keeping, however, a little to the west of the cave and taking my line by a certain very tall tree which, as I had noted, towered up against the sky at the back of the graveyard.

As it happened my calculations were accurate and in the end I directed the bow of the canoe into the rushes behind which I had left my companions. Just then the moon began to struggle out through the thinning rain-clouds, and by its light they saw me, and I saw what for a moment I took to be the gorilla-god himself waddling forward to seize the boat. There was the dreadful brute exactly as he had appeared in the forest, except that it seemed a little smaller.

Then I remembered and laughed and that laugh did me a world of good.

"Is that you, Baas?" said a muffled voice, speaking apparently from the middle of the gorilla. "Are you safe, Baas?"

"Of course," I answered, "or how should I be here?" adding cheerfully, "Are you comfortable in that nice warm skin on this wet night, Hans?"

"Oh! Baas," answered the voice, "tell me what happened. Even in this stink I burn to know."

"Death happened to the Motombo, Hans. Here, Stephen, give me your hand and my clothes, and, Mavovo, hold the rifle and the canoe while I put them on."

Then I landed and stepping into the reeds, pulled off my wet shirt and pants, which I stuffed away into the big pockets of my shooting coat, for I did not want to lose them, and put on the dry things that, although scratchy, were quite good enough clothing in that warm climate. After this I treated myself to a good sup of brandy from the flask, and ate some food which I seemed to require. Then I told them the story, and cutting short their demonstrations of wonder and admiration, bade them place the Holy Flower in the canoe and get in themselves. Next with the help of Hans who poked out his fingers through the skin of the gorilla's arms, I carefully re-loaded the rifle, setting the last cap on the nipple. This done, I joined them in the canoe, taking my seat in the prow and bidding Brother John and Stephen paddle.

Making a circuit to avoid observation as before, in a very short time we reached the mouth of the cave. I leant forward and peeped round the western wall of rock. Nobody seemed to be stirring. There the fires burned dimly, there the huddled shape of the Motombo still crouched upon the platform. Silently, silently we disembarked, and I formed our procession while the others looked askance at the horrible face of the dead Motombo.

I headed it, then came the Mother of the Flower, followed by Hans, playing his part of the god of the forest; then Brother John and Stephen carrying the Holy Flower. After it walked Hope, while Mavovo brought up the rear. Near to one of the fires, as I had noted on our first passage of the cave, lay a pile of the torches which I have already mentioned. We lit some of them, and at a sign from me, Mavovo dragged the canoe back into its little dock and tied the cord to its post. Its appearance there, apparently undisturbed, might, I thought, make our crossing of the water seem even more mysterious. All this while I watched the doors in the sides of the cave, expecting every moment to see the women rush out. But none came. Perhaps they slept, or perhaps they were absent; I do not know to this day.

We started, and in solemn silence threaded our way down the windings of the cave, extinguishing our torches as soon as we saw light at its inland outlet. At a few paces from its mouth stood a sentry. His back was towards the cave, and in the uncertain gleams of the moon, struggling with the clouds, for a thin rain still fell, he never noted us till we were right on to him. Then he turned and saw, and at the awful sight of this procession of the gods of his land, threw up his arms, and without a word fell senseless. Although I never asked, I think that Mavovo took measures to prevent his awakening. At any rate when I looked back later on, I observed that he was carrying a big Pongo spear with a long shaft, instead of the copper weapon which he had taken from one of the coffins.

On we marched towards Rica Town, following the easy path by which we had come. As I have said, the country was very deserted and the inhabitants of such huts as we passed were evidently fast asleep.

Also there were no dogs in this land to awake them with their barking. Between the cave and Rica we were not, I think, seen by a single soul.

Through that long night we pushed on as fast was we could travel, only stopping now and again for a few minutes to rest the bearers of the Holy Flower. Indeed at times Mrs. Eversley relieved her husband at this task, but Stephen, being very strong, carried his end of the stretcher throughout the whole journey.

Hans, of course, was much oppressed by the great weight of the gorilla skin, which, although it had shrunk a good deal, remained as heavy as ever. But he was a tough old fellow, and on the whole got on better than might have been expected, though by the time we reached the town he was sometimes obliged to follow the example of the god itself and help himself forward with his hands, going on all fours, as a gorilla generally does.

We reached the broad, long street of Rica about half an hour before dawn, and proceeded down it till we were past the Feast-house still quite unobserved, for as yet none were stirring on that wet morning. Indeed it was not until we were within a hundred yards of the harbour that a woman possessed of the virtue, or vice, of early rising, who had come from a hut to work in her garden, saw us and raised an awful, piercing scream.

"The gods!" she screamed. "The gods are leaving the land and taking the white men with them."

Instantly there arose a hubbub in the houses. Heads were thrust out of the doors and people ran into the gardens, every one of whom began to yell till one might have thought that a massacre was in progress. But as yet no one came near us, for they were afraid.

"Push on," I cried, "or all is lost."

They answered nobly. Hans struggled forward on all fours, for he was nearly done and his hideous garment was choking him, while Stephen and Brother John, exhausted though they were with the weight of the great plant, actually broke into a feeble trot. We came to the harbour and there, tied to the wharf, was the same canoe in which we had crossed to Pongo-land. We sprang into it and cut the fastenings with my knife, having no time to untie them, and pushed off from the wharf.

By now hundreds of people, among them many soldiers were hard upon and indeed around us, but still they seemed too frightened to do anything. So far the inspiration of Hans' disguise had saved us. In the midst of them, by the light of the rising sun, I recognised Komba, who ran up, a great spear in his hand, and for a moment halted amazed.

Then it was that the catastrophe happened which nearly cost us all our lives.

Hans, who was in the stern of the canoe, began to faint from exhaustion, and in his efforts to obtain air, for the heat and stench of the skin were overpowering him, thrust his head out through the lacings of the hide beneath the reed-stuffed mask of the gorilla, which fell over languidly upon his shoulder. Komba saw his ugly little face and knew it again.

"It is a trick!" he roared. "These white devils have killed the god and stolen the Holy Flower and its priestess. The yellow man is wrapped in the skin of the god. To the boats! To the boats!"

"Paddle," I shouted to Brother John and Stephen, "paddle for your lives! Mavovo, help me get up the sail."

As it chanced on that stormy morning the wind was blowing strongly towards the mainland.

We laboured at the mast, shipped it and hauled up the mat sail, but slowly for we were awkward at the business. By the time that it began to draw the paddles had propelled us about four hundred yards from the wharf, whence many canoes, with their sails already set, were starting in pursuit. Standing in the prow of the first of these, and roaring curses and vengeance at us, was Komba, the new Kalubi, who shook a great spear above his head.

An idea occurred to me, who knew that unless something were done we must be overtaken and killed by these skilled boatmen. Leaving Mavovo to attend to the sail, I scrambled aft, and thrusting aside the fainting Hans, knelt down in the stern of the canoe. There was still one charge, or rather one cap, left, and I meant to use it. I put up the largest flapsight, lifted the little rifle and covered Komba, aiming at the point of his chin. *Intombi* was not sighted for or meant to use at this great distance, and only by this means of allowing for the drop of the bullet, could I hope to hit the man in the body.

The sail was drawing well now and steadied the boat, also, being still under the shelter of the land, the water was smooth as that of a pond, so really I had a very good firing platform. Moreover, weary though I was, my vital forces rose to the emergency and I felt myself grow rigid as a statue. Lastly, the light was good, for the sun rose behind me, its level rays shining full on to my mark. I held my breath and touched the trigger. The charge exploded sweetly and almost at the instant; as the smoke drifted to one side, I saw Komba throw up his arms and fall backwards into the canoe. Then, quite a long while afterwards, or so it seemed, the breeze brought the faint sound of the thud of that fateful bullet to our ears.

Though perhaps I ought not to say so, it was really a wonderful shot in all the circumstances, for, as I learned afterwards, the ball struck just where I hoped that it might, in the centre of the breast, piercing the heart. Indeed, taking everything into consideration, I think that those four shots which I fired in Pongo-land are the real record of my career as a marksman. The first at night broke the arm of the gorilla god and would have killed him had not the charge hung fire and given him time to protect his head. The second did kill him in the midst of a great scrimmage when everything was moving. The third, fired by the glare of lightning after a long swim, slew the Motombo, and the fourth, loosed at this great distance from a moving boat, was the bane of that cold-blooded and treacherous man, Komba, who thought that he had trapped us to Pongo-land to be murdered and eaten as a sacrifice. Lastly there was always the consciousness that no mistake must be made, since with but four percussion caps it could not be retrieved.

I am sure that I could not have done so well with any other rifle, however modern and accurate it might be. But to this little Purdey weapon I had been accustomed from my youth, and that, as any marksman will know, means a great deal. I seemed to know it and it seemed to know me. It hangs on my wall to this day, although of course I never use it now in our breech-loading era. Unfortunately, however, a local gunsmith to whom I sent it to have the lock cleaned, re-browned it and scraped and varnished the stock, etc., without authority, making it look almost new again. I preferred it in its worn and scratched condition.

To return: the sound of the shot, like that of John Peel's horn, aroused Hans from his sleep. He thrust his head between my legs and saw Komba fall.

"Oh! beautiful, Baas, beautiful!" he said faintly. "I am sure that the ghost of your reverend father cannot kill his enemies more nicely down there among the Fires. Beautiful!" and the silly old fellow fell to kissing my boots, or what remained of them, after which I gave him the last of the brandy.

This quite brought him to himself again, especially when he was free from that filthy skin and had washed his head and hands.

The effect of the death of Komba upon the Pongos was very strange. All the other canoes clustered round that in which he lay. Then, after a hurried consultation, they hauled down their sails and paddled back to the wharf. Why they did this I cannot tell. Perhaps they thought that he was bewitched, or only wounded and required the attentions of a medicine-man. Perhaps it was not lawful for them to proceed except under the guidance of some reserve Kalubi who had "passed the god" and who was on shore. Perhaps it was necessary, according to their rites, that the body of their chief should be landed with certain ceremonies. I do not know. It is impossible to be sure as to the mysterious motives that actuate many of these remote African tribes.

At any rate the result was that it gave us a great start and a chance of life, who must otherwise have died upon the spot. Outside the bay the breeze blew merrily, taking us across the lake at a spanking pace, until about midday when it began to fall. Fortunately, however, it did not altogether drop till three o'clock by which time the coast of Mazituland was comparatively near; we could even distinguish a speck against the skyline which we knew was the Union Jack that Stephen had set upon the crest of a little hill.

During those hours of peace we ate the food that remained to us, washed ourselves as thoroughly as we could and rested. Well was it, in view of what followed, that we had this time of repose. For just as the breeze was failing I looked aft and there, coming up behind us, still holding the wind, was the whole fleet of Pongo canoes, thirty or forty of them perhaps, each carrying an average of about twenty men. We sailed on for as long as we could, for though our progress was but slow, it was quicker than what we could have made by paddling. Also it was necessary that we should save our strength for the last trial.

I remember that hour very well, for in the nervous excitement of it every little thing impressed itself upon my mind. I remember even the shape of the clouds that floated over us, remnants of the storm of the previous night. One was like a castle with a broken-down turret showing a staircase within; another had a fantastic resemblance to a wrecked ship with a hole in her starboard bow, two of her masts broken and one standing with some fragments of sails flapping from it, and so forth.

Then there was the general aspect of the great lake, especially at a spot where two currents met, causing little waves which seemed to fight with each other and fall backwards in curious curves. Also there were shoals of small fish, something like chub in shape, with round mouths and very white stomachs, which suddenly appeared upon the surface, jumping at invisible flies. These attracted a number of birds that resembled gulls of a light build. They had coal-black heads, white backs, greyish wings, and slightly webbed feet, pink as coral, with which they seized the small fish, uttering as they did so, a peculiar and plaintive cry that ended in a long-drawn *e-e-é*. The father of the flock, whose head seemed to be white like his back, perhaps from age, hung above them, not troubling to fish himself, but from time to time forcing one of the company to drop what he had caught, which he retrieved before it reached the water. Such are some of the small things that come back to me, though there were others too numerous and trivial to mention.

When the breeze failed us at last we were perhaps something over three miles from the shore, or rather from the great bed of reeds which at this spot grow in the shallows off the Mazitu coast to a breadth of seven or eight hundred yards, where the water becomes too deep for them. The Pongos were then about a mile and a half behind. But as the wind favoured them for a few minutes more and, having plenty of hands, they could help themselves on by paddling, when at last it died to a complete calm, the distance between us was not more than one mile. This meant that they must cover four miles of water, while we covered three.

Letting down our now useless sail and throwing it and the mast overboard to lighten the canoe, since the sky showed us that there was no more hope of wind, we began to paddle as hard as we could. Fortunately the two ladies were able to take their share in this exercise, since they had learned it upon the Lake of the Flower, where it seemed they kept a private canoe upon the other side of the island which was used for fishing. Hans, who was still weak, we set to steer with a paddle aft, which he did in a somewhat erratic fashion.

A stern chase is proverbially a long chase, but still the enemy with their skilled rowers came up fast. When we were a mile from the reeds they were within half a mile of us, and as we tired the proportion of distance lessened. When we were two hundred yards from the reeds they were not more than fifty or sixty yards behind, and then the real struggle began.

It was short but terrible. We threw everything we could overboard, including the ballast stones at the bottom of the canoe and the heavy hide of the gorilla. This, as it proved, was fortunate, since the thing sank but slowly and the foremost Pongo boats halted a minute to recover so precious a relic, checking the others behind them, a circumstance that helped us by twenty or thirty yards.

"Over with the plant!" I said.

But Stephen, looking quite old from exhaustion and with the sweat streaming from him as he laboured at his unaccustomed paddle, gasped:

"For Heaven's sake, no, after all we have gone through to get it."

So I didn't insist; indeed there was neither time nor breath for argument.

Now we were in the reeds, for thanks to the flag which guided us, we had struck the big hippopotamus lane exactly, and the Pongos, paddling like demons, were about thirty yards behind. Thankful was I that those interesting people had never learned the use of bows and arrows, and that their spears were too heavy to throw. By now, or rather some time before, old Babemba and the Mazitu had seen us, as had our Zulu hunters. Crowds of them were wading through the shallows towards us, yelling encouragements as they came. The Zulus, too, opened a rather wild fire, with the result that one of the bullets struck our canoe and another touched the brim of my hat. A third, however, killed a Pongo, which caused some confusion in the ranks of Tusculum.

But we were done and they came on remorselessly. When their leading boat was not more than ten yards from us and we were perhaps two hundred from the shore, I drove my paddle downwards and finding that the water was less than four feet deep, shouted:

"Overboard, all, and wade. It's our last chance!"

We scrambled out of that canoe the prow of which, as I left it the last, I pushed round across the water-lane to obstruct those of the Pongo. Now I think all would have gone well had it not been for Stephen, who after he had floundered forward a few paces in the mud, bethought him of his beloved orchid. Not only did he return to try to rescue it, he also actually persuaded his friend Mavovo to accompany him. They got back to the boat and began to lift the plant out when the Pongo fell upon them, striking at them with their spears over the width of our canoe. Mavovo struck back with the weapon he had taken from the Pongo sentry at the cave mouth, and killed or wounded one of them. Then some one hurled a ballast stone at him which caught him on the side of the head and knocked him down into the water, whence he rose and reeled back, almost senseless, till some of our people got hold of him and dragged him to the shore.

So Stephen was left alone, dragging at the great orchid, till a Pongo reaching over the canoe drove a spear through his shoulder. He let go of the orchid because he must and tried to retreat. Too late! Half a dozen or more of the Pongo pushed themselves between the stern or bow of our canoe and the reeds, and waded forward to kill him. I could not help, for to tell the truth at the moment I was stuck in a mud-hole made by the hoof of a hippopotamus, while the Zulu hunters and the Mazitu were as yet too far off. Surely he must have died had it not been for the courage of the girl Hope, who, while wading shorewards a little in front of me, had turned and seen his plight. Back she came, literally bounding through the water like a leopard whose cubs are in danger.

Reaching Stephen before the Pongo she thrust herself between him and them and proceeded to address them with the utmost vigour in their own language, which of course she had learned from those of the albinos who were not mutes.

What she said I could not exactly catch because of the shouts of the advancing Mazitu. I gathered, however, that she was anathematizing them in the words of some old and potent curse that was only used by the guardians of the Holy Flower, which consigned them, body and spirit, to a dreadful doom. The effect of this malediction, which by the way neither the young lady nor her mother would repeat to me afterwards, was certainly remarkable. Those men who heard it, among them the would-be slayers of Stephen, stayed their hands and even inclined their heads towards the young priestess, as though in reverence or deprecation, and thus remained for sufficient time for her to lead the wounded Stephen out of danger. This she did wading backwards by his side and keeping her eyes fixed full upon the Pongo. It was perhaps the most curious rescue that I ever saw.

The Holy Flower, I should add, they recaptured and carried off, for I saw it departing in one of their canoes. That was the end of my orchid hunt and of the money which I hoped to make by the sale of this floral treasure. I wonder what became of it. I have good reason to believe that it was never replanted on the Island of the Flower, so perhaps it was borne back to the dim and unknown land in the depths of Africa whence the Pongo are supposed to have brought it when they migrated.

After this incident of the wounding and the rescue of Stephen by the intrepid Miss Hope, whose interest in him was already strong enough to induce her to risk her life upon his behalf, all we fugitives were dragged ashore somehow by our friends. Here, Hans, I and the ladies collapsed exhausted, though Brother John still found sufficient strength to do what he could for the injured Stephen and Mavovo.

Then the Battle of the Reeds began, and a fierce fray it was. The Pongos who were about equal in numbers to our people, came on furiously, for they were mad at the death of their god with his priest, the Motombo, of which I think news had reached them and at the carrying off of the Mother of the Flower. Springing from their canoes because the waterway was too narrow for more than one of these to travel at a time, they plunged into the reeds with the intention of wading ashore. Here their hereditary enemies, the Mazitu, attacked them under the command of old Babemba. The struggle that ensued partook more of the nature of a series of hand-to-hand fights than of a set battle. It was extraordinary to see the heads of the combatants moving among the reeds as they stabbed at each other with the great spears, till one went down. There were few wounded in that fray, for those who fell sank in the mud and water and were drowned.

On the whole the Pongo, who were operating in what was almost their native element, were getting the best of it, and driving the Mazitu back. But what decided the day against them were the guns of our Zulu hunters. Although I could not lift a rifle myself I managed to collect these men round me and to direct their fire, which proved so terrifying to the Pongos that after ten or a dozen of them had been knocked over, they began to give back sullenly and were helped into their canoes by those men who were left in charge of them.

Then at length at a signal they got out their paddles, and, still shouting curses and defiance at us, rowed away till they became but specks upon the bosom of the great lake and vanished.

Two of the canoes we captured, however, and with them six or seven Pongos. These the Mazitu wished to put to death, but at the bidding of Brother John, whose orders, it will be remembered, had the same authority in Mazitu-land as those of the king, they bound their arms and made them prisoners instead.

In about half an hour it was all over, but of the rest of that day I cannot write, as I think I fainted from utter exhaustion, which was not, perhaps, wonderful, considering all that we had undergone in the four and a half days that had elapsed since we first embarked upon the Great Lake. For constant strain, physical and mental, I recall no such four days during the whole of my adventurous life. It was indeed wonderful that we came through them alive.

XIX

THE TRUE HOLY FLOWER

When I came to myself again it was to find that I had slept fifteen or sixteen hours, for the sun of a new day was high in the heavens. I was lying in a little shelter of boughs at the foot of that mound on which we flew the flag that guided us back over the waters of the Lake Kirua. Near by was Hans consuming a gigantic meal of meat which he had cooked over a neighbouring fire. With him, to my delight, I saw Mavovo, his head bound up, though otherwise but little the worse. The stone, which probably would have killed a thin-skulled white man, had done no more than knock him stupid and break the skin of his scalp, perhaps because the force of it was lessened by the gum man's-ring which, like most Zulus of a certain age or dignity, he wore woven in his hair.

The two tents we had brought with us to the lake were pitched not far away and looked quite pretty and peaceful there in the sunlight.

Hans, who was watching me out of the corner of his eye, ran to me with a large pannikin of hot coffee which Sammy had made ready against my awakening; for they knew that my sleep was, or had become of a natural order. I drank it to the last drop, and in all my life never did I enjoy anything more. Then while I began upon some pieces of the toasted meat, I asked him what had happened.

"Not much, Baas," he answered, "except that we are alive, who should be dead. The Maam and the Missie are still asleep in that tent, or at least the Maam is, for the Missie is helping Dogeetah, her father, to nurse Baas Stephen, who has an ugly wound. The Pongos have gone and I think will not return, for they have had enough of the white man's guns. The Mazitu have buried those of their dead whom they could recover, and have sent their wounded, of whom there were only six, back to Beza Town on litters. That is all, Baas."

Then while I washed, and never did I need a bath more, and put on my underclothes, in which I had swum on the night of the killing of the Motombo, that Hans had wrung out and dried in the sun, I asked that worthy how he was after his adventures.

"Oh! well enough, Baas," he answered, "now that my stomach is full, except that my hands and wrists are sore with crawling along the ground like a babyan (baboon), and that I cannot get the stink of that god's skin out of my nose. Oh! you don't know what it was: if I had been a white man it would have killed me. But, Baas, perhaps you did well to take drunken old Hans with you on this journey after all, for I was clever about the little gun, wasn't I? Also about your swimming of the Crocodile Water, though it is true that the sign of the spider and the moth which your reverend father sent, taught me that. And now we have got back safe, except for the Mazitu, Jerry, who doesn't matter, for there are plenty more like him, and the wound in Baas Stephen's shoulder, and that heavy flower which he thought better than brandy."

"Yes, Hans," I said, "I did well to take you and you are clever, for had it not been for you, we should now be cooked and eaten in Pongo-land. I thank you for your help, old friend. But, Hans, another time please sew up the holes in your waistcoat pocket. Four caps wasn't much, Hans."

"No, Baas, but it was enough; as they were all good ones. If there had been forty you could not have done much more. Oh! your reverend father knew all that" (my departed parent had become a kind of patron saint to Hans) "and did not wish this poor old Hottentot to have more to carry than was needed. He knew you wouldn't miss, Baas, and that there were only one god, one devil, and one man waiting to be killed."

I laughed, for Hans's way of putting things was certainly original, and having got on my coat, went to see Stephen. At the door of the tent I met Brother John, whose shoulder was dreadfully sore from the rubbing of the orchid stretcher, as were his hands with paddling, but who otherwise was well enough and of course supremely happy.

He told me that he had cleansed and sewn up Stephen's wound, which appeared to be doing well, although the spear had pierced right through the shoulder, luckily without cutting any artery. So I went in to see the patient and found him cheerful enough, though weak from weariness and loss of blood, with Miss Hope feeding him with broth from a wooden native spoon. I didn't stop very long, especially after he got on to the subject of the lost orchid, about which he began to show signs of excitement. This I allayed as well as I could by telling him that I had preserved a pod of the seed, news at which he was delighted.

"There!" he said. "To think that you, Allan, should have remembered to take that precaution when I, an orchidist, forgot all about it!"

"Ah! my boy," I answered, "I have lived long enough to learn never to leave anything behind that I can possibly carry away. Also, although not an orchidist, it occurred to me that there are more ways of propagating a plant than from the original root, which generally won't go into one's pocket."

Then he began to give me elaborate instructions as to the preservation of the seed-pod in a perfectly dry and air-tight tin box, etc., at which point Miss Hope unceremoniously bundled me out of the tent.

That afternoon we held a conference at which it was agreed that we should begin our return journey to Beza Town at once, as the place where we were camped was very malarious and there was always a risk of the Pongo paying us another visit.

So a litter was made with a mat stretched over it in which Stephen could be carried, since fortunately there were plenty of bearers, and our other simple preparations were quickly completed. Mrs. Eversley and Hope were mounted on the two donkeys; Brother John, whose hurt leg showed signs of renewed weakness, rode his white ox, which was now quite fat again; the wounded hero, Stephen, as I have said, was carried; and I walked, comparing notes with old Babemba on the Pongo, their manners, which I am bound to say were good, and their customs, that, as the saying goes, were "simply beastly."

How delighted that ancient warrior was to hear again about the sacred cave, the Crocodile Water, the Mountain Forest and its terrible god, of the death of which and of the Motombo he made me tell him the story three times over. At the conclusion of the third recital he said quietly:

"My lord Macumazana, you are a great man, and I am glad to have lived if only to know you. No one else could have done these deeds."

Of course I was complimented, but felt bound to point out Hans's share in our joint achievement.

"Yes, yes," he answered, "the Spotted Snake, Inhlatu, has the cunning to scheme, but you have the power to do, and what is the use of a brain to plot without the arm to strike? The two do not go together because the plotter is not a striker. His mind is different. If the snake had the strength and brain of the elephant, and the fierce courage of the buffalo, soon there would be but one creature left in the world. But the Maker of all things knew this and kept them separate, my lord Macumazana."

I thought, and still think, that there was a great deal of wisdom in this remark, simple as it seems. Oh! surely many of these savages whom we white men despise, are no fools.

After about an hour's march we camped till the moon rose which it did at ten o'clock, when we went on again till near dawn, as it was thought better that Stephen should travel in the cool of the night. I remember that our cavalcade, escorted before, behind and on either flank by the Mazitu troops with their tall spears, looked picturesque and even imposing as it wound over those wide downs in the lovely and peaceful light of the moon.

There is no need for me to set out the details of the rest of our journey, which was not marked by any incident of importance.

Stephen bore it very well, and Brother John, who was one of the best doctors I ever met, gave good reports of him, but I noted that he did not seem to get any stronger, although he ate plenty of food. Also, Miss Hope, who nursed him, for her mother seemed to have no taste that way, informed me that he slept but little, as indeed I found out for myself.

"O Allan," she said, just before we reached Beza Town, "Stephen, your son" (she used to call him my son, I don't know why) "is sick. The father says it is only the spear-hurt, but I tell you it is more than the spear-hurt. He is sick in himself," and the tears that filled her grey eyes showed me that she spoke what she believed. As a matter of fact she was right, for on the night after we reached the town, Stephen was seized with an attack of some bad form of African fever, which in his weak state nearly cost him his life, contracted, no doubt, at that unhealthy Crocodile Water.

Our reception at Beza was most imposing, for the whole population, headed by old Bausi himself, came out to meet us with loud shouts of welcome, from which we had to ask them to desist for Stephen's sake.

So in the end we got back to our huts with gratitude of heart. Indeed, we should have been very happy there for a while, had it not been for our anxiety about Stephen. But it is always thus in the world; who was ever allowed to eat his pot of honey without finding a fly or perhaps a cockroach in his mouth?

In all, Stephen was really ill for about a month. On the tenth day after our arrival at Beza, according to my diary, which, having little else to do, I entered up fully at this time, we thought that he would surely die. Even Brother John, who attended him with the most constant skill, and who had ample quinine and other drugs at his command, for these we had brought with us from Durban in plenty, gave up the case. Day and night the poor fellow raved and always about that confounded orchid, the loss of which seemed to weigh upon his mind as though it were a whole sackful of unrepented crimes.

I really think that he owed his life to a subterfuge, or rather to a bold invention of Hope's. One evening, when he was at his very worst and going on like a mad creature about the lost plant—I was present in the hut at the time alone with him and her—she took his hand and pointing to a perfectly open space on the floor, said:

"Look, O Stephen, the flower has been brought back."

He stared and stared, and then to my amazement answered:

"By Jove, so it has! But those beggars have broken off all the blooms except one."

"Yes," she echoed, "but one remains and it is the finest of them all."

After this he went quietly to sleep and slept for twelve hours, then took some food and slept again and, what is more, his temperature went down to, or a little below, normal. When he finally woke up, as it chanced, I was again present in the hut with Hope, who was standing on the spot which she had persuaded him was occupied by the orchid. He stared at this spot and he stared at her—me he could not see, for I was behind him—then said in a weak voice:

"Didn't you tell me, Miss Hope, that the plant was where you are and that the most beautiful of the flowers was left?"

I wondered what on earth her answer would be. However, she rose to the occasion.

"O Stephen," she replied, in her soft voice and speaking in a way so natural that it freed her words from any boldness, "it is here, for am I not its child"—her native appellation, it will be remembered, was "Child of the Flower." "And the fairest of the flowers is here, too, for I am that Flower which you found in the island of the lake. O Stephen, I pray you to trouble no more about a lost plant of which you have seed in plenty, but make thanks that you still live and that through you my mother and I still live, who, if you had died, would weep our eyes away."

"Through me," he answered. "You mean through Allan and Hans. Also it was you who saved my life there in the water. Oh! I remember it all now. You are right, Hope; although I didn't know it, you are the true Holy Flower that I saw."

She ran to him and kneeling by his side, gave him her hand, which he pressed to his pale lips.

Then I sneaked out of that hut and left them to discuss the lost flower that was found again. It was a pretty scene, and one that to my mind gave a sort of spiritual meaning to the whole of an otherwise rather insane quest. He sought an ideal flower, he found—the love of his life.

After this, Stephen recovered rapidly, for such love is the best of medicines—if it be returned.

I don't know what passed between the pair and Brother John and his wife, for I never asked. But I noted that from this day forward they began to treat him as a son. The new relationship between Stephen and Hope seemed to be tacitly accepted without discussion. Even the natives accepted it, for old Mavovo asked me when they were going to be married and how many cows Stephen had promised to pay Brother John for such a beautiful wife. "It ought to be a large herd," he said, "and of a big breed of cattle."

Sammy, too, alluded to the young lady in conversation with me, as "Mr. Somers's affianced spouse." Only Hans said nothing. Such a trivial matter as marrying and giving in marriage did not interest him. Or, perhaps, he looked upon the affair as a foregone conclusion and therefore unworthy of comment.

We stayed at Bausi's kraal for a full month longer whilst Stephen recovered his strength. I grew thoroughly bored with the place and so did Mavovo and the Zulus, but Brother John and his wife did not seem to mind. Mrs. Eversley was a passive creature, quite content to take things as they came and after so long an absence from civilization, to bide a little longer among savages. Also she had her beloved John, at whom she would sit and gaze by the hour like a cat sometimes does at a person to whom it is attached. Indeed, when she spoke to him, her voice seemed to me to resemble a kind of blissful purr. I think it made the old boy rather fidgety sometimes, for after an hour or two of it he would rise and go to hunt for butterflies.

To tell the truth, the situation got a little on my nerves at last, for wherever I looked I seemed to see there Stephen and Hope making love to each other, or Brother John and his wife admiring each other, which didn't leave me much spare conversation. Evidently they thought that Mavovo, Hans, Sammy, Bausi, Babemba and Co. were enough for me—that is, if they reflected on the matter at all. So they were, in a sense, for the Zulu hunters began to get out of hand in the midst of this idleness and plenty, eating too much, drinking too much native beer, smoking too much of the intoxicating *dakka*, a mischievous kind of help, and making too much love to the Mazitu women, which of course resulted in the usual rows that I had to settle.

At last I struck and said that we must move on as Stephen was now fit to travel.

"Quite so," said Brother John, mildly. "What have you arranged, Allan?"

With some irritation, for I hated that sentence of Brother John's, I replied that I had arranged nothing, but that as none of them seemed to have any suggestions to make, I would go out and talk the matter over with Hans and Mavovo, which I did.

I need not chronicle the results of our conference since other arrangements were being made for us at which I little guessed.

It all came very suddenly, as great things in the lives of men and nations sometimes do. Although the Mazitu were of the Zulu family, their military organization had none of the Zulu thoroughness. For instance, when I remonstrated with Bausi and old Babemba as to their not keeping up a proper system of outposts and intelligence, they laughed at me and answered that they never had been attacked and now that the Pongo had learnt a lesson, were never likely to be.

By the way, I see that I have not yet mentioned that at Brother John's request those Pongos who had been taken prisoners at the Battle of the Reeds were conducted to the shores of the lake, given one of the captured canoes and told that they might return to their own happy land. To our astonishment about three weeks later they reappeared at Beza Town with this story.

They said that they had crossed the lake and found Rica still standing, but utterly deserted. They then wandered through the country and even explored the Motombo's cave. There they discovered the remains of the Motombo, still crouched upon his platform, but nothing more. In one hut of a distant village, however, they came across an old and dying woman who informed them with her last breath that the Pongos, frightened by the iron tubes that vomited death and in obedience to some prophecy, "had all gone back whence they came in the beginning," taking with them the recaptured "Holy Flower." She had been left with a supply of food because she was too weak to travel. So, perhaps, that flower grows again in some unknown place in Africa, but its worshippers will have to provide themselves with another god of the forest, another Mother of the Flower, and another high-priest to fill the office of the late Motombo.

These Pongo prisoners, having now no home, and not knowing where their people had gone except that it was "towards the north," asked for leave to settle among the Mazitu, which was granted them. Their story confirmed me in my opinion that Pongo-land is not really an island, but is connected on the further side with the continent by some ridge or swamp. If we had been obliged to stop much longer among the Mazitu, I would have satisfied myself as to this matter by going to look. But that chance never came to me until some years later when, under curious circumstances, I was again destined to visit this part of Africa.

To return to my story. On the day following this discussion as to our departure we all breakfasted very early as there was a great deal to be done. There was a dense mist that morning such as in these Mazitu uplands often precedes high, hot wind from the north at this season of the year, so dense indeed that it was impossible to see for more than a few yards. I suppose that this mist comes up from the great lake in certain conditions of the weather. We had just finished our breakfast and rather languidly, for the thick, sultry air left me unenergetic, I told one of the Zulus to see that the two donkeys and the white ox which I had caused to be brought into the town in view of our near departure and tied up by our huts, were properly fed. Then I went to inspect all the rifles and ammunition, which Hans had got out to be checked and overhauled. It was at this moment that I heard a far-away and unaccustomed sound, and asked Hans what he thought it was.

"A gun, Baas," he answered anxiously.

Well might he be anxious, for as we both knew, no one in the neighbourhood had guns except ourselves, and all ours were accounted for. It is true that we had promised to give the majority of those we had taken from the slavers to Bausi when we went away, and that I had been instructing some of his best soldiers in the use of them, but not one of these had as yet been left in their possession.

I stepped to a gate in the fence and ordered the sentry there to run to Bausi and Babemba and make report and inquiries, also to pray them to summon all the soldiers, of whom, as it happened, there were at the time not more than three hundred in the town. As perfect peace prevailed, the rest, according to their custom, had been allowed to go to their villages and attend to their crops. Then, possessed by a rather undefined nervousness, at which the others were inclined to laugh, I caused the Zulus to arm and generally make a few arrangements to meet any unforeseen crisis. This done I sat down to reflect what would be the best course to take if we should happen to be attacked by a large force in that straggling native town, of which I had often studied all the strategic possibilities. When I had come to my own conclusion I asked Hans and Mavovo what they thought, and found that they agreed with me that the only defensible place was outside the town where the road to the south gate ran down to a rocky wooded ridge with somewhat steep flanks. It may be remembered that it was by this road and over this ridge that Brother John had appeared on his white ox when we were about to be shot to death with arrows at the posts in the market-place.

Whilst we were still talking two of the Mazitu captains appeared, running hard and dragging between them a wounded herdsman, who had evidently been hit in the arm by a bullet.

This was his story. That he and two other boys were out herding the king's cattle about half a mile to the north of the town, when suddenly there appeared a great number of men dressed in white robes, all of whom were armed with guns. These men, of whom he thought there must be three or four hundred, began to take the cattle and seeing the three herds, fired on them, wounding him and killing his two companions. He then ran for his life and brought the news. He added that one of the men had called after him to tell the white people that they had come to kill them and the Mazitu who were their friends and to take away the white women.

"Hassan-ben-Mohammed and his slavers!" I said, as Babemba appeared at the head of a number of soldiers, crying out:

"The slave-dealing Arabs are here, lord Macumazana. They have crept on us through the mist. A herald of theirs has come to the north gate demanding that we should give up you white people and your servants, and with you a hundred young men and a hundred young women to be sold as slaves. If we do not do this they say that they will kill all of us save the unmarried boys and girls, and that you white people they will take and put to death by burning, keeping only the two women alive. One Hassan sends this message."

"Indeed," I answered quietly, for in this fix I grew quite cool as was usual with me. "And does Bausi mean to give us up?"

"How can Bausi give up Dogeetah who is his blood brother, and you, his friend?" exclaimed the old general, indignantly. "Bausi sends me to his brother Dogeetah that he may receive the orders of the white man's wisdom, spoken through your mouth, lord Macumazana."

"Then there's a good spirit in Bausi," I replied, "and these are Dogeetah's orders spoken through my mouth. Go to Hassan's messengers and ask him whether he remembers a certain letter which two white men left for him outside their camp in a cleft stick. Tell him that the time has now come for those white men to fulfil the promise they made in that letter and that before to-morrow he will be hanging on a tree. Then, Babemba, gather your soldiers and hold the north gate of the town for as long as you can, defending it with bows and arrows. Afterwards retreat through the town, joining us among the trees on the rocky slope that is opposite the south gate. Bid some of your men clear the town of all the aged and women and children and let them pass though the south gate and take refuge in the wooded country beyond the slope. Let them not tarry. Let them go at once. Do you understand?"

"I understand everything, lord Macumazana. The words of Dogeetah shall be obeyed. Oh! would that we had listened to you and kept a better watch!"

He rushed off, running like a young man and shouting orders as he went.

"Now," I said, "we must be moving."

We collected all the rifles and ammunition, with some other things, I am sure I forget what they were, and with the help of a few guards whom Babemba had left outside our gate started through the town, leading with us the two donkeys and the white ox. I remember by an afterthought, telling Sammy, who was looking very uncomfortable, to return to the huts and fetch some blankets and a couple of iron cooking-pots which might become necessities to us.

"Oh! Mr. Quatermain," he answered, "I will obey you, though with fear and trembling."

He went and when a few hours afterwards I noted that he had never reappeared, I came to the conclusion, with a sigh, for I was very fond of Sammy in a way, that he had fallen into trouble and been killed. Probably, I thought, "his fear and trembling" had overcome his reason and caused him to run in the wrong direction with the cooking-pots.

The first part of our march through the town was easy enough, but after we had crossed the market-place and emerged into the narrow way that ran between many lines of huts to the south gate it became more difficult, since this path was already crowded with hundreds of terrified fugitives, old people, sick being carried, little boys, girls, and women with infants at the breast. It was impossible to control these poor folk; all we could do was to fight our way through them. However, we got out at last and climbing the slope, took up the best position we could on and just beneath its crest where the trees and scattered boulders gave us very fair cover, which we improved upon in every way feasible in the time at our disposal, by building little breastworks of stone and so forth. The fugitives who had accompanied us, and those who followed, a multitude in all, did not stop here, but flowed on along the road and vanished into the wooded country behind.

I suggested to Brother John that he should take his wife and daughter and the three beasts and go with them. He seemed inclined to accept the idea, needless to say for their sakes, not for his own, for he was a very fearless old fellow. But the two ladies utterly refused to budge. Hope said that she would stop with Stephen, and her mother declared that she had every confidence in me and preferred to remain where she was. Then I suggested that Stephen should go too, but at this he grew so angry that I dropped the subject.

So in the end we established them in a pleasant little hollow by a spring just over the crest of the rise, where unless our flank were turned or we were rushed, they would be out of the reach of bullets. Moreover, without saying anything more we gave to each of them a double-barrelled and loaded pistol.

XX

The Battle of the Gate

B y now heavy firing had begun at the north gate of the town, accompanied by much shouting. The mist was still too thick to enable us to see anything at first. But shortly after the commencement of the firing a strong, hot wind, which always followed these mists, got up and gradually gathered to a gale, blowing away the vapours. Then from the top of the crest, Hans, who had climbed a tree there, reported that the Arabs were advancing on the north gate, firing as they came, and that the Mazitu were replying with their bows and arrows from behind the palisade that surrounded the town. This palisade, I should state, consisted of an earthen bank on the top of which tree trunks were set close together. Many of these had struck in that fertile soil, so that in general appearance this protective work resembled a huge live fence, on the outer and inner side of which grew great masses of prickly pear and tall, finger-like cacti. A while afterwards Hans reported that the Mazitu were retreating and a few minutes later they began to arrive through the south gate, bringing several wounded with them. Their captain said that they could not stand against the fire of the guns and had determined to abandon the town and make the best fight they could upon the ridge.

A little later the rest of the Mazitu came, driving before them all the non-combatants who remained in the town. With these was King Bausi, in a terrible state of excitement.

"Was I not wise, Macumazana," he shouted, "to fear the slave-traders and their guns? Now they have come to kill those who are old and to take the young away in their gangs to sell them."

"Yes, King," I could not help answering, "you were wise. But if you had done what I said and kept a better look-out Hassan could not have crept on you like a leopard on a goat."

"It is true," he groaned; "but who knows the taste of a fruit till he has bitten it?"

Then he went to see to the disposal of his soldiers along the ridge, placing, by my advice, the most of them at each end of the line to frustrate any attempt to out-flank us. We, for our part, busied ourselves in serving out those guns which we had taken in the first fight with the slavers to the thirty or forty picked men whom I had been instructing in the use of firearms. If they did not do much damage, at least, I thought, they could make a noise and impress the enemy with the idea that we were well armed.

Ten minutes or so later Babemba arrived with about fifty men, all the Mazitu soldiers who were left in the town. He reported that he had held the north gate as long as he could in order to gain time, and that the Arabs were breaking it in. I begged him to order the soldiers to pile up stones as a defence against the bullets and to lie down behind them. This he went to do.

Then, after a pause, we saw a large body of the Arabs who had effected an entry, advancing down the central street towards us. Some of them had spears as well as guns, on which they carried a dozen or so of human heads cut from the Mazitus who had been killed, waving them aloft and shouting in triumph. It was a sickening sight, and one that made me grind my teeth with rage. Also I could not help reflecting that ere long our heads might be upon those spears. Well, if the worst came to the worst I was determined that I would not be taken alive to be burned in a slow fire or pinned over an ant-heap, a point upon which the others agreed with me, though poor Brother John had scruples as to suicide, even in despair.

It was just then that I missed Hans and asked where he had gone. Somebody said that he thought he had seen him running away, whereon Mavovo, who was growing excited, called out:

"Ah! Spotted Snake has sought his hole. Snakes hiss, but they do not charge."

"No, but sometimes they bite," I answered, for I could not believe that Hans had showed the white feather. However, he was gone and clearly we were in no state to send to look for him.

Now our hope was that the slavers, flushed with victory, would advance across the open ground of the market-place, which we could sweep with our fire from our position on the ridge. This, indeed, they began to do, whereon, without orders, the Mazitu to whom we had given the guns, to my fury and dismay, commenced to blaze away at a range of about four hundred yards, and after a good deal of firing managed to kill or wound two or three men. Then the Arabs, seeing their danger, retreated and, after a pause, renewed their advance in two bodies. This time, however, they followed the streets of huts that were built thickly between the outer palisade of the town and the market-place, which, as it had been designed to hold cattle in time of need, was also surrounded with a wooden fence strong enough to resist the rush of horned beasts. On that day, I should add, as the Mazitu never dreamed of being attacked, all their stock were grazing on some distant veldt. In this space between the two fences were many hundreds of huts, wattle and grass built, but for the most part roofed with palm leaves, for here, in their separate quarters, dwelt the great majority of the inhabitants of Beza Town, of which the northern part was occupied by the king, the nobles and the captains. This ring of huts, which entirely surrounded the market-place except at the two gateways, may have been about a hundred and twenty yards in width.

Down the paths between these huts, both on the eastern and the western side, advanced the Arabs and half-breeds, of whom there appeared to be about four hundred, all armed with guns and doubtless trained to fighting. It was a terrible force for us to face, seeing that although we may have had nearly as many men, our guns did not total more than fifty, and most of those who held them were quite unused to the management of firearms.

Soon the Arabs began to open fire on us from behind the huts, and a very accurate fire it was, as our casualties quickly showed, notwithstanding the stone *schanzes* we had constructed. The worst feature of the thing also was that we could not reply with any effect, as our assailants, who gradually worked nearer, were effectively screened by the huts, and we had not enough guns to attempt organised volley firing. Although I tried to keep a cheerful countenance I confess that I began to fear the worst and even to wonder if we could possibly attempt to retreat. This idea was abandoned, however, since the Arabs would certainly overtake and shoot us down.

One thing I did. I persuaded Babemba to send about fifty men to build up the southern gate, which was made of trunks of trees and opened outwards, with earth and the big stones that lay about in plenty. While this was being done quickly, for the Mazitu soldiers worked at the task like demons and, being sheltered by the palisade, could not be shot, all of a sudden I caught sight of four or five wisps of smoke that arose in quick succession at the north end of the town and were instantly followed by as many bursts of flame which leapt towards us in the strong wind.

Someone was firing Beza Town! In less than an hour the flames, driven by the gale through hundreds of huts made dry as tinder by the heat, would reduce Beza to a heap of ashes. It was inevitable, nothing could save the place! For an instant I thought that the Arabs must have done this thing. Then, seeing that new fires continually arose in different places, I understood that no Arabs, but a friend or friends were at work, who had conceived the idea of *destroying the Arabs with fire*.

My mind flew to Sammy. Without doubt Sammy had stayed behind to carry out this terrible and masterly scheme, of which I am sure none of the Mazitu would have thought, since it involved the absolute destruction of their homes and property. Sammy, at whom we had always mocked, was, after all, a great man, prepared to perish in the flames in order to save his friends!

Babemba rushed up, pointing with a spear to the rising fire. Now my inspiration came.

"Take all your men," I said, "except those who are armed with guns. Divide them, encircle the town, guard the north gate, though I think none can win back through the flames, and if any of the Arabs succeed in breaking through the palisade, kill them."

"It shall be done," shouted Babemba, "but oh! for the town of Beza where I was born! Oh! for the town of Beza!"

"Drat the town of Beza!" I holloaed after him, or rather its native equivalent. "It is of all our lives that I'm thinking."

Three minutes later the Mazitu, divided into two bodies, were running like hares to encircle the town, and though a few were shot as they descended the slope, the most of them gained the shelter of the palisade in safety, and there at intervals halted by sections, for Babemba managed the matter very well.

Now only we white people, with the Zulu hunters under Mavovo, of whom there were twelve in all, and the Mazitu armed with guns, numbering about thirty, were left upon the slope.

For a little while the Arabs did not seem to realise what had happened, but engaged themselves in peppering at the Mazitu, who, I think, they concluded were in full flight. Presently, however, they either heard or saw.

Oh! what a hubbub ensued. All the four hundred of them began to shout at once. Some of them ran to the palisade and began to climb it, but as they reached the top of the fence were pinned by the Mazitu arrows and fell backwards, while a few who got over became entangled in the prickly pears on the further side and were promptly speared. Giving up this attempt, they rushed back along the lane with the intention of escaping at the north-gate. But before ever they reached the head of the market-place the roaring, wind-swept flames, leaping from hut to hut, had barred their path. They could not face that awful furnace.

Now they took another counsel and in a great confused body charged down the market-place to break out at the south gate, and our turn came. How we raked them as they sped across the open, an easy mark! I know that I fired as fast as I could using two rifles, swearing the while at Hans because he was not there to load for me. Stephen was better off in this respect, for, looking round, to my astonishment I saw Hope, who had left her mother on the other side of the hill, in the act of capping his second gun. I should explain that during our stay in Beza Town we had taught her how to use a rifle.

I called to him to send her away, but again she would not go, even after a bullet had pierced her dress.

Still, all our shooting could not stop that rush of men, made desperate by the fear of a fiery death. Leaving many stretched out behind them, the first of the Arabs drew near to the south gate.

"My father," said Mavovo in my ear, "now the real fighting is going to begin. The gate will soon be down. *We* must be the gate."

I nodded, for if the Arabs once got through, there were enough of them left to wipe us out five times over. Indeed, I do not suppose that up to this time they had actually lost more than forty men. A few words explained the situation to Stephen and Brother John, whom I told to take his daughter to her mother and wait there with them. The Mazitu I ordered to throw down their guns, for if they kept these I was sure they would shoot some of us, and to accompany us, bringing their spears only.

Then we rushed down the slope and took up our position in a little open space in front of the gate, that now was tottering to its fall beneath the blows and draggings of the Arabs. At this time the sight was terrible and magnificent, for the flames had got hold of the two half-circles of huts that embraced the market-place, and, fanned by the blast, were rushing towards us like a thing alive. Above us swept a great pall of smoke in which floated flakes of fire, so thick that it hid the sky, though fortunately the wind did not suffer it to sink and choke us. The sounds also were almost inconceivable, for to the crackling roar of the conflagration as it devoured hut after hut, were added the coarse, yelling voices of the half-bred Arabs, as in mingled rage and terror they tore at the gateway or each other, and the reports of the guns which many of them were still firing, half at hazard.

We formed up before the gate, the Zulus with Stephen and myself in front and the thirty picked Mazitu, commanded by no less a person than Bausi, the king, behind. We had not long to wait, for presently down the thing came and over it and the mound of earth and stones we had built beyond, began to pour a mob of white-robed and turbaned men whose mixed and tumultuous exit somehow reminded me of the pips and pulp being squeezed out of a grenadilla fruit.

I gave the word, and we fired into that packed mass with terrible effect. Really I think that each bullet must have brought down two or three of them. Then, at a command from Mavovo, the Zulus threw down their guns and charged with their broad spears. Stephen, who had got hold of an assegai somehow, went with them, firing a Colt's revolver as he ran, while at their backs came Bausi and his thirty tall Mazitu.

I will confess at once that I did not join in this terrific onslaught. I felt that I had not weight enough for a scrimmage of the sort, also that I should perhaps be better employed using my wits outside and watching for a chance to be of service, like a half-back in a football field, than in getting my brains knocked out in a general row. Or mayhap my heart failed me and I was afraid. I dare say, for I have never pretended to great courage. At any rate, I stopped outside and shot whenever I got the chance, not without effect, filling a humble but perhaps a useful part.

It was really magnificent, that fray. How those Zulus did go in. For quite a long while they held the narrow gateway and the mound against all the howling, thrusting mob, much as the Roman called Horatius and his two friends held the entrance to some bridge or other long ago at Rome against a great force of I forget whom. They shouted their Zulu battle-cry of *Laba! Laba!* that of their regiment, I suppose, for most of them were men of about the same age, and stabbed and fought and struggled and went down one by one.

Back the rest of them were swept; then, led by Mavovo, Stephen and Bausi, charged again, reinforced with the thirty Mazitu. Now the tongues of flame met almost over them, the growing fence of prickly pear and cacti withered and crackled, and still they fought on beneath that arch of fire.

Back they were driven again by the mere weight of numbers. I saw Mavovo stab a man and go down. He rose and stabbed another, then fell again for he was hard hit.

Two Arabs rushed to kill him. I shot them both with a right and left, for fortunately my rifle was just reloaded. He rose once more and killed a third man. Stephen came to his support and grappling with an Arab, dashed his head against the gate-post so that he fell. Old Bausi, panting like a grampus, plunged in with his remaining Mazitu and the combatants became so confused in the dark gloom of the overhanging smoke that I could scarcely tell one from the other. Yet the maddened Arabs were winning, as they must, for how could our small and ever-lessening company stand against their rush?

We were in a little circle now of which somehow I found myself the centre, and they were attacking us on all sides. Stephen got a knock on the head from the butt end of a gun, and tumbled against me, nearly upsetting me. As I recovered myself I looked round in despair.

Now it was that I saw a very welcome sight, namely Hans, yes, the lost Hans himself, with his filthy hat whereof I noticed even then the frayed ostrich feathers were smouldering, hanging by a leather strap at the back of his head. He was shambling along in a sly and silent sort of way, but at a great rate with his mouth open, beckoning over his shoulder, and behind him came about one hundred and fifty Mazitu.

Those Mazitu soon put another complexion upon the affair, for charging with a roar, they drove back the Arabs, who had no space to develop their line, straight into the jaws of that burning hell. A little later the rest of the Mazitu returned with Babemba and finished the job. Only quite a few of the Arabs got out and were captured after they had thrown down their guns. The rest retreated into the centre of the market-place, whither our people followed them. In this crisis the blood of these Mazitu told, and they stuck to the enemy as Zulus themselves would certainly have done.

It was over! Great Heaven! it was over, and we began to count our losses. Four of the Zulus were dead and two others were badly wounded—no, three, including Mavovo. They brought him to me leaning on the shoulder of Babemba and another Mazitu captain. He was a shocking sight, for he was shot in three places, and badly cut and battered as well. He looked at me a little while, breathing heavily, then spoke.

"It was a very good fight, my father," he said. "Of all that I have fought I can remember none better, although I have been in far greater battles, which is well as it is my last. I foreknew it, my father, for though I never told it you, the first death lot that I drew down yonder in Durban was my own. Take back the gun you gave me, my father. You did but lend it me for a little while, as I said to you. Now I go to the Underworld to join the spirits of my ancestors and of those who have fallen at my side in many wars, and of those women who bore my children. I shall have a tale to tell them there, my father, and together we will wait for you—till you, too, die in war!"

Then he lifted up his arm from the neck of Babemba, and saluted me with a loud cry of *Baba! Inkosi!* giving me certain great titles which I will not set down, and having done so sank to the earth.

I sent one of the Mazitu to fetch Brother John, who arrived presently with his wife and daughter. He examined Mavovo and told him straight out that nothing could help him except prayer.

"Make no prayers for me, Dogeetah," said the old heathen; "I have followed my star," (i.e. lived according to my lights) "and am ready to eat the fruit that I have planted. Or if the tree prove barren, then to drink of its sap and sleep."

Waving Brother John aside he beckoned to Stephen.

"O Wazela!" he said, "you fought very well in that fight; if you go on as you have begun in time you will make a warrior of whom the Daughter of the Flower and her children will sing songs after you have come to join me, your friend. Meanwhile, farewell! Take this assegai of mine and clean it not, that the red rust thereon may put you in mind of Mavovo, the old Zulu doctor and captain with whom you stood side by side in the Battle of the Gate, when, as though they were winter grass, the fire burnt up the white-robed thieves of men who could not pass our spears."

Then he waved his hand again, and Stephen stepped aside muttering something, for he and Mavovo had been very intimate and his voice choked in his throat with grief. Now the old Zulu's glazing eye fell upon Hans, who was sneaking about, I think with a view of finding an opportunity of bidding him a last good-bye.

"Ah! Spotted Snake," he cried, "so you have come out of your hole now that the fire has passed it, to eat the burnt frogs in the cinders. It is a pity that you who are so clever should be a coward, since our lord Macumazana needed one to load for him on the hill and would have killed more of the hyenas had you been there."

"Yes, Spotted Snake, it is so," echoed an indignant chorus of the other Zulus, while Stephen and I and even the mild Brother John looked at him reproachfully.

Now Hans, who generally was as patient under affront as a Jew, for once lost his temper. He dashed his hat upon the ground, and danced on it; he spat towards the surviving Zulu hunters; he even vituperated the dying Mavovo.

"O son of a fool!" he said, "you pretend that you can see what is hid from other men, but I tell you that there is a lying spirit in your lips. You called me a coward because I am not big and strong as you were, and cannot hold an ox by the horns, but at least there is more brain in my stomach than in all your head. Where would all of you be now had it not been for poor Spotted Snake the 'coward,' who twice this day has saved every one of you, except those whom the Baas's father, the reverend Predikant, has marked upon the forehead to come and join him in a place that is even hotter and brighter than that burning town?"

Now we looked at Hans, wondering what he meant about saving us twice, and Mavovo said:

"Speak on quickly, O Spotted Snake, for I would hear the end of your story. How did you help us in your hole?"

Hans began to grub about in his pockets, from which finally he produced a match-box wherein there remained but one match.

"With this," he said. "Oh! could none of you see that the men of Hassan had all walked into a trap? Did none of you know that fire burns thatched houses, and that a strong wind drives it fast and far? While you sat there upon the hill with your heads together, like sheep waiting to be killed, I crept away among the bushes and went about my business. I said nothing to any of you, not even to the Baas, lest he should answer me, 'No, Hans, there may be an old woman sick in one of those huts and therefore you must not fire them.' In such matters who does not know that white people are fools, even the best of them, and in fact there were several old women, for I saw them running for the gateway. Well, I crept up by the green fence which I knew would not burn and I came to the north gate. There was an Arab sentry left there to watch.

"He fired at me, look! Well for Hans his mother bore him short"; and he pointed to a hole in the filthy hat. "Then before that Arab could load again, poor coward Hans got his knife into him from behind. Look!" and he produced a big blade, which was such as butchers use, from his belt and showed it to us. "After that it was easy, since fire is a wonderful thing. You make it small and it grows big of itself, like a child, and never gets tired, and is always hungry, and runs fast as a horse. I lit six of them where they would burn quickest. Then I saved the last match, since we have few left, and came through the gate before the fire ate me up; me, its father, me the Sower of the Red Seed!"

We stared at the old Hottentot in admiration, even Mavovo lifted his dying head and stared. But Hans, whose annoyance had now evaporated, went on in a jog-trot mechanical voice:

"As I was returning to find the Baas, if he still lived, the heat of the fire forced me to the high ground to the west of the fence, so that I saw what was happening at the south gate, and that the Arab men must break through there because you who held it were so few. So I ran down to Babemba and the other captains very quickly, telling them there was no need to guard the fence any more, and that they must get to the south gate and help you, since otherwise you would all be killed, and they, too, would be killed afterwards. Babemba listened to me and started sending out messengers to collect the others and we got here just in time. Such is the hole I hid in during the Battle of the Gate, O Mavovo. That is all the story which I pray that you will tell to the Baas's reverend father, the Predikant, presently, for I am sure that it will please him to learn that he did not teach me to be wise and help all men and always to look after the Baas Allan, to no purpose. Still, I am sorry that I wasted so many matches, for where shall we get any more now that the camp is burnt?" and he gazed ruefully at the all but empty box.

Mavovo spoke once more in a slow, gasping voice.

"Never again," he said, addressing Hans, "shall you be called Spotted Snake, O little yellow man who are so great and white of heart. Behold! I give you a new name, by which you shall be known with honour from generation to generation. It is 'Light in Darkness.' It is 'Lord of the Fire.'"

Then he closed his eyes and fell back insensible. Within a few minutes he was dead. But those high names with which he christened Hans with his dying breath, clung to the old Hottentot for all his days. Indeed from that day forward no native would ever have ventured to call him by any other. Among them, far and wide, they became his titles of honour.

The roar of the flames grew less and the tumult within their fiery circle died away. For now the Mazitu were returning from the last fight in the market-place, if fight it could be called, bearing in their arms great bundles of the guns which they had collected from the dead Arabs, most of whom had thrown down their weapons in a last wild effort to escape. But between the spears of the infuriated savages on the one hand and the devouring fire on the other what escape was there for them? The blood-stained wretches who remained in the camps and towns of the slave-traders, along the eastern coast of Africa, or in the Isle of Madagascar, alone could tell how many were lost, since of those who went out from them to make war upon the Mazitu and their white friends, none returned again with the long lines of expected captives. They had gone to their own place, of which sometimes that flaming African city has seemed to me a symbol. They were wicked men indeed, devils stalking the earth in human form, without pity, without shame. Yet I could not help feeling sorry for them at the last, for truly their end was awful.

They brought the prisoners up to us, and among them, his white robe half-burnt off him, I recognised the hideous pock-marked Hassan-ben-Mohammed.

"I received your letter, written a while ago, in which you promised to make us die by fire, and, this morning, I received your message, Hassan," I said, "brought by the wounded lad who escaped from you when you murdered his companions, and to both I sent you an answer. If none reached you, look around, for there is one written large in a tongue that all can read."

The monster, for he was no less, flung himself upon the ground, praying for mercy. Indeed, seeing Mrs. Eversley, he crawled to her and catching hold of her white robe, begged her to intercede for him.

"You made a slave of me after I had nursed you in the spotted sickness," she answered, "and tried to kill my husband for no fault. Through you, Hassan, I have spent all the best years of my life among savages, alone and in despair. Still, for my part, I forgive you, but oh! may I never see your face again."

Then she wrenched herself free from his grasp and went away with her daughter.

"I, too, forgive you, although you murdered my people and for twenty years made my time a torment," said Brother John, who was one of the truest Christians I have ever known. "May God forgive you also"; and he followed his wife and daughter.

Then the old king, Bausi, who had come through that battle with a slight wound, spoke, saying:

"I am glad, Red Thief, that these white people have granted you what you asked—namely, their forgiveness—since the deed is greatly to their honour and causes me and my people to think them even nobler than we did before. But, O murderer of men and woman and trafficker in children, I am judge here, not the white people. Look on your work!" and he pointed first to the lines of Zulu and Mazitu dead, and then to his burning town. "Look and remember the fate you promised to us who have never harmed you. Look! Look! Look! O Hyena of a man!"

At this point I too went away, nor did I ever ask what became of Hassan and his fellow-captives. Moreover, whenever any of the natives or Hans tried to inform me, I bade them hold their tongues.

Epilogue

I have little more to add to this record, which I fear has grown into quite a long book. Or, at any rate, although the setting of it down has amused me during the afternoons and evenings of this endless English winter, now that the spring is come again I seem to have grown weary of writing. Therefore I shall leave what remains untold to the imagination of anyone who chances to read these pages.

WE WERE VICTORIOUS, AND HAD indeed much cause for gratitude who still lived to look upon the sun. Yet the night that followed the Battle of the Gate was a sad one, at least for me, who felt the death of my friend the foresighted hero, Mavovo, of the bombastic but faithful Sammy, and of my brave hunters more than I can say. Also the old Zulu's prophecy concerning me, that I too should die in battle, weighed upon me, who seemed to have seen enough of such ends in recent days and to desire one more tranquil.

Living here in peaceful England as I do now, with no present prospect of leaving it, it does not appear likely that it will be fulfilled. Yet, after my experience of the divining powers of Mavovo's "Snake"— well, those words of his make me feel uncomfortable. For when all is said and done, who can know the future? Moreover, it is the improbable that generally happens[*]

Further, the climatic conditions were not conducive to cheerfulness, for shortly after sunset it began to rain and poured for most of the night, which, as we had little shelter, was inconvenient both to us and to all the hundreds of the homeless Mazitu.

However, the rain ceased in due time, and on the following morning the welcome sun shone out of a clear sky. When we had dried and warmed ourselves a little in its rays, someone suggested that we should visit the burned-out town where, except for some smouldering heaps that had been huts, the fire was extinguished by the heavy rain. More from curiosity than for any other reason I consented and accompanied by Bausi, Babemba and many of the Mazitu, all of us, except Brother

---

[*] As the readers of "Allan Quatermain" will be aware, this prophecy of the dying Zulu was fulfilled. Mr. Quatermain died at Zuvendis as a result of the wound he received in the battle between the armies of the rival Queens.—Editor.

John, who remained behind to attend to the wounded, climbed over the debris of the south gate and walked through the black ruins of the huts, across the market-place that was strewn with dead, to what had been our own quarters.

These were a melancholy sight, a mere heap of sodden and still smoking ashes. I could have wept when I looked at them, thinking of all the trade goods and stores that were consumed beneath, necessities for the most part, the destruction of which must make our return journey one of great hardship.

Well, there was nothing to be said or done, so after a few minutes of contemplation we turned to continue our walk through what had been the royal quarters to the north gate. Hans, who, I noted, had been ferreting about in his furtive way as though he were looking for something, and I were the last to leave. Suddenly he laid his hand upon my arm and said:

"Baas, listen! I hear a ghost. I think it is the ghost of Sammy asking us to bury him."

"Bosh!" I answered, and then listened as hard as I could.

Now I also seemed to hear something coming from I knew not where, words which were frequently repeated and which seemed to be:

"*O Mr. Quatermain, I beg you to be so good as to open the door of this oven.*"

For a while I thought I must be cracked. However, I called back the others and we all listened. Of a sudden Hans made a pounce, like a terrier does at the run of a mole that he hears working underground, and began to drag, or rather to shovel, at a heap of ashes in front of us, using a bit of wood as they were still too hot for his hands. Then we listened again and this time heard the voice quite clearly coming from the ground.

"Baas," said Hans, "it is Sammy in the corn-pit!"

Now I remembered that such a pit existed in front of the huts which, although empty at the time, was, as is common among the Bantu natives, used to preserve corn that would not immediately be needed. Once I myself went through a very tragic experience in one of these pits, as any who may read the history of my first wife, that I have called *Marie*, can see for themselves.

Soon we cleared the place and had lifted the stone, with ventilating holes in it—well was it for Sammy that those ventilating holes existed; also that the stone did not fit tight. Beneath was a bottle-shaped and cemented structure about ten feet deep by, say, eight wide. Instantly through the mouth of this structure appeared the head of Sammy with his mouth wide open like that of a fish gasping for air. We pulled him out, a process that caused him to howl, for the heat had made his skin very tender, and gave him water which one of the Mazitu fetched from a spring. Then I asked him indignantly what he was doing in that hole, while we wasted our tears, thinking that he was dead.

"Oh! Mr. Quatermain," he said, "I am a victim of too faithful service. To abandon all these valuable possessions of yours to a rapacious enemy was more than I could bear. So I put every one of them in the pit, and then, as I thought I heard someone coming, got in myself and pulled down the stone. But, Mr. Quatermain, soon afterwards the enemy added arson to murder and pillage, and the whole place began to blaze. I could hear the fire roaring above and a little later the ashes covered the exit so that I could no longer lift the stone, which indeed grew too hot to touch. Here, then, I sat all night in the most suffocating heat, very much afraid, Mr. Quatermain, lest the two kegs of gunpowder that were with me should explode, till at last, just as I had abandoned hope and prepared to die like a tortoise baked alive by a bushman, I heard your welcome voice. And Mr. Quatermain, if there is any soothing ointment to spare, I shall be much obliged, for I am scorched all over."

"Ah! Sammy, Sammy," I said, "you see what comes of cowardice? On the hill with us you would not have been scorched, and it is only by the merest chance of owing to Hans's quick hearing that you were not left to perish miserably in that hole."

"That is so, Mr. Quatermain. I plead guilty to the hot impeachment. But on the hill I might have been shot, which is worse than being scorched. Also you gave me charge of your goods and I determined to preserve them even at the risk of personal comfort. Lastly, the angel who watches me brought you here in time before I was quite cooked through. So all's well that ends well, Mr. Quatermain, though it is true that for my part I have had enough of bloody war, and if I live to regain civilized regions I propose henceforth to follow the art of food-dressing in the safe kitchen of an hotel; that is, if I cannot obtain a berth as an instructor in the English tongue!"

"Yes," I answered, "all's well that ends well, Sammy my boy, and at any rate you have saved the stores, for which we should be thankful to you. So go along with Mr. Stephen and get doctored while we haul them out of that grain-pit."

Three days later we bid farewell to old Bausi, who almost wept at parting with us, and the Mazitu, who were already engaged in the re-building of their town. Mavovo and the other Zulus who died in the Battle of the Gate, we buried on the ridge opposite to it, raising a mound of earth over them that thereby they might be remembered in generations to come, and laying around them the Mazitu who had fallen in the fight. As we passed that mound on our homeward journey, the Zulus who remained alive, including two wounded men who were carried in litters, stopped and saluted solemnly, praising the dead with loud songs. We white people too saluted, but in silence, by raising our hats.

By the way, I should add that in this matter also Mavovo's "Snake" did not lie. He had said that six of his company would be killed upon our expedition, and six were killed, neither more nor less.

After much consulting we determined to take the overland route back to Natal, first because it was always possible that the slave-trading fraternity, hearing of their terrible losses, might try to attack us again on the coast, and secondly for the reason that even if they did not, months or perhaps years might pass before we found a ship at Kilwa, then a port of ill repute, to carry us to any civilized place. Moreover, Brother John, who had travelled it, knew the inland road well and had established friendly relations with the tribes through whose country we must pass, till we reached the brothers of Zululand, where I was always welcome. So as the Mazitu furnished us with an escort and plenty of bearers for the first part of the road and, thanks to Sammy's stewardship in the corn-pit, we had ample trade goods left to hire others later on, we made up our minds to risk the longer journey.

As it turned out this was a wise conclusion, since although it took four weary months, in the end we accomplished it without any accident whatsoever, if I except a slight attack of fever from which both Miss Hope and I suffered for a while. Also we got some good shooting on the road. My only regret was that this change of plan obliged us to abandon the tusks of ivory we had captured from the slavers and buried where we alone could find them.

Still, it was a dull time for me, who, for obvious reasons, of which I have already spoken, was literally a fifth wheel to the coach. Hans was an excellent fellow, and, as the reader knows, quite a genius in his own way, but night after night in Hans's society began to pall on me at last, while even his conversation about my "reverend father," who seemed positively to haunt him, acquired a certain sameness. Of course, we had other subjects in common, especially those connected with Retief's massacre, whereof we were the only two survivors, but of these I seldom cared to speak. They were and still remain too painful.

Therefore, for my part I was thankful when at last, in Zululand, we fell in with some traders whom I knew, who hired us one of their wagons. In this vehicle, abandoning the worn-out donkeys and the white ox, which we presented to a chief of my acquaintance, Brother John and the ladies proceeded to Durban, Stephen attending them on a horse that we had bought, while I, with Hans, attached myself to the traders.

At Durban a surprise awaited us since, as we trekked into the town, which at that time was still a small place, whom should we meet but Sir Alexander Somers, who, hearing that wagons were coming from Zululand, had ridden out in the hope of obtaining news of us. It seemed that the choleric old gentleman's anxiety concerning his son had so weighed on his mind that at length he made up his mind to proceed to Africa to hunt for him. So there he was. The meeting between the two was affectionate but peculiar.

"Hullo, dad!" said Stephen. "Whoever would have thought of seeing you here?"

"Hullo, Stephen," said his father. "Whoever would have expected to find you alive and looking well—yes, very well? It is more than you deserve, you young ass, and I hope you won't do it again."

Having delivered himself thus, the old boy seized Stephen by the hair and solemnly kissed him on the brow.

"No, dad," answered his son, "I don't mean to do it again, but thanks to Allan there we've come through all right. And, by the way, let me introduce you to the lady I am going to marry, also to her father and mother."

Well, all the rest may be imagined. They were married a fortnight later in Durban and a very pleasant affair it was, since Sir Alexander, who by the way, treated me most handsomely from a business point of view, literally entertained the whole town on that festive occasion. Immediately afterwards Stephen, accompanied by Mr. and Mrs. Eversley and his father, took his wife home "to be educated," though what that process consisted of I never heard. Hans and I saw them off at the Point and our parting was rather sad, although Hans went back the richer by the £500 which Stephen had promised him.

He bought a farm with the money, and on the strength of his exploits, established himself as a kind of little chief. Of whom more later—as they say in the pedigree books.

Sammy, too, was set up as the proprietor of a small hotel, where he spent most of his time in the bar dilating to the customers in magnificent sentences that reminded me of the style of a poem called "The Essay on Man" (which I once tried to read and couldn't), about his feats as a warrior among the wild Mazitu and the man-eating, devil-worshipping Pongo tribes.

Two years or less afterwards I received a letter, from which I must quote a passage:

"As I told you, my father has given a living which he owns to Mr. Eversley, a pretty little place where there isn't much for a parson to do. I think it rather bores my respected parents-in-law. At any rate, 'Dogeetah' spends a lot of his time wandering about the New Forest, which is near by, with a butterfly-net and trying to imagine that he is back in Africa. The 'Mother of the Flower' (who, after a long course of boot-kissing mutes, doesn't get on with English servants) has another amusement. There is a small lake in the Rectory grounds in which is a little island. Here she has put up a reed fence round a laurustinus bush which flowers at the same time of year as did the Holy Flower, and within this reed fence she sits whenever the weather will allow, as I believe going through 'the rites of the Flower.' At least when I called upon her there one day, in a boat, I found her wearing a white robe and singing some mystical native song."

Many years have gone by since then. Both Brother John and his wife have departed to their rest and their strange story, the strangest almost of all stories, is practically forgotten. Stephen, whose father has also departed, is a prosperous baronet and rather heavy member of Parliament and magistrate, the father of many fine children, for the Miss Hope of old days has proved as fruitful as a daughter of the Goddess of Fertility, for that was the "Mother's" real office, ought to be.

"Sometimes," she said to me one day with a laugh, as she surveyed a large (and noisy) selection of her numerous offspring, "sometimes, O Allan"—she still retains that trick of speech—"I wish that I were back in the peace of the Home of the Flower. Ah!" she added with something of a thrill in her voice, "never can I forget the blue of the sacred lake or the sight of those skies at dawn. Do you think that I shall see them again when I die, O Allan?"

At the time I thought it rather ungrateful of her to speak thus, but after all human nature is a queer thing and we are all of us attached to the scenes of our childhood and long at times again to breathe our natal air.

I went to see Sir Stephen the other day, and in his splendid greenhouses the head gardener, Woodden, an old man now, showed me three noble, long-leaved plants which sprang from the seed of the Holy Flower that I had saved in my pocket.

But they have not yet bloomed.

Somehow I wonder what will happen when they do. It seems to me as though when once more the glory of that golden bloom is seen of the eyes of men, the ghosts of the terrible god of the Forest, of the hellish and mysterious Motombo, and perhaps of the Mother of the Flower herself, will be there to do it reverence. If so, what gifts will they bring to those who stole and reared the sacred seed?

P.S.—I shall know ere long, for just as I laid down my pen a triumphant epistle from Stephen was handed to me in which he writes excitedly that at length two of the three plants are *showing for flower*.

Allan Quatermain

A Note About the Author

Sir Henry Rider Haggard, (1856–1925) commonly known as H. Rider Haggard was an English author active during the Victorian era. Considered a pioneer of the lost world genre, Haggard was known for his adventure fiction. His work often depicted African settings inspired by the seven years he lived in South Africa with his family. In 1880, Haggard married Marianna Louisa Margitson and together they had four children, one of which followed her father's footsteps and became an author. Haggard is still widely read today, and is celebrated for his imaginative wit and impact on 19th century adventure literature.

A Note from the Publisher

Spanning many genres, from non-fiction essays to literature classics to children's books and lyric poetry, Mint Edition books showcase the master works of our time in a modern new package. The text is freshly typeset, is clean and easy to read, and features a new note about the author in each volume. Many books also include exclusive new introductory material. Every book boasts a striking new cover, which makes it as appropriate for collecting as it is for gift giving. Mint Edition books are only printed when a reader orders them, so natural resources are not wasted. We're proud that our books are never manufactured in excess and exist only in the exact quantity they need to be read and enjoyed. To learn more and view our library, go to minteditionbooks.com

bookfinity & MINT EDITIONS

Enjoy more of your favorite classics with Bookfinity,
a new search and discovery experience for readers.
With Bookfinity, you can discover more vintage
literature for your collection, find your Reader Type,
track books you've read or want to read,
and add reviews to your favorite books.
Visit www.bookfinity.com, and click on
Take the Quiz to get started.

Don't forget to follow us
@bookfinityofficial and @mint_editions